Poor Mary - A Tale of Schizophrenia

by

Sylvia Hoole

authorHOUSE®

AuthorHouse™ UK Ltd.
500 Avebury Boulevard
Central Milton Keynes, MK9 2BE
www.authorhouse.co.uk
Phone: 08001974150

© 2008 Sylvia Hoole. All rights reserved.

No part of this book may be reproduced, stored in a retrieval system, or transmitted by any means without the written permission of the author.

First published by AuthorHouse 2/28/2008

ISBN: 978-1-4343-3882-2 (sc)

Printed in the United States of America
Bloomington, Indiana

This book is printed on acid-free paper.

PART 1

1. BIRTH OF A BABY.

It was the seventh of March, 1936. The weather was typical of the time of year, cold and blustery. A smattering of snow, blown on the wind, lashed the faces of the men tramping home from the night shift at the pit, and the women who were scurrying to the corner shop to buy their four and a half penny loaves and perhaps a couple of rashers of fatty bacon.

"A bit o' fat keeps ye warm in this 'ere weather", they would declare.

No talk then of cholesterol or healthy diets and the like. They ate what they could afford to buy and some weeks it might be very little. Perhaps indeed the fat which they ate was less harmful than that which we try to avoid today. After all, the food chain had not been tampered with by the use of pesticides and so forth, and pollution did not exist on the levels which we know today. These hard working people certainly seemed to live a long time in spite of their so called bad diet.

The small mining town in Yorkshire was one of England's ugly places – really ugly – ugly and depressing with its row upon row of squat terraced houses blackened by the perpetual belching smoke from both domestic and pit chimneys. Soot and grime were everywhere and nothing would stay clean for long. The air was permanently pervaded by an acrid smell and if one wished to fill one's lungs with real fresh air then it had to be a visit to the Yorkshire moors or the seaside.

These occasions were few and far between for most of these people.

The lives of those struggling to exist in this environment were harsh to say the least, and it showed in their faces – hard faces, grim unsmiling faces as they went about their daily business. Unemployment – being 'laid off' – miner's strikes – the dole – all were common place to these people. Yes it was hard, but they had learned how to handle it long ago, and they could cope, whereas people in fairer and more affluent towns would be on their knees with only half of these deprivations.

Towards the bottom end of the town, down the hill and quite near the pit, stood a row of terrace houses by the name of Fowlstone Row – an unattractive name for an equally unattractive street. The small houses consisted of 'one up, one down', that being a general purpose living room and one bedroom. There was no bath room. One washed at the kitchen sink with hot water from a kettle which was always simmering on a grid over a coal fire. Using a flannel, or face cloth, one would wash 'as far as possible one way and as far as possible the other'. A weekly bathe would be achieved by bringing in the tin bath which usually hung on the wall of the small back yard, and buckets of water would be heated in the oven to fill it. What a performance! The whole family used the same water and there would be endless squabbles as to who should have the luxury of being first in the bath with nice, clean hot water. It can't have been too pleasant for the last person to step into tepid and scummy water. The hair was usually washed also on this occasion, and with ordinary common soap which was also used for scrubbing floors. The water was particularly hard but there was never the luxury of some sweet smelling bubble bath to soften it, nor of shampoo and conditioning lotions.

Imagine being taken ill in the middle of the night with a tummy problem! There was no W.C. in the house at all. Instead one would have to creep down the stairs, open the back door, walk through the yard to a back gate, and then down to the end of the passage to a communal W.C. which served the whole row of houses. One can only imagine the quarrels with neighbours as to whose turn it was to clean the 'lav' this week, if indeed it was ever cleaned! Of course one could always keep a 'gerry' or 'po' under the bed, as most people did, but that had to be emptied into a slop bucket each morning and then delivered to the W.C. – not an enviable chore to have to perform each day.

How many people might there be living in each of these 'one up, one down' houses, might you ask? A family with however many children they might produce would be the answer. It seemed to be that the poorer the people the more children they had. These offspring could be seen playing and quarrelling on the pavement outside their houses. Some of the children were permanently black and dirty. Some of them started off their day clean enough but soon became covered in grime as they rolled and tumbled and fought each other, shouting and squealing, and in and out of friendships a dozen times a day.

The broad Yorkshire dialect of these people was a foreign language not always understood by others who had not been born and bred there. There was the little boy who was taken by his mother to see the doctor who asked the child to open his mouth and show his tongue. The child did not respond to the doctor's request and the gentleman began to show signs of impatience as the boy continued to stand mute. Then the boy's mother cried out,

"Cum on lad, open tha gob an' pull out tha licker"

The boy instantly opened his mouth and stuck out his tongue. On another occasion a traveller was baffled by being told'

"It's rate down in t' coil oil where t' muck slarts on t' windas"

The man eventually worked out that whatever it was happened to be down in the coal hole, or cellar, where the dirt splashes on the windows.

Each small house of Fowlstone Row could have told its own tale of love and sorrow, laughter and sadness, life and death, toil and redundancy. A hundred books could be written about a hundred different lives. Like a camera lens zooming in, we focus on just the one house, Number 1 at the end of the terrace. Entering through the door from the street we would find ourselves in the tiny living room furnished with the usual dining table and four chairs with matching sofa and a sideboard. Everything was neat, clean and orderly, unlike some of the houses down the street where dirt, untidiness and chaos went hand in hand with poverty. On the top of the sideboard which gleamed with polish, was a runner which was a long strip of embroidered material trimmed with lace, to protect the surface from being scratched. There were several ornaments resting there, a pretty multi coloured rose - bowl, a matching jug and bowl made of peach coloured glass shot through with mother of pearl effect, and a tall, slender specimen vase in clear glass. In the centre of the sideboard stood a framed photograph bearing the likeness of a handsome couple posing together in evening attire, he in a smart dark suit and she in an elegant long gown. The photograph was in sepia so it was impossible to know the colour of the gown except that it was pale. An old wireless set sat on one end of the sideboard and from it could be heard the strains of music and a male voice singing a popular song of the day.

Above the words of the song other sounds were coming from the upstairs bedroom. Two women were in the room. One of the women, a middle aged plump lady with greying hair in tight crinkly curls, was the local midwife. Mrs. Firth, for that was her name, was busy with all the necessary preparations for delivering a baby and clucking reassuring words like a mother hen. The woman who was about to give birth was lying on the bed, her eyes closed as she tried to rest in between contractions. Her hands were clutching at a roller towel which had been slotted through the brass bars of the bed head, and secured tightly so that she could pull hard upon it to aid her contractions.

"It won't be long now luv! When t' next contraction cums I want ye to pull on t' towel with all yer might"

The woman was becoming exhausted, for she had been in labour most of the day, and now the contractions were coming strongly and frequently as she reached the final stages of her labour. With no drugs to dull the senses every pain seered through her body like a sword. At first she thought that she would die and then she wished that she could die. Another fierce contraction gripped her body like a vice and she screamed to God for it to stop.

"Pull on that towel an' push as 'ard as ye can lass – ye won't be long now".

The woman, drenched in sweat, pulled and pushed, gathering strength from somewhere to make one last valiant effort to expel the new young life from her body. She could hear her own screams of agony inside her head and was aware that the room was spinning round and round as she struggled with the final throes of her labour. Suddenly, for a minute, she thought her body would split in two, and then came a new sound, and a merciful release.

"It's a little lass!" declared Mrs. Firth as she took the new born child to clean, weigh and wrap up in a shawl. " There's nowt wrong wi 'er. She's got all 'er fingers and toes – she's right bonny! What are ye goin' to call 'er?"

From the wireless down stairs came the strains of a song,

'Who is Sylvia? What is she?'

"I'll call 'er Sylvia", murmured the woman as she took the child to her arms for the first time and gazed at the baby in wonderment.

And so, on Saturday 7th of March, 1936, was born Sylvia who was destined to suffer more than her fair share of physical pain and mental anguish at the hands of the woman who had just borne her.

2. OUR MARY

Mary looked at her baby and was filled with a fierce, possessive love – a selfish love – a love which was to stifle, restrict and impair the emotional development of another human being. This little child was to be 'the be all and end all' of Mary's life – to be set on a pedestal to be worshipped and adored – a model of perfection not to be spoilt! Let not the child reach out and tipple from her mount, or she would have to be punished to make sure that she stayed put.

Mary Alice Copley was born in 1907, the second child of Arthur and Lucy. She was usually called by her full name, Mary Alice, by her mother and 'our Mary' by the rest of the family. From an early age she had been a difficult child, having an obstinate and wilful streak in her nature, and would never listen to reason or accept advice, which is why she always ended up in trouble. Trying to cope with her two younger, boisterous children on top of this proved hard going for Lucy. When Grandma Haytack, a severe, no nonsense lady, came to stay, she declared that she would take Mary back home with her for a few weeks and get her sorted out.

This was a great novelty for Mary initially – she being the only one to be singled out to go and stay with 'Gramma Haytack' – and for a long visit! Borough Bridge, where Grandma Haytack lived, was much nicer than dirty old Cudworth. Gramma had a garden and there were fields close by. However, it did not take long for the novelty to wear off. There was no one to play with her, no one to torment, and Mary soon became bored – besides which Gramma Haytack wouldn't let her do anything exciting and had the time to make sure that she couldn't. Mary threw many a tantrum but to no avail – Gramma Haytack was immoveable!

At last Mary decided that she'd had enough and in order to create as much nuisance as possible she packed her small bag and ran away in the early hours of the morning, once again demonstrating that she was not going to be disciplined by anyone, not even the fierce Grandma Haytack. There was a great fuss when Mary arrived back at Arthur and Lucy's house, but she did not care, and so her life continued as before.

Mary's elder brother was Ted and he presented no more than average teenage problems as he grew up. As soon as he left school at the age of thirteen he went to work 'down t' pit' as did his dad, thus having no time to go round making a nuisance of himself. He eventually married a girl called Rose and they had two children, Colin and Irene. Ted and his family rented a little terrace house a block away from his parent's home.

Georgie was born two years after Mary. As a child he was known as Georgie Porgie because of his plumpness, and he was certainly extremely greedy. One day the children were given an unusual and special treat – a day trip to Blackpool one summer Sunday. Sandwiches were packed and the family set off to catch a special train to the coast. There was great excitement all round, resulting in petty squabbles as to who was going to sit near the window, who was going to carry this or that, who had more or less sweets than anyone else, and so on. It was all quite wearing for Mum and

Dad who proceeded to scold accordingly. At last they were there! They could hardly believe it when they finally settled down on the beach, and they pinched each other to make sure that they were not dreaming. Out came buckets and spades and the next hour was spent industriously building an enormous sand castle.

"Let's go an' look fo' shells to pur on t' top o' t' castle", suggested Ted.

"I'll stay an' guard it", said Georgie as the other three scampered away with their buckets. " Mam an' Dad need guardin' as well 'cos they've gone to sleep"

Sure enough, Mam and Dad were fast asleep on their rug, their faces turned up to the warm sunshine. This was a rare treat indeed for a couple whose normal days were nothing but drudgery. Another half hour passed and the three shell seekers came racing back, rattling their buckets and shouting at the tops of their voices.

"Mam – Dad – we're 'ungry. Can we 'ave us dinner?"

"Awe dear! Did ye 'ave to wake us up like that? We was just enjoyin' that forty winks", grumbled Arthur. "We dun't get much chance at 'ome!"

"There won't be no peace till they've 'ad their dinner", sighed Lucy. "Mary Alice, get the bag an' bring it 'ere an' I'll sort out t' sandwiches".

Three of the children were hopping about excitedly, their mouths drooling at the thought of the cold meat sandwiches to come. Georgie did not seem very interested, which was most unusual. The packets of sandwiches were opened and, with the exception of Georgie, the children dived in, fighting and pushing each other to be the first to grab a sandwich. They couldn't wait.

Everyone took their first bite. There came an instance of silence followed by exclamations of disgust. The children had taken mouthfuls of bread – and SAND! Whilst Mam and Dad had slept and the others were gathering shells, greedy Georgie had raided the packets of sandwiches, taking out all the meat and eaten it all to the last scrap. Not content with that naughtiness he had filled up the sandwiches with sand and then carefully returned them to their packets.

What an uproar! No one was in any doubt as to who was responsible. Fred jumped on Georgie and the two of them rolled over and over in the sand whilst Mary and little Connie wept tears of frustration and disappointment. Their day was spoilt!

"Just you wait till we get you 'ome me lad", scolded Arthur. "You'll feel t' buckle end o' me belt on yer backside. No more seaside for you Georgie Copley".

Georgie was the culprit of many such tricks during his childhood. However, as he grew up he lost his fatness and with it his delight in practical jokes. He became quite a serious young man and married a lass called Doreen, generally known as "our Dor" by the rest of the family. Georgie lived the least eventful life of the foursome, perhaps because he did not produce any children!

Connie was the youngest of the Copley family, a rather plain child with mouse coloured hair. Being the youngest, the baby of the family, she found it easy to get her own way, particularly with the two boys. She did not always get on with her sister Mary who was

Poor Mary

inclined to be jealous of this younger sibling who could twist her brothers, and Mam and Dad, around her little finger. As Connie grew into adolescence she became precocious and always 'knew it all'. She was fiery and quick tempered with anyone who crossed her and therefore she and Mary were always at loggerheads with each other. Like Mary, Connie had a wilful streak but she was luckier in the way that fate treated her.

In her early teens Connie started to court a young lad who was called Eric whom she eventually married at a very young age. They had two sons, Ralph and Ronnie.

Let us now take a look at Mary's parents, Arthur and Lucy Copley. They had married when Lucy was but eighteen years old and she had borne six children in all. Two of them had died in infancy and so never became part of this story.

The couple had struggled through more hard times than good but had always stuck together through thick and thin. People did in those days – they had no other choice! Arthur Copley was a hard worker and very, very straight. He worked down the mine and he refused to go on strike during the great miner's strike of 1926. He had his principals and he stuck to them in spite of abuse and jeers from fellow work mates as he single mindedly made his way to the colliery, his pit boots clip clopping on the pavement, for his early morning shift. He was strictly teetotal and had never smoked a cigarette in the whole of his life and he deplored the habit in others. He never ceased to rebuke his daughter, Connie, for smoking like a chimney and continued to remonstrate with her over this for the whole of his life.

Arthur had two hobbies, gardening and breeding budgerigars. He had an allotment behind the house and there he built himself an aviary for his budgies and a hen house where he kept chickens thus providing a goodly supply of fresh eggs for his family. Instead of spending his leisure hours in the pub, or in the Working Men's Club, as did the average miner, he would spend his time in his allotment attending to his budgies or preparing the garden where he grew vegetables and a profusion of flowers – a bright scene amidst the drabness of the sooty houses and concrete backyards.

Arthur was a good looking man with twinkling blue eyes with laughter lines, and he was blessed by a head of jet black curly hair. He was full of fun and forever playing tricks upon his children, and also his wife who, sad to say, did not usually appreciate his joviality and she would become exceedingly cross with him at times.

During the First World War Arthur was called up and sent to the Front Line to fight in the trenches in France. He was one of the lucky ones who came home alive having suffered no serious wounds. He was not unscathed though. His lovely black hair had turned snow white during the four years of that dreadful war. This was due to the shock of seeing many of his comrades in arms being blown to pieces or badly maimed before his very eyes. He was not by nature pugilistic, being a very gentle person who hated violence of any kind – but he was called to fight for his country and he did his duty to the last letter.

Poor Mary

Whilst Arthur was fighting in France, Lucy struggled to make ends meet for the family. Whatever else she was – or was not – Lucy was not afraid of hard work, and she used to take in washing to earn a few shillings. There were many days when all she was able to give the children to eat was dry bread with a little brown sauce. Meat was a rare treat during that period of their lives and would be supplemented by Yorkshire puddings, served before the meat course, with lashings of gravy in order to satisfy their appetites. This was common practice within the mining families of Yorkshire, and even now in more affluent times it is traditional to eat Yorkshire puddings with gravy before the main course.

The older Lucy grew the harder she became and it showed in the grim expression on her face, the thin set line of her lips, mouth turned down at the corners. Had she been pretty when she was young there was no evidence of this now. Apart from the toil of her life Lucy was riddled with arthritis, and the perpetual nagging pain that goes with it. Her hands were coarse with hard work, gnarled with the arthritis, and her legs were bowed with the same. Her constant cry of ' Ee, me legs is bad today!' caused the children to keep out of her way. She was often bad tempered and would have moods when she would speak to no one for days at a time. In the household Lucy ruled the roost and if ever there was a henpecked husband then it was Arthur. Having a peace loving nature he always let her have her own way, taking refuge in his garden and talking to his budgies.

Talking of budgies, there was one more character in the Copley household who deserves a mention. His name was Billy – Billy Copley – the budgie who lived in a cage in the house and not in the aviary. Arthur spent a great deal of time in teaching Billy to talk, and not without success. The bird chattered away all day saying the usual things like, " Whose a pretty boy then?" or "Hello Billy!" but his prize saying was, "Cheeky bugger, naughty boy, what the 'ell yer doin?" Fortunately this was not a household where the vicar came to tea!

3. WILFUL MARY

Whilst Ted, Connie and George were all rather plain in their appearance, like their mother, Mary was singularly striking. She had the good fortune to take after her father and had inherited his jet black hair which cascaded down her back in natural waves and curls. She had high cheek bones and a fine complexion which gave her a youthful appearance lasting well beyond her middle years.

Mary was living at home when it was arranged that Arthur and Lucy should take Connie's baby, Ralph, into their care so that his mother was free to work. This little child brought out the better side of Mary's nature and she thought the world of him, being more of a mother to him than Connie ever was. Thus Ralph always had a deep affection for his Auntie Mary, lasting for the rest of his life, no matter what havoc and distress she caused in other people's lives. Mary was always very generous towards him and gave him many a treat which he never would have had otherwise.

As Mary grew into her teens she became extremely fashion conscious and also aware how attractive she was. She began to earn her own living 'in service', working for a notable family in the larger town of Barnsley. She lived with the Rawlings family during the week and went home for the weekends. All the money she earned was saved in order to buy clothes of the very latest 1920's fashion. One day she examined her appearance in the mirror.

"It's got to go", she thought. "It's not fashionable at all. What's the use of all these fashion clothes without t' hairstyle to match!"

As soon as possible Mary went to the hairdresser and looked at the pictures of glamorous girls in the salon window, each picture showing a girl sporting the very latest Twenties hair style, the short and sleek bob.

"That's it!" she thought, and before she had the time to get too nervous and change her mind, she marched into the shop and asked if she could have an immediate appointment. As she sat down in front of the mirror she felt a moment of trepidation at the thought of losing her fine locks which had always been her father's pride and joy. Whatever would her father say? She quickly dismissed that thought from her mind.

"I want it all cut off", she declared quickly. "I want it bobbed – like the pictures in the window".

Since working for the Rawlings family Mary had made a determined effort to lose the coarseness of her Yorkshire accent and had acquired a more gentle way of speaking.

"Are ye sure luv?" queried the young hairdresser. "It seems a right shame to cut off all this luvly 'air".

"'Course I'm sure. I look old fashioned like this", Mary cried with more confidence than she was feeling inside herself.

At the weekend Mary clad herself in her latest new clothes so that she could 'show off' at home to family and friends. She tossed her head to feel the freedom of her new short hairstyle, just one tiny curl fashionably gracing her forehead on the left hand side. Her mother looked up at the sound of the door opening.

"Oh my God! Whatever 'ave ye done to ye sen Mary Alice? Arthur – Arthur – Look what our Mary's done to 'er 'air!"

Arthur looked at his daughter in horror. He rarely showed anger but this was one of the few exceptions.

"Whatever did tha do that fo' our Mary? Tha's made tha sen look rate common. I'm disgusted wi' thee!"

"It's my hair, and my life, and I can do as I like", exclaimed his daughter. "Anyway, it's the latest fashion, anyone who is anybody wears their hair like this, and I think it suits me, and so do the Rawlings. Both their daughters 'ave 'ad it done and you don't think they're common do ye! Ye're both too old fashioned for words. I hate you!"

"Now that's enough o' that Mary Alice. Ye're not too old to feel me belt on tha backside lass. What's done's done, but I dun't like it, and yer Mam and me won't be spoke to like that!"

Mary stomped upstairs to put her things in her bedroom.

"I wish I hadn't bothered to come 'ome", she muttered under her breath. "They're always the same! I bet if it'd been our Connie they wouldn't 'ave grumbled. They never did like me!"

"Gramma, what's up wi' Auntie Mary?" asked the toddler, Ralph, who had observed the row without understanding what it was all about. "Why is 'er 'air all gone, and why is Granddad mad wi' 'er?"

"Never you mind our Ralph, it's nowt to do wi' you", scolded Lucy.

"Ee, I don't know!" bemoaned Arthur. "These lasses 'ave been nowt but trouble. There's our Connie not looking after 'er own bairn – an' she smokes like a chimney wi' them filthy cigarettes, and now our Mary's 'ad all 'er 'air cut off. Whatever next our Lucy? Where's it all goin' to end? Our Ted an' Georgie 'aven't caused us this much bother".

"It's time our Mary wa' settled down", replied Lucy. "She's that flighty wi' lads an' she's vain, allus standin' in front o' mirror combing 'er 'air, an' spendin' all 'er money on fancy clothes. It'll cum to no good, you mark my words!"

One thing to be said for Mary, she did have an eye for good clothes and never bought anything cheap and tatty, even though it might take her several weeks to save up what she needed. As a result, when she was dressed up she looked very smart indeed. Mary thought that her sister, Connie, had no taste at all and made herself look common, particularly with a "ciggy" permanently hanging from her lips and curlers worn in her hair for most of the day. She covered the latter by means of a scarf tied into a turban. Connie and Eric were trying to make the best of their teenage marriage, though they fought like cat and dog most of the time, Connie being so bossy. However, Eric loved her very much and they managed to weather the storms. For some reason known only to Connie, there was never any question of young Ralph going back to live with them so he continued to live with his grandparents. He always acknowledged Connie and Eric as his parents but 'Gramma and Granddad' were his stability. What his personal thoughts about this situation were as he grew up we shall never know.

Once a year, for one week, the whole family went to Blackpool, having saved up every spare penny throughout the whole year to pay for it. Now that the family had grown up and were earning it was possible to do this. They always stayed in the same little boarding house which was situated about ten minute's walk from the sea front. Every day, come rain, wind or shine, they all trooped off to the sea front. Arthur and Lucy sat on the promenade, drinking in the view of the sea with their eyes, and tasting the salt spray on their lips. Their faces became as red as turkey cocks, but this would be proof that they had been for a week by the sea! Sometimes other families they knew would be there also, as it was the annual holiday – or 'Wakes Week' as it was called. The youngsters would get together and go off on their own, either on the sands, paddling in the sea, or looking round the shops. Mary, Connie and Eric would usually take young Ralph with them and help him to make sand pies on the beach, or pay for him to have a ride on a donkey.

In her usual form, Mary wore the latest fashion in holiday clothes – well cut shorts and striped cotton tops for the beach. She enjoyed showing off her shapely legs, much to her father's consternation, and was for ever declaring that she " had a nice leg for a stocking" – as someone had once told her.

After the evening meal, they all went out for a stroll on the promenade, the youngsters eating candy floss or toffee apples, or sometimes visiting the famous Pablo's Ice Cream Parlour where they made themselves feel sick with eating giant sundaes with long, slender handled spoons from tall glasses. They saved as much money as they could for their last evening when they went to the Pleasure Beach. Here they sampled as many 'hairy rides' as possible, the Fun House, the House of Mirrors, the Ghost train, and then fell about laughing as they stood and listened to the Laughing Clown who performed in his glass case after the insertion of a silver sixpence. No one could keep a serious face for long at the sound of this life size clown dummy which rolled about with hearty laughter.

The thing that Mary most lived for during this week was the visit to Blackpool Tower Ballroom where she could dance all evening to the strains of organ dance music played by Reginald Dickson. She saved up to buy a really special dress for this occasion, usually of flowing chiffon or crushed velvet. She wore glittering diamante clips in her dark short bobbed hair, together with a matching clip attached to her dress. Her stockings were of the finest silk and accompanied by pretty court shoes to tone with the colour of her dress. How Mary loved to dance and to show off her skills, never minding if she and her partner were the sole dancers on the ballroom floor when she could really attract attention. It has to be admitted that she made a striking picture of elegance, perfectly groomed, and expertly made up, eyebrows plucked to a fine line and her glossy black hair gleaming under the lights. Many a head turned to look at her and she was never short of partners. Nevertheless, Arthur worried a great deal about his elder daughter. Somehow something was not quite right but he could not put his finger on it.

Mary had many young men dancing attendance on her so she could pick and choose her escorts. In her early twenties she began courting seriously a young man by the name of Roland who absolutely doted on her. Eventually they became engaged to be married and everything seemed to be going well for a while.

Roland was an ambitious young man who wanted to make something of his life. He did not want to spend the rest of his life in the pit. He hated it, but it was a job and there was nothing else except the dole. One day he saw an advertisement in the local newspaper for good job opportunities in Canada. Whilst he was grovelling for coal in the darkness of the bowels of the earth, choking with coal dust and longing for the natural light of the day, he kept thinking and thinking about the advertisement.

"Anything's better than this", he thought. "Canada! A new start – an' if I don't go now I'll be stuck in this pit fo' the rest o' me working life!"

When he arrived home after his shift at the pit he took out the advertisement from the drawer where he had placed it for safe keeping.

"I'll write for details, it can do no harm", he muttered to himself as he studied the paper carefully.

So he put pen to paper and wrote a presentable letter in reply to the advertisement. Two weeks later he received the reply for which he had been anxiously waiting. As yet he had not said anything to Mary about his plans for he did not know how she would react. Also he wanted to be armed with all the details before confronting her. It worried him a great deal that she might not take too kindly to his plans. At last he received all the information from the agency and he was filled with great excitement, It all seemed so right for him, he couldn't let this opportunity go by. He sent for the job application form and made enquiries about emigration, passports and so on.

"Mary luv, I've got summat to talk to you about". Roland shuffled his feet uneasily as he wondered how Mary would react to his news.

"Well, go on then", mumbled Mary as she smoothed her hair in front of the mirror and adjusted her stocking seams. "Whatever it is, get on with it or we'll be late for the pictures and I don't want to miss the beginning of the film".

"I've got this chance o' doing a better job than working down t' pit, and it is better paid as well – an' it's got prospects". Roland went bright red as he stammered out these words to Mary.

"Oh let's get off quickly Roland. I've told you we'll be late. Tell me about it as we go", Mary grabbed his arm and hurried him out of the house.

Roland did not get a chance to say anymore as they met some friends on their way to the cinema. After the film had ended Roland took Mary's arm as they strolled home passed the garden allotments.

"About this new job Mary -"

"What about this new job?" Mary asked. "Have you really got it – and what is it?"

Roland became very uncomfortable – "I've got to talk to you about it Mary".

"Well, provided it brings in a good wage then it's got to better than working down the pit. I'd like that – it's not so common. Is it a white collar job? I don't fancy 'aving all those white shirts to wash, starch and iron every week".

"It definitely brings in a good wage and I can 'ave it if I want it – and I want it more than anything Mary. I don't want to work down t' pit all me life".

"Well, what's botherin' ye then, ye daft pie-can? Take the job if they've offered it to ye. Where is it any way? I didn't think there was much going round here except at the pit".

"That's just it Mary – where it is!"

"Oh for goodness sake Roland! What's the matter with ye tonight? Where – is – the – job?"

"Canada", Roland mumbled into his tie.

"Canada". Then with realisation – "CANADA! You've got to be joking! You are joking aren't ye? 'Course you are!" cried Mary.

"No", Roland muttered. "No I'm not joking Mary. I want us to get married right away and then we'll emigrate to Canada. Just think about it – a new life in a new country! It'd be a good life Mary – we'd be summat!"

Mary went deathly quiet, her face pale and her lips set in a grim line. Roland was dismayed, his worst fears realised, the reason he had hesitated for so long before telling her. She did not want to go! He was torn apart! He loved Mary and did not want to lose her, but he was also ambitious and here was the best opportunity he was ever going to have – a chance to break away from the mould set by his father, and his grandfather. He couldn't turn it down.

"Mary, I want to go. Please come wi' me!"

"You mean you'll go anyway", spat Mary, "whether I go with you or not?"

At that moment Roland made up his mind. "Yes", he said, his voice breaking. "I've got to Mary".

"That's it then isn't it?" and Mary wrenched his engagement ring from her finger and flung it into the hedge which bordered the allotments. Full of anger she ran from him and did not stop running until she reached her parent's home.

Roland never found the ring. He sailed for Canada one month later. Mary never saw him again. She received a single post card from him about a year later – and she wept!

4. LEWIS

The Princess Marina green dress, with its frilled collar and flowing long skirt, had been carefully laid out on the bed. It was of Mary's favourite colour and complimented her jet black hair which was immaculately groomed, and showed off to the best effect the milky whiteness of her skin. Mary had plucked her eyebrows and was just applying her vivid red lipstick before powdering her nose. New silk stockings were taken from the drawer and very carefully put on to make sure that they were not snagged. Finally Mary took the dress and carefully slipped it over her head, taking care not to disturb her sleek hair, and then she fastened up the zip at the back. She took stock of herself in the mirror, turning to observe all possible views, and she was pleased with what she saw. The dress fitted perfectly, showing off her tiny waist and then falling gently into soft fullness at ankle length. It was in no way flashy for she never bought flashy clothes. Modelling her self on the wealthy Rawlings girls all her clothes were in good taste. After a final adjustment to her hair, Mary stepped into her white court shoes, picked up her matching evening bag and went down the stairs.

"Where's tha going now – all dressed up like a dog's dinner – our Mary?" her father chuntered from behind his newspaper.

He was seated in his favourite chair, a large, shabby, leather wing back chair situated close by Billy's bird cage. There he could talk to his best friend, Billy, in between reading bits out of the newspaper.

"A few of us are goin' to a dance at the Town Hall Dad, and I'm just goin' to call for my friend, Ray, an' she'll be waiting for me so I'm in a hurry" Mary said.

"Spendin' all tha money again! Tha's got more money than sense our Mary – out every night – it's time tha settled down now. Ye Mam and me were married and wi' kids at your age! Ye spend all ye time gallivantin' about and never stay wi' a lad fo' more than five minutes", complained Arthur.

"I court all and marry none!" retorted Mary perkily. "Anyway, who wants to be settled down wi' kids? Look at our Connie, grindin' away tryin' to make ends meet, and not even looking after her own lad. Besides, I earn all the money I spend, and I work 'ard at Rawlings' and Mrs. Rawlings thinks a lot about me. I think I deserve some fun on me days off."

During this speech Mary was studying her own reflection in the mirror over the fireplace, patting her hair and smoothing her eyebrows.

"Bye Dad!" she said. The back door slammed behind her and she was away.

Arthur laid down his paper and sighed.

"Ee dear! I don't know what will become o' the lass", and he drifted into an uneasy doze as he contemplated on his elder daughter's flightiness.

The band struck up a waltz as the group of young people chattered away in the corner of the dance hall. Mary's feet were tapping in time to the music, she was impatient to be on the dance floor, swirling and turning, her long dress billowing around her ankles. How she loved to dance!

"Cum on then Mary lass, let's give it a whirl. I can see tha's rarin' to go", shouted one of the lads.

Lewis Howell was staring intently across the dance room floor at the girl with raven black hair. Her eyes were sparkling and her red lips parted showing even white teeth as she laughed gaily under the flickering lights of the spinning mirror ball. Now she was really something – a cut above the rest. He liked an elegant woman – and she was a good dancer – he liked that too.

Mary sat down breathlessly, picked up her evening bag, opened it and took out a pretty silver plated powder compact which had been given to her on her twenty first birthday. She dusted her nose and cheeks with powder and reassured herself from her mirror that her appearance was satisfactory.

"Would ye like to dance?" spoke a soft voice.

Mary looked up and found herself looking into the softest brown eyes – laughing eyes, wickedly teasing! Lewis Howell was twenty nine years old, a handsome man, dark and swarthy. He was well built, not too tall, but a fine smart figure of a man. Mary's heart missed a beat! She stood up and Lewis led her on to the dance floor. As they began to dance Mary felt a sudden thrill at his closeness. Now here was a man worth knowing, really good looking – and he wasn't common!

"I'm Lewis – Lewis Howell. What's your name?"

"Mary – Mary Copley", she replied, and found herself blushing much to her consternation. This wasn't like her at all; she usually had the upper hand.

"I haven't seen you 'ere before. Where've you been hiding yerself?" asked Lewis.

"Well I work most of the time. I'm in service with the Rawlings' family. Mr. Rawlings is the Mayor of Barnsley", explained Mary proudly. "When I get a few days off I come to my Mother's. Where do you live?"

"I live here – in Cudworth", replied Lewis.

"Where do you work?" asked Mary.

"Well, I do get around a bit. I go to sea from time to time, as part of a ship's crew", he answered. "I've been all over the world at some time or other. I've also worked down t' pit and my trade's a shot fire really, but I don't think much to that life. I'd much rather be sailing. I love the freedom of it. I hate being cooped up down t' pit, I feel so stifled".

Mary felt excited. Here was someone worth bothering with, someone different from the run of the mill lad she usually encountered. They danced together for the rest of the evening, and then Lewis walked her home.

"Can I take you out Mary? We could go to t' pictures tomorrow night if ye like. I think there's a Shirley Temple film on – if your like most girls you'll like that, though I can't say I'm struck on 'er myself".

"I'd really like that", Mary replied. "I luv Shirley Temple with all her curls and lovely clothes. If I had a little girl I'd make her look just like Shirley".

And so Mary and Lewis began their courtship. Although at last Mary had found someone she really liked, Arthur continued to be uneasy. There was something not quite right, and somehow he didn't trust Lewis – and he didn't know why.

5. "I CAN'T BE!"

Mary was madly in love with Lewis. He could do no wrong in her eyes and she would never hear a word said against him. He was her idol to worship and adore. Lewis decided to return to working in the colliery for the time being so that they could spend all their spare time together. He hated the pit though but it brought in the money and perhaps something better would turn up if he stuck at it for a while, for he was not without ability. Mary did not like him working there either but she realised that if he returned to sea then he would be away for weeks at a time and she couldn't bear the thought of that.

They both loved dancing and every weekend Lewis would pick up Mary, either from the Rawlings' house, should she be having a working weekend, or from her mother's. They would then go to a dance in the evening, perhaps in Barnsley, or even in Leeds. Once a week they went to the pictures to see a film. Next to Mary, Lewis's great love was his motor bike and sidecar. Having their own transport made it easy for them to go further afield to places where there was more life than in their dreary old home town. Mary loved the excitement of the motor cycling – this was real living – and she preferred to ride on the pillion seat, unless of course she was dressed up in a long gown when she would ride in the sidecar.

There were occasional weekends when they rode to Blackpool where Mary was in her element – the Pleasure Beach – the Arcades – the shops – and best of all the Tower Ballroom where they could dance the hours away to their heart's content. Mary would boast to her friends at home, and to fellow workers, how she and Lewis were always the first couple on the dance floor. She enjoyed the attention that this created, for they made a striking couple together. Yes, life was now really exciting – all she had ever dreamed of – and she wanted it to go on for ever and ever.

All good things must come to an end eventually. Life never stays the same indefinitely and Mary's life was about to change drastically. She did not know then, at the age of twenty eight, that she had reached her highest pinnacle and that from hereafter her life was to take a backward spiralling downward course which would eventually bring her to the very depths of human despair, suffering and degradation. If proud Mary had been able to look through a crystal ball and see what she was to become, then she would not have wished to live.

It was after their last whirlwind weekend in Blackpool that Mary began to feel unwell.

"I must have eaten something a bit off", she thought as she experienced waves of nausea throughout the day. "I'd feel a lot better if I could be sick".

Mary wasn't sick but the nauseous feelings continued, making her irritable, tired and edgy.

"Is something wrong Mary dear?" queried Mrs. Rawlings as Mary took in her early morning tea. "You look a trifle pale and down in the mouth. Have you had a quarrel with your Lewis?"

"I'll be all right Ma'am. No, we haven't quarrelled or anything. I just don't feel too grand this morning, but it'll pass".

"I do hope that you are not sickening for something Mary. We have a busy week ahead with two very large dinner parties to arrange. If you don't feel better tomorrow then I think a visit to Dr. Smedley might be in order".

"I don't think it will come to that Mrs. Rawlings. I'm sure I'll feel better in the morning" said Mary.

Mary struggled through the day as best she could. There were all the fire grates to clean out, the black leading to do on the Yorkist range in the kitchen – then she mustn't forget that all the silver needed to be cleaned in preparation for the dinner parties next week. There were some very important people coming to them, she knew that. Mary was always intrigued by these occasions, taking careful note of the very latest fashions worn by the grand ladies so that she could emulate them – as far as she could with her meagre earnings. She would spend hours looking round the fashion stores in Barnsley, and she was never satisfied until she had found something similar to what she might have seen worn by one of Mrs. Rawlings' lady guests. Not for Mary the common 'cheap and cheerful' clothes that all her female friends wore. She did not want to look common. She wanted to dress like a real lady. This attitude did not make Mary too popular with the girls back home.

"Mary Copley tries to get above 'erself", they would say to each other. "Who the 'eck does she think she is – Lady Muck?"

Mary did not wish to let Mrs. Rawlings down by giving in to her feelings of lethargy and the waves of nausea which continued to envelop her. Give her credit for Mary was a hard worker, never shirking any duties or trying to cut corners as some of the younger maids were inclined to do. It was important to her that Mrs. Rawlings thought well of her. Whilst Mary behaved in a very superior manner within her family circle and socio group, she was always very subservient towards people of a higher status, professional people – doctors, dentists, teachers and the like.

At the end of a very long day, Mary climbed the steep stairs to her attic bedroom and opened the door. She paused for a moment before entering the room and closing the door behind her. She leaned on the door and closed her eyes. Opening them again she took stock of her tiny bedroom which had been her own private domain for the last ten years since entering into service with the Rawlings' family. The room was sparsely furnished but neat and tidy and comfortable enough. Hanging on her wardrobe was Mary's latest acquisition which she had collected from the departmental store the previous day. It was an evening dress which she had seen weeks before and couldn't afford to buy it at the time. She had managed to put down a deposit on the dress which had been 'put by' for her, then she had paid as much as she could on a weekly account and at last paid up fully and the dress was hers.

Mary gazed at the dress which was made up in the softest satin crepe, pale peach in colour, with a slim fitting bodice, the skirt falling into fullness at the hem. The style was absolute simplicity except for the double frilled collar which embraced the shoulders also. Lewis was taking her to a big dance in Leeds on the following Saturday night, and she felt sure that she would be the 'belle of the ball' in this beautiful dress.

At this moment the usual thrill she experienced when looking at a latest new garment was missing. She felt too poorly to care. Mary stopped propping up the door and moved over to her bed where she sat down. She removed her shoes and stockings and then the rest of her garments, letting them drop on the floor and leaving them where they fell instead of putting them on the clothes hangers as she usually did. Having struggled into her night shift she crawled between her sheets and rested her head on the pillow.

"I aven't even brushed my hair", she reflected. "That's not like me. I've never missed doing that before. I hope I feel better in the morning".

Mary slept fitfully that night, tossing and turning, her mind uneasy. She awoke feeling unrefreshed and again with this deep down gut feeling of nausea. She sat up and viewed with dismay her crumpled clothes on the floor. Dragging herself out of bed, she picked them all up to hang them on a hanger, hoping that the creases would have fallen out by the time she had completed her toilet. Pouring cold water from the large jug into the equally large wash bowl on her dressing table, she began to wash herself.

"This should wake me up", she thought as she splashed her eyes with the icy cold water.

When she had finished and dressed herself, Mary went down to the kitchen to make herself a cup of tea. She didn't fancy any breakfast at all but her mouth was very dry. The tea didn't taste like tea at all but she forced herself to drink it, thinking it would do her good.

All the fire grates had to be cleaned and then laid ready for the day. The dining room fire would be lit first before the family came down to breakfast. Then Mary prepared the breakfast table and went back to the kitchen to lay the early morning tea tray for Mrs. Rawlings. The kitchen fire was already crackling and as Mary put the kettle on to boil Mrs. Foster, the cook, came through the door to start work on the family breakfast.

"Mornin' Mary! All right are ye?"

"I'm still feeling a bit out o' sorts", replied Mary. "I reckon I'm sickening for something".

"Th'ad better not be Mary. We've got a lot on next week wi' these big dinner parties. Pull yourself together lass; it's not like you to be skiving!"

"You know I wouldn't do that Mrs. Foster. I just feel a bit rough that's all. I'll be all right – and I've done everything that needs to be done so far so nobody can grumble", retorted Mary.

"I'm right sorry Mary lass. I know tha's not afraid o' work like some o' these young uns!"

Mary picked up the tea tray to take up to Mrs. Rawlings' room. As she turned round quickly she felt suddenly giddy and another wave of nausea swept over her.

"I'm going to be sick, I know I am", she thought, "but perhaps I'll feel better then!"

"Mary, you look perfectly ghastly!" exclaimed Mrs. Rawlings. "I insist that you make an appointment to see Dr. Smedley as soon as possible".

The next morning found Mary sitting in the waiting room at Dr. Smedley's surgery. Her condition was no better, in fact she actually had been sick that morning but it had not improved the situation. Today was Saturday, and that evening was the special dance to which Lewis was taking her. Perhaps the doctor would give her some medicine which would make her feel better by the evening. Lewis was going to be right peeved if she should be too sick to go! The tickets had cost him an arm and a leg and she doubted that he would be able to sell them at this late stage. Besides, there was all that money she herself had spent on the dress which was far too posh to wear for their usual Saturday night hops!

"Mary Copley, it's your turn. Would you go into Dr. Smedley's room please", shouted the receptionist.

This sudden announcement startled Mary who had been deep in thought. She felt very nervous as she entered Dr. Smedley's consulting room.

"Now then Miss Copley, do sit down, What can I do for you?" queried the elderly man who had been doctor to the Rawlings family for many years.

"I haven't been feeling too grand Doctor, an' Mrs. Rawlings said I should come an' see you. She gave me this morning off specially.

"What appears to be the trouble my dear?" questioned the old doctor in a kindly manner.

"Well – I've been feeling sick all the week – an' really tired an' everything. I thought at first I must have eaten something which didn't agree with me. I was hoping I could be sick to make me feel better – but this morning I was sick an' I don't feel right", stammered Mary, in a rush to get the explanation over with.

How old are you now Mary?" Dr. Smedley asked in a fatherly way, hoping to put her at ease.

"Twenty eight Sir – an' I've never ailed much in my life before – not since I was a child anyway".

"Could you tell me when your last period was Mary?"

Mary thought for a while, trying to calculate, and shuffled her feet in embarrassment.

"I think it was about five weeks ago, but I've never been regular, an' I often go for six weeks without seeing anything, so it's hard to reckon".

"I see. Well I think I should examine you Mary. There are all kinds of problems which could occur in that department which could make you feel sick. One of life's little unfair inconveniences of being a woman I'm afraid".

Dr. Smedley gave Mary a thorough examination and then asked her to sit down after she had dressed again.

"Can you give me something for it Doctor? I'd like to feel better by tonight. I'm going to this posh dance ye see – in Leeds – it's right expensive – the tickets I mean – and Lewis – he's my boy friend – and I have been looking forward to it for ages". Mary gabbled away, trying to hide her discomfort.

"I can give you some tablets to help the sickness Mary, but I'm afraid they're not going to cure your condition my dear", said Dr. Smedley.

Mary suddenly began to sweat with fear and her face turned a shade paler than it already was.

"What do you mean Doctor? Have I got cancer then? I've been really worried deep down".

"No Mary, you haven't got cancer – you are a perfectly healthy young lady – but I do have to tell you that you are pregnant – and I think that you must have miscalculated the date of your last period".

There was a stunned silence from Mary, and then –

"I'm pregnant? You mean - a baby? I'm going to have a baby? Oh no Doctor – you're kidding me aren't you? - I can't be!"

"I'm afraid there is no doubt about it Mary, and as far as I can tell your baby will be born in March. Now you'd better tell your boyfriend – Lewis do you call him? Also Mrs. Rawlings will need to know as soon as possible. I want you to make another appointment to come and see me in one month's time. Regular check ups are very important. The tablets I've given to you should help you through this sickly period which should only last a week or two until your hormones have adjusted to your new condition. Don't forget to eat well and to drink plenty of milk".

6. "OH MARY!"

Mary was sitting on a park seat, blind and deaf to all activity going on all around her. She did not see the bees attracted by the brilliant colours of high summer flowers, nor the butterflies delicately poised on silken petals. She did not hear the blackbird singing high up in the elm tree behind her, nor the laughter of the children as they raced across the open spaces, free from the restrictions of their over populated dwelling areas of brick, concrete and high walls. Two little boys were flying a kite which had become entangled in the branches of a large old oak tree, but Mary saw none of this. Normally she would have helped them to retrieve the kite.

'Poor Mary sat a weeping on a bright summer's day' – so the nursery rhyme tells us. Our Mary was too shocked for tears. Whatever was she going to do? What was Lewis going to say? However would she tell Mrs. Rawlings, and what would that lady think of her? Oh the shame of it! She – Mary – who had always held her head so high, and had heaped scorn on other unfortunate girls who had, ' got into trouble'. She – Mary – was now in trouble herself. There wasn't even the excuse that she was young and ignorant – she was after all twenty eight years old and should have known the risk of spending weekends with Lewis, booked into Blackpool hotels as man and wife! She had been oblivious to everything except her love for him and wanted to please him in every way, afraid of losing him if she did not!

How could she face going home? Her mother and father would be mortified to have to go through the agonies of a daughter in trouble. Her sister, Connie, was due to have a second child in December and Arthur and Lucy were troubled enough about that as they regarded Connie and Eric as still too irresponsible to care for children. The couple liked to enjoy themselves and did not like to be restricted.

Mary trudged back to the Rawlings' house with a very heavy heart. She had never felt so wretched in the whole of her life. When she reached the house she slipped through the back door, through the kitchen to the back staircase, hoping that she wouldn't bump into Mrs. Foster or the scullery maid. She did not want to talk to anyone, and certainly did not want to answer any questions. Reaching her bedroom safely she entered her room, quietly closing the door behind her. Her new and expensive dress hanging ready for the evening seemed to mock her. She took hold of it and shoved it out of sight inside the wardrobe. Curling up on the bed Mary rested, feeling exhausted from her trip to the surgery and still trying to take in the reality of her situation. Ten minutes later there was a light tap on her bedroom door.

"Mary, are ye there? Mrs. Rawlings wants to 'ave a word wi' ye. She's in t' sitting room an' she asked me to get you. She's rate worried about ye".

Mary did not stir or even answer Mrs. Foster who tapped on the door again, this time a little more loudly.

"I know ye're in there Mary lass. I saw ye comin' in so stop foolin' about. Hurry up an' get down stairs before Mrs. Rawlings gets mad!"

"I'm coming. Just leave me alone an' I'll be down in a minute", said Mary.

Mary did not want a confrontation with the cook just yet, nor at any time for that matter. When she was quite sure that Mrs. Foster had gone back down stairs, Mary got up from her bed and carefully opened the door, peering out into the corridor to make sure that all was clear before venturing out. She did not want to have to go through the kitchen, so she went via the top landings until she reached the main staircase. There was no one in that part of the house so she descended the wide oak stair case and slipped along the passage to Mrs. Rawlings' sitting room. Her heart was pounding like mad as she gently tapped on the door and she thought that she would suffocate.

"Come in – oh hello Mary – I thought it might be you. Sit over there my dear and tell me how you got on with Dr. Smedley".

Mrs. Rawlings was a kindly person, very dignified, and rarely showed anger. Nevertheless, Mary was shaking in her shoes as she crossed the room and sat down on the chair opposite to her employer.

"You look extremely pale Mary. I'm really quite worried about you. Did Dr. Smedley give you anything to help you?"

"Yes ma'am – some tablets – for the sickness!" Mary's voice was scarcely audible.

"Oh good! Did he say how long this sickness might last – bearing in mind the heavy work load we have in store for us next week?"

Mary was hesitant before she ventured to speak. "Dr. Smedley said it would last for a bit – until - - - "

"Until what Mary?" asked Mrs. Rawlings gently.

"Until my 'ormones – whatever they are – have adjusted – and then it will settle down", Mary went a shade paler as she uttered these words.

"Your hormones have adjusted Mary! Adjusted to what? Whatever do you mean?"

Mary hung her head and said nothing. Realisation began to dawn on Mrs. Rawlings.

"I hope he doesn't mean what I'm beginning to think he means Mary. You're not pregnant are you?"

Mary's bowed head and silence were answer enough.

"Oh Mary! Why ever did you let a thing like this happen? You will have to tell Lewis of course – as soon as possible – and he will have to marry you - and the sooner the better! When will you be seeing him next?"

Mary replies quietly," We're supposed to be going out tonight ma'am. I've got me dress an' everything, but – well – well – well I don't think I can go ma'am – not feeling like this, and besides – it doesn't seem right now! Oh what am I going to do, and how am I going to tell him? "

Mrs. Rawlings' kind heart bled for the wretchedness of Mary's plight. She understood more than Mary could realise the shame that she was feeling.

"I've known you for many years Mary. You're a good girl at heart and all this is most unfortunate, but it's not the end of the world. These things happen and I'm sure everything will turn out well when you have told Lewis. When he come to call for you this evening I think it would be wise if you were to take him into the day room and tell him your news immediately. A trouble shared is a trouble halved and I'm quite sure he will want to do the right thing by you. Now, I think you should carry out your duties for the rest of the day, but don't over do things. Run along now – oh – I don't think that you should tell the others in the kitchen – the least they know the better – and we don't want any gossip do we?"

7. DECEPTION

"I'm sorry Mary, I can't marry ye!"

Mary could not believe what Lewis was saying. She suddenly felt that she was being sucked down into nothingness. This just could not be happening to her.

"You can't marry me Lewis? But Lewis, we have to get married now – what about the baby?" she pleaded helplessly. "I thought you loved me!"

"I can't marry you Mary because – "

"Because what Lewis? What are you keeping from me?"

Lewis could not meet her eyes as he uttered his next words –

"Mary – I'm – already married!"

There was a moment of stunned silence from Mary. Her head began to swim and her heart was beating so fast that she thought she was going to faint. She couldn't be hearing these words – she couldn't! She heard herself crying, "No! No! No!" and she was vaguely aware of his strong arms around her, guiding her to a chair and gently sitting her down. Her pent up tears of the past few days began to spill and she began to sob hysterically. He held her close, trying to soothe her and eventually her sobbing ceased and she rested against him, exhausted.

"Now listen to me Mary. I'm not goin' to desert you. We'll work something out together. Believe me, I do love you an' I didn't mean to get us into this mess".

"Why didn't ye tell me before?" whispered Mary miserably. "Ye know I'd never 'ave gone with ye if I'd known ye were married. I'm not like that!"

"It's because you're not that I never said anything," replied Lewis. "I knew ye wouldn't have looked at me if you'd known, and I wanted you more than anything. The longer we were together the more impossible it was to tell ye. I didn't want to lose ye!"

"But what about your wife?" Mary asked. "Where is she, and what's she going to say? Doesn't she need you too?"

"We split up a few years ago", said Lewis, "– but she won't divorce me 'cause she doesn't believe in divorce. Her father is a vicar ye see – and she's very religious – and that's one o' the reasons things didn't work out between us. She didn't like me going out for a drink with the lads and I felt stifled. So we agreed to go our separate ways. I didn't mind at first – her not agreeing to give me a divorce – I didn't want to get wed again. Once bitten, twice shy, as they say!"

"I didn't know ye went out drinking", said Mary – and then almost to herself – "My Dad never drinks!"

"Well I haven't been as much since I've been taking you out Mary. I know ye don't like folks who drink a lot and I've tried to stay off the booze – and I think I've succeeded, haven't I?"

Mary began to cry again. This was a side to Lewis that she had not known existed and she began to realise the helplessness of her situation. How could she ever face her family and friends? How could she ever lift up her head again?

"Don't cry lass – I can't bear to see ye crying like that. Look – there's nothing to stop us from living together as man an' wife. We can find a little house to rent and I'll buy you a wedding ring, and nobody'll know any different. The only thing missing will be a wedding ceremony. Nobody in this area, except me Mam and Dad, know I'm already married, and we don't have to say a word to anyone! Me Mam an' Dad will keep quiet 'cos they won't want any scandal".

"But", stammered Mary "– what's my family going to say? They'll expect a wedding, and a party an' all that! My Mam and Dad won't want me to be living in sin!"

"We could go to Blackpool for a weekend", Lewis said, " and when we get back we can tell 'em we suddenly decided to get married – an' that we went to a registry office in Blackpool on t' spur o' the moment. They'll never know any different – an' when the baby's born I'll register it like normal, and it will have my name legally".

"Do ye really think it will work?" Mary asked.

"I don't see what other choice we've got Mary", said Lewis, "and the sooner we get on with it the better!"

And so Mary and Lewis laid their plans and carried them out, not without some trepidation in Mary's heart. She did not of course tell Mrs. Rawlings the truth, for she was too ashamed. She said that they had decided to get married as quickly as possible and in the circumstances they did not want any fuss. Mrs. Rawlings thought it all sounded very wise and in her ignorance was pleased for a solution to Mary's problems. Arthur and Lucy displayed great consternation at the whole procedure, being extremely baffled. It was totally out of character for their elder daughter not to want a big splash on her wedding day! All this did not reassure Arthur about his headstrong daughter, nor did it alleviate his mistrust of Lewis!

The little terraced house in Fowlstone Row was acquired for rent and Mary and Lewis moved in as Mr. and Mrs. Howell. The house was very dirty and poorly decorated, but the rent was cheap due to the close proximity of the pit. Mary knew well how to scrub, clean and polish and before long the little house was spick and span. She was now feeling much better with the help of the tablets from Dr. Smedley. Lewis gave all the paint work a fresh coat of paint and together they stripped off the old, dirty and tattered wall paper and replaced it with some pretty new wall paper of the latest design.

They visited the Coop. Furniture Department and put down deposits on basic furniture requirements – the balance to be paid off during the next three year period. Mary invested every penny of all her savings of the past ten years into this project. At last she began to feel happy again, although deep down her happiness was shadowed by a niggling feeling of doubt and uncertainty.

"I've no other choice", she kept telling herself, "and nobody knows any different – except I think me Mam and Dad are a bit suspicious – and I'm sure me Mam knows I'm expecting. That's perhaps why she's not saying too much. I've got a feelin' that our Connie knows as well. She hasn't said anything, but I keep seeing a smug look in her eyes. She doesn't miss much".

Lewis continued to work in the colliery as a shot firer and this brought home a good wage. With care they were able to meet the monthly payments to the Coop. Mary took a pride and joy in her little home, and though its situation was not one in which she had ever imagined she would live, inside it was kept like a proper little palace. Initially their lives carried on as before with plenty of dancing and visits to the cinema. As they had not had a wedding ceremony, and therefore no wedding pictures, they went to the photographers and had studio photographs taken.

Mary wore her latest peach coloured evening gown with the double frilled collar. Lewis wore his best dark suit with matching waist coat, a pocket watch installed in the latter, and the chain across his chest. They made a handsome couple and they agreed that it was as good as any wedding photograph and proudly displayed it on their smart new sideboard. To Mary it seemed a symbol to show to the rest of the world that they were man and wife. Who would doubt it with a picture like that?

After a suitable time had elapsed, Mary announced to her family that she was expecting a baby. Her Mother was not fooled but it was easier to go along with Mary. After all, she did not want it to be common knowledge that her elder daughter had had to get married, did she? If Mary chose to play it this way then it seemed easier all round to accept things as they appeared!

8. THE WIFE

Lewis had gone to work and Mary, now six months pregnant, was happily making her little house sparkle and thinking what to give him for his dinner when he came home. She would have to put on her coat and nip up to the corner shop for a few potatoes to make some chips. It was bitterly cold outside in this early December, and there might be a white Christmas yet. Things seemed to be working out better than she had anticipated. No one had ever suggested that they might not be married, and as Mary's confidence grew she was even beginning to believe that they really were. They were now well known as Mr. and Mrs. Howell and regarded by all as a respectable married couple. Mary picked up the photograph of them both as she dusted the sideboard top and caressed it lovingly before replacing it. As she gently placed it down there was a sudden knock at the front door.

"I wonder who that can be?" thought Mary. "I'm not expecting anyone this morning. I hope it's not one of those door to door salesmen, or a gypsy selling pegs. They're so hard to get rid of, particularly if they stick their foot in the door!"

Mary gingerly opened the door just far enough to see who might be there. Standing on the pavement was a woman whom she had never seen before, and with her was a little girl of about five years old. Mary's heart lurched when she looked at the child. She did not need to be told whose child it was. The big soft brown eyes gazing back at her with interest were identical to Lewis's. This child was the image of her father to the last detail. All Mary's feelings of happiness dissipated, taking flight like a butterfly which pauses only briefly on each flower as it passes by. And if the child were Lewis's daughter, and there was no doubt in Mary's mind about this, then the woman whose hand she was holding must be his wife. What shame burned through Mary's mind, filling the space which happiness had vacated.

"You don't know me, but I need to talk to you. I would be grateful if you would spare me a few minutes of your time. May I come in? It's extremely cold standing out here with that icy wind whistling round the corner".

The speaker was an attractive woman, perhaps in her early thirties, and she spoke a good Standard English with only the slightest hint of a Yorkshire intonation. She was wearing a thick, navy blue winter coat, very plain in style, and on her feet were sensible walking shoes of brown leather. On her hands she wore plain leather gloves and she carried a brown leather shoulder bag. The child also was simply but warmly dressed, for it was the beginning of December and the weather was quite raw.

"By the sound of her voice I really do believe she is a vicar's daughter", Mary thought. "I only half believed Lewis when he told me that!"

Mary opened the door fully and invited the woman and her child to come and sit down by the fire and get warm. She studied the child closely and there was no doubt at all in Mary's mind about her parentage. As though to confirm her supposition, a slow smile spread from the child's dark eyes to her lips and then to her dimpled cheeks. That was Lewis's smile all right – the smile that would melt any heart and disarm its owner.

"You must be wondering who I am and why I have come", said the woman.

The child was now gazing around the room, as children will, and her gaze rested on the photograph of Mary and Lewis on the sideboard and she stared intently at it. The woman's attention was drawn to the photograph, but she quickly looked away.

"You are Lewis's wife", said Mary in a flat voice. "I recognise his child – but he never told me he had a little girl – he never told me he was married until it was too late. Please believe me – I wouldn't have had anything to do with him if I'd known! I didn't want to be responsible for breaking up anyone's marriage!"

"You didn't break up my marriage – it was already finished – four years ago – in fact when Audrey was quite small. My name is Joan by the way, and I know you're Mary – please may I call you that?"

"How did ye know that, and how did ye know where we lived? Lewis said ye lived miles away from here", said Mary.

"I do occasionally visit Lewis's parents so that they can see their grand daughter from time to time. They told me where to find you, but they did not want me to come and spoil things for you both now that you are settled – and they have at last accepted that Lewis and I will never be reconciled".

"Why didn't they tell me about the child?" queried Mary. "I would never have agreed to live with him if I'd known he 'ad a bairn. He should be with you, helping to look after her. Oh dear – what a mess! I don't know what to do!"

"I haven't come here to suggest that Lewis should come back to Audrey and me", said Joan. "We've managed a long time without him now, thanks to my parents who have been very supportive. No – I came here to warn you about Lewis – before it's too late. You really should not be with him once your child is born. He will become very jealous of all the attention you have to give to your baby, and because you won't be able to go out with him very much he will probably go out drinking – and believe me he will return in a violent mood, and both you and your child will be at risk. I know that he will be absolutely charming to you now, and it's hard to believe that he could raise a hand to anyone, but he has a very dark side to his nature – which comes out when he's had too much to drink. I had to flee with my baby and take refuge in my parent's home! The drink turns him nasty and if he thinks he is lacking your sole attention – because of your baby – he will lash out physically. That is why I had to leave him. I couldn't risk him hurting Audrey. I will never marry again because I believe in my wedding vows. In the sight of God I will always be Lewis's wife until death. You are not hampered by such ties - you could leave now, have your baby, and eventually marry someone else. I urge you to leave him as soon as possible!"

"I can't", said Mary. "As long as you and the child don't want him back, then I must stay with him. I know he loves me – and perhaps he will have learnt his lesson this time. He won't want a second home broken up will 'e now? Besides, he says he's really looking forward to our baby coming. P'rhaps he really misses Audrey. She's a lovely little girl an' so like him".

"Well I can see your mind is made up Mary. I'm sorry to be upsetting you like this, but I just felt I had to try and warn you. As you say, he might have learned his lesson, but I do have grave misgivings for you. We will be on our way now so – good luck!"

As they left the house Mary heard Audrey say to her mother, "Mummy, why has that lady got a picture of my daddy in her house?"

These words cut Mary to the quick. She now knew that she would never feel like Lewis's wife again, having come face to face with his true wife and child. She went back into the little sitting room and sat down in front of the fire, silent tears streaming down her cheeks. A sword was piercing her very soul. When her grief was spent a little she pulled herself together, washed her face and combed her hair. She then busied herself with the preparations for dinner, resolving to say nothing of Joan's visit, or of the fact that she now knew Lewis had a little daughter. Some gut feeling told her that she would be treading on dangerous ground if she were to confront him with this knowledge.

"What else is there for me to do but carry on?" she thought." We've told too many lies to undo now! I must hope an' pray that everythin' will come right in the end!"

The next day Mary had a visit from her mother.

"I'm just goin' down to our Connie's", she said. "Eric's just ridden up on 'is bike to get me 'cause she's gone into labour".

Later that day Connie gave birth to another son who was named Ronald, and who came to be known generally as "our Ron".

Christmas preparations were now afoot. Because of Connie's new baby, and Mary being tired with her own pregnancy, Lucy said she would make up all the puddings and cakes, and that all the family should go to her for the Christmas and New Year celebrations. From her parents for Christmas, Mary received a matching jug and sugar bowl made of peach coloured glass shot through with a mother of pearl effect. Mary placed them on display on her sideboard as they were so pretty and she enjoyed looking at them.

Christmas came and went and Mary struggled through the last three months of her pregnancy, all be it with a heavy heart. She showed a bright and cheerful face to the world, telling no one of her fears.

On the morning of March 7th, Lewis said cheerio to Mary and set off for the early morning shift at the pit. Shortly after he had gone Mary felt what she thought must be the first pangs of pain of the first stage of labour. As she became surer, she collected everything together, both for her confinement and for the new baby. Then she slipped out of the house to ask a neighbour if someone would go and fetch Mrs. Firth, the midwife.

PART 2

1. 1989 A FUNERAL

Far up in the sky a lark was singing and the few clouds that were drifting across the great arc of blue were fluffy and white. The trees were in their full glory, massive with foliage, and the bees were humming busily as they extracted the nectar from the various blossoms. The grass in the meadows had grown tall, full of buttercups, moon daisies and cowslips. The little lane turned and twisted and there was a fresh earthy smell after last evening's shower.

A sleek Volvo saloon car of pale metallic green slid quietly down the lane. It turned into the entrance of the pretty little cemetery which was completely hidden from the road by tall hedges where the bird song rang and echoed. The cemetery was extremely well kept, everything neat and tidy, and the tall cherry trees which lined the driveways were like fountains against the blue of the sky.

The car came to a standstill and the driver, a woman in her mid fifties, emerged. She was smartly dressed in clothes of quality – a Burberry trench coat as there was still a nip in the air, brown leather court shoes, and a silk Hermes scarf draped around her shoulders. People said that she looked younger than her years and that she had a good skin – probably because she had never smoked, neither had she clogged her pores with heavy make up. Her hair was a dark brown, with help now from an occasional tint to ward off the onset of grey, and she wore it shoulder length. At this particular moment it looked extremely sleek as she had just left the hairdressers. Left alone, her hair would wave and curl in all the wrong places and she felt like a gypsy. She had strong regular features, dark eyes and strongly marked eyebrows which she had never plucked. More often than not her face wore a stern expression, born of years of self control in a classroom situation when she had often wanted to laugh but must not. However, when she did smile her whole face lit up and her soft brown eyes twinkled with merriment. Due to a bad childhood diet she had always had a struggle to keep her weight under control, but she worked hard at it and other people said that they did not know what she was worrying about – but no one is ever satisfied with their own appearance! Although in her fifties she had managed not to develop the usual middle age 'spare tyre' so perhaps looked slimmer than she actually felt!

She walked across the muddy grass to a row of graves and came to a standstill by the fifth one along the line.

"Yes", she thought, "that's absolutely right – simple with no gush! She would have liked that – it's what she wanted – and she would have appreciated this pretty last resting place – had she been in her right mind! She had a horror of being cremated – it would have been cleaner somehow! Well – I've kept my promise, and now that at last the stone has been erected there is nothing more I can do for her!"

Sylvia, for that was the woman's name, stepped back to get a better view of the white marble headstone. It was not too big or ostentatious in any way – adorned only with the simple carving of a single rose in the top right hand corner. The inscription on the stone read quite simply;

MARY ALICE COPLEY

1907 – 1989

REST IN PEACE

"I hope that at last she can", Sylvia murmured as she arranged a bunch of mixed flowers in the pristine new vase at the base of the stone. "Her whole life that I remember was full of turmoil, and she certainly knew how to create havoc in other people's lives. I always wonder how it is that Richard ever stayed with me in the circumstances. Most men would have walked away from it all, but he did his best for her and she hated him for it. He couldn't win – nobody could win – she wouldn't let them!"

Satisfied that everything was in order, Sylvia returned to her car. As she climbed into it she thought how lucky she had been in many other ways, a husband who thought the world of her, in spite of her problems of which there were many, a good career, and a good life style in general.

"We've come a long way since Fowlstone Row Mother, but how much more we could have done for you if only you had let it happen! You wouldn't be happy would you – no matter how hard we tried!"

Sylvia sat for a while, deep in thought. The end had come suddenly and unexpectedly, not in the least how she had imagined it would be. After conscientiously looking after her mother's needs since she had been fourteen, Sylvia had fully expected a long, drawn out and messy ending, and she could barely take in the fact that the burden she had carried for forty three years of her life had at last slipped from her shoulders.

Her mind drifted back to the day of the funeral last August. It was such a day as this, with the larks singing riotously high up in the sky. She remembered the warmth of the sun, the green moss on the banks, and the heavy scent of all the flowers which arrayed all the other graves around. There had not been a church service, somehow it had not seemed appropriate as Mary had refused to set foot in church for many, many years. Instead, the local vicar of this little Somerset town had conducted the burial service at the graveside, and it was all very simply beautiful.

Sylvia had struggled to the edge of the grave on her crutches to take a last look at the coffin bearing her mother's name, before it was covered up. She had been extremely ill herself, and almost at death's door, but she was strong and had fought hard to survive, although now she was very weak. No tears would come as she made her last farewell. Her cousin, Ralph, came to her and put his arm around her shoulder, and they both stood for a moment, gazing down at the coffin. Ralph had always loved his Auntie Mary and never forgot how good she had been to him in the days of his youth, before she had lost her mind!

As she turned at last from the grave, Sylvia became aware that her own three daughters were sobbing into their handkerchiefs. She remembered vaguely wondering why they were all crying so much when she could not cry at all. After all, they had never been involved in looking after her. If she were lucky one of them might cut her lawn, or muck out the bathroom, but it was once in a blue moon! They were always glad to receive the weekly pocket money that their Nanna gave to them, and the numerous bars of chocolates and sweets, and the nice presents at Christmas and birthdays. Give Mary her due, she had thought a great deal about her grandchildren and was excessively generous towards them, to the point of starving herself had it been allowed!

"This is their first experience of the death of someone close – except of course their sister Jayne, but then they were too young to take that in! Nevertheless, I hope that I will never give to my children the troubles that my mother gave to me. If I did I don't think they would tolerate it anyway!"

Richard, Sylvia's husband, came forward to guide her back to the car and to remove her crutches as she got in. He had been her tower of strength throughout their married life together, warm hearted and dependable. He took her hand for a second and his, as always, felt strong and comforting. She did not know what she would ever have done without him.

Sylvia leaned out of the window and said goodbye to the only other visitor to the little service – her friend Madge. Madge lived close by but had never met Mary. She had only come to the funeral to offer Sylvia some moral support. There was no one else present except Ralph's son who had driven his father down to Somerset from Yorkshire. Mary had had no friends and never wanted any! She had only ever wanted her daughter, and Sylvia had grown to hate the words, "I only love you luv!" which Mary had constantly repeated to her daughter throughout her life.

As Sylvia sat in her car, enjoying the few minutes of peace and quiet, she began to think upon her childhood days with Mary. It hadn't been all bad in the very early days, but Mary's illness had become progressively worse, for years being untreated, and the situation becoming more intolerable for all concerned.

"I must try to remember the good times and what she used to be like when I was very young. She did her best for me as far as she was able. If only she'd been in her right mind in later years she would have been proud of my achievements. As it was she let everything one said flow over her and nothing ever got through to her. I suppose that could have been the drugs though, as she was on extra large doses of Largactil in the end. It wasn't her fault that she became mentally ill – though it was hard to believe that as she could be positively evil at times."

Sylvia's thoughts drifted back to her very earliest memories, and she tried to piece together the events of her mother's life after she'd had her child. Sylvia had vague recollections of moments in her infancy. All her other knowledge she had gleaned from Mary, her grandparents, and various other relations, in particular her Auntie Connie who had died a few years before Mary. Had Arthur Copley been alive he would have been convinced that his daughter, Connie, had smoked herself to death and he was most probably right!

"I wonder what course Mother's life would have taken if I had not been conceived?" Sylvia thought. "Would she still have lost her mind if her life had been smoother, or was it inevitable? I'll never know!"

2. 1936. "I DON'T KNOW WHAT TO DO!"

Mary was panicking. Her baby was unable to keep down the milk she was offered from the bottle. She had tried in vain to feed the child herself but she just had not made enough milk and her breasts had now dried up completely. The child had weighed a good eight pounds at birth but was now losing weight at an alarming rate. Mrs. Firth, who acted as District Nurse as well as midwife, had said that she must go on the bottle at once, but it wasn't working! The milk just did not suit the child. Mary was also very frightened of this little scrap of humanity – she did not feel comfortable handling her and was afraid that she might drop her. As Mary became more and more agitated so did the child who cried incessantly because she also was not at ease, and indeed was very hungry. Mary had had no idea just how much time a baby takes up in every twenty four hours – particularly when there are feeding problems. Her housework was neglected and Lewis's meals were not always on the table on time. At first he was quite patient but as the situation grew, worse instead of getting better, he began to be irritated.

"Mary, I do live 'ere as well ye know!" he crossly spoke when Mary went to pick up the crying baby from her crib. "Can't yer leave 'er alone for a minute and attend to me. Leave 'er to cry – it won't hurt 'er!"

The tears pricked in Mary's eyes and fear clutched at her heart as she remembered what Lewis's wife had told her of his behaviour within his marriage to Joan.

Poor Mary

"I'm sorry Lewis, but I think we might lose her if she goes on like this. I don't know what to do!"

"Well take 'er to see the doctor then, an' let him sort 'er out – but right now I wouldn't mind my dinner if tha doesn't mind!"

Mary put Lewis's somewhat dried up meal on the table.

"I'm sorry about that Lewis – I made the meal earlier whilst she was sleeping for a while – I thought I'd better 'cos she doesn't sleep for long and then I've no chance of doing it!"

"OK!" said Lewis, his annoyance dissipating at the sight of Mary's crestfallen face. "I tell ye what – why don't we go down to the photographers with our Sylvia and 'ave a family picture taken – while she's still little. They grow up quick tha knows, an' it'll be nice to look back on"

A few days later they were in the photographer's studio ready for a family photograph. Lewis was standing by Mary who was sitting on a chair with the tiny child on her knee. Lewis was wearing his smart dark suit and Mary an elegant dark blue dress with small polka dots and a white lace collar. As always her sleek black hair looked impeccable with a diamante clip catching back the waves. Mary did not look at all comfortable holding her baby and she was afraid that she might drop her. Behind her forced smile could be detected a deep anxiety. The baby appeared to gaze at the camera with eyes which looked a little sunken.

Mary had taken her baby to the doctor's and he told her to keep trying different brands of baby food until one was found which suited the child.

"It's no good trying it for a day or two though", he said." You've got to give the baby's system chance to adapt to it".

Mary did as advised but still nothing was working. The baby had lost three pounds in weight since birth and now looked like a shrivelled up old man. Mary's sister, Connie, brought her new baby Ron to see her. Ron was a fine bouncing boy of four and a half months old. Connie was shocked to see her small niece looking so frail and weak, obviously having deteriorated drastically since her last visit.

"My God Mary! You'll never rear that bairn; she's small enough to go in a pint pot". She broke down and wept which did not make Mary feel any better. Mary looked at little Ron who was chuckling contentedly in his pram, and her fears for her own child deepened.

The next day Lewis was not working so Mary asked him if he would look after Sylvia whilst she went to the chemist shop to buy a different brand of baby milk which had been recommended by the midwife.

"It'll be quicker if I don't 'ave to get her ready to go out", Mary said, "and I'll get something for your dinner while I'm out".

Lewis was agreeable so she set off to the chemist shop with a heavy heart.

"Nothing seems to agree with my baby", she said to the chemist. "I've tried all sorts an' she can't keep it down. I know I'm going to lose her – she only weighs five pounds now, and she was over eight pounds at birth". Mary couldn't help herself and she began to cry.

"Well Mrs. Howell", said the chemist, "there is a new brand of milk formula now on the market. It's homogenized and therefore as near as possible to a mother's milk. Unfortunately it is much more expensive than all the other brands, but it would be worth trying for at least a few weeks, then if your baby accepts it you could wean her back on to the cheaper brand when she's strong enough to cope".

"I'll take some", said Mary. "I don't care how much it costs, an' I'll keep her on it as long as she needs it if it works".

"If it does work Mrs. Howell, give her a few weeks on it and then introduce a teaspoonful of Virol into her bottle. That will help to rebuild her body weight and is very good for muscles, bones and teeth".

The chemist did not mention to Mary his concern for the child who had lost weight so drastically, and of the possible damage which could occur in severe cases of malnutrition. It is perhaps as well that she remained in ignorance of this.

Mary opened her front door and could hear Sylvia crying.

"Oh dear! Where is Lewis and why has he left her to cry like that?" thought Mary, going into the sitting room and heading for the pram. The pram was empty! "He must have her upstairs", she thought. "Lewis, I'm back. You can bring our Sylvia down now. I've got some new milk to try – the chemist said it's very good. It's expensive though – I hope you don't mind. He says it's hom – hom- homogenic or something like that. I don't know what that means but he says it's as near as possible to a mother's milk".

Lewis did not appear and she could still hear Sylvia crying – a rather muffled cry – and she wasn't sure from whence it came! It sounded to be from upstairs. Mary climbed the stairs to the bedroom and there was Lewis, fast asleep and snoring on the bed – but no baby! She looked all round and couldn't find her anywhere, but she could still hear the wailing.

"Lewis! Lewis! Wake up! Where's our Sylvia?" Mary shook him as she spoke.

"Aw leave me alone, I'm tired!", and Lewis turned over and continued to snore.

Mary went through the whole house again, looking in cupboards and wardrobe and under the bed, but the child whose cries were becoming desperate was no where to be seen. Mary tried not to panic and to fight down the alarm within her. She stood and listened very carefully and then she realised that the cries were coming from the blanket box on the landing. She rushed to open it and there, lying amidst the spare blankets, her tiny face flushed and almost purple, was Sylvia. Mary snatched her up and rushed into the bedroom, blazing with anger.

"How could you be so stupid?" she cried. "She was suffocatin' in there. She's weak enough without you doing that to her! I just don't understand you Lewis!"

"Well – she wouldn't stop cryin'", mumbled Lewis from under the sheets, "so I put 'er in there so I wouldn't hear 'er. I'm not like you, fussing over every little whimper!"

Again Mary was filled with foreboding. If he had loved the child he would never do a thing like that to her. She was so tiny and defenceless.

Mary made up the new milk in Sylvia's bottle and began to feed her. The child took comfort from sucking at the teat. She was not yet strong enough to guzzle greedily like the average healthy baby. After she had finished sucking Mary sat with her on her knee for about half an hour. The milk did not come back as it usually did and the baby had fallen into a contented sleep. Mary was elated as she gently lowered her into the pram where she slept for two hours. At last Mary had found a milk formula which suited the child who gradually began to gain weight. After a few weeks, Mary introduced a spoonful of Virol into each feed and eventually Sylvia regained all the weight she had lost – and more!

Now that Sylvia had grown stronger Mary thought it was time for her to be christened. Lewis had registered her in his own name, so she bore the name of Sylvia Howell. The christening took place one Sunday afternoon at the local Church of England and again the child's name was officially confirmed. The family went back to Mary and Lewis's little house for a simple christening party, and everyone rejoiced to see how well Sylvia was coming on now, and delighted in her dimpled smiles and chuckles. Mary looked on, feeling a great relief and satisfaction.

3. THE LAST MEMORIES

Lewis had started going out drinking. He had asked Mary to go with him on several occasions, but she was totally absorbed in looking after her baby and said she could not possibly leave her.

"Why don't ye get yer mother to come an' sit in so that we can go out together? We 'aven't been to a dance or the pictures since our Sylvia wa' born, an' ye know ye love dancing", Lewis grumbled.

"Ye know me mother won't do things like that. She'll only come to look after the bairn if I were going out to work – but never for pleasure. You ask our Connie. She likes to go out a lot and she leaves our Ron, but she has to ask a neighbour to sit in. I wouldn't like to do that – not with our Sylvia after all the troubles we've had with her", protested Mary.

"Suit yerself", growled Lewis – "but I've 'ad enough o' this stayin' in every night. Ye think o' nobody but that kid. I'm off out on my own!"

Mary's heart sank as Lewis went out, slamming the door behind him. When he came home, very late, he was extremely drunk and abusive towards Mary, taunting her for the way she panicked over Sylvia, and telling her that she couldn't cope. Her heart felt like a stone within her, she had never known him to be so nasty.

The next morning, which was Sunday, Lewis was his usual charming self, as though nothing had happened between them.

"Let's take our Sylvia for a walk in the park Mary – it'll do ye both good to get some fresh air".

Mary felt so relieved at the change in him and she readily agreed. She quickly prepared her baby for her pram and put on her own coat and scarf. Sylvia was now nine months old and could sit up in her pram. Her face was now chubby with dimpled cheeks, and she already had a mischievous look in her brown eyes. She strongly resembled her father in appearance and Mary realised that she was a duplicate of his other little daughter, Audrey. Mary had never mentioned the visit by Lewis's wife and he did not know that she knew of Audrey's existence.

I do not know how old one is supposed to be before one can retain memories of one's first experiences. At any rate the following occasion was one which Sylvia was able to vaguely remember when she grew older. She remembered being pushed in her pram by her father, with her mother walking by the side of him. She even thought that she remembered what they were wearing, but this image in her mind could be confused with a photograph taken at a similar time. As they walked along, Lewis produced a bar of milk chocolate from his pocket. Sylvia knew that it was milk chocolate because he had said so as he passed it to Mary who accidentally dropped it on the floor.

"Oh dear, I think it's broken!" exclaimed Mary, "But it's well wrapped up so it won't be dirty!"

Sylvia remembered leaning over the side of the pram to look at the broken bar of chocolate, and she fully expected to see white milk spilling from it – but of course it wasn't. She remembered feeling very puzzled that there was no milk on the floor, but her attention was soon to be on the lovely taste of the chocolate which

Mary gave to her in small pieces so that it wouldn't dribble down her nice clean coat.

"I think it's about time we 'ad another photo taken", said Lewis. "Our Sylvia's altering that fast we ought to go and 'ave one done"

Mary readily agreed as she was only too pleased that he was interested enough in his daughter to want to do this. A few days later they visited the same photographer's studio again. Mary wore her new coat of imitation leopard skin and a multi- coloured velvet scarf at her throat. She had dressed Sylvia in a pale green knitted coat with matching leggings. A matching bonnet was taken off in order to reveal her pretty curls to the best advantage. This was the last photograph of the three of them together, and indeed the last one ever to be taken of Lewis!

By now Sylvia was able to toddle around on strong, sturdy legs. Everyone was amazed at how she had come on after such a bad start. She was a very chubby child, and had overtaken her cousin, Ron, in size. Mary attributed Sylvia's chubbiness to the Virol and in her ignorance kept stuffing more and more of it into the child to make sure that she stayed that way. She became obsessed about it – there was no happy medium – everything to excess!

Sylvia had one more fleeting memory of her father and it was to be her last. One Sunday afternoon Lewis took her by the hand and they went for a walk in the park. Sylvia trotted along on her chubby little legs but she was unused to walking this distance and Lewis had not taken her pushchair.

"Cum on, it'll do ye good lass to walk some o' that fat off ye", said Lewis as his daughter began to drag her feet. "In my opinion ye Mam's feeding ye too much now and you're going to end up too fat if she's not careful. She's no reasoning yer mother, once she gets something in 'er head!"

Sylvia gamely struggled on for she was not a complaining child, being generally placid by nature, but her legs really did hurt and ache. Nevertheless she enjoyed being in the park. There were soft murmurings and rustlings in the tall trees as a cool breeze was blowing from the south west. The grass was golden and flowers like jewels decorated the edges of the spacious lawns. Lilacs grew in a tangle of heady perfume as the breeze gently swayed the purple and white blossom.

At last it was time to go home and Sylvia's pace grew slower and slower, but Lewis would not pick her up to carry her. He did at least realise that he'd overdone her though, and when they reached home he sat her down on a little stool whilst he went to fetch a bowl of warm, soapy water. He then proceeded to bathe her tiny feet with the utmost gentleness. Sylvia remembered so clearly the feeling of comfort that the warm water gave to her aching feet, and the gentleness of her father in that moment. Providence was kind that this should be her last memory of him.

4. THE DEMON DRINK

One morning Mary took Sylvia to the shops, and now that the child was bigger and stronger she didn't use the pushchair unless they were going any distance. There was no self service in those days, and it was necessary to wait in a long queue of people before reaching the counter to be served. Each customer would be involved in often long conversations with the shopkeeper so getting served was usually a lengthy process. Outside the shop could be heard the sound of a brass band playing as the musicians marched down the street. They made a colourful procession with their red tunics and navy blue trousers, and silver buttons glinting in the sun. The usual dingy, grimy street was momentarily transformed, giving a few moments of joy to the occupants.

Mary finished paying for her provisions and turned round to take hold of her daughter's hand – but she wasn't there! Panicking, she looked all round the shop but the child was nowhere to be seen. Her heart pounding with fear, Mary dashed outside, fearful about the road and possible traffic. There were often heavy lorries passing to and from the colliery. Sylvia wouldn't stand a chance if she ran in front of one of them. The band was playing a stimulating march to the delight of the onlookers who for some reason were beginning to laugh with amusement. Mary pushed her way through the crowd, her eyes scanning the pavement and the road. Then she stopped in amazement, looking on as her young daughter, marching in time to the music, head held high and her arms swinging, was leading the band down the road. Although she laughed about the incident and proudly related the escapade to family and friends, Mary felt inwardly annoyed that she had actually lost control of the child for a while, and thought that in future she would have to watch her more closely.

Lewis continued to go out in the evening on his own and more often than not he came back in a drunken state and nasty with it. He had hit Mary on several occasions but was always full of remorse the next day. He had been known to kneel with his head on her lap and weep, begging for forgiveness, and vowing that he would never do it again, but he always did.

"I can put up with it", Mary thought, "as long as 'e doesn't hurt our Sylvia!"

One Sunday lunch time Lewis said that he was going down to the pub with his mates. At tea time Sylvia was sitting in her high chair and chewing her bread and butter fingers which had been spread with honey. Mary was at the kitchen sink washing up when the front door was flung open and in lurched Lewis. He staggered over to the sofa which was quite near Sylvia's highchair. She grinned at him and he grinned back, then he took his cigarette from his mouth and deliberately stubbed it on her bare foot. Sylvia screamed out and Mary turned round just in time to see him do this monstrous thing again to her other foot.

"Stop it! Stop it!" Mary cried, and snatched the screaming child from her chair and ran to the other side of the room. Lewis picked up the jar of honey and hurled it across the room at them, narrowly missing Sylvia's head. Mary ran out of the room, up the stairs and into the bedroom, locking the door securely behind her. Both she and the child trembled and wept as Lewis persistently hammered on the door, demanding to be let in. At last the banging ceased as Mary cowered on the bed with the child in her arms. Lewis had obviously fallen into a drunken stupor.

Mary examined the child's burns and gently put on some soothing ointment and some cotton socks to protect them. She did not stir from the room all night, and didn't even get undressed.

"I can't let this happen again", thought Mary. "I don't care if he hurts me, but I can't have our Sylvia hurt – but what are we going to do? I can't take another bairn home to me mother's – she's got enough on with our Ralph". And so were her thoughts throughout the long and sleepless night.

The decision was taken out of Mary's hands sooner than expected. Lewis had sheepishly gone off to his early morning shift after breakfast which was accompanied by stony silence. Mary began to put the house to rights as Lewis had certainly created a great deal of havoc the night before and a great many things had been thrown around, and some pots broken.

"We can ill afford to have this sort o' damage – it's taking us all our time to pay for the furniture without him smashing everything up"

As she was thinking these thoughts there was a loud knocking at the front door. When Mary opened it she was confronted by two burly looking men, both wearing navy blue overalls. On the top pocket of their overalls was embroidered the word "COOPERATIVE". Parked at the side of the road was an enormous furniture van also bearing the word "COOPERATIVE" in large letters written across its side.

"Mrs. Howell?" they asked.

"Yes", replied Mary. "Whatever do you want?"

"We've cum to collect yer furniture Mrs. Howell", the larger of the two men stated.

"Collect my furniture? Whatever do ye mean?" said Mary, her heart giving a sickening lurch.

"Well, it 'asn't been paid fo' Mrs. Howell", said the second man who had a cigarette dangling from his lips.

"Of course it's being paid for", said Mary. "My husband's been down to Coop. every week with the money".

"Ye're well behind wi' the payments luv. No money's come in for months now, an' yer 'usband signed an agreement that if payments weren't kept up then Coop. as a right to redeem all the goods supplied on credit".

Mary went weak at the knees and began to tremble. This just could not be happening!

"But I know it's been paid for regularly", she cried. "I've seen my husband put the money aside from his wage packet every week, and then he's taken it to the Coop."

"Well, he may 'ave taken money out of 'is wage packet Mrs. Howell, but it never got as far as the Coop. He's 'ad several letters to remind 'im of overdue payments but there's been no reaction. We're sorry luv, but we'll 'ave to remove these items which are on our list 'ere!" The taller man produced a very official looking document containing a list of all the furniture they had acquired from the Coop.

Mary was utterly bewildered. Certainly she had noticed official looking letters arriving at the house but when she had questioned Lewis about them he had whisked them away and said they were nothing to worry about. It had never entered her head that he wasn't keeping up with the weekly instalments to the Coop. He must have used the money for the drink and also betting on the horses which he had taken up recently. Perhaps he had gotten into bad debt at the betting office – though when she had reproached him about his gambling on the horses he had replied that he only had a little flutter and that wouldn't hurt anyone!

The two men pushed their way passed Mary and began to remove the chairs and table from the room. Mary ran to the sideboard and snatched the photographs and precious ornaments, including the peach coloured bowl and jug, and quickly stuffed them into the built in wall cupboard at the side of the fireplace. She then stood by helplessly whilst they removed her beautiful sideboard and then went upstairs to retrieve the bedroom furniture.

Apart from Sylvia's pram and cot, various small articles, personal things and the bed covers which were strewn around the bedroom floor, everything was gone! Mary looked round the house in disbelief, and when she reached the bedroom something snapped inside her head and she began to scream, and scream and then collapsed on the pile of bedding on the floor in a fit of hysteria. Sylvia, who had been placed on the floor, joined in with a loud wailing, feeling very frightened and insecure.

After about half an hour of uncontrolled sobbing, Mary at last calmed down. She collected all her personal things together and put them into a suitcase. Then she gathered Sylvia's clothes and her few toys and put them in another case and then struggled down the stairs with the heavy cases and put them by the door. Going up the stairs once more, Mary went to rouse the child from the uneasy sleep into which she had cried herself. The tears again coursed down Mary's cheeks as she looked down on Sylvia who was curled up on the pile of bed linen and sucking her thumb for comfort. Her closed eyes were still wet with tears. Having awakened the child, Mary dressed her in her outdoor clothes and then secured her in the pram. She then went to the cupboard in the bedroom, took out her leopard skin coat and velvet scarf and put them on. Ten minutes later saw her bowed figure struggling up the steep hill to reach the main road towards her mother's house. The heavy cases were balanced on the front of the pram and Sylvia was peering out from behind them, looking very bewildered.

Mary pushed open the back door of her mother's house and went in.

"Hello our Sylvie", said Arthur, twinkling at his well beloved grand daughter. "'Ave ye come to see yer granddad?"

"I've left 'im Dad", said Mary. "I've left Lewis and I don't know what to do!"

In between sobs she told her parents what had been going on for the past few months, culminating in the events of the last two days.

"You'd better take ye things up t' bedroom Mary Alice", said Lucy. "I'll look after our Sylvia whilst ye sort yerself out. Ee dear Arthur! Whatever is to do? Our poor Mary!"

"I told ye I never trusted that Lewis", said Arthur whose blue eyes, usually full of fun, were now bright with unshed tears. "– but yer couldn't tell 'er, an' now she's payin' for it! It's our Sylvia I worry about, poor bairn! It's not 'er fault, any o' this, an' she'll be the one to suffer for it".

5. BLACK LEAD

Whilst Mary was staying with her parents Lewis came many times to beg her to go back to him. She loved him still and could have put up with any situation on her own, but she loved her child more and would never again risk her being hurt at his hands. Every time he came he tore Mary apart with his pleas and she realised that if she were going to have any peace, then she must leave the area. But how could she do this with a small child in tow?

Living a block away, in a larger than usual terraced house, lived an elderly widow by the name of Mrs. Adams. She was an educated lady who was comfortably off compared to most of her neighbours. She had set herself up as counsellor to all who might need the benefit of her 'expert' advice and opinions. Every community has such a person – doesn't it! Lucy Copley hung on to every word the good lady uttered. Everything she said had to be right, and indeed the lady did offer a great deal of good advice. Mary's problems had come to the ears of Mrs. Adams who had known her since she was a little girl. She paid a visit to the Copley family household to see if she could be of any assistance.

"What Mary needs to do is to look for a position as companion housekeeper to someone who will accept a child into their home. She's had a great deal of experience in service with Mrs. Rawlings for all those years, and I'm quite sure that she will be given an excellent reference from her. I myself would also vouch for Mary's character. I know she's been headstrong in the past, but she's an honest girl, hard working and conscientious, and she keeps herself smart". Mrs. Adams paused to take a sip of tea before carrying on.

"I think if you buy a Sheffield newspaper you will find people advertising their requirements under the column 'Situations Vacant'. The paper will cover a large area well beyond Sheffield, and I'm sure it is best Mary if you get well away from here. If you stay you will be continually pestered by Lewis and getting yourself really upset. Besides, it's not good for the child. You both need a new start somewhere else".

Mary began to buy a Sheffield paper regularly, and each evening she perused the 'Situations Vacant' column for a likely position. In the meantime she helped her mother with the housework, taking some of the burden from her as Lucy was getting on in years now, and her arthritic condition was worsening. For a house proud person it was a very dirty area in which to live, and if one wanted to be spick and span it meant regular hard work to keep it so.

Now that times were a little better for the Copleys, their children all being grown up, they were able to afford a little more for themselves. Every Sunday lunch saw a roast joint of beef, lamb or pork on the table, but it was still preceded by the traditional Yorkshire pudding served with lashings of gravy. If the roast joint happened be lamb then the pudding was taken with mint sauce. Sometimes a handful of raisins was thrown into the pudding mixture, and believe it or not - this was quite delicious served with the gravy and the mint sauce! If you haven't tried it then you don't know what you're missing!

The remains of the joint were taken down to the cool cellar and preserved for the next day – Monday Wash Day! Wash Day was the biggest domestic event of the week, and had to be completed all in the one day, including the ironing. On Sunday evening, before retiring to bed, Arthur's job was to go down into the cellar and bring up the 'peggy' tubs, rubbing board and any other equipment needed for Wash Day. He would place them in the kitchen after taking up the kitchen mats.

At three o'clock in the morning – without fail – Lucy would get up and dress quickly, go into the kitchen and light the copper which stood in the corner. The copper was built into the kitchen and was made of bricks. Underneath was a small area for a fire which heated up the water. The water had been poured into the copper by means of a bucket filled from the tap and it was soon brought to boiling pint by the fire. When not in use the copper was covered by a board, which in turn was covered by a cloth, and used as a shelf. Lucy would pour some ammonia into the boiling water to ensure that her 'whites' were whiter than white! She would then collect more water into the bucket to put on the fireplace to heat up, as there was no hot water in the house at all. Whilst the copper was heating up its water, and the fire heating up the bucket ready for the 'peggy' tubs, Lucy sorted out all the dirty clothes into piles according to colour. The white sheets and any white shirts and collars were then put into the bubbling water in the copper, and left there until they were well and truly bleached.

At this point Lucy would have her breakfast. Afterwards she would carry the heavy bucket of hot water from the fire and pour it into one of the 'peggy' tubs. Then she would refill the bucket ready for the fire to heat up. She would then place a selection of coloured garments into the solution of hot water and soap suds and 'posh' them, as they say, with a 'peggy' stick. The latter was a wooden contraption bearing three short legs on a round piece of wood attached to a long wooden handle. Any heavily soiled garments would then receive an application of green washing soap and then rubbed hard against the rubbing board in the tub.

By this time the second lot of water would be ready and poured into the second 'peggy' tub, but no soap was added. All the clothes had to be put through a heavy mangle with big rollers in order to extract as much soapy water as possible before placing them in the tub with clear water for rinsing. Turning those heavy rollers was hard enough work, particularly with voluminous sheets going through them. As soon as the clothes were rinsed they were once more put through the mangle and then hung up outside to dry. It was heaven help the household should it be raining! The whole living room would be filled with steaming clothes drying by the heat of the fire and this did not improve Lucy's temper!

If you think that was the end of Wash Day, and give a sigh of relief, then you are wrong! Heavy irons were heated up in the oven and as soon as any washing was dry then the ironing process would begin. When the iron cooled down it was put back in the oven and another one taken out. Everything was carefully ironed and folded and then arranged on the ceiling rack which was suspended by means of two pulleys from the ceiling enabling it to be pulled up or down as required. Not until every last garment was hanging up on the clothes rack, and all the equipment in the kitchen emptied of water and transferred back down the cellar, the lid back on the copper, the kitchen rugs replaced, could one give that sigh of relief that Wash Day was over.

What would you do without your electric automatic washing machine, tumble dryer, electric steam iron and water heated by your central heating system? Would you do what Lucy did – or just go and buy new clothes every week !!!!!

Tuesday was Upstairs Day and all the furniture was moved about so that carpets could be thoroughly swept by use of a hand brush and dust pan. During Spring Cleaning times all carpets were taken up, brought downstairs and hung on the washing line outside. Here they were beaten hard with a carpet beater and when they were deemed to be free from dust they were taken indoors and re-layed. Then the furniture would be thoroughly dusted and polished until it gleamed and a pleasant smell of polish pervaded the air. The downstairs rooms went through the same process each Wednesday. In addition to this, daily dusting had to be done because of the smoke and dust created by the coal fires.

Thursday was Black Lead Day, and the large Yorkist range was devoid of its fire and every piece which would come apart was taken apart, brushed with a wire brush and reassembled. Black lead polish was then applied to all surfaces, rubbed in and then buffed hard until they were a nice, shiny black. Only after all that was the fire rekindled.

We mustn't forget the ritual of the steps! The steps up to the front door, the back door step and the step to the back gate were evidence of a housewife's cleanliness – or lack of it! If one wished to be thought to be clean by one's neighbour then these steps must be kept well scrubbed at all times and then scoured, the latter being a yellow line created on the edge of each step by the scouring stone. Dirty and unscoured steps were indicative of a dirty housewife!

Friday was the day that Lucy liked best. It was her Shopping Day! She would walk down into the town for her weekly provisions, visiting the market, the butcher, the chemist or any other shop she might need. It took her hours to do this for the simple reason that every few yards she would meet someone she knew and she would stand there gossiping for ages. It had been known for a member of her family to pass her on the street as she was engrossed in her 'tittle tattle' and on their return, perhaps an hour later, she was still rooted to the same piece of ground, pulling the world to pieces with the same person! Eventually she would return home, her baskets heavily laden, moaning as to how her poor legs ached and how crowded were the shops! Arthur would smile to himself – he knew Lucy and how she enjoyed this social occasion of the week!

6. SWALLOW NEST

Mary replied to several advertisements from the Sheffield paper. She had taken Sylvia along to see Mrs. Rawlings who was very concerned at Mary's plight. A great fuss was made of Sylvia, Mrs. Rawlings exclaiming in delight what a lovely child she was. The kind lady was more than happy to supply Mary with a good reference and she wrote it there and then. She wished Mary every success.

Frank Stewart was a bookmaker and he owned a betting shop in Sheffield where he had made a pile of money from people who gambled on horses. He had bought for himself a little smallholding in a small village a few miles into the country side near Sheffield. The bungalow which went with the smallholding was called 'Swallow Nest' and was situated on several acres of land. Frank kept hundreds of laying hens and an enormous curly haired black and brown Airedale dog which had the best of temperaments. The dog was known by the name of Nellie Blye, for some reason best known to Frank. Frank spent all the working week in Sheffield at his business but enjoyed going down to his country home at the weekends. This he found to be the best relaxation after the hustle and bustle of cars and lorries, restless people scurrying to and fro, and the fumes from factory chimneys and steel works of Sheffield. He needed someone to care for his bungalow and to feed the hens and dog, not to mention the collecting of the numerous eggs from the hen houses when he wasn't there.

Mary had replied to his advertisement and so he wrote to ask her to go along to 'Swallow Nest' to be interviewed. Mary took Sylvia with her as she wanted to make sure that the child would be welcome into an employer's home. Frank took an immediate liking to Mary, and her child who was in no way precocious and had a winning smile for anyone she met. In her early thirties now, Mary was still very attractive and smart. Frank liked that and so offered her the post, declaring that he had no objection to the child being there also.

"After all, I'm not here during the week", he said, "so it's hardly going to bother me, and you'll have the house to yourselves. I'm quite happy for you to have friends and relatives to visit you, and even stay if you want – during the week. There's plenty of room".

"I don't think I'll be having any friends to stay", said Mary. "I've lost touch with most of them since our Sylvia was born. It would be nice though if my sister, Connie, could bring her little boy occasionally. He's no trouble and he would be company for Sylvia."

"All problems solved for both of us then – what did you say you're full name was?" queried Frank.

"Mary – Mary Copley", she stammered, as her name had not entered her head until this moment. She could hardly call herself Mrs. Howell now as she had never been legally married to Lewis. There had been enough deception! From that moment her child was also known as Sylvia Copley.

Mary moved her few possessions to 'Swallow Nest' the following weekend. It seemed an ideal situation where she would have time to be on her own and give all her attention to her daughter. Frank was a kindly man in his mid forties, short in stature, and balding. He made a big fuss of Sylvia when they arrived, and took some sweeties from his pocket to give to her.

"She's a bonnie little lass", he said to Mary, "– a real credit to ye".

Mary glowed with pride; he could not have said anything better as far as she was concerned.

"She's as good as gold." she said, "She won't be any bother".

Mary took their cases into the pretty bedroom which she would share with her daughter, Sylvia sleeping in the big double bed with her. It was a pleasant home set in its few acres of meadow and grassland, and a small stream trickled through the bottom of the garden. It was a far cry from the grimness of Fowlstone Row, and Mary's aching heart began to ease a little.

"I think I'm going to enjoy being here", she thought, "and I'm sure our Sylvia will".

Mary did enjoy being there, feeding the hens and collecting the eggs was pleasure rather than a chore. Sylvia adored the big brown shaggy dog, Nellie Blye, and the dog returned her affection. Frank only ever came to the bungalow at the weekends and Mary cooked his meals for him. He found Sylvia an endearing little girl whose hair now hung in ringlets around her face. Mary had not lost her admiration for the child star, Shirley Temple, and she modelled Sylvia's appearance on this precocious character. As she grew up, Sylvia began to hate this image and was often teased by her peers about it. Frank would often bring her a present when he came at the weekend, and he would sit with her on his knee and tell her stories. On one occasion he brought her a large stuffed toy monkey which danced up and down when its strings were pulled. She loved it.

Mary had bought a new dress for Sylvia. She was as keen to make sure that she would be the best dressed child in town as she had been about herself in days gone by. All her spare money went into this fetish. The child's hair was immaculately groomed into shiny ringlets, usually with a large ribbon perched upon the top of her head. Sometimes she wore a straw bonnet decorated with artificial flowers and a silk ribbon to tie under the chin. Always she wore white leather bar shoes of the best quality, and spotless white socks. Poor Sylvia was not allowed to get dirty, and if she did then Mary would be very angry with her. Imagine a childhood with no mud pies and no splashing in puddles! If only Mary had allowed her to wear suitable clothes in which to play and get dirty then it would have saved a great deal of unhappiness all round!

The new dress which Mary had bought for Sylvia was very unusual. In the shop it had been described as an 'umbrella dress' because of the sharp pleats which fell all round from the yoke. The dress was of a gold satin material with a white satin inlet within each pleat. Thus, when its wearer spun around, the effect was like an umbrella. The dress had little puffed sleeves and a white satin collar. Mary put the dress on Sylvia and it fitted perfectly. The child ran out into the garden and twirled round and round, watching the pleats swirl round her legs as she danced.

"You be careful ye don't fall down in that dress", said Mary. "I don't want it dirtied up or I shall be cross!"

Nevertheless she felt a glow of pride at the image of her daughter.

"Ooh! Look Mummy – see the pleats. Oh I wish my Daddy could see me in this pretty dress!" cried Sylvia,

Mary's smile faded. She was suddenly devastated and felt bereft. She had thought that Sylvia must have forgotten about Lewis and her daughter's words cut her to the quick! She fell to her knees on the grass, drew the child towards her, and wept – her heart was breaking! Sylvia put out her hand and patted her mother's face.

"Don't cry Mummy – you've got me – and I love you!"

7. "YOU LITTLE BITCH!"

Once Mary was properly settled in her new home her sister, Connie, came to visit, bringing young Ron with her. Connie was going to stay for one night and then leave Ron with Mary for the rest of the week. Both children were so excited, for they had always enjoyed each other's company.

"How are ye our Mary?" said Connie. "Ye look a lot better than ye did anyway!"

"I'm fine Connie", replied Mary. "It's lovely here for our Sylvia with lots of space to run around in, an' she really likes the dog and the chickens".

"I must say, she's the image o' Lewis", said Connie. "By the way, he's still looking for ye, but nobody will tell 'im where you are. Last week he came round to our house, drunk as a lord, asking where ye were. I wouldn't tell him an' do ye know what 'e did? He threw a brick through our front room window! I had to get police to 'im. A right mess it were as well, glass in everything. It took ages to clean it up and it cost our Eric a lot to put some new glass in. Eric was right mad I can tell ye!"

Although her heart ached with longing for him, Mary realised that she and Sylvia were better off out of Lewis's way.

Young Ron stayed for the week and he and Sylvia had a whale of a time. Ron was much quicker than Sylvia who tried to keep up with him on her sturdy little legs. She did seem to have a problem with running and certainly was not as agile as a child of her age ought to be.

"Come on, I'll race ye to bottom o' garden", shouted Ron. He set off at great speed, taking a running jump over the stream and landing safely on the other side. Sylvia followed his example – she ran – she jumped – and SPLASH – she landed right in the middle of the stream. Ron was doubled over with laughing at her plight, and watched her pick herself up, her pretty dress soaking wet and covered in mud, and those white shoes and socks were not fit to be seen! Mary was far from amused and roughly dragged her daughter back into the house, took off her wet and dirty clothes and sent her to bed for the rest of the day.

"Just look what you've done – you little bitch – all your nice clothes dirty. You know I don't like dirty clothes!"

For the first time in her short life, Sylvia felt a wave of fear of her mother at such rough treatment, and she cried herself to sleep.

All was forgiven by the next morning and the children were allowed to go egg collecting, and also to feed the hens. Sylvia loved the feel of the grain running through her fingers, and also the smell of the hen house. Nelly Blye came bounding after them, barking in sheer delight at their young energy. They each had a little bowl into which to gather the eggs. Somehow it was comforting to put one's hand into the soft warm straw of the hen box and to find a warm brown egg. They were shouting and laughing, and becoming more and more excited when suddenly, Nelly Blye leapt up at them to join in the excitement and they both dropped their bowls, smashing about twenty eggs between them. They stared in dismay at the mangled mess on the floor, broken shells and yellow yolks, and the whites all oozing everywhere.

"Auntie Mary's goin' to be right mad!" said Ron – and she was livid!

They were both sent to bed for the rest of the afternoon and not allowed any sweets that evening.

All too soon for Sylvia her Auntie Connie came to collect Ron and take him home. There were kisses all round and promises of further visits.

"You'll 'ave to let our Sylvia come an' stay with us soon", said Connie.

"Oh I don't think so Connie. I can't do without her", replied Mary.

There was nothing Sylvia liked better than a visit to the village shop. Here she could spend her Saturday penny on a round lollipop on a stick, taken from a large glass jar containing lollipops of all different colours. She always chose the really dark red, almost black ones, for she liked that flavour the best. Another time she might buy a pennyworth of jelly babies and again she preferred the black ones. Somehow she always felt guilty about eating the heads off the jelly babies – it seemed cruel – but nevertheless she always ate the head first. More of her favourite sweets were the white milk chocolate buttons, or better still a white chocolate

Poor Mary

mouse which she would keep for ages before she could bear to eat it.

In the same shop were cases of pop or fizzy drinks. The different coloured liquids fascinated her, from the bright Orangeade to the green Limeade, the red Cherryade, and best of all the black Dandelion and Burdock. One thing she was not allowed to buy and that was chewing gum. It was only common little girls who chewed that, How Sylvia longed to try some!

"I'm thirsty Mummy. Please may I have a drink of milk?"

Mary poured some milk into a cup, gave it to her daughter and then went outside to hang up some washing to dry. Sylvia started to drink the milk and after she had drunk about half of it she decided that she'd had enough. She had seen her mother pour the dregs from tea cups down the sink, so she thought it would be the right thing to do to pour the unwanted milk down there too. The sink was very high for her to reach but she stood on her tip toes and carefully stretched up as far as she could and just about managed to pour away the milk without making a mess on the floor. She felt very pleased with her achievement – for it was a long way up to the sink for a little girl!

Mary came in from the garden and Sylvia said to her, "I couldn't drink all my milk Mummy, so I poured the rest of it down the sink".

Nothing could have prepared the child for what happened next. Sylvia did not know what had hit her! She was briefly aware of a sudden change in her mother's face, then Mary went absolutely wild, grabbing hold of her and shaking her like a dog would shake a rat.

"YOU LITTLE BITCH!" screamed Mary. "'How dare you waste milk like that?" and she struck the child across the head again and again and again!

"Get out of the house", she screamed. "I don't want to see you near me!"

Sobbing her heart out as much from bewilderment as from physical hurt, Sylvia fled from the house and to her sandpit. She was trembling all over and could not understand what she had done that was so bad! She picked up her dolly, cradling it in her arms, and began to rock backwards and forwards, tears coursing down her cheeks. At last her sobbing ceased and she began to play with her dolly and talk to it. After about half an hour Mary came out, all smiles, and took Sylvia into her arms and hugged her.

"I'm sorry Mummy", said Sylvia, feeling relieved that perhaps things were back to normal. "I won't do it again. Do you love me Mummy?" was her anxious plea.

"I don't love anyone else but you luv", said Mary.

This was the first of many such incidents with her mother and Sylvia developed a state of deep anxiety which showed itself in a little pucker on her brow. She was always uncertain about how her mother would react to anything, and she couldn't understand! She had heard her mother say that she had left her daddy because he had hurt her, and there she was, now being hurt by her mother!

8. PROPOSAL

Frank came home as usual the following weekend. Having had a good week at the race course he came bearing gifts for Mary and Sylvia. The child was delighted to see him for he was always the same, kindly and jolly and never any changes of mood. She felt secure when he was there. After he had eaten his meal Frank put down his knife and fork and looked at Mary who had almost finished hers.

"I enjoyed that Mary lass! Chips and eggs always taste good". He hesitated, and then continued, "Do you like living 'ere Mary?"

"Yes, it's lovely Frank – I'm very happy here, and it's lovely for our Sylvia – there's so much space for her to run about in. It's nice that she doesn't have to play out on the street like children back home"

Frank fiddled with his knife and fork, he seemed very ill at ease, and then he suddenly burst out, "I'd like ye to marry me Mary. I'm right fond o' ye, and I think the world o' your Sylvia".

Mary was stunned. She hadn't been expecting this and nor did she want it. She'd finished with all men, and only wanted her daughter.

"Please say yes Mary. I'd be a good father to Sylvia and she could 'ave anything she wanted – clothes galore, toys, piano lessons – anything – and so could you Mary. I'm not short o' money!"

Of course it could have been the solution to all Mary's problems, but if she loved any man then she still loved Lewis. Besides, Lewis had hurt his own child so how much more chance would there be of a step father hurting her. She did not choose to remember how she herself had begun to hurt her daughter.

"No I can't Frank! I'm grateful for your offer, but I don't want to marry anyone. It's nothing I've got against you, you're a good man! I just had such a bad time with Lewis – I don't want to get involved with anyone ever again in that way".

The next day, when Frank had gone back to Sheffield, Mary gathered all her and Sylvia's things together, packed them into her two suit cases, left a letter for Frank, and left 'Swallow Nest' for ever. She couldn't stay here now after last evening. She would feel too uncomfortable around Frank. Her independence had been threatened. As they left Sylvia wondered what was going to happen to her much loved Nelly Blye if they were not there to look after her and feed her. Then what about the hens? They would need feeding too.

"I'll call in at the corner shop as we go", said Mary, "and tell them we're gone. They will know someone who'll come and feed the animals until Frank can find someone else".

Suddenly Sylvia felt the loss of the toy monkey which Mary had left behind, along with one or two other things that she couldn't manage to carry. She did not dare to say anything in case her mother turned on her again. She was learning at the tender age of three to be long suffering!

Once more they found themselves complete with bags and baggage, struggling on and off buses until they reached Mary's home town. Once more they trudged up the High Street until they reached Lucy's house.

Poor Mary

"Whatever 'ave ye cum back for now?" exclaimed Lucy, seeing the entire luggage on her door step. "I thought ye liked that job!"

9. JOB HUNTING – AGAIN!

Sylvia liked to stay with her grandparents. She loved her granddad who was full of fun and always teasing her. She loved his twinkling blue eyes and the laughter lines in his kind face. She also liked talking to Billy, the budgie, and enjoyed it very much when Granddad let him out of his cage and he flew round and round the room, rejoicing in his momentary freedom from the cage. She thought it was really funny when Billy landed on the top of Granddad's head and pecked at his hair, and she squealed with delight when he landed on her own head – it tickled so! She liked the feel of this little creature, except sometimes his claws might be a trifle sharp, or he might peck her quite hard, but she never grumbled if he did.

"Now Arthur, don't get our Sylvie over excited, and don't let 'er mess up 'er dress. Ye know our Mary will be mad with 'er. She can't stand the bairn to be dirty for a minute. It doesn't seem natural for a bairn to be as clean as a new pin all day long!" exclaimed Lucy.

Mary had gone job hunting and had left Sylvia with her parents. At the end of the row of houses where they lived stood a large Coop. grocer's shop with a house for the manager attached to it. This particular row of houses where Arthur and Lucy lived was nicknamed 'Nobility Row' by people who lived in worse conditions. Each house was strongly built of stone, rather than the usual cheap red bricks, and each sported a reasonable sized front garden. The houses were all owned by the Coop. and if one ever managed to get hold of one of them to rent - then one really had arrived!

"Grandma, please may I have a penny for some sweeties from the Coop?" Sylvia wheedled.

"Ee – I suppose so", said Lucy, going to the cupboard where she kept her purse. "Be careful near that road when ye go. I don't know what ye mam would do if anything 'appened to you. And don't make a mess on yer dress or ye're mam'll blame me!"

Sylvia scampered off happily to the Coop. shop, thinking what she might buy with her penny - a lollypop - a white chocolate mouse perhaps - or some dolly mixtures? Her eyes eagerly scanned the large glass sweet containers, and then she saw it. CHEWING GUM!

"Mum'll never let me have that - it's common!" she thought, "But she won't know if I try some today", and she bought some chewing gum with her penny.

She gleefully took it back to Grandma's and excitedly peeled off the silver paper and popped the gum into her mouth. It tasted really good initially, and she chewed and chewed, but suddenly the lovely taste was gone and she was left with what seemed like a piece of rubber in her mouth. Nevertheless she really had enjoyed that minty taste and wanted to experience it again.

"Grandma, please could I have another penny for some more sweeties?"

"Ye've eaten 'em all up so soon?" said Lucy. "All right then, 'ere's another penny, but don't gobble 'em all up so quick this time."

Back to the shop Sylvia went and bought some more chewing gum. This did not last long either, for as soon as the taste had disappeared then she threw the gum on to the fire. All in all this occurred five times, though why Lucy was giving in to her grand daughter's requests was a mystery as she was usually as hard as nails and did not soften easily. Perhaps in her way she was trying to make up for the hard time her little granddaughter had been having, being dragged from pillar to post, On Sylvia's sixth visit to the Coop. for yet some more chewing gum, the manager, a balding portly man wearing half rimmed spectacles, intervened. He looked down at the small child on the other side of the counter and she gave him a big grin.

"Don't you think that you've had enough chewing gum for one day young lady? Too much is not good for you, particularly if you swallow it".

"Oh I don't swallow it", said Sylvia. "I just throw it away on the fire when all the taste has gone out of it!"

"Well this time I'm going to give you a bar of chocolate instead, whether you like it or not!" said the manager.

Sylvia accepted the chocolate most cheerfully, gave him the penny, and skipped happily back to Grandma's. She really did prefer the chocolate anyway!

"Grandma! Grandma! He wouldn't give me anymore chewing gum. He gave me chocolate instead - but I like the chocolate better anyway!"

"Chewin' gum! Chewin' gum! I didn't know tha'd been spendin' pennies on that muck. Ye mustn't tell ye're mam or she'll 'ave a fit", said Grandma, "– and no more pennies for you today!"

Poor Mary

Ralph was allowed to have a weekly comic, either 'Beano' or 'Dandy'. He loved the comic strip stories of 'Corky the Cat', 'Desperate Dan' and 'Keyhole Kate'. Sylvia liked to look at the pictures too but of course she couldn't read yet so sometimes Ralph would read them to her. He was very fond of his little cousin and, being six years older than she, he felt protective towards her. Sometimes he would take her for walks, and even to the Saturday afternoon showing at the cinema. Here he had to protect her, if he could, from the hard peas issuing forth from the pea shooters of other little boys. His retaliation was to take out his own pea shooter and score direct hits on their noses. He was a crack shot! When the film began they would all settle down to watch the Cowboys and Indians sweeping across the screen, shooting each other with guns or bows and arrows.

One Tuesday morning, Ralph's 'Beano' comic arrived after breakfast, just as he was about to go school. Like many people he liked the experience of being the first person to turn the nice new pages of his comic or book.

"Don't touch my comic when I'm at school our Sylvia. I want to read it myself first", he said to her as she clamoured to get it. At the time he was sitting on the floor resting his back on Arthur's old leather chair. He put the comic behind his back and surreptitiously slipped it underneath the chair out of sight, hoping that Sylvia wouldn't notice, But of course she had noticed and as soon as she was sure that he was well on the way to school she retrieved the comic from its hiding place and had a good look at it, being very careful not to crease the pages, and then slipped it back underneath the chair.

Ralph came home from school at four o'clock and sat down at the table with Granddad and Sylvia, ready for his tea. There was bread and butter on the table, and jam or honey to spread on it. Sylvia was quietly getting on with her tea whilst Ralph was chattering away about the events of his school day. Suddenly Ralph stopped talking and looked intently at Sylvia and what she had been quietly doing. He then let out a yell.

"Granddad! Look what our Sylvia's doin'. She's eaten all 'er bread an' jam but she's left all 'er crusts an' hidden 'em under 'er saucer so that you won't see 'em"

Arthur always told the children that they should eat up the crust of bread because it was good for them and it would 'make their hair curl'! He put on a stern voice and remonstrated with his granddaughter for leaving her crusts and also for trying to hide them under her saucer. His eyes then twinkled as he said, "If ye don't eat yer crusts lass, your hair won't curl!"

Sylvia did remember thinking that her hair was already curly enough, and that anyway she'd rather have straight hair so that she could wear it in plaits instead of her silly ringlets!

Mary came home later that day, not having had much success with her job hunting. It wasn't easy to find work where one could also take a small child. The next morning Connie brought Ron up to see Grandma and Granddad, his brother Ralph, and of course Sylvia and Auntie Mary. Connie and Mary decided to go to the shops together, Ralph went off to play with some friends and Grandma was busy doing something in the attic. This left Granddad with young Ron and Sylvia to entertain. He did not mind in the least as he loved fooling about with them, being young at heart himself.

They were playing hide and seek, using under the table, behind Granddad's chair, the bottom of the stair case and, if they were brave enough, the cellar head. Sylvia was frightened of the cellar with its well of darkness and shadows looming down the steep steps. She wasn't quite big enough to reach the light switch, so she avoided hiding there as she thought she might fall down the cellar steps into the arms of who knows what! Granddad suddenly caught both the youngsters up in his arms and carried them down into the dark cellar. He then popped one squirming wriggling little body into each of the two 'peggy' tubs at the bottom of the cellar steps. He then ran back up the steps, and before he reached the top young Ron, being agile and fleet of foot, was running up the steps behind him, leaving Sylvia stuck in her 'peggy' tub because she was unable to climb out. How she squawked, being fearful of any possible 'bogey men' who might be lurking in that dark place. As soon as Arthur realised that she was becoming really distressed he hurried back down into the cellar to rescue her, for he never had any intention to frighten her. After he had calmed her down, and reassured her that it was only a game, and that of course no 'bogey men' lived in the cellar, for it was only a cool place for storing food and 'peggy' tubs, he found some sweeties for both of them and they then resumed their play.

10. MAGGOTS

One evening Mary was scanning the 'Situations Vacant' column in the newspaper when her eyes alighted on an interesting advertisement. An invalid widower required a living in housekeeper to look after him and his home. She was attracted to the statement – 'Child not objected to'. The only drawback that she could see at the moment was that the address was in her home town. She did not really want to work locally in case she ran into Lewis and this would open old wounds again, but she couldn't stay with her parents forever. She decided to visit the widower and find out about the work involved and if it would be a suitable home for Sylvia.

"I think I'll take our Sylvia with me today", said Mary the following morning. "It's not too far, only to the other side of town".

It was quite a long walk for Sylvia and by the time they had reached the house her little legs ached curiously, but she was getting used to this recurring discomfort so she suffered in silence. She had become aware that these aches and pains often occurred after she had been running a great deal, and she certainly did not seem to have the agility of the average child of her age. Mary was totally unaware that her daughter had any physical problems.

The house was in the middle of a terraced row of houses all looking rather dark and foreboding; some of them extremely uncared for. The front garden of the house was choked with weeds and the windows were smeared with dirt and grime. Certainly the front

Poor Mary

doorsteps had been neglected for a very long time and Mary was in two minds whether or not to turn back, but having walked all that way she thought that she may as well go through with the interview at least. After all, she wasn't afraid of hard work and could soon clean up those windows and steps. She took Sylvia round to the back of the house and knocked on the door and it was opened by a woman who gave Mary a hard stare. The woman's hair was steely grey and was rolled up in curling pins. Her skin was wrinkled and coarse and her down turned mouth held a cigarette which had a great deal of ash on the end of it. She took the cigarette from her mouth and flicked the ash on to the floor. She was shabbily dressed and wearing a not too clean sleeveless overall. The sleeves of her grubby looking cardigan were frayed at the edges and there was a hole in the elbow of one of them. Her stony eyes took in Mary - smart, elegant and immaculate, and then drifted down to the child - impeccably dressed - white shoes - white socks!

Mary's attention was fleetingly directed to a small child playing on her own in the corner of the communal yard. The child was wearing a tatty, grubby dress, no shoes or socks, and when she bent down Mary noticed that she had no knickers either. Her hair was matted and she was scratching her head a great deal, and though her skin would have been white one could not tell because of the grime ingrained in it. Mary shuddered and held Sylvia's hand more tightly less she dash off to talk to the child.

"What do yer want?" growled the woman.

"I've come about the job advertised in the paper", replied Mary, now wishing that she had turned back.

"Humph! Well I'm just a neighbour – I live nex' door – I jus' look in on t' old man from time to time. He's bedridden an' he's upstairs. I don't think this job'll be your cuppa tea lady, but ye'd best go up an' see for yer self!"

Mary entered the house which was amazingly dirty. The place had a dank, sour smell and a sickly stench came from the bedroom where the old man lay on a double bed. He was propped up on some pillows, his eyes were sunken and his yellow skin was stretched tightly over the bones of his face. All about was the smell of dirty clothes, dirty bed linen, an unwashed body and incontinence. Mary nearly wretched and told Sylvia to go and stay outside in the back yard – even if she did talk to the grubby little girl who was hovering in the yard and had eyed them with curiosity – it was preferable to this!

"I need someone to look after me", wheezed the old man through his colourless lips. "I'm jus' lying 'ere on my own all day long an' I've nobody to care. You'd 'ave a nice big bedroom for yerself an' yer bonnie little lass. Go an' 'ave a look at it if yer like an' see what ye' think"

Mary went into the bedroom next door. It had obviously been quite nice at one time, but now it stank of dankness, mould and decay. The floor boards were rotting and she could even see fungus growing in one corner of the room. She gingerly turned back the bedclothes to inspect the mattress for bed bugs which she was quite sure must be lurking there – and horror of horrors – the mattress was alive with maggots, a writhing mass protesting at their disturbance! At this point Sylvia came up the stairs looking for her mother. The child in the yard had proved to be most unfriendly, sticking out her tongue at Sylvia and calling her rude names. Mary took her hand and they went back to the old man's room. Sylvia recognized a pleading in his eyes and voice as he begged Mary to stay and care for him. She always remembered feeling very, very sorry for the old man when her mother refused, and she could not bear his hurt.

11. THE BLACK MAN IN THE CELLAR

Mary's luck turned and another decent housekeeping job became available. This time it was in a small town called Greenford near Sheffield. Mary went along to be interviewed, was offered the post and accepted it. She was to be housekeeper to a man called Arthur Mason who had recently lost his wife and needed his home cleaned and his meals cooked whilst he was at the colliery. He did not work down the pit but in the pit offices where he was in charge of the wages department.

Arthur's house was an end terrace house with a long front garden and the usual communal yard at the back. Each of the houses had its own lavatory across the yard. There was a wall at the end of the yard, separating it from a large field beyond where grazed a couple of horses and a few cows. Adjacent to the field across its other side was an enormous muck tip where all the waste from the colliery was deposited.

"Not so nice as 'Swallow Nest'", thought Mary, "but it'll do", and she and Sylvia moved in with their few possessions. As before, they had to share a bedroom, both of them sleeping in the double bed within. Downstairs was an extra spare room where Sylvia was allowed to play and keep her toys.

In the next row of houses along the road lived Arthur's sister, Annie, and her husband Randolph Green. They had been married many years, loved children, but never managed to produce one of their own. They were desperate to have a child and were now seriously thinking of adopting one. Sylvia soon learned to find her way down to "Auntie Annie and

Uncle Randolph's" as she now called them. Whenever she went to see Annie and Randolph they spoilt her to death. Randolph would make her cowboy hats and Indian outfits out of newspapers and play with her for hours. She would be lavished with sweets and chocolates and they also indulged her in allowing her to eat Nestlé's condensed milk with a spoon from the tin – very sweet and sickly but Sylvia loved it! All this was very fattening of course, and as Mary still plied her with Virol every day she was now quite a chubby three year old. However, people said that her chubbiness was becoming and that it just made her cuddlier. In any event she was bound to grow out of it, for it was only puppy fat! Annie and Randolph knew of Mary's situation with Lewis and would like to have adopted Sylvia for their own, but Mary wouldn't hear of it. For the rest of their lives they always kept in touch with Sylvia, no matter where she was living, even after they eventually did adopt a little girl named Susan.

Mary's continuing outbursts of violence towards Sylvia made the child increasingly insecure because she never knew when they might happen or what might trigger them off. Sylvia did not complain to anyone about this, accepting it as normal and expected to have to put up with it. As she grew older she gradually learned which certain things would ignite her mother's short fuse and tried to avoid doing them, but it wasn't always possible.

On her third birthday, Grandma had sent her a pretty ring of which the child was extremely proud. It was just a little too big for her but she was allowed to wear it. She went out to play in the front garden and pretended that she was trimming the hedge which separated the garden from the main road. This game lasted for ten minutes or so and, when Sylvia returned to playing with her dolls at the top of the garden, she noticed that the ring was missing from her finger. She immediately felt apprehensive and went back to the hedge to search for it, but it was no where to be found. With her heart in her stomach she went into the house to find her mother who was busy in the kitchen.

"Mummy - I've - I've - lost my ring", she faltered.

"Oh you've never lost that lovely ring! You little bitch! I'll teach ye not to lose things!" Mary vent forth her anger, giving Sylvia a good hiding and sending her upstairs to bed. Sylvia lay there quietly sobbing until at last she fell asleep. She awoke to find her mother by her bedside and her heart felt some relief to see that she was smiling as though nothing had happened, and bidding her to come downstairs for her tea now that she'd had a good sleep.

There was a cellar to this house, and in the cellar was an old well covered by a wooden lid which was easy to pick off. One day Mary told Sylvia that a nasty black man lived in this well and should she be naughty then she would be given to him. Sylvia was very frightened of the Black Man in the cellar.

"I'll either give ye to the Black Man in the cellar, or to the Rag and Bone Man, or I might even put you in a home", Mary said in an evil manner!

Sylvia was petrified. She never went near the door of the cellar if she could help it, and should she be playing in the front garden and hear the cry of the Rag and Bone Man as he trudged the streets with his pony and cart, she would run into the house in terror. She wasn't quite sure what her mother meant by 'a home', but she was sure it wouldn't be very nice.

Sylvia could never remember exactly what she might have done wrong, if anything, to bring down her mother's wrath upon herself one day. I'm sure that if she'd done anything really bad she would have remembered it as vividly as the event which followed.

"Come here you little bitch. I'll teach you to be good!" and Mary grabbed her little daughter under her arm, opened the cellar door, walked down the steps with her and kicked away the lid from the well. A thin shaft of light from a tiny window was the only means of being able to see, and dark shadows loomed in every corner, and the well was a bottomless pit of inky blackness.

"I'm going to give ye to the Black Man this time", Mary snarled. Sylvia screamed out in terror as her belief in the Black Man was so strong that she actually saw two enormous black hands reaching up out of the darkness of the well to grab her and drag her down, and down and down into the darkest of nightmares. Who knows what other monsters might be lurking down there – if the Black Man did not eat her first!

"I'll be good! I'll be good Mummy!" she cried, terror struck. With that, satisfied that she had Sylvia well under control, Mary kicked the lid of the well back into place and took the trembling child back up the cellar steps. She began to make the tea as though nothing had happened! Mary's moods like this swung back and forth. Not a single person knew any of these things and Mary proclaimed to the world that "Our Sylvia's as good as gold!"

12. "THERE'S A WAR ON!"

Sylvia enjoyed listening to the wireless, and even enjoyed the News broadcasts although she couldn't understand them. Somehow she found the voices comforting, and when she was frightened in her bed at night she would be reassured by the sound of the news reader's voice should the wireless happen to be on. If dance music came on the radio during the day, Mary would pick her up and gaily dance round the room with her in her arms.

"This is how your daddy and I used to dance", Mary would say, and she would whirl and twirl with her daughter laughing in her arms until the music stopped. These were enjoyable moments spent with her mother, and Sylvia couldn't get enough of those!

Listening to the News one day, Sylvia heard a very solemn announcement stating that England was now at war with Germany. She did not know what this meant and Mary explained to her that English soldier men would be fighting with German soldier men, just like Granddad had done in the last war. Still not fully understanding the implication of this, Sylvia skipped off down the road to see Auntie Annie and Uncle Randolph.

"Will you make a cowboy costume for me out o' newspaper please Uncle Randolph?" she asked. Always pleased to play with her, Randolph obliged and very soon Sylvia was prancing around pretending to shoot him with a pretend gun.

"I'm an English soldier and I'm going to kill you 'cos you're a germ. My Granddad used to kill germs with a real gun", shouted Sylvia. "Have you got any sweeties Uncle Randolph?" she wheedled.

"No lass, I 'aven't – not now", he replied.

"Well have you got any Nestlés milk then?" Sylvia asked.

"I'm sorry luv, but there's none o' that either".

"Why not Uncle Randolph?"

"Well there's a war on now, an' ye can't buy things like that easily anymore. Ye won't be able to have any more bananas either until after the War's over", he explained. The country has to be careful with our food so we don't run out, so everyone 'as to go on Rations to make sure that we all get a fair share of what there is!"

"When will it be over Uncle Randolph? Next week?"

"Ee I don't know luv! As soon as Winston Churchill's beaten them Gerries I suppose!"

"You mean germs Uncle Randolph", corrected Sylvia.

Greenford was very close to Sheffield which of course was badly hit by German bombers trying to destroy the steel and munitions factories there. There was a communal air raid shelter at the end of the street and when the air raid warning went off during the night, everyone left their beds and moved into the shelter, taking with them a pillow and a rug for they did not know how long they might be there. Sometimes the blitz on Sheffield went on all through the night until the breaking of the dawn. Not realising all the implications of this, Sylvia found it very exciting and jumped for joy as she walked along the dark street wearing her pyjamas. She was quite tickled by this. The air raid shelter was dark and damp, the walls sweating with condensation and the air smelling rancid with the smell of numerous bodies in there. The whole atmosphere was seething with germs.

Sylvia developed a very bad cough accompanied by a high temperature and the doctor said that she had a good dose of 'shelter sickness'. From that moment Mary decided that no matter what happened she would not take Sylvia to the shelter anymore, declaring that if they were going to die they might as well die in the comfort of their own bed.

The next night, when the air raid warning sounded again, Mary grabbed Sylvia from the bed, snatched up all her precious photographs, and ran to the outside lavatory which was strongly built with double thickness walls. There they stayed in fear and trembling as the German bombers whined over head. Suddenly there was an ear splitting explosion close by, and they could hear the tinkling of broken glass as many windows of adjacent houses were blown out. The lavatory remained intact although a great deal of damage was done to many of the nearby houses. Mary learned the next morning that a German aircraft had been shot out of the sky and had landed in the field on the other side of their back wall, burying itself in the muck tip before exploding into flames. Several of the cows in the field were torn apart by the impact of the explosion and it was not a pretty sight!

Poor Mary

Food rationing was well established now. Everyone had a ration book containing coupons which they exchanged for their weekly quota of butter, meat, sugar, sweets and so on. Clothing was also rationed and likewise coupons had to be surrendered before articles of clothing or material could be bought. Shopping was a real chore because one spent hours on end standing in long queues at the various food counters.

On day Mary took Sylvia to the local Cooperative store in order to buy the weekly provisions. The queue was long and slowly being served. Sylvia grew tired of standing and her legs began to ache again so she was fidgeting around with discomfort. Nearby was a large wicker laundry basket so Mary sat Sylvia on top of it and took a seat herself to take the weight off her own feet. All at once, the lid of the basket gave way and Sylvia disappeared into the basket. Mary was too big to disappear but she was well and truly wedged inside the basket and all Sylvia could see as she looked up were her mother's legs sticking straight up in the air. Neither she nor her daughter was hurt but there was riotous laughter throughout the shop and the incident took the gloom out of everyone's day. Even Mary found it funny and could laugh at herself!

13. THE SCHOOL BELL

A few yards up the road from where Mary and Sylvia lived was situated the local infant school. Often when they were passing they would stand and watch the children at play in the school yard. There was nothing more that Sylvia wanted other than to be allowed to go to school, but of course, at only three years old, she was far too young. Nevertheless she was fascinated by the school and even if the children were not at play she would beg her mother to linger outside the school railings for a while. She was often rewarded by a glimpse of something exciting going on in that mysterious place, and even if she did not see anyone she liked to look at the classroom windows which were usually decorated with something intriguing which the children had produced. How she longed to be part of the little world inside those grey stone walls.

One bright sunny morning of early Spring, Sylvia went out to play in the back yard. At first she rode on her tricycle carrying her teddy bear, and a tiny suit case which she dangled by its handle from the handle bars. She pretended that she was going to stay with Grandma and the suitcase was her luggage. After a while she became bored with that game and thought that her teddy would like a change of scenery, so she wondered round to the front garden with him.

In the borders of the garden were growing bright yellow daffodils and hyacinth of blue, pink and white. What a lovely scent wafted across the garden in the mild warmth of the spring sunshine. Sylvia could hear the ring of bird song from some distant trees, and the sparrows were twittering away on the grey slate roof tops. She looked up to see the merry little birds and noticed the smoke from the chimneys coiling lazily up above the red chimney pots and disappearing somewhere into a blue, blue sky. She sat her teddy on the grass and then ventured to the front gate and peered through, for she was not yet tall enough to see over the top. Through the gate she saw a cat strolling languidly up the main road which was very quiet at this time of day.

"Pussy!" she called. "Pussy come here!" but the black and white cat disdainfully chose to ignore her, as is the way with cats. Sylvia pulled on the gate and it swung back with ease as the catch had not been properly secured. Peeping out to see the cat she then took it into her head to go after it. Catching up with it she gently stroked its soft fur and the little creature purred with pleasure and rubbed itself against her legs. A bell began to ring just up the road.

"The school bell!" thought Sylvia. "The children are coming out to play. I'll go and watch them through the railings". Abandoning the cat she skipped up the road towards the school. Boys and girls were just pouring through the big double doors and into the playground. They then quickly joined up with their usual friends and began to play. One group of girls had a large skipping rope and they were chanting skipping rhymes as they took turns to skip in the rope. Other girls chose to remain upside down for most of their playtime, showing their knickers as they performed handstands up against the wall or skillfully cart-wheeling across the playground. A few were playing with a ball, catching, throwing, shrieking and squabbling. It seemed that all that most of the boys wanted to do was to fight each other, playing war games, rolling and tussling with each other all over the dirty floor. A couple of boys were having a game with some shiny, brightly coloured marbles, and one boy was playing by himself with a whip and top which spun merrily as he skillfully lashed it into motion with his whip.

"I wish my mummy would let me do things like that", thought Sylvia. "P'raps I will be able to when I start school, but I'd better not get dirty like those boys".

She continued watching intently and was fascinated by all that she saw. Suddenly a little girl of about six years old spotted Sylvia peering through the railings.

"Aw! Look at that little girl – Isn't she sweet?" she exclaimed to her friend. The pair of them dashed over to the railings. They seemed very big girls to Sylvia who was only three.

!'Ello! What's your name?" one of them asked.

"Sylvia", she answered.

"Would yer like to come in an' play with us? Just go up to the gate and we'll let you in", said the second girl.

Without a moment's hesitation Sylvia ran to the gate which was quickly opened by the two girls. Sylvia gleefully entered the play ground whereupon a whole crowd of six year old girls descended upon her, petting her, cuddling her, patting her curls and admiring them.

"We like yer dress", one of them said, "and ye've got lovely white shoes on. My mam would never let me 'ave white shoes. You are lucky!"

"She looks just like Shirley Temple doesn't she?" another girl exclaimed.

At this point a shrill whistle was blown by the teacher on playground duty to summon the children to their class lines in order to file into their classrooms.

"Come with us Sylvie", said the girl who had first spoken to her, leading her towards the lines of children. This was really so exciting. She was at last to enter that great big door and discover the mysteries of school. Sylvia slipped into the line with her new found friends and marched with them through the great big doors into a dimly lit corridor with a red tiled floor. The children filed down the corridor until they came to a large classroom and on entering they each sat down at their own desk. At this point Sylvia felt suddenly bemused and did not know what to do.

"What – or who have we here?" spoke a kindly voice, and Sylvia looked up into the merry, bespectacled eyes of Miss Brown, the class teacher.

"We brought 'er in Miss", came a chorus of voices. "Can she stay for a bit 'cos it's only a painting lesson?"

"I suppose so", said Miss Brown." if she's good!"

"I am good", said Sylvia. Indeed with Mary as her mother how would she dare be otherwise!

"Well, sit down here then", said Miss Brown, pointing to an empty desk. "Sandra is away today so you can sit there. What's your name? Sylvia? Right then Sylvia, here is a large sheet of plain paper for you and you may share Jane's paints and water pot. Find her a paint brush please Jane".

Everything was ready for the lesson to begin. Sylvia could hardly believe that she was in this wondrous place, and her eyes drank in every detail of that classroom. She liked the smell of the chalk dust, the paint and the books. She liked the look of the teacher and the way she spoke with calm authority. Above all she was enjoying the companionship of other children, for she rarely had the opportunity to play with young people of her own age, unless her cousin came to stay. Her mother always said that she couldn't have anyone to play because it was not their own house. In reality Mary looked down on the children who lived nearby and did not think that they were good enough to play with her daughter. She considered them too rough. And further more they might teach Sylvia bad habits or worse still – bad language!

"This morning we are going to paint a pattern", said Miss Brown, "a repeat pattern – that means that you paint one thing in exactly the same way in a series of twelve squares. First, using your ruler, divide up your page into twelve squares – and remember to measure carefully. Each square will be three inches. When you have done that you must think what you would like to paint in your first square. Keep it simple so that you can easily repeat the design in all the squares".

Joan helped Sylvia to make her squares on the paper. Sylvia was engrossed in all that was going on and she made up her mind on this day that she wanted to be a teacher when she grew up.

"I see that your squares are ready now Sylvia. What are you going to paint in your first square?" asked Miss Brown kindly.

Poor Mary

Sylvia remembered the aeroplanes which were continually droning across the sky like swarms of bees now that the War was on. She also remembered the aeroplane which had crashed in the field beyond their home and feeling sorry for the cows which had been killed by its explosion.

"An aeroplane", she said.

Sylvia picked up the paint brush with the long wooden handle and looked at the pots of paint on Joan's desk. She chose ultramarine blue, dipped her paint brush into it and then very carefully made the simple shape of an aeroplane in her first square.

"That's very good Sylvia", said Miss Brown, "I can see that you are going to be artistic. Now see if you can carefully copy your aeroplane into all the other squares on your paper, then you will have made a pattern".

With the utmost care and concentration, Sylvia continued with her pattern and when she had finished it was almost as good as the patterns made by the older children.

In the meantime Mary went to find Sylvia only to discover that she was no where in sight.

"She must have gone down to Annie's", she thought. "I'll give it her when I get hold of her, going off like that without saying anything", and Mary, with a very grim face, slipped down the road and knocked at Annie's door.

"Is our Sylvia here?" said Mary in a very irate manner.

"No luv", said Annie, "I haven't seen her this morning. She hasn't been here at all today".

"Oh dear!" said Mary, some of the sting dissipating from her manner as her annoyance turned to genuine worry. "I wonder where she can be. I hope she hasn't gone off with anyone. There are some funny people about these days, and ye read such a lot of bad things happening to children. I'd better go and look for her".

By now Mary was extremely agitated and there was a red line of stress streaked down the centre of her forehead. Just as she was, in her working overall and her hair tied up in a turban to protect it from the dust, she set off down the road to look for her daughter. There was no sign whatsoever of the little girl as Mary peered over each gate to the gardens. Panic stricken, she began to fear the worst, that some pervert had abducted her child.

As she approached the school she saw an old lady outside in her front garden, sunning herself in the new warmth of the Spring sunshine. Mary crossed the road and asked her if she had seen a three year old child with hair in ringlets and wearing a green dress.

"I think I did see a little tot dressed like that. She was standing near the school railings and watching children playing in the playground", said the old lady who had permanently waved white hair. She was wearing a shawl around her shoulders just in case there was one of those tricky little spring winds around to tease the bones. "I didn't take too much notice but I think she might have gone in to the school playground with the children. What happened to her when the children went back into school I don't know. I didn't see her again".

Poor Mary

Mary thanked the old lady and went back across the road towards the school gate. There was no sign of Sylvia now in the playground. Surely she hadn't gone inside! Hurrying across the now deserted playground she hesitated for a second before entering those large double doors. Never in a thousand years would she normally have entered that establishment dressed as she was – for spring cleaning – and she felt very dirty and shabby, but for once in her life she did not care too much what people might think of her.

Sylvia had just completed a very skilled little pattern with the aeroplane design – albeit simple. She looked up as the classroom door suddenly burst open and her mother's irate face appeared. Her heart quailed within her as she observed the familiar stress signs upon her mother's brow but suddenly they disappeared to be replaced by a look of great relief.

"Oh thank goodness – you're here! I'll take her now Teacher. I've been looking for her everywhere. I hope she hasn't been any trouble", said Mary.

"Not at all", said Miss Brown. "We've enjoyed having her haven't we children? Don't forget to take your lovely picture with you Sylvia. Your mummy should be very pleased with that! Goodbye!"

There was a chorus of "Goodbyes" from Sylvia's new found friends as her mother took her out of the classroom.

On their way back home Sylvia's feelings were of deep anxiety as to what might happen to her. Would her mother give her a good hiding? Mary was struggling with mixed feelings, one which said that her child should be punished and the other of relief and joy that she was safe! Fortunately on this occasion Mary's feelings of relief predominated and Sylvia was spared the rod. The picture which she had painted was treasured by Mary for the rest of her life.

14. BAD NEWS

Mary picked up a letter addressed to Mr. Arthur Mason. It was very important looking and had H.M.S. printed on the envelope. She put it on the mantelpiece so that he would see it on his return home from work that evening. He arrived home about six o'clock and was obviously extremely tired.

"A cup o' tea would go down well Mary. I'm gagging for a drink", he said.

"There's a letter for you on the mantelpiece", called out Mary as she filled the kettle from the kitchen tap. "It looks important!

Arthur took down the letter from the mantelpiece and wearily sat down in his armchair with a sigh. After examining the envelope and the post mark he opened it with a knife taken from the drawer in the table. When Mary came in from the kitchen she saw him staring into the fire, the letter on his lap and a pensive look on his face and his mind obviously miles away. He came to himself as Mary handed him a cup of tea.

"I'm afraid there's bad news Mary, and it affects you too".

Mary felt herself grow uneasy as she enquired as to the nature of the news.

"These are my Calling Up papers Mary. I've got to go an' fight in the War. It means of course that I won't be able to keep you on 'ere when I'm gone!"

"Oh!" said Mary in a small voice, "Oh dear! I'm sorry you've got to go Arthur and – Oh dear! Whatever will I do now? We'd got used to it here and our Sylvia's right fond of yer sister Annie and her husband".

"And I know they think the world of 'er Mary. Why don't ye think seriously about letting them adopt Sylvia? It would make life a lot easier for you and they'd give 'er a good home and everything she wanted", said Arthur.

"I couldn't let our Sylvia go", said Mary. "She's all I've got and I don't want anybody else. When do you have to go Arthur?"

"In two weeks time", he replied. "That will give you a bit o' time to get yourself sorted out".

Once again saw Mary packing up their few possessions like a wondering nomad, and once again Sylvia had to leave behind some of her treasured toys, leaving her feeling very bereft. It was bad enough to leave a house where she had begun to feel secure, but to have to leave behind her little treasures was another sorrow to bear, but her complacent nature prevented her from making a fuss as many children might have done.

They never saw Arthur again, though Sylvia did visit her Auntie Annie and Uncle Randolph when she was older. By then they had adopted a little girl called Susan, but they never lost their affection for Sylvia and always welcomed her as their own.

Mary and Sylvia had been back with Lucy and Arthur now for several weeks. Mary was job hunting again, but good jobs did not come easily when one has a small child in tow. Lucy was not too unhappy that Mary was at home for a while because it was spring cleaning time. Her arthritis continued to become worse as she grew older, so it was good to have some help with the shifting of heavy furniture, and the beating of those heavy carpets. She could not say either that Sylvia was any bother about the place because she wasn't. Sylvia was used to amusing herself for hours on her own with her dollies and teddy bear called Rupert. Lucy did notice that Mary was over strict with the child in her opinion, but that was none of her business.

One Friday morning Mary's sister, Connie, walked down the back yard with Ron. It was an unusual time for her to visit her mother. Mary sensed that something was badly wrong and experienced a strange sense of foreboding.

"What's wrong Connie?" Mary said. "You look as white as a sheet".

"I've got some bad news for ye Mary", Connie blurted out, and there were tears pricking in her eyes.

"Bad news! For me? What do you mean?" Mary said apprehensively.

"I don't know 'ow to tell ye Mary", and Connie began to cry.

"Don't keep me in suspense Connie. Pull yourself together and tell me what it is", Mary cried.

"It's Lewis an' his brother", stammered Connie, between sobs. "Lewis an' his brother Harold!"

"What about them?" Mary felt as cold as ice.

"Lewis an' his brother were both called up at the beginning o' War, both being youngish like! As they'd both been to sea before they were conscripted to the Naval Forces an' the ship they were on was a mine sweeper. It got torpedoed by the Germans in the North Atlantic!" and Connie began to sob again.

"You mean - ?" Mary said quietly.

"They were both killed our Mary – blown to bits wi' ship. Lewis an' Harold are both dead. I know Lewis were a bad un to ye, but he didn't deserve that, and 'e was all right when he wasn't drinking!"

Mary smiled a strange colourless smile but her eyes were deadly dull. She left Connie to her mother and went upstairs to the very top of the house and entered the attic. The sudden emptiness within her gripped her body like a vice. Yes, she had left Lewis of her own free will, but somewhere deep down there had always been hope – hope that one day they might get together again, and he would have stopped drinking, and they would live happily ever after as one united family. And now hope had flown away never to return, and there was nothing – nothing but this awful emptiness, and the certain knowledge that death was final. When she began to weep at last, her body, wracked by convulsive sobbing, felt to be torn apart.

15. DOUGLAS

Mary was successful in acquiring another housekeeping position, this time in the small town of Wath several miles away. It no longer mattered where she went now that Lewis was gone. She felt no joy at her prospects, and she could only look ahead to endless years of emptiness stretching in front of her, and her unhappiness buried itself deep within her like a worm burrowing into an apple. Her one ray of sunshine was her daughter and she must work hard to provide her with beautiful clothes and nice toys – but if the child strayed from perfection then she must be severely punished.

Mr. Adams, a wealthy widower, was Mary's new employer. He had a young son, Douglas, who was confined to a wheelchair having contracted polio when he was very small. Now at eight years of age, and with callipers on both his withered legs, it was necessary to have someone to care for him as his mother was dead and his father worked away from home. Sylvia was welcomed into this quiet and lonely household by Douglas. He delighted in her constant chatter for she was a naturally friendly child. He liked nothing better than to play board games with her – the favourite being 'Snakes and Ladders', though she was frightened of the snakes! Douglas used to read her stories and together they would invent games which he could join in from his wheelchair. Sylvia accepted his crippled state, never questioning him as to why he was not like other boys. To her he was just Douglas and she loved him!

Sylvia always remembered the particular smell of that house and she liked it. The house was large and detached, with a very big garden in which she spent a good deal of her time when Douglas was at school. It was at this house that she celebrated her fourth birthday. She was so excited when the postman came with a pile of envelopes addressed to her, and a big parcel from Grandma and Granddad. Some of the envelopes contained money as well as a birthday card so she felt really grown up. Douglas watched her opening her presents and rejoiced with her over every one, with promises to play the new games with her. He himself gave her a pretty bag made up of beads of every colour. There was no birthday party, no birthday cake, but Sylvia had never experienced those things so she did not miss them.

Sylvia never did know why her mother made a sudden decision to terminate her employment with Mr. Adams. All she did remember was the usual ritual of packing up their possessions yet again, and being bundled back to Grandma's house. She remembered clearly her own concern for Douglas's hurt and what he would do without them to look after him, and her little heart bled for him. As they arrived at Grandma's back gate and entered the yard, Lucy was just taking in some washing from the clothes line. She turned as she heard them and saw Mary with her two suitcases and Sylvia struggling with a bag full of toys and her teddy bear under her arm.

"Oh my God! Whatever 'ave ye come back for this time?" Lucy exclaimed.

All Sylvia knew was that Mr. Adams and Douglas had not wanted them to leave, and indeed they had begged Mary to stay, but she had no idea, nor understanding, what had triggered off something in her mother's unstable mind to cause her to take flight once again.

PART 3

1. TIME TO STAY

1990. Sylvia was suddenly aware of the singing of the birds as she came out of her reverie. She sighed as she settled back into the driving seat of her Volvo car and pulled on her gloves. She was very much disturbed by the wave of forgotten memories which had flooded through her mind. For a while she had forgotten herself and was once more the child of over forty years ago.

"Time I was getting home", she thought, and she straightened up, started the car, and drove slowly out of the cemetery, up the leafy lane and back on to the main road. It was a good half hour's drive home, through winding country lanes mud splattered by farm tractors or splashed by cow pats from the herd driven along there earlier that day.

"I wonder why it is that one remembers mainly the bad things and all the rest fades into a pale grey?" she thought. "Mother did have my best interests at heart – at least that was her intention. She was basically a good woman who had fallen prey to the evil of insanity". As she drove along Sylvia's thoughts once again slipped back to the past events of her mother's life – to the time when Mary had made up her mind to find a position where she felt she could stay.

1940. The rational side of Mary realised that her daughter needed a more stable existence, particularly now that she was almost ready to start school. Mary was ambitious for Sylvia and she wanted her to have a good education. She knew that the latter would suffer if the child continued to be dragged around from pillar to post.

"I'll try and get a job with a lady", said Mary to her mother. "I've really got to find somewhere where I feel I can stay. I think I'll be better off with a lady. I've 'ad enough of men!"

One day she saw an advertisement in the local paper and it seemed to be just what she was looking for. An elderly lady required a living in companion housekeeper, and a child would not be objected to! Mary wrote to the lady, whose name was Mrs. Baker, recently widowed, who asked her to go along for an interview. Mary was overjoyed to be accepted for the post and resolved that she would stick to this job through thick and thin for the sake of Sylvia's future schooling.

Sylvia's first memory of this new phase in her life was of being driven in a car up a very steep hill. She and Mary had taken a train to Chesterfield in Derbyshire. At the station they were met by Mrs. Baker and her son who had a car to take them to the small town of Bolsover. Half way up the hill Mrs. Baker pointed out to them the ancient castle which was sitting on the crest, commanding spectacular views of the plain below, and surrounded by a thick protective plantation of trees.

"It's just like Sleeping Beauty's castle", Sylvia thought. "I wonder if there is a sleeping princess there, and if so would the prince manage to fight his way through all those prickly looking trees!"

A few minutes later they arrived at Mrs. Baker's house in Castle Street, and in fact the gates of the castle were only a few yards away. The house was a very large one, detached but rather austere in appearance. It had a sizeable front garden, but not the sort you play in, and at the back was a small enclosed concrete yard which in turn led down to an area of land where stood outbuildings and a chicken shed. Chickens strutted and squawked as they pecked the dusty ground in search of food. At the side of the house was a large garage which sheltered a couple of lorries as Mrs. Baker's husband had been a coal merchant. After his death Mrs. Baker carried on the business with the help of her youngest son, Bob. Her elder son, Eddie, who had collected them in the car, was a farmer.

As in previous employment, Mary was given a large bedroom containing a double bed which she and Sylvia would share. It was a much bigger room than they had enjoyed before, big enough for Sylvia to play in as well as sleep. Meals were taken in the large living kitchen and afterward Mrs. Baker would retire to her own front sitting room, leaving the kitchen to Mary and Sylvia. There was another very large and unused room downstairs and Sylvia was allowed to use this for play and storage of toys.

Mrs. Baker was a portly seventy year old lady, a formidable figure and a very strict disciplinarian. Not that Sylvia ever needed the latter, but she was quick to recognise the lady's stern character and therefore determined never to get on the wrong side of her if she could help it. The old lady had borne four children, two sons already mentioned, and two daughters, Maureen and Edna. They were all married with children of their own who were all equally respectful of their grandmother's authority.

Sylvia had now reached her fifth birthday and was ready to start school at last. Mary registered her at the local infant school where she quickly settled in, loving every minute of the day. The War continued so each child had to take a gas mask to school every day, and there was the daily practice of taking them out of the cases, fitting them over their faces, and sitting quietly in this manner for fifteen minutes or so whilst the teacher read them a story. They all looked exceedingly funny and there were many giggles and much shuffling of bottoms, and scrapings of chair legs on the wooden floor, for most of the children could not stand the rubbery smell inside the gas masks and felt that they would choke. Should the air raid siren warning go, then the whole school would be temporarily evacuated to an underground air raid shelter. Here they all sang songs until the 'All Clear' siren was sounded.

Although in no way brilliant, Sylvia performed well at school. She felt secure within its walls, and worked hard to produce good results and to please her teachers.

"Sylvia, will you go and empty the water out of this vase please?" asked the teacher as she removed the dead flowers. Always pleased to be singled out to do something, Sylvia took the vase and carefully carried it down the corridor so as not to let the water slop out on to the tiled floor. Once outside in the playground she had to negotiate a step and as she was keeping her eye on the water in the vase, her foot missed the step and she fell.

"Oh dear! The vase!" she thought, and as she felt herself falling she somehow managed to keep hold of the vase and prevent it from making contact with the hard ground, thus saving it from being broken. In doing so, she tipped the vase up and all the water poured out, mainly running down her neck and saturating her dress. Sylvia fretted for the rest of the day about the state of her dress and her mother's possible reaction! She also felt wet and uncomfortable.

The good hidings administered to Sylvia by Mary continued from time to time. They were compensated for – or perhaps Mary's conscience was eased – by an over indulgence of material things, particularly at Christmas time when the child was given far more than was necessary.

Sylvia had acquired a little friend called Joan. She was a publican's daughter and lived only a few doors away. Joan was never allowed to play at Sylvia's home but she would invite Sylvia to play at her apartment home above the pub. Very often Sylvia would be asked to stay for tea with Joan, but Mary did not feel that she could return the hospitality as Mrs. Baker did not relish the presence of more than one youngster in her house.

A favourite uncle came to stay with Joan's family one weekend, and on the Saturday afternoon Sylvia was invited to stay for tea. For dessert they were served with tinned pears and lashings of cream, much to the children's delight. Unfortunately Sylvia spilt some pear juice on her dress and she began to cry.

"Whatever is the matter?" asked Jane's mother.

"I've spilt some juice on my dress and my mummy will hit me", Sylvia stammered.

"Don't be silly, of course she won't hit you", said Joan's mother.

"I'm sure she won't", declared Uncle Tom, an elderly lightly built person with hair greying at the temples. "You didn't do it on purpose. When it's time to go home I will come with you and explain that it was an accident. Your mother will understand".

Feeling a little more confident with the promise of protection from her friend's Uncle Tom, Sylvia relaxed into enjoying the rest of the tea, making short work of the jam sponge cake which had been made by Joan's grandma. When it was time to go, Uncle Tom took Sylvia by the hand and led her up the road to where she lived. Taking her round to the back of the house he knocked on the door which was opened by Mary.

"Hello!" he said. "I'm Joan's Uncle Tom. I've brought Sylvia home for you. She's a little upset because she spilt some fruit juice on her dress. I told her that I would explain to you that she didn't do it on purpose"

"It's all right", said Mary unctuously. "It doesn't matter".

Closing the door on Uncle Tom as he said goodbye, Mary turned angrily on her daughter who cringed from the following onslaught upon herself. Mary picked up a cane walking stick, a child's toy belonging to Sylvia, and began to beat her with it, lashing it across the backs of her legs, bringing up vivid red weals. She then dragged the child to the bottom of the stairs and gave her a great kick which sent her sprawling upon the steps. Sylvia picked herself up as best she could and stumbled up the rest of the stairs, her mother shouting abuse at her from behind. Distressed and sobbing, Sylvia went into the bedroom where she huddled up in a chair where she remained until Mary shouted to her to go downstairs.

A few days later, Sylvia was playing outside with the little cane which had been used to beat her. She walked down the street towards her friend's house and suddenly she stopped by a large wooden gate. She looked at the little walking stick which she quite liked as a play thing, she looked at the large wooden gate – then – quick as a flash – she stood on her tip toes and deftly dropped the stick over the top of the gate, knowing full well that she would not be able to retrieve it. Her only thought at the time was that her mother would not be able to beat her with it any more. Then she began to worry about the possibility of her mother discovering that the stick was missing and questioning her about it. However, nothing was ever said about the missing stick, but out of the blue appeared a bigger weapon – a large knobby stick which Mary chose to wield over her daughter, and did not refrain from whacking her hard with it whenever she considered that Sylvia should be punished.

2. AIR RAID

Mary was very lavish with the gifts which she showered upon Sylvia at Christmas time. She did not earn much money, but she joined a Christmas club at a small nearby toy shop. Every year she had set ideas on what she wanted to buy for her daughter, and whatever she decided upon had to be bigger and better and more expensive than the average. If Sylvia's friend, Joan, had a scooter for Christmas, then the one Mary bought would be bigger and smarter. Likewise she bought dolls of excellent quality, expensively dressed and with real hair, whereas Joan's dolls were of a cheaper variety, though her parents were comparatively rich. Not that there was anything wrong with buying good quality items, on the contrary – but Sylvia might have been happier with less toys and less good hidings!

In spite of everything, Sylvia thought that Christmas mornings were pure magic, and she appreciated every single gift, always taking the greatest care that toys should not get broken or books torn. After the opening of the presents, which Mary watched with great satisfaction as she observed the pleasure and excitement on her daughter's face, they went downstairs for breakfast. The meal being over, Sylvia would go to call for Joan, taking with her the latest new doll. They would then go to the Christmas Day Service at church together and later they would meet up again to compare and examine each other's presents.

Some Christmases were spent at Grandma's. Mrs. Baker was not too pleased when this happened as she did not relish being on her own at Christmas. Going

Poor Mary

to Grandma's for Christmas was wonderful for Sylvia and she became very excited. She could not wait to get there to see Grandma's Christmas tree which was adorned with sparking baubles, ornaments shaped like birds with silken tails, and of course the angel crowning the topmost branch. The delicate silver tinsel shimmered in the fire light, as did all the other glittering things. The tree proudly sat on the sideboard of the living room, paper garlands hung from the ceiling and holly was stuck behind the pictures and over the mirror. On Christmas Eve, stockings were hung from the mantelpiece of the fireplace which sported a crackling bright fire. All the family – aunts, uncles and cousins came to Grandma's for Christmas Day, Boxing Day and New Year's Eve and Day, so it was all so much more exciting for a little girl who was not allowed to have many friends.

Mary took Sylvia to visit her parents about twice a year, and as the War was still raging throughout Europe it could be a very hazardous journey. They had to take a bus to Sheffield and then they had to walk to the other side of the city in order to catch another bus to Mary's home town. Sylvia remembered vividly one nightmarish episode. As the bus in which they were travelling approached the city there was a sudden air raid by German bombers. The bus arrived in the middle of a blitz on Sheffield and, as they alighted from the bus, the whole city seemed to be ablaze. Even as they ran fearfully through the streets, bombs were falling on nearby buildings and fires were raging everywhere. Mary was terrified and clinging to her small case, she ran as fast as she could as she dragged her child behind her until they eventually reached the bus stop. As they waited for the bus to come they could hear loud explosions and buildings went up in flames before their eyes. Amidst all this could be heard the clanging of numerous fire engines and the wailing of ambulance sirens, and everywhere people were scurrying for shelter. Mary felt that they were very vulnerable and was shaking in her shoes. Like most wartime children, Sylvia accepted it as a way of life, not of course fully comprehending the danger they were in.

At last the bus appeared, trundling along later than it should have been. It had been necessary to make detours because some streets were suddenly no longer there, instead were gaping bomb craters and rubble from destroyed homes. No one thought that the bus should be cancelled. People tried to live through the Blitz as normally as possible and they became quite philosophical about the possibility of each moment being their last! Mary was very relieved to reach her parents' home that night, and to still be alive to tell the tale!

3. "PLEASE DON'T SCRUB MY KNEES"

At seven years old Sylvia left the infant school and continued her schooling at the small Church of England school nearby. Sylvia's friend, Joan, did not move up to the junior school. Instead she was sent to a convent school in Chesterfield. Being publicans her parents could afford to pay for her education. This was the beginning of the end of the two children's friendship as they began to take separate paths in their lives.

During her few years at the junior school, Sylvia began to be troubled by pains in her legs and back, but everyone said that she was suffering from growing pains. On the games' field she performed very badly, always coming last in races and finding difficulty in jumping and climbing. Thus she was subjected to a great deal of teasing from her peers, so much so that she began to hate games lessons. She very easily stumbled and would fall badly and make a mess of her knees and clothes, much to her consternation. She was more worried about the consequences at home with her mother than about the initial injury.

It was the end of the school day. Spring was in the air and the children were in high spirits as they poured out into the school playground to the brilliant sunshine and a bright blue sky.

"Come on Sylvia, let's play chasing. Bet you can't catch me!" cried a class mate as she shot across the playground.

Sylvia gave chase after her friend and their shrieks of laughter echoed across the playground as they twisted and turned to avoid each other. Sylvia made a sudden dash towards the centre of the playground which was rough and uneven with loose stones. Her slippery shoes lost their grip and she was thrust forward, falling with a dull thud which shook every bone in her body, the shock reverberating through her head. For a moment she lay there, stunned, and her friend came to help her up. Slowly she began to collect herself together and turned over, remaining in a sitting position as she examined the damage to her legs. Both her hands were grazed and full of grit, and each knee bore an enormous hole full of blood, dirt and grit. Sylvia hardly dared to look at her dress which was badly soiled. Her face went a bright pink and tears came into her eyes as she was filled with dismay. She was not so much distressed by her injuries, painful though they were, but by the thought of what would happen to her when she got home. Struggling to her feet and looking at her scuffed shoes and dirty white socks, Sylvia burst into tears.

"Never mind", comforted her friend, "it's home time an' ye can go straight home and your mum will clean ye legs up and put some plasters on".

"I daren't go home", wept Sylvia. "My mum will hit me!"

"'Course she won't", said her friend, "Ye didn't fall down on purpose".

"She will – I know she will – she always does", cried Sylvia.

"Well I'll come home with ye", said the other girl, "an' I'll tell her that ye couldn't help it".

Sylvia allowed herself to be led home by her friend, knowing in her heart that it would not make any difference and that her mother would hit her for making such a mess of herself. As they approached the back door of the house her heart quailed and not without good reason, for Sylvia recognized that set, stern look on Mary's face as she regarded the state of her daughter. Mary's lips stated that there was nothing to worry about, but her eyes belied her words.

As soon as Sylvia's friend had gone, Mary dragged her into the kitchen and flung her on to a chair near the sink.

"I'll teach you to make a mess of yourself like this, ye little bitch", she cried. Then, opening the cupboard under the sink, she took out the floor scrubbing brush and proceeded to scrub the wounds on Sylvia's knees as hard as she could, ignoring the sobs and pleas to stop. When she had done that she attacked the child's sore hands in a similar fashion. Her face blotchy with tears, Sylvia was sent upstairs to sit alone in the bedroom, her bruised knees throbbing with pain, and her hands still stinging from the effect of the hard bristles of the scrubbing brush. She had not had a good hiding this time, but the treatment had been worse!

4. WHAT'S IN A NAME?

Mary religiously brushed and curled Sylvia's hair into ringlets every night and every morning. If the child moved an inch during this process then Mary would strike her sharply on the head with the brush. Sylvia began to hate her ringlets and longed to have plaits like the other girls at school, or even to have her hair cut short, but Mary would not hear of it.

One morning before school started, Mary was busily grooming Sylvia's hair when a letter appeared on the door mat. It was from Mary's mother and Sylvia asked if she could open and read Grandma's letter. Mary consented to this and continued curling her ringlets. Sylvia opened the envelope, trying to keep as still as possible. She could now read silently and well, but she did find Grandma's scrawling writing a little difficult to decipher in places. She slowly read each sentence to herself and they were the usual Grandma type expression as to how the weather had been, how expensive everything had become, and how bad her arthritic legs were! Then there was a sentence which Sylvia read twice because she couldn't understand it. There was some reference to Mrs. Adams, Grandma's near neighbour who was always advising everyone, and words to the effect that the name 'Sylvia Howell' could be changed to 'Sylvia Copley' by Deed Poll.

"What does this mean Mummy?" asked Sylvia.

Mary turned scarlet and she snatched the letter from Sylvia's hand and shoved it into her apron pocket.

"Never you about that – you wouldn't understand! Now off ye go to school or else you'll be late".

Sylvia set off for school feeling puzzled by not only Grandma's letter but by her mother's attitude towards it.

"Well I'm Sylvia Copley", she thought, "so who is Sylvia Howell?"

She did not speak to anyone about this mystery but she never forgot about it, continuing to puzzle over it from time to time.

That same evening Mary found some small reason to punish Sylvia again. This time she had acquired a leather belt with which to whip her, but not satisfied with that, she used the buckle end of the belt to strike the backs of her legs. The next day Sylvia went to school showing enormous red weals down the backs of both legs which were by then stiff and painful. No teacher noticed, or if they did there were no queries!

5. SUCCESS

Sylvia eventually reached the last and most important year of her junior school – the 'eleven plus' year which would decide the course of her future education. If she passed the 'eleven plus' examination then she would go on to one of the grammar schools in Chesterfield. If she did not pass then she would have to go to the local secondary modern school which was situated at the bottom of a very, very steep hill. Sylvia's heart was still set on being a teacher and she realised that it was important to pass the examination so that she could have a grammar school education. Mary wanted her to pass the exam because that would be prestigious and it would give her something to boast about, plus the fact that she did not want her to be mixing with the 'rough girls' she had seen on their way to the local school!

"If ye don't pass that exam Sylvia, then you'll have to go to that awful school at the bottom of the hill where all those rough girls go – and I won't let you stay for school dinners either – you'll have to walk all the way back up that steep hill for your dinner everyday!"

Sylvia did not need threats of this sort to make her try hard at school, but nevertheless, the thought of having to walk up and down that steep hill twice every day was pretty daunting! The 'Big Day' came at last and she looked forward to the challenge of the examination. She set off to school carrying in her pocket a tiny glass black cat for luck. All the desks were set out in the school hall, far enough apart so that no one could cheat. The boy sitting at the desk nearest to hers was a tall, pale and lanky lad called Tom Shepherd.

Poor Mary

The first part of the examination was Mathematics and Sylvia waded through the hundred questions, undaunted by the paper. Tom Shepherd did not appear after lunch for the next part of the test.

"How could he stay away this afternoon and miss his exam?" everyone was saying.

What they did not know was that Tom had met with a terrible accident during his lunch break. He had gone home for his lunch as usual and when he had finished eating he disappeared into the garden shed. There, unknown to his parents, he had hidden a hand grenade which he had found during a weekend visit to Sherwood Forest. He took the grenade from its hiding place and put it in the work bench. Then he took a hammer and - there was a tremendous explosion!

Tom's hand was blown off and he was permanently blinded by the blast. No one at school ever saw him again. When he eventually recovered from his fearful injuries he was sent to finish his education in a school for the blind in York. Sylvia experienced a sense of loss at the sight of his desk standing empty for the rest of the term.

Three weeks later, a brown envelope appeared through the letter box and it was addressed to Mary. She opened it with trembling fingers as Sylvia looked on apprehensively.

"You've passed!" Mary cried excitedly. "You've passed yer Scholarship exam and you have to go for an interview at your new school next week. Tapton House

Grammar School! My goodness – I'm right proud of ye Sylvia luv!"

Sylvia felt a great depth of relief which overwhelmed her for the moment, and she had to admit that part of it was due to the fact that now she wouldn't be faced with that awful school, where there were really rough children, nor would she have to walk back up that laboriously steep hill twice a day! Then she had visions of starting life in her new school, wearing a smart uniform, and being able to have dinner at school with all the other children, and learning French and Latin. It was all too wonderful for words and she hopped and skipped around the house in sheer delight.

Uniform! That was going to be a costly business, but Mary was determined that her daughter would be correctly uniformed no matter how much it cost. No second hand uniform for her daughter, everything would be new, smart, and from a quality shop. It is a fact that the people who can least afford it are usually the ones who buy their children the perfect new uniform, whilst the really wealthy people are content to delve around for second hand clothes and 'hand me downs'!

"There won't be any flies on my daughter!" Mary explained. "Nobody will be able to point a finger at her and say she's not properly dressed!" So Mary's meagre earnings were now carefully saved until she had sufficient money to take Sylvia to the department store and buy the necessary requirements.

6. THE SCARF

In the September of 1947 Sylvia began a new chapter in her life at Tapton House Grammar School. She had never wavered in her ambition to be a teacher and knew that she would have to work hard to achieve this goal. Mary had not received much schooling and therefore would not be able to help her with her studies.

The school was housed in a red bricked eighteenth century building, the former home of George Stephenson, the 'Father of Railways'. George Stephenson was the self educated son of a colliery mechanic. He built his own steam locomotive and called it Blucher after the Prussian field marshal who played a crucial role in the Napoleonic Wars. His pioneer engine, Locomotion, was eventually succeeded by his engine called The Rocket. Quiet and retiring, Stephenson refused most of the honours offered to him in his old age, including a knighthood and a seat in Parliament. He retired to Tapton House, near Chesterfield in Derbyshire. The house overlooked a stretch of the North Midland Railway and it allowed him to watch his beloved trains go by. He spent his last years enjoying the magnificent gardens of his home.

The red brick house was situated on high ground and surrounded by several acres of parkland. It was a lovely environment in which to work – springtime being particularly beautiful as there were masses of golden daffodils growing everywhere. At this time of the year Sylvia always remembered Wordsworth's poem 'Daffodils' and the words –

> 'Ten thousand saw I at a glance,
> Tossing their heads in sprightly dance'

On the lower slopes of the extensive school grounds was a steeply wooded area which was thickly carpeted with bluebells in the spring. It was at the very bottom of these woodland slopes that the railway ran, and as it had been Stephenson's favourite pass-time to walk down there and watch the trains go by, so it was with the pupils of the school, and many of them would wonder down there during their lunch break. Sylvia enjoyed having her school dinners in the school canteen, though she did her share of grumbling about the lumpy custard and the 'frog spawn' tapioca pudding – who wouldn't? She could have received free school dinners but Mary was much too proud for that, and every Monday morning she gave her daughter some dinner money to take to school.

It was good to make so many new friends and to encounter all the types of characters. Sylvia also experienced some who were down right dishonest, and often bitter lessons were learned that not everyone was to be trusted. In her early years at the school her closest friend was Pat who could be very spiteful on occasions, but nevertheless they remained very close. One day Pat came to school wearing a new scarf of the school colours, black and purple, hand knitted by Pat's mother.

"What a lovely scarf!" Sylvia exclaimed, "I wish I had one like that. Please may I try it on?"

"OK!" said Pat, and wrapped the scarf around Sylvia's neck.

"It's so warm and cosy, and I love the way it's long enough to hang down at the back", said Sylvia.

"I'll ask my mum to knit one for your birthday", said Pat.

On Sylvia's birthday, which happened to fall on a school day, Pat gave her a parcel which was beautifully wrapped in pretty paper. Excitedly Sylvia opened it and there, to her great delight, was a hand knitted school scarf.

"Oh thank you, thank you!" cried Sylvia. "It's just what I wanted. Please thank your mum for knitting it for me".

The two girls scampered off across the playground, their long scarves flying in the high March wind.

On Sunday, Sylvia proudly wore her new scarf when she went to church. Being somewhat bored during the Sermon, she began messing around with the ends of her scarf and amused herself by counting the number of tassels on each end. The next day at school Pat and Sylvia went to the cloakroom at break time to pick up their scarves before going outside in the cold. Sylvia's scarf was not on the peg where she had left it. She could not believe it. How could it disappear like that? The two girls searched the cloakroom to no avail and at last decided to report the scarf as missing to the headmaster.

"Did the scarf have your name on it Sylvia?" queried Mr. Mellor, the headmaster.

"No Sir", Sylvia replied.

"Well that is really very foolish", continued Mr. Mellor. "If things are not named then it is extremely difficult to trace them – isn't it?"

"Yes Sir", said Sylvia meekly. Feeling really deprived without her precious scarf, she went out to play with Pat and they mooched around the playground together, both of them disgruntled.

A few days later, during the lunch break, a small scrap of a girl who was thin and pale, her hair unkempt and straggly, ran passed Pat and Sylvia.

"Hey! Look! She's wearing my scarf!" cried Sylvia. "It's exactly like yours, hand knitted and everything!"

They ran after the scrawny child who glared at them with hard eyes. When they tackled her about the scarf she of course denied it and told them to 'Get lost!'

"Let's go and tell Mr. Mellor", said Pat, so off they went to his study. They told him that they had seen the missing scarf being worn by Jean Smith in Class 1C. Mr. Mellor sent for Jean and told her to bring the scarf to him. Pat produced her own scarf which was of course identical, and said that they had both been knitted by her mother.

"Well Sylvia", said the Head, "there's no name on this scarf and, as I said before, it makes things very difficult to prove it's yours".

Sylvia had a sudden flash of inspiration as she remembered the tassels.

"There are twenty two tassels on each end Mr. Mellor. I counted them when I was in church last Sunday".

The Headmaster counted the number of tassels on each end of the scarf and sure enough there were twenty two. He handed the scarf to Sylvia with instructions to get it named and, dismissing the two friends, he turned his attention to the scruffy individual named

Jean Smith. They never knew what was said to her but Sylvia did not care about that. She was overjoyed to get back her beautiful scarf!

7. "I CAN'T STAND PEOPLE LIKE YOU!"

The Headmaster, Mr. Mellor, was a person one could never forget. He was a Churchillian character, both in appearance and in his distinctive way of speaking, even down to the almost permanent cigar. He was short in stature and rotund , and he stalked the school and its grounds in his cap and gown, ready to pounce on anyone who might look as though they were about to break the rules. He might walk into any lesson and take over from the teacher, and woe betides anyone who was not working hard – or had not learnt their French verbs! Not having too much talent for languages, one of the few French verbs that Sylvia would never forget was the verb 'Finir' – To Finish' – simply because Mr. Mellor had pounced on her one day and discovered that she didn't know it. He demanded that she learn it thoroughly by the next day when she would report to his study and repeat it to him. One did not ignore this – one learnt it thoroughly! The proof of the pudding was that whatever else Sylvia did not know about the French language, she never forgot the conjugation of the verb 'Finir'.

Two of Mr. Mellor's sayings also remained firmly fixed in Sylvia's memory forever.

"Hard work hurts no one. Worry kills!" he said one morning in Assembly.

"Always leave a place as you would wish to find it", he said on another occasion .He continued to instil into his pupils the importance of good manners.

Poor Mary

"Manners maketh man", he would say, and instructed them to always give up their seat for adults, particularly on a bus, and to hold doors open for people instead of selfishly barging through in order to be first. It has to be said that a big percentage of pupils who were taught by Mr. Mellor retained his lessons in good manners and practiced them for the rest of their lives.

"Let's go down to the railway track and watch the trains", suggested Pat after lunch one day.

"OK!" said Sylvia," but it's a long way so we'd better not stay too long or we'll be late for French".

The two girls set off across the park till they came to the steep woodland area bordering the railway track. In the wood a woodpecker was laughing and wood doves were cooing. They could see paths like aisles in the woods, leaves shot with sunlight, and green ferns and brambles. In a break within the trees could be seen a glimpse of sunlit fields, yellow with buttercups, across the other side of the railway line. They lingered from time to time as their interest was captured by this or that as they made their way to the railway line. Suddenly the path was lost to them as low growing brambles crowded upon it. They had to retrace their steps until they found another pathway which was clear.

Eventually they reached the bottom and they ran alongside the fence until they came to the railway bridge. Here they mounted the steps and stood looking down from the top of the bridge, hoping that a train might pass beneath them, but one didn't. Sylvia suddenly shivered as a cool breeze sprang up and whipped round their bare legs. The sun had disappeared and mountainous clouds were piled upon each other in the now grey sky.

"I think we ought to be getting back", said Sylvia. "We took ages getting here and it looks as though it's going to rain any minute and we have no coats".

As she said this the first large spots of rain began to fall. Suddenly the heavens opened and as the two girls fled from the bridge they were caught in the deluge of rain which descended upon them. As they raced alongside the fence again, a two coach train was loudly chugging eastwards, dragging its plume of smoke behind it, but the girls did not even glance at it in their haste to escape the rain. What had been a happy and exciting adventure down to the railway had turned into a cold and uncomfortable uphill trek on their return and, of course, it took them much longer.

Two bedraggled girls, soaked to the skin, hair dripping wet, stood in some trepidation outside the classroom door. They were fifteen minutes late for their French lesson. Sylvia gingerly knocked on the door and they entered the room. There was a sudden momentary silence from the rest of the class at the appearance of the girls who looked like a couple of drowned rats. Then could be heard the titters and sniggers and caustic comments from one or two boys. However, Mademoiselle was not amused! She sent them both down to the headmaster to explain themselves. They were each given some extra homework to do, and of course, Sylvia was in further trouble from Mary at home because of the state of her clothes and her hair.

One of Sylvia's favourite lessons was Domestic Science. This was not because she was particularly good at cooking; on the contrary, she usually ended up making a muddle of her cooking. At home she was never allowed to participate in cooking or baking and therefore, compared to her contemporaries she hadn't had any experience. The reason why she enjoyed these lessons was that she idolized the teacher who was young and pretty and very kind. Ironically, the teacher's name was Miss Howell. Sylvia would go home and extol the virtues of Miss Howell to Mary who appeared to become extremely uncomfortable at the mention of her name. Sylvia had momentarily forgotten about the letter referring to herself as Sylvia Howell. Of course there was no connection but the constant reference to Miss Howell caused Mary some distress.

It was apparent that one particular teacher took a strong dislike to Sylvia. Her name was Miss Loft and she was a most unattractive person with coarse short cropped hair, a hairy face, and she was stocky in stature. She was perhaps in her early fifties. In one particular Scripture lesson Sylvia took her book to be marked and, without even reading the work, Miss Loft put a red line through it and sent her back to her desk to do it again. This happened several times before Miss Loft eventually condescended to read and mark the work. Her parting shot to Sylvia was scathing.

"I can't stand people like you who always have to be different!"

Sylvia knew that Miss Loft was referring to the fact that she always wore her hair in ringlets whilst all the other girls wore plaits or bobbed hair. Little did Miss Loft realise how Sylvia herself despised the Shirley Temple look which her mother still insisted on giving her. Eventually Mary relented now that her daughter was growing up, and the despised ringlets were cut off to be replaced with a short layered style which curled prettily round her face.

8. DISAPPOINTMENT AND TRIUMPH.

Mrs. Baker decided that the house in Castle Street was far too big and too expensive to maintain. She had finally retired from the coal business which she had successfully run since her husband died, so she no longer needed the large garages and all the out buildings. She was getting on in years now and she desired a nice retirement house, but she still wanted Mary to continue working for her as housekeeper companion. She found a suitable place, a modern semi detached house situated half way down the very steep hill called Castle Lane which curled round and down below the castle.

Sylvia found the move very exciting and, though she still had to share a bedroom with her mother, she loved the view from their bedroom window. It looked over the long back garden, at the top of which stood a group of apple trees, to fields beyond, and on the crest of a hill could be seen the church spire. The church bells could be heard clearly every Sunday, calling people to worship.

Every Sunday morning Sylvia went to the church service and also to afternoon Sunday school. As she grew older she began to go to the evening service which was later followed by the church youth club. One Sunday afternoon the Sunday school teacher, Miss Rutledge, announced that the class would be performing a Christmas play and that the following week she would be choosing people for the parts. Sylvia was so excited and after class she ran all the way home and gleefully told her mother.

"Oh I do hope that she'll choose me to be an angel", she said to Mary.

"You'll just have to wait an' see", said Mary. "Anyway, your teacher's bound to give you a part, even if it's a little one - you do go to Sunday school every week without missing!"

The next week eventually passed and on Sunday afternoon Sylvia set off to her class in eager anticipation. At last the moment came when Miss Rutledge said she was going to sort out the parts for the play. Several children who did not normally attend Sunday school came that day, having heard that there was going to be a play and hoping that they would have a part in it.

"Stand up everyone", said Miss Rutledge who also happened to be the headmistress of a nearby school. "I want to see how tall you all are then I can choose people for suitable parts."

Everyone stood up as tall as possible and Miss Rutledge began to make her choices. Sylvia did not expect to get a main part, an angel would do, and she waited anxiously as the main characters were chosen – Mary, Joseph, the Three Kings and the shepherds. All around her the children were being selected, including those children who hardly came to the classes, if ever!

"Surely she'll pick me next", thought Sylvia.

"Right! Now I will choose the angels", declared Miss Rutledge. "Jane, Anne, Dorothy, Betty, Jean and – let me see – Maureen. That will be enough I think. The one or two who are left can work behind the scenes".

Sylvia nodded, the tears pricking her eyelids as her hopes were dashed. She instinctively felt that, for some reason unknown to herself, she was being discriminated against. She contained her tears and bitter disappointment within her, but her heart was constricted and she felt that her chest would burst. As soon as class had finished she fled from the church hall and again ran all the way home, this time the tears falling freely down her cheeks as she tried to stifle the sobs which were choking her.

"Whatever is the matter our Sylvia?" cried Mary as her daughter burst through the back door and threw herself into her mother's arms. Between sobs Sylvia related to her mother how Miss Rutledge had totally ignored her and had chosen for the play the children who rarely went to Sunday school. Mary comforted her daughter as best she could, but in her own heart she felt that Sylvia was being a victim of prejudice.

"P'raps you'd better not go to Sunday school anymore", said Mary.

"I agree", said Mrs. Baker who had come to see what all the fuss was about. "It's obvious that the woman doesn't like her. I wouldn't let her go again if I were you".

Nevertheless Sylvia did continue to go to the church and the Sunday school. Mary had risen above the prejudice and she had encouraged her daughter to do the same.

"Ye go to church to worship God, an' that's all that matters in the end!"

At twelve years old Sylvia began to go to Confirmation classes in preparation for her Confirmation.

The Vicar gave her a form to be filled in by her mother. Sylvia took it home and gave it to Mary.

"What's all this?" asked Mary.

"The Vicar would like you to answer all the questions on the form before I can be confirmed", answered Sylvia. "It's about when I was christened and everything".

Mary began to read the questions which she had to answer and one question in particular leaped up at her from the paper.

"Was the child baptised in any other name than the one with which he or she will be confirmed?"

Mary's heart lurched as she read this and she became agitated and turned quite pale. Of course Sylvia had been baptised with the name of Sylvia Howell, and now she was known as Sylvia Copley. Mary made a quick decision and wrote "NO" by the offending question. Of course she was worrying unduly as the question was referring to Christian names, but Mary did not realise that and was convinced that she had just committed a great sin.

In due time Mary proudly watched her daughter, clad in a simple white dress, being confirmed by the Bishop of Derby. She gave Sylvia a beautiful Book of Common Prayer with a cover of white ivory embellished with letters of gold leaf. During the 'laying on of hands' Mary experienced twinges of guilt as she remembered the circumstances of Sylvia's birth which had been surrounded by lies and deception.

Poor Mary

Shortly after Sylvia's Confirmation, the Vicar announced that there would be a voluntary Scripture examination set by the clergy of the Diocese, and there would be prizes for those who did well in the test. Children from all over the Diocese would be entering and so Sylvia thought that she also would 'have a go'. At the due time she went to the vicarage, where the examination was to take place, and rang the front door bell. The door was opened by an extremely pretty girl with short, black curly hair and dark eyes. It was Sarah, the Vicar's daughter. Her flashing black eyes looked Sylvia up and down disdainfully and she haughtily bade her to come in. Then she led her to a large, shabby room which was obviously a study. The walls were lined with books, and a large wooden table stood in the centre of the room. Rugs were scattered on the wooden floor and an enormous floor to ceiling window overlooked the pretty vicarage garden. The room was full of culture – and dust!

"The test paper is on the table", said Sarah. "You have just one hour to complete the test and you're not allowed to ask any questions. I am here to make sure that you don't cheat!" Sarah settled herself down in an easy chair and buried her head in a book.

Sylvia felt somewhat aggrieved at Sarah's last remark as it was not in her nature to cheat. She settled down to tackle the paper and became deeply absorbed as she began to answer the questions, writing her answers at great length. She finished well before the time limit.

"I've finished the test", she said.

"Well go then", mumbled Sarah ungraciously, not lifting her head from her book. "Just leave it on the table!"

Sylvia felt herself well and truly dismissed as she quietly let herself out through the front door of the vicarage. The vicar's wife happened to be a teacher of English at Sylvia's school. About three weeks later Sylvia was sitting at her desk in the classroom when Mrs. Drew, the vicar's wife, came in and sought her out.

"I've got some good news for you Sylvia. You know the test which you did at the vicarage a short while ago? You came top in the whole Diocese. I'm really proud of you!"

Sylvia experienced a feeling of warmth within her. She could hardly believe that she had done so well and she didn't know what to say. On the following Sunday she was presented with the First Prize by the Reverend Drew. It was a book token for three pounds which was a considerable sum of money in those days. The whole occasion did a great deal to raise Sylvia's self esteem, and certainly it seemed that she was regarded in a new light by all in authority at the church, including Miss Rutledge who had treated her so unfairly before!

9. "NEVER GO WHERE IT'S LONELY"

Mary had many times lectured Sylvia on the dangers of frequenting lonely places.

"Never go in lonely places, and never talk to strange men or go anywhere with them", Mary would say. She had not talked to Sylvia about the facts of life, or of the possibilities of what might happen to her should she meet and go off with the wrong person. Sylvia had read newspaper reports about young girls who had been found murdered in remote places so she assumed that this could be her fate if she disobeyed her mother on this point. Thus she generally took care not to venture into the woods or fields unless she was with a group of young people or adults that she knew. She held a deep fear of strange men; even should their intentions be honourable ones.

It was a Sunday afternoon in May and Sylvia went off to Sunday school as usual. As the weather had emerged from winter into the mildness of early spring, she was wearing a new pink and white candy striped dress of a very flimsy material and for warmth she wore a navy blue woollen cardigan. After the class had finished she began to talk with Catherine, a girl who went to her school. Catherine was a year younger than Sylvia. She was not very tall and was quite plump, and she had short, straight flaxen hair. She had the potential of becoming quite attractive, when she eventually grew out of her plumpness. Being the child of much older parents than usual, Catherine tended to be very old fashioned in her ways. Her father was well over sixty whilst she was only eleven so she was virtually brought up with previous generation values.

"It's a lovely spring day and really warm. Shall we go for a walk?" Sylvia suggested.

"OK! Where shall we go?" said Catherine.

"I don't know yet, but I must go home first and let my mum know or she'll go mad", said Sylvia. "Are you able to come with me, or would you like to go and ask your mum first?"

"Oh my mum won't mind if I go for a walk now so long as I'm in by five o'clock. I'll come with you to your house".

The two girls set off from the church and walked down the very steep hill by the castle to Sylvia's home.

"Is it all right if I go for a walk with Catherine?" Sylvia asked her mother, hoping that she was in a reasonable frame of mind!

"All right luv – but don't go where it's lonely, and don't be late for tea".

"We won't go far", shouted Sylvia as they went out of the garden gate.

The two girls walked back up the steep hill until they came to the path which skirted round the bottom of the woodland which protected the castle. They decided to take this path which led to open fields where cattle were grazing peacefully in the warm sunshine. There was the wonderful smell of new mown grass in the air, after the first cut of the season. The larks were singing riotously above their heads, and the banks alongside the path were green with moss and starred with primroses. The whole beauty of the day seemed to flow through the two young girls as they skipped along the narrow path. Far up in the trees was a faint rustling of leaves blown gently in the May breeze. At this point they were literally five minutes away from Sylvia's home!

They reached the end of the path and came to a stile where they paused for a while to look at the cows in the field, and wondered if they actually dare to cross over.

"You never know", said Sylvia, "one of those cows might be a bull. My mum and I were chased by a bull in this field when I was younger!"

The cherry blossom was now gone but in the woods the bluebells were not yet over. Wafts of bluebell scent came to the girls as they leaned on the stile. They turned towards the fence which bordered the woodland and stood on the bottom bar, looking over to see the bluebells and lured by the wonderful scent.

"Gosh! Look at the lovely bluebells!" cried Sylvia. "Shall we go and pick some for our mums?"

Catherine readily agreed so they clambered over the fence into the silver birch wood roofed with green and gold. Shafts of refracted sunlight fell on to the froth of cow parsley growing by the hedge and they heard a cuckoo calling. They looked up and saw the rose colour of a chaffinch's breast as he called down to them from the branches over their heads. A butterfly settled on a long stalked toadstool of pale lavender, and there were trails of creamy wild roses entwined in the brambles. A cluster of bluebells grew under a nearby tree and the girls each reached to pick a few.

"Oh look, those are bigger over there!" exclaimed Catherine.

Deeper and deeper they went into the woods as the bluebells beckoned, promising bigger and better ones a little further ahead. They came to the edge of a clearing and stood gazing upon a carpet of blue, and they were stunned by the beauty there.

"Hello", said Catherine.

Sylvia looked at Catherine and then turned to follow her gaze which rested on a man who was standing poised as though to spring upon them. He was a burly red faced man and he was dressed in an ill fitting dark blue striped suit which was shabby and dirty. On his head he wore a flat cap and round his neck was wound what should have been a white scarf but was now dirty and grey. All her mother's warnings flashed through Sylvia's mind and she could only think that they were about to be murdered – but she wasn't going to hang around and wait for it to happen. Quick as a flash, she grabbed hold of Catherine and shoved her in front of her, giving her a great push.

"Run!" she cried – "As fast as you can!"

Catherine needed no further bidding and ran, being guided from behind by Sylvia who knew that they would eventually reach the low hedge overlooking the fields where people were walking. They could not go back the way they had come, for the man was in hot pursuit of them. They tore through the undergrowth, the brambles tearing at their bare legs and clothes, but they did not feel the pain in their haste to escape their pursuer. It seemed as though fear had caused them to grow wings on their heels and at last they reached the low hedge. Here they kicked up such a shindig that the people on the lower slopes of the field looked up in

Poor Mary

astonishment. The man caught up with them and told them to stop making all that noise.

"I'm the caretaker of the castle grounds", he said. "I followed you 'cos I thought ye were birds' nesting and pinching their eggs!"

Sylvia was now convinced that they really were going to be murdered, for she knew that he was lying. She had known the real caretaker of the castle and its grounds for years, and he had always been happy for her, and her friends, to play there. This man she had never seen before in her life. Whatever he had intended, the man decided to make a hasty retreat, the girls having attracted such unwanted attention. He ran off further into the woods and disappeared from sight, but Sylvia knew that there was no way out from the direction in which he had gone.

Shaken and trembling, the two girls made their way back through the undergrowth to the nearest fence suitable for climbing over. What had started off as a wonderful afternoon had turned into a nightmare which they would never forget. They had lost all their lovely bluebells but they were too upset even to think about that.

"Whatever have you done to yourselves?" exclaimed an elderly lady who was taking a Sunday afternoon stroll with her dog.

Sylvia looked down and saw that her legs were pouring with blood coming from numerous deep wounds inflicted upon her by the cruel brambles. Her new dress was torn to shreds. Catherine had not fared quite as badly as she was wearing her long, thick winter coat which had offered her more protection.

"There was an awful man in the woods and he chased us", sobbed Catherine.

"Well, you'd both better get home quickly and get yourselves cleaned up", said the lady. "Those scratches look really nasty".

The girls separated at the point where the path joined the lane, Catherine turning left to climb the steep hill homewards, Sylvia turning right to walk the few yards down the hill to her home. The incident had happened less than five minutes away from the front door of her home. As she opened the garden gate, Sylvia now felt more apprehensive about what her mother's reaction would be than about her wounds, though by now they were beginning to sting terribly.

"Oh my God Sylvia! What have ye done?" cried Mary when she laid eyes upon her daughter. Sylvia related what had happened, feeling nothing but surprise that her mother for once was concerned and sympathetic.

"Mrs. Baker! Come an' look at our Sylvia's legs", shouted Mary.

"Good Heavens!" exclaimed Mrs. Baker. "Get her straight into a hot bath Mary, and put disinfectant into the water. However did she do that?"

A few minute later , Sylvia was in a bath of water which was turned a vivid purple in colour by the fluid made from Potassium Permanganate, an old fashioned remedy for wounds, but highly poisonous if taken internally. Her ruined dress lay in a heap on the floor. Sylvia was still too bemused by the fact that her mother was obviously not going to thrash her to notice the pain coming from her legs. She was also thankful to be home and alive! Once she had had a good soak to cleanse the wounds, the water was drained from the bath and Marry wrapped her in a large bath towel and told her to sit down on the bathroom chair. Examining her legs for the first time, Sylvia was shocked at their appearance. They were crisscrossed from top to bottom with scratches, some of these being extremely red and angry. There were many thorns from the brambles embedded into her flesh and the wounds were throbbing painfully.

In bed that night the deeper abrasions began to tighten up and Sylvia spent an uncomfortable and sleepless night, hardly daring to move as she could not bear the weight of the bed covers on her legs. The next morning Mary took her to see the doctor who examined her legs carefully.

"There are too many thorns embedded in there to try to get them out", he said. "They may work themselves out in time, but if any start to fester then you'll have to bring her in again. In the meantime keep the wounds clean and I'll give you some soothing ointment for them".

The doctor was very concerned to hear about the man in the woods and thought that the situation could have been much worse for the two girls!

Eventually the scratches and abrasions healed, the smaller ones fading away completely, the deeper ones leaving permanent scars. Many of the thorns remained in Sylvia's legs for the rest of her life but fortunately did not cause any further bother. Sylvia never forgot that awful day which had begun so beautifully, but her biggest wonderment was that her mother had remained so reasonable and sympathetic!

10. TOTAL BREAKDOWN

Something was really wrong now. Sylvia had never questioned her mother's erratic behaviour, her periods of dark and light. She had accepted things as they were – but now there was something different about Mary. It seemed that a dark gloom had settled on Mary's spirits and she became morose and ever more moody. Mary was of course experiencing hormonal changes due to the menopause which might have accounted for it, and indeed people assumed that this was the cause of her depression. Sylvia was fast asleep in bed one night when she was awakened by the quiet weeping of her mother.

"What's the matter", she asked.

"Nothing. Go back to sleep", mumbled Mary between sobs.

Sylvia tried to do this but until the early hours of morning she was aware that her mother was silently crying. These incidents now started happening almost every night and Sylvia began to get very tired from the constant disturbances.

"Why won't you tell me why you keep crying every night?" Sylvia sighed in despair one night.

"Will you promise that you'll always love me, no matter what?" said Mary.

"Of course I will. Now please can we go to sleep?" murmured Sylvia, her eye lids heavy with exhaustion.

A few nights later Sylvia was yet again awakened by Mary's weeping and she felt herself grow irritable at being disturbed once more. She turned over and tried to cover her ears but was unsuccessful in blocking out the sounds of her mother's sniffles which irritated her no end!

"Mother, what is the matter? Why do you keep crying every single night?" exclaimed Sylvia. "If you tell me then I might be able to help you".

"You'll promise that you'll always love me?" said Mary miserably.

"Yes", Sylvia sighed, not without some irritation. "You know I will!"

"Well", began Mary, "when you were a baby – and we still lived with your father --------------------------! Well – I found out that I was having another baby", said Mary haltingly.

Sylvia pricked up her ears at these words. "Well?" she inquired.

"I felt that I couldn't cope with another baby – not with your father being like he was – ".

"What did you do then?" asked Sylvia.

"I went to this woman – an' she - - - -".

"She what?" asked Sylvia.

"She got rid of it", said her mother in the smallest of voices.

"Oh!" said Sylvia sleepily. Perhaps with that confession they might enjoy some better nights. Perhaps everything would be all right now. Somehow, things which had happened so long ago were too remote to concern her and she couldn't see what all the fuss was about. She was too young to understand the implications of her mother's desperate act all those years ago, nor could she possibly understand the mental trauma – the anguish which had been buried deep inside Mary all these years. She did not ask herself what could have brought it to the surface after all these years. Like most teenagers, only the present mattered to her, and all she wanted now was to be allowed to sleep.

"Do you still love me?" asked Mary.

"Yes", said Sylvia irritably, "now can we go to sleep?"

If Sylvia thought for one moment that the situation with her mother would now improve then she could not have been more wrong. The nightly crying continued and for Mary there seemed only the evil of the dark abyss of the night. Her mind was tormented by strange fears and weird nightmares in which she heard frightening voices – voices which laughed cruelly – taunting her and instructing her that the whole world was against her. These fearful feelings began to extend into the daylight hours and Mary would go about her work with tears continuously pouring down her cheeks. Mrs. Baker could not shake her out of it and she herself was now showing signs of intense irritation.

It was about six o'clock in the morning when Sylvia awoke to find that her mother was not in bed. Feeling very puzzled she got up and went to the bathroom which was empty, and then she crept quietly downstairs, not wishing to disturb Mrs. Baker. Downstairs there was still no sign of Mary. Sylvia could not understand this at all but thought that she had better get ready for school. When she was ready she went into the sitting room, opened the curtains and looked outside to the promise of a beautiful day. The grass was golden, the white moon daisies pearl coloured, and the trees and bushes were a warm pinkish grey. The sun was just beginning to break through pale luminous clouds. It was a sight which should have raised the spirits and gladdened the heart – but not this morning for Sylvia. She could only feel a deep anxiety.

At this point the ample figure of Mrs. Baker appeared through the sitting room door and there was no smile on her colourless lips. Sylvia knew instinctively that she was going to say something serious about her mother, something bad, and she felt scared as in a bad dream.

"Where's Mum?" she almost whispered.

"Well it's like this Sylvia – your mother seems to be having a nervous breakdown. The reason that she is in a state is that she and your father were never legally married, and she's worried that she told the Vicar a lie when you were confirmed. She thinks that you were christened in a different name from what she told him. Anyway, she's run off to the vicarage to confess. God knows what he'll think of being disturbed at this early hour – though he ought to do something to earn his living! I'm sorry to have to tell you this Sylvia, but I can't stand much more of her odd behaviour and I'm going to have to ask her to leave if she doesn't improve".

Whereupon Mrs. Baker made a hasty retreat into the kitchen and busily began with making breakfast. She did not want Sylvia to see the tears in her eyes. Mary and Sylvia had been with her now for nearly ten years and losing them would be like losing part of her family.

As Sylvia digested Mrs. Baker's words, her bright brown eyes were fixed unseeingly on the colourful garden which was now lit up by the early morning sun. To her, as a sensitive teenager living in an era when families stayed together and there was even a stigma to being divorced, this news devastated her. She was mortified and ashamed and did not know how she could face the world with this knowledge.

Mary returned from the vicarage before Sylvia left for school.

"I've told Sylvia", said Mrs. Baker to Mary as she came into the room. Mary's face reflected a mixed picture of relief and anxiety as she looked at her daughter.

"I've got to go now", mumbled Sylvia, not looking at her mother, "otherwise I'll miss the school bus", and she fled from the house and hurried up the steep hill. Her mind was in turmoil as she reflected on the events of the past few weeks, culminating in this morning's episode. She did not know what to think or how to handle the situation, nor did she know of anyone in whom she could confide, for she was too ashamed.

One could be forgiven for expecting that things would begin to improve now that Mary had unburdened herself, but sadly this was not the case. Mary's mental state grew worse and she began to suffer severely from paranoia and then developed delusions of grandeur. She claimed that she was the first grandchild of Queen Victoria and that her daughter was the Princess Sylvia of Wales. One day came the moment which Sylvia had been dreading, when Mrs. Baker called her into her sitting room.

"I'm very sorry Sylvia, but I really cannot cope with your mother anymore. She's obviously very sick indeed and needs treatment. She'll have to go home to her parents!"

"That means that I will have to go too", said Sylvia. "I'll have to leave my school and all my friends – and I'm right in the middle of my examination course".

"I'm sorry Sylvia", said Mrs. Baker again, "but I can't see any other alternative".

Mary was packed off to her parents immediately whilst Sylvia went to stay with a friend so that she could at least finish off the term at school. Sylvia had hoped that she would be allowed to go back to her friend's house after the summer holidays, and continue her education at Tapton House, but it was not to be. Mr. and Mrs. Beal, her friend's parents, drove Sylvia to her grandparent's house in their car.

"We'd love to have you back next term dear, but we're afraid it just isn't practical. It might take years for your mother to recover, and besides she needs you to be with her. You are all she's got!"

With a sinking heart Sylvia realised the finality of these words. Her eyes ached with held tears, knowing that she had left her childhood place for ever, and she hadn't even said goodbye to her friends at school!

PART FOUR

1. TRAUMATIC DAYS

1990. Sylvia had cleared her mother's house of all her personal things and brought them home. She put the tiny suitcase in her sitting room and went into the kitchen to make a cup of coffee. When it was ready she returned to the sitting room and sat down in her easy chair, her two cats already occupying the settee. As she drank her coffee she looked round the comfortably furnished sitting room of her detached house. The floors were covered with a tasteful fitted carpet in a restful shade of green. The walls, painted in a delicate shade of apricot, were hung with numerous pictures. Antique chests of dark oak provided resting places for her Royal Daulton figurines and vases of flowers, and a seventeenth century grandfather clock with an exquisite brass face stood by the side of the fireplace.

The tiny suitcase, alone and forlorn, stood in the centre of the room. In the case were all of Mary's things. Eighty two years of a life, and this was all there was left of it. Everything else – her house, furniture and equipment had been provided for Mary by Sylvia and her husband. Their intention now was to redecorate the house and then rent it out. It was going to be a big job, and expensive. The place needed going through with a fine tooth comb, for Mary had created one big mess in that house!

Having finished her coffee, Sylvia knelt by the little suitcase and opened it with a deep despairing sigh and her eyes full of unshed tears. She had tried hard with her mother, tried to make her happy, but she might just as well have hit her head against a brick wall.

The first thing that she picked out from the suitcase was the pretty multi coloured velvet scarf which she remembered Mary wearing when she was young and smart. Indeed it was worn by Mary in one of the old photographs which Sylvia had kept in an album. Next she took out a bowl. It was of peach coloured glass with a mother of pearl effect. Once upon a time there had been a matching jug but what had happened to that she had no idea. Sylvia then picked out of the case a multi coloured glass rose bowl and a slender specimen vase of clear glass. These few things had been in Mary's possession since before Sylvia's birth. These had been her treasures – the things that she had clung to because they were all she had left of her short time with Lewis. He was the only man that she had ever truly loved, and she had never known another man since their parting.

There were several other things in the case but they meant nothing to Sylvia, except the photographs! There was one photograph in sepia of 'Grandma Haytack', Sylvia's great grandmother. She could not remember her of course, but she had been told that she herself bore a strong resemblance to that lady. She stared hard at the stern face which gazed back at her with unsmiling and unseeing eyes. The woman was magnificently dressed in the stiff and starchy Victorian clothes of her day. This was the woman with a reputation of being a strict no nonsense lady, but even she had not been able to handle Mary as a child.

The next photograph was of a family group, again the clothes being heavy Victorian garb. There was a young version of Sylvia's grandparents, Arthur and Lucy, posing stiffly and surrounded by their four children. Mary was a young child sitting on Lucy's knee. Sylvia looked closely at this childhood picture of her mother, trying to fathom the nature of the child who grew up to cause such misery to others. Was she imagining it, or was there really something rather strange about the eyes of the little girl who grew up to be her mother? Sylvia's eyes then rested on the faces of her grandparents staring back at her from the photograph. Her grandmother, even at that young age, bore the miserable expression which Sylvia remembered so well. Her mind cast back to the time when she and Mary had gone back to live with her grandparents because of Mary's mental breakdown.

1951. When she was very young Sylvia had always been excited at the prospect of visiting her grandparents in her mother's home town. Now, being forced to stay there, having been ousted from her childhood home, she saw things in a different light. She did not like what she saw and felt very resentful at this sudden change in her life. Her dislike of the place grew more intense every passing week. She hated the oppressive atmosphere charged with pollution and dirt from the numerous collieries, and she hated the sound of the harsh broad Yorkshire accent. Whereas Arthur, her grandfather, continued to be full of fun, she found her grandmother to be awkward and cantankerous. Of course it wasn't until much later in life that Sylvia understood what it must have been like for the aging Arthur and Lucy to have two more people thrust into their lives when they had become used to their own company and routine. Certainly Lucy made it clear that both Mary and Sylvia were there on sufferance.

Next door to Arthur and Lucy lived a couple with four children, all girls. Eddie Jones was a miner and his pretty young wife, Helena, was already careworn, having borne four daughters in quick succession. Sylvia enjoyed the company of the young sisters, Eileen, Maureen, Judith and Anne, and would often take them for walks or play games with them.

The summer holidays eventually came to an end and one September morning found Sylvia on a bus, about to face her first day at a new school – the High School for Girls. She could not help feeling resentful as she made the journey. She kept wondering about her friends at Tapton House. What would they be doing now? She wished desperately that she were with them at the beginning of this new term. The High School was situated on the outskirts of the town and was an enormous red bricked building which Sylvia approached with some trepidation.

After entering the building she was eventually ushered into the study of the headmistress, Miss Bedford. Her full name was Catherine Patricia Bedford and she was known to her friends as Cathy. Cathy Bedford was an attractive woman in her mid forties and Sylvia took to her immediately. Little did either of them realise at this first meeting that it would be the beginning of a life long friendship until Cathy died in her eighties. Miss Bedford was always kindly towards Sylvia, helping and supporting her ambition to be a teacher. Sylvia, who by now was being starved of her own mother's love and support, subconsciously regarded her as a mother substitute, clinging to her for support when things were at their worst. The tables were completely reversed many years later when Sylvia, in her prime, was able to give Cathy Bedford some support when she was old, alone and afraid!

"What is your full name my dear?" queried Miss Bedford.

"Just Sylvia Copley", was the reply.

"At which school were you?"

"Tapton House Grammar School, in Chesterfield", answered Sylvia.

"Why did you leave there?" continued Miss Bedford.

"Well – my mother became ill and had to leave her job. We had to come and live with my grandparents".

"What about your father?" probed Miss Bedford.

Sylvia blushed with discomfort as she replied that he had been killed at the beginning of the war. This of course was quite true, but Sylvia always felt mortified at the thought of having to tell someone that her parents had not been married. The stigma of illegitimacy was very strong in those days.

"Have you any idea what you want to do when you leave school Sylvia" asked the Head.

I would like to go to a teacher training college, if I pass the necessary exams", replied Sylvia.

"You do realise that it is going to be a little difficult for you being as you have left your old school whilst in the middle of the examination course. The work here will be somewhat different as this school uses the Northern Universities Syllabus. I believe that Chesterfield uses the Cambridge Syllabus!"

"Oh!" said Sylvia, her heart sinking. That possibility had not occurred to her.

"Well you'll just have to do the best you can and see what happens. I would suggest that you do a maximum of five subjects which is the minimum requirement for entry into training college, plus a couple of A Levels in the Sixth Form. I will put you into Form 5E2 where most of the girls are working towards a place at a teacher training college.

After her interview with the headmistress, Sylvia was taken to her new classroom by a Sixth Form prefect. The girls of Form 5E2 welcomed her pleasantly enough and two of them, Margaret and Rosemary, were destined to become her life long friends. Having been previously educated in a coeducational school, with a good balance of male and female staff, Sylvia initially found the teachers at her new school somewhat 'spinsterish and fuddy-duddy', and of course most of them were spinsters in their middle years, or even older. However as time passed by and they became more familiar to her, she began to recognize their good qualities and she warmed towards them.

The problems of pain and discomfort, which Sylvia had experienced in her legs from being quite small, still continued. The pain often reached to the lower half of her back. This caused her much difficulty in Games and Physical Education lessons and she found that her legs had no spring compared to other girls, so she could never vault over gym boxes and horses, nor could she climb ropes. These lessons proved to be a great embarrassment to her, for she was often teased or ridiculed by the teacher. Because Sylvia's mother was now totally switched off to the difficulty her daughter was experiencing and her grandparents were too old to bother, these discomforts were never investigated and she continued to suffer uncomplainingly.

Mary was growing worse by the week and she was driving everyone to despair. No one could reason with her, for she no longer saw reason.

"Ee I don't know! Our poor Mary!" said Lucy to Arthur. "Whatever is wrong with 'er? She never used to be like this. Oh dear oh dear! Whatever can we do?"

"I always thought there were somethin' wrong with 'er", said Arthur, "but I've never known 'er like she is now. There's no reasonin' with 'er at all. She gets these weird notions in 'er head and no one can shift 'em. I'm sure I don't know what will become of 'er!"

Sylvia said nothing and tried to concentrate on her homework. She was utterly bewildered by her mother's strange behaviour, and exasperated by the stupid things that she was saying.

"I'm not right, I'm left", said Mary.

Sylvia inwardly cringed as her mother started babbling utter nonsense.

"They're all getting at me ye know!" continued Mary.

"Who are?" said Sylvia.

"They are, out there. They come in and take my things, an' dirty my clothes when I've just washed 'em!"

"Who are THEY?" asked Sylvia irritably as she struggled to concentrate on her homework.

"They know! Mam and Dad know! They're all against me!" shouted Mary.

"Oh don't be silly, of course they're not", said Sylvia, trying to calm her mother down.

"Mary! Pull yerself together an' stop talkin' so daft!" said Arthur with a sigh.

Mary suddenly went berserk and physically attacked her father who turned quite dizzy and fell reeling into his chair. Sylvia looked on in horror.

"Stop it! Stop it!" she cried, whereupon Mary dashed to the front door of the house, opened it and fled in her bare feet, out into the cold dark night.

For the first time Sylvia felt the sudden weight of responsibility for her mother. She abandoned her school work and hurried out into the night, calling after her. It was exceedingly cold without a coat, and by now Mary was well down the street, although she wore no shoes. Sylvia could hear her shouting obscenities and swearing at astonished passers by. She broke into a run, calling and pleading with her mother to come back. She had yet to discover that her mother would never yield to persuasion, but rather to a command or threat, but it took her years to learn this. At the moment she herself was a highly sensitive teenager who had hitherto been totally dominated by her mother. One could not switch roles overnight!

At last Mary stopped her mad dash, turned round and saw her daughter running towards her.

"For goodness sake, come back Mother!" shouted Sylvia whose teeth were now chattering with cold. "It's too cold to be out here, and you haven't got your shoes on. You'll get your death of cold, and so will I – and I've got all my homework to finish. It has to be in tomorrow!"

Mary's mood suddenly switched and for a while she became quite rational .In her right mind she wanted Sylvia to be successful at school. She was very proud of her daughter and wanted her to be a teacher, but she also realised that Sylvia needed to work hard. Meekly she followed Sylvia back to the house and did not say another word, and then went straight upstairs to bed. Sylvia went back into the living room to see how her granddad was. Lucy was giving him a cup of tea laced with whisky.

"Are you all right Granddad? Mum seems to have settled down now".

"I'm all right lass – but I'm worried about yer mam".

"They say they always go for the one they think most about", said Lucy," – and our Mary 'as always been right fond of 'er dad. Our poor Mary! Whatever shall we do?"

Sylvia sat down at the table in order to finish her school work – but it was no good – she couldn't concentrate and didn't make a very good job of it.

"I won't get a very good mark for this lot", she thought as she packed away her books into her school bag. "How can I explain why I have done so badly?"

She felt very depressed and lonely, and there was no one she could talk to. She went upstairs and when she was ready she climbed into the big double bed and lay down beside her mother. Sylvia now longed for a room and a bed of her own. She hated sharing with Mary, especially in the present circumstances. Throughout the night she was disturbed by her mother's nonsensical mutterings and tried to cover her ears, but it was no good. She couldn't block it out and Mary seemed intent on giving her another bad night.

2. THE WEDDING AND 'UNCLE JACK'

Mary's favourite nephew, Ralph, was to marry his childhood sweetheart, Doreen. It was to be a December wedding, just before Christmas. Sylvia was very excited for she was to be a bridesmaid, along with three other girls. She had always loved dressing up and this was for real! Doreen was a good seamstress and so would be making the four bridesmaid dresses, and also her own wedding dress. Sylvia had never attended a wedding let alone been a bridesmaid and she couldn't wait for the big day.

Ralph was very hurt and upset by his Auntie Mary's attitude towards his forthcoming marriage, and even more so by her cutting remarks to his bride to be.

"I'm not men!" said Mary to Doreen one day. Doreen looked bewildered and did not try to answer. She had not known Mary in the days before her illness, so it was difficult for her to realise that once upon a time Ralph's Auntie Mary would have been only too delighted at the prospects of his wedding. Perhaps now Mary bore a deep resentment that she herself, who had once been so proud, had not had the satisfaction of her own wedding day.

"I'm not men!" repeated Mary insistently. "No men for me, I'm left luv, I'm not right!"

"Your telling me", thought Dorothy. "You are not right – and a bitch into the bargain!" However she kept these thoughts to herself and made an excuse to leave the room. Mary continued to sit in the chair and snigger to herself.

At last the big day arrived and everyone awoke very early so that all the final preparations could be made for a smooth running day. There was a whisper of dampness in the cool air of the December day and at this early hour the roads were empty in the grey light. The rain of the night had spent itself, and a thin sun was beginning to show through the clouds. For once, and thankfully, Mary was in a reasonably rational mood and she was being very helpful with the organization.

The wedding ceremony took place at the local church and everything went according to plan. With due accord the photographer flourished his camera about, taking endless pictures of the bride, bride and groom, bride with bridesmaids, bridesmaids alone, bridesmaids together, family of the bride, family of the groom, and so on and so on!

After all this performance, the wedding party continued in a hired hall where everyone made merry and no doubt took more to drink than was good for them. Mary was very quiet during all of this, and remained sitting in a chair for the whole of the evening. She was looking round at everyone and wore a strange smile on her lips and a cold look in her eyes. At least she stayed quiet and that was something to be thankful for – though Sylvia was on tenterhooks when she saw the expression on her mother's face.

Mary's sister had a lodger who had been staying with her and her husband ever since Sylvia could remember. Sylvia had always known him as 'Uncle Jack', and as he had been like part of the family for many years naturally he was invited to the wedding. On several occasions during the course of the evening

Sylvia observed 'Uncle Jack' to be staring at her in a way which made her feel really uncomfortable and she did not know why. When he was not looking, she surreptitiously studied him and discovered that she did not like what she saw. Jack was a divorcee and in his forties. He wore a slick moustache and his rather bulbous nose which was purplish in colour, suggested that he was more than a little fond of his drink. He was certainly drinking more than his share on this occasion. Sylvia noticed that his salt and pepper coloured hair was thinning at the crown and she didn't like the sly expression on his face. He was of course dressed up in his Sunday best – a blue pin striped suit and a garish tie. Something about the suit, and the expression on Jack's face, stirred a hidden memory and she shuddered as she recalled a mental image of another man – a man in a dirty pin striped suit – the man who had chased her through the woods two years ago!

The celebrations continued until midnight, and then the wedding party began to disband.

"Time for us to go now", said Arthur as the last of the guests disappeared through the door. Jack was hovering on the pretext of waiting for Eric, Mary's brother in law. On the way home Sylvia found herself walking ahead of her grandparents, Mary and the rest. Suddenly Jack caught up with her and put his arm round her as they walked along. She felt herself recoil from this action and knew instinctively that 'Uncle Jack' was up to no good. She stiffened and kept her arm close to her side as his hand sought her breast, and she managed to stave him off.

"How do I handle this?" she thought. She was young, inexperienced, shy and vulnerable, and he was her 'Uncle Jack', a trusted friend of the family. Sylvia tried to slow down her pace so that the rest of the family would catch up with them, but they were all laughing and joking, taking their time, and lagged behind considerably.

When Sylvia and Jack reached the house, there was no alternative but to go in as the door was unlocked. Sylvia put on the lights and went into the living room, Jack following close on her heels. From her bag she took out a small package which was her bridesmaid's gift from Ralph and Doreen. As she began to open it she could feel Jack's eyes burning into the back of her neck. Tearing the paper from the package, Sylvia then opened a little box to reveal a pretty brooch of three emeralds surrounded by diamonds. They were imitation of course, but the brooch was to remain one of Sylvia's treasures.

"Come 'ere a minute", said Jack huskily. Sylvia turned round and was immediately caught up in his arms, his body pressed close to hers.

"You're beautiful, did ye know that? You're really beautiful", mumbled Jack, and her pressed his wet slack lips on her mouth in a passionate embrace. Sylvia experienced feelings of helplessness and revulsion at the same time as not wishing to offend 'Uncle Jack' by being rude and shaking him off! She also felt angry that he had spoilt for her what had been a wonderful day. Fortunately she was released from this compromising position by the sound of the voices of the rest of the family who were coming down the back yard and into

Poor Mary

the house. All Sylvia wanted to do now was to end this thing with the minimum of fuss and thought that the best thing she could do would be to disappear upstairs to bed, hoping that by doing that it would make it clear to 'Uncle Jack' that she had no desire to encourage him.

She lay in bed and a silent tear slid down her cheek as she listened to the rest of the family deep in conversation. She felt so alone and longed to tell someone of the incident with Jack. It was no good talking to her mother who was 'away with the fairies' most of the time. She dare not say anything to her grandmother, firstly because she was too embarrassed, and secondly because she would not have believed her. 'Uncle Jack' was a grand lad and could do no wrong in Lucy's eyes. Sylvia's thoughts drifted to life at school, a place where she felt safe and secure. She thought of her kindly headmistress whom she greatly admired.

"One day I will be like her", she thought, "I'll be a teacher, perhaps a headmistress eventually, and I'll have my own car and my own house, and my own bed. I'll be miles and miles away from this dirty old town with its horrible houses. If only I had a mother like Miss Bedford, cultured and educated, someone who would understand when I talked to her, and - - -", she drifted into an uneasy sleep.

Poor Mary! She was desperate for Sylvia's love and affection. She felt a desolation and sadness as she regarded her sleeping daughter. She too was depressed and lonely. At the root of this feeling was the chasm that had opened up within her family. They, including her daughter, were all standing on one side, whilst she,

Mary, stood alone on the other side. She was tormented by the strange voices inside her head, and by feelings which altered her whole perception of life. She no longer knew what was real, in fact the dark side of her mind was engulfing her, and she was afraid!

3. DAYTRIP TO BLACKPOOL

There were a couple more incidents with 'Uncle Jack' which caused Sylvia some discomfort. One Sunday afternoon she was seated at the table trying to concentrate on a heavy load of school work which had to be in on the following day. There was a knock at the door and Jack walked into the house.

"'Ello Jack", said Lucy. "Would ye like a cup o' tea? Kettle's on t' boil an' it won't take a minute".

"That would be grand", said Jack, sitting down in Arthur's easy chair.

"Hello Sylvia. What are ye doin' then?" he asked.

"I'm trying to do my homework", replied Sylvia with the faintest trace of acidity in her voice. She buried her head deeper into her work but she could feel his eyes boring through her and inwardly she squirmed.

"'Here you are Jack! Drink it whilst it's hot", said Lucy, handing him his cup of tea.

"Thanks Lucy. It's just what I was ready for." As he drank his tea, Jack continued to stare at Sylvia who pretended not to notice. He tried to engage her in conversation but without success. Then he fished in his pocket and took out a half crown coin and threw it on the table towards Sylvia. "A bit o' pocket money for ye luv!"

Sylvia froze as she regarded the silver coin on the table. It humiliated her to think that he was trying to buy her 'friendship' and she hated him for it.

"No thank you. I don't want it", she said.

"Don't be so ungrateful our Sylvia, when yer Uncle Jack is so generous. Ye know ye need it", scolded Lucy.

"Sorry", muttered Sylvia, "and thank you -", but she left the money on the table when she had finished her work after Jack had gone. Seeing it there untouched, Lucy picked it up and put it in her own purse!

The Easter holiday was due and on Easter Monday Sylvia was going for a country ramble with the Church Youth Group. It meant getting up very early and preparing two sandwich meals for the day. Sylvia had been looking forward to this day for ages, and on that Monday morning she rose very early and went down to the kitchen to get washed. Lucy was already up and had some hot water all ready in the kettle and this she poured into the bowl for Sylvia to wash. Sylvia was clad only in her bras and pants as she stood at the kitchen sink in readiness to complete her toileting. She nearly jumped out of her skin at the sound of a loud knock at the door. Lucy took the door chain off the catch, unlocked the door and opened it.

" 'Ello Jack! What are you doin' 'ere so early. Come in lad".

"No, no!" cried Sylvia in horror – but it was too late. Jack was in the kitchen and ogling her state of undress. How could her grandmother do this to her? She quickly grabbed the towel and rushed out of the kitchen, her face bright red with embarrassment.

Poor Mary

"Eric's thrown me out o' house!" Sylvia heard Jack say to her grandmother as she dashed up the stairs.

"Whatever for?" asked Lucy. "All the years you've lived there – why would he do that?"

Sylvia did not hear his reply, nor did she care. "It serves him right! He must have deserved it", she thought.

Jack was hoping that Lucy would offer him a bed in her house but he was disappointed, it never entered her head! By the time that Sylvia was dressed and ready to go, she found that Jack had left, much to her relief. She put him out of her mind as she made her way to the meeting place for the ramble. There was no one about yet, and the silent streets dankly glistened from a light rain which had fallen with the coming of the dawn.

"I'm always too early", thought Sylvia who liked to be ready in good time. She looked anxiously at the sky but there was a good patch of blue – enough to make a sailor a pair of trousers, as the saying goes – so it would probably be a fine day for the ramble. Suddenly she froze! She couldn't believe it! There was Jack on the other side of the street, and walking towards her. Hoping that he had not noticed her, she quickly stepped into a deep recess of a shop doorway, and busied herself looking at the displays in the windows. She prayed that he would go away without seeing her.

"Hello again Sylvia. Why are you out so early?" Jack was suddenly behind her.

Sylvia looked up to be confronted with Jack's eyes which flashed like cold blue jewels. She lowered her own eyes and stared blindly into the shop window again.

"What's the matter with ye lass? Why are ye so taciturn with yer Uncle Jack these days?"

All at once Sylvia caught a glimpse of three members of the Youth Group making their way towards the church where everyone was to meet.

"I must go! My friends have arrived", she muttered, and diving passed Jack, she ran across the road towards her friends. She was briefly aware of one blue, hard glance from 'Uncle Jack', but she did not look behind her. She never saw him again. For one reason or another, Eric had seen fit to throw him out of his house. Not getting any satisfaction from Lucy, he left the area never to return.

As Sylvia returned from the day's rambling, there was a sullen red-streaked sky with banks of clouds building up on the horizon.

"It looks like rain again", remarked one of the happy crowd of youngsters," but it kept fine for our ramble, thank goodness!"

"It's been a lovely day", answered Sylvia, her cheeks glowing from the fresh air of the countryside. "I really enjoyed getting out into the country away from all this", and she pointed to the nearby muck stacks, and belching chimneys of the adjacent colliery. As they passed the news agent's shop, Sylvia saw a large poster advertising a day trip to Blackpool and it wasn't very expensive.

"I wonder if my mum would like to go on that trip?" she pondered. "It might do her the world of good to have a change of scenery, and I wouldn't mind another day out before the school term begins again. It's going to be a heavy term with all the exams coming up!"

Hoping to find her mother in a receptive mood, Sylvia entered the house to find her grandmother putting some supper on the table.

"Gosh! I'm really hungry now Grandma. Please may I have some apple pie? Where's Mum?"

Mary appeared at that moment and she appeared to be in a reasonable mood.

"Have you enjoyed your day luv?" she asked. "Ye look as though you've been out in the sunshine; your cheeks are right rosy".

"It's been really lovely Mum. You would have enjoyed it. Would you like to go on a day trip to Blackpool before I go back to school? I've seen a cheap day trip advertised in the news agent's shop".

"Yes, I'd like that very much", said Mary. "I haven't been to the seaside for a long time".

The next day Sylvia went down to the news agent to book two places on the day trip to Blackpool on the following Sunday. It was to be another early start to the day, and the first red splashes of dawn appeared as Sylvia and her mother rose from their bed to make ready for their trip. Sylvia was full of eager anticipation – Mary was very quiet!

When they had gathered their things together, they left the house and made their way to the local bus station from where the coach would begin its journey to Blackpool. It was surprising how many people were about so early on this Sunday morning. Mary had a strange smile playing on her lips and Sylvia's heart sank, for this was not a good sign. As a group of people were coming towards them on the other side of the road, Mary began to laugh, and suddenly she stuck out her tongue at the passing crowd, and began shouting swear words at them.

"Oh no!" thought Sylvia, her high spirits now completely dissipated. "I can't believe this is happening." She hoped that the people on the other side of the road were too busy chattering to notice her mother's absurd behaviour. They did not seem to have noticed, but a bus passed by and again Mary put out her tongue, and some of the passengers stared in astonishment at the bizarre woman on the pavement.

"Behave yourself Mother, and hurry up or we'll miss the bus". By now Sylvia's enthusiasm for the day had vanished and she felt very depressed and anxious, wondering what other unpleasantness and embarrassment Mary might bring during the day. At last they were established on the bus, Sylvia having found a seat at the back thinking it might be better to keep her mother out of sight as far as possible. She had yet to understand that if no one could see her, then Mary would make sure that she was noticed. On this occasion she continued to laugh out loudly for no reason, and to shout obscenities at the other passengers.

"Shut up Mother!" Sylvia pleaded, wishing with all her heart that they had never come. She was mortified by her mother's behaviour, and beset with anxiety. Eventually they arrived in Blackpool and, with great relief, Sylvia alighted from the bus and hurried her mother away from the other passengers, and into the crowds on the beach. When she felt that they were

Poor Mary

comfortably out of sight, Sylvia slowed down her pace and took stock of their surroundings. She looked for a place where they could sit and eat their sandwich lunch. The weather was fine, though breezy, and she saw Blackpool Tower soaring into a tranquil sky.

"I used to go dancing in there", said Mary, "– with yer father".

"Yes", said Sylvia, fishing in the bag for the sandwiches. Why did her mother have to be like this? Why couldn't she have a normal mother like all her friends?

As they ate their sandwiches, a beach photographer came by and photographed them. Sylvia tried to put on a happy smile for the camera whilst Mary leered into the lens of the camera with a sickening grimace. Sylvia had a distinctive feeling that her mother was doing all these outrageous things with the deliberate intention of embarrassing her. It was very hard to draw the line between her mental disorder, and what would appear to be calculated intentions to upset and embarrass her. Which ever it was, Sylvia did not know how to handle the situation.

"One day it will be all right", she thought. "One day, when I'm a teacher, and can provide for her properly, then she'll be all right!"

4. "OUR SYLVIA 'AS DONE WELL!"

The attic was stifling and airless. The hot sun beat down on to the skylight through which one could see the blue of the sky and perhaps an occasional bird flying high.

"The whole town is stifling in this heat wave", thought Sylvia, sighing as she resumed work with her books. She was revising the year's course work as hard as she could in preparation for the impending examinations. Because she had missed a year of the course work, her subjects had been limited to five, but that was all she needed for entry to the Sixth Form. Then she could work for two or three Advanced Levels for entry into Teacher Training College – hopefully!

Sylvia had retreated to the attic, hot though it may be, as it was the only place where she could work undisturbed. A bottle of Lucozade stood on the marble slab on the dressing table which she was using as a desk. Mary, in a more rational frame of mind for once, had decided that this drink would be good for her daughter whilst she was studying. Sylvia did not know about that, but it was a welcome drink in the heat of the day, and a little treat in between bouts of studying. It helped her to pace herself and keep going.

At last all the exams were completed, and now began the nail biting period until the results were published in August.

Poor Mary

"What are ye goin' to do when ye leave school this year?" said Auntie Connie one evening when she was visiting Lucy.

"I'm not leaving school this year", replied Sylvia, "– that is not if I pass my exams!"

"Not leavin' school! Why ever not? Don't ye think it's about time ye were earnin' your keep and bringin' in some money? There's plenty o' factory work about!"

"But I want to go to college", said Sylvia. "I want to be a teacher".

Connie laughed derisively. "You – be a teacher! You'll never be a teacher! Besides, who is goin' to pay for it all?"

"If I pass my exams, then I'll be able to get a grant for my college education", said Sylvia, now feeling very threatened by her Aunt's aggressiveness toward her.

"Well, if ye do get a grant ye'll 'ave to pay all the money back when ye do start work", said Connie.

"Not any more!" said Sylvia. "Everything changed this year. Once I've qualified then I'll have a good income, and I won't have to repay the grant".

Connie snorted again, "Umph! I still say it's time ye were working! What can ye do? Ye're good for nothing! Ye can't even wash a pot, let alone cook a meal. Ye're useless!"

Sylvia felt hurt by these remarks. It wasn't her fault that she'd always lived in someone else's house. She'd never been allowed to do things like that. "Children should be seen and not heard", had been Mrs. Baker's rule, and therefore Sylvia had had to remain in the background and by doing so she didn't get under anyone's feet in the kitchen.

"Leave our Sylvia alone!" broke in Mary, "She wants to be a teacher an' that's what she'll be if she can pass her exams. I don't want our Sylvia working in a factory!"

"You always were too big for ye boots our Mary!" shouted Connie, "An' look where it got you!"

And so another family row developed!

To keep everybody happy, Sylvia thought it would be a good idea if she could get a job during the long summer holiday. That way she would be from under everyone's feet as well as earning some money. It was suggested by a friend that she should try the General Post Office as students were often employed there during the holidays. After the school term had finished, Sylvia made her way to the Post Office which was in the centre of the town. She entered the building somewhat nervously and asked the first person she saw if there were any temporary jobs to be had. After being asked to wait for a few minutes she was eventually led to a small room where she was interviewed by the General Post Master. He was a small insignificant man in appearance, about forty years of age. He studied her over his spectacles.

"What sort of job do you want lass?" he asked of the nervous girl sitting on the other side of the desk.

Poor Mary

"I'm prepared to do any work that you have to offer", answered Sylvia. "I'm a student and I need to earn some money during the holidays".

"It can be very heavy work here, and you'd have to be down here by 4.30 each morning!"

"That's all right", said Sylvia, "I can manage that"

"Can you start on Monday lass?" said the Post Master.

"Yes", she answered, "I'll be here at 4.30 on Monday morning". She never thought to ask how much the pay was.

Her alarm clock was set for 3.30 on Monday morning and by 4.15 Sylvia was waiting at the Post Office for the doors to be opened. The first job was to sort out the sacks and sacks of letters into areas of distribution, and then into piles for each street. There was a pigeon hole for each street, and Sylvia found it fascinating to see letters addressed to people she knew, and there was even one for herself from an old school friend in Chesterfield. After all the letters had been put into bundles, they were stuffed into post bags together with relevant parcels. By six o'clock everyone was ready to begin their deliveries. One of the postmen helped Sylvia to adjust her heavy mail bag round her shoulders.

"One consolation", thought Sylvia, "the bag will become lighter and lighter as I get rid of the letters".

"I wouldn't let my daughter do this job", remarked a fellow postman. "These sacks are far too heavy for a young girl!" What he didn't know was that Sylvia had no father to object to her doing an unsuitable job.

The mail bag was heavier than Sylvia could have imagined it to be, and it was already cutting into her shoulders as she began the delivery of letters and parcels.

"Once I get rid of some of these parcels my load will be much lighter", she kept telling herself, determined not to give in. One would think that delivering letters was an uncomplicated business but it was not always the case. It was very early in the morning and not all the residents of the houses were up and about. There was no problem if there were only letters to pop through the letter box – unless there happened to be a fierce dog in the garden! If there should be a parcel to deliver it entailed knocking and knocking at the door until someone eventually awoke to the sound. People were not always happy to be disturbed so early in the morning, and Sylvia often received the brunt of an abrasive tongue!

"Why do you 'ave to bring it at this ungodly hour? A man needs his sleep when he's been on nights at t' pit!"

Sometimes there appeared to be no one at home, in which case there was no alternative but to put the parcel back into the mail bag and carry it around for the rest of the delivery, so the load was not always lightened!

At the end of the first morning Sylvia was exhausted but equally determined to see the job through for the duration of the school holiday. At the end of the week she received her very first pay packet. It contained the total sum of nineteen shillings and in those days there were twenty shillings to the pound! Sylvia was doing exactly the same work as the adult postmen who received ten times that amount. She did not grumble, and when she arrived home she put the money on the table for her grandmother who took it without a word!

As Sylvia's work began so early in the morning her hours had finished by lunch time. One afternoon, Mary was in the front sitting room making a minor adjustment to one of her dresses which was hanging on a hanger behind the door. As she reached up to straighten the collar of the dress, Mary suddenly cried out in pain and doubled up, clutching her side. At first Sylvia thought that it was just another display of her mother's irrational behaviour, and then she thought that she had pricked herself with a pin. It was neither of these, for Mary's face had become grey and drawn, and she collapsed on the floor.

Sylvia called for her grandmother and together they decided that Mary was genuinely in trouble. Sylvia ran down the street to the nearest telephone box and called for a doctor. By the time he arrived Mary was rolling around on the floor in agony. The doctor diagnosed a strangulated hernia and sent for an ambulance which whisked Mary away to the General Hospital.

When she had gone, Sylvia sat down in a chair, dropped her hands into her lap and sighed deeply, but more with relief than anxiety. She was aware of a feeling of buoyant lightness within herself, as though she had been relieved of a burden.

"Now at last it will be all right", she thought. "At last she'll be in the right place and they'll be able to make her better as well!" That night she slept better than she had done for months.

She visited her mother the next day with high hopes. Mary had had a minor operation for the strangulated hernia, and was sitting up in bed in the hospital ward. Sylvia's heart sank as Mary began to shout at the nurses who took not the slightest notice of the torrent of abuse which came from her lips. They continued with their work as though they had not heard. This was a hospital for the physically sick, and as soon as Mary was on the mend she was discharged and had to be taken home.

When Mary arrived home her mental state was ten times worse than before, and she saw to it that everyone's lives were made a misery.

"How long will things carry on like this?" thought Sylvia. "Surely something can be done to make her better". She visited the local doctor one day in order to talk to him about her mother.

"Your mother is suffering from what we call a degeneration of the nervous system, brought on by the menopause", she was told.

Sylvia did not quite understand that. She agreed that her mother had been much worse with the onset of the menopause, but what about all the years before that, when her reactions to happenings had often been irrational? What about the stories of her mother's strange behaviour as a child?

"Is it hereditary?" queried Sylvia anxiously.

"Not at all my dear", answered the doctor.

"But will she ever get better?" asked Sylvia.

"That is very hard to say. Only time will tell. In the meantime she should take her tablets which will sedate her a little, and she should continue to see me once a week. Can you make sure that she does that?"

"I'll try", said Sylvia, "but she doesn't always listen, and she can be very obstinate". She left the doctor's surgery, her heart feeling as heavy as lead. He had not given her any hope that her mother would ever be normal and she was beginning to realise what a heavy burden this was going to be.

Two good things happened to shed a ray of light on all the gloom and doom of the Copley household. Baby Paula was born to Ralph and Doreen, and Sylvia was thrilled to have a baby in the family. Every spare moment she had would be spent at her cousin's house helping with the baby. How she loved this baby girl and one of her greatest pleasures was to wheel Paula in her pram whenever she could. As the child grew Sylvia felt a strong kinship with her.

The next good thing was that the examination results came and Sylvia had passed in all her subjects, thus enabling her to continue with her education in the Sixth Form at the High School. Sylvia was overjoyed and even Mary showed signs of elation as this knowledge sank in. Also Sylvia was very surprised one day to hear her grandmother bragging to a neighbour.

"Ee our Sylvia 'as done well. She's passed all 'er exams and she wants to go to college!"

Perhaps under her hard exterior, her grandmother cared more than Sylvia realised!

5. "WHY MUST IT BE LIKE THIS?"

Full of enthusiasm, Sylvia started the new term as a member of the Sixth Form. She thoroughly enjoyed the school routine and by now she had quite a circle of good friends. Many of her friends had boy friends with whom they went out in the evenings or at the weekends.

"I would love to have a boy friend", thought Sylvia who was now seventeen. "The trouble is, if I get too involved with a boy I would probably be distracted from my work which might spoil my chances, and I really do want to get on and be somebody". So she resigned herself to her studies for the time being, occasionally going to the theatre with a school friend if she could afford it. Lucy was very disapproving of her staying the night with any of her girl friends, quite sure that she would be messing about with boys.

"I'm not interested in boys yet Grandma. I don't want to spoil my chance of going to college, having got this far, so you don't have to worry! I only want to stay with Rosemary after going to the theatre because it will be too late to get a bus back. I'll get her mother to write a note to you about it if you want!"

Out of the blue, Mary decided that she wanted to work again, and began to look for a suitable position. Sylvia did not feel that this would work in the circumstances, but there was no curbing her mother who was liable to terrible waywardness and outrageous whims. Mary acquired a housekeeping post with a frail and gentle old lady who was desperate for some help and company in the house. During the interview, Mary somehow managed to contain herself and presented a meek and docile front to the vulnerable old lady.

Mrs. Ridgeway lived in a large, detached Victorian house situated within walking distance of the High School. This would have been ideal for Sylvia in normal circumstances, as it meant that she would not have to catch a bus to school each morning. If she had not had such misgivings about her mother's latest venture, then she would have been over the moon about the prospects of being able to meet up with school friends more easily after school hours.

Mrs. Ridgeway showed Mary and Sylvia what was to be their shared bedroom. Sylvia was dismayed when she saw the bed – a single bed with an iron frame and a very thin mattress!

"I'm afraid you'll have to share this rather small bed", said Mrs. Ridgeway. "Do you think it will be all right for you?"

"Oh we'll manage", said Mary.

Sylvia said nothing and her spirits were low. At least at her grandmother's they had the use of a large double bed with a soft mattress, soft pillows and nice warm blankets. This bed looked like something out of a prison cell, in fact the whole room was not much better – small, dark and sparsely furnished.

"One day I'll do better than this", she thought. "One day I'll have my own bed, and my own room in my own house – but I must work hard to earn enough money. I mustn't let anything distract me!"

Downstairs they were confined to what had once been the servants' quarters, a dark and uncomfortable kitchen – a depressing place for anyone! There was no place really conducive to studying but Sylvia made the best of a bad job and tried to make the most of the benefits of living so close to school and friends. Each Sunday she went to the nearby church and she was rewarded by the presence of her beloved headmistress who always had a kindly word for her, thus brightening her day.

Mary was a very thorough worker, and ordinarily Mrs. Ridgeway would have been delighted with her. However, it soon became apparent that Mary was extremely unbalanced, as Sylvia feared that it would. The night time ravings of Mary began again, and then they were extended into the daytime with her shouting obscenities at no one in particular, but loud enough to be heard by Mrs. Ridgeway.

One evening Sylvia was seated at the kitchen table, doing her homework, when Mary began to shout and swear and utter strange nonsense. She was pacing up and down wildly and she had opened the door wide to make sure that she could be heard in the rest of the house. Sylvia tried to close her ears to it all at first then, when Mary became even louder, she tried to calm her down, being afraid that Mrs. Ridgeway would hear. It was so embarrassing! Having no success, Sylvia fled from the kitchen and let herself out of the back door and went out into the freshness of the night. The first stars were out but the afterglow of the sun was still in the west. Sylvia gazed up at the stars and from the depths of her soul cried out to God.

Poor Mary

"Why, oh why must it be like this? Why can't I have a normal mother?"

Her heart felt as though it were being slowly and painfully dragged from her body. She could hardly contain the pain of it, such was her distress. In the normal course of life Sylvia gave no hint of the anguish that was devouring her, but at this moment she was in the very depths of despair. She found herself suddenly incredibly tired, but after a while her resilient nature came to the fore and she forced herself to go back into the depressing kitchen. By now Mary had calmed down and Sylvia decided to abandon her books for the evening and go to bed, hoping that her mother would not keep her awake again. It was bad enough being poised on the edge of the small bed, almost falling out, without having to listen to her mother's ravings as well.

The next occasion that peaked in Sylvia's memory was the one which finally led to Mary's dismissal. Mrs. Ridgeway's daughter, Janet, came to visit her mother one day. She asked Sylvia if she would like to do some baby sitting for her on the following week. Sylvia jumped at the chance of earning some pocket money and thought that she could combine the job with her homework if she took the latter with her. She was sure that the youngsters were reasonably well behaved because she had already met them.

"Mrs. Ridgeway's daughter has asked me to baby sit for her next week, and she'll pay me for it", said Sylvia excitedly to her mother.

"You're not to do it!" said Mary severely.

Sylvia was dumbfounded. "But why not? I need to earn some money. What's wrong with doing it?"

At this point Mary began to shout at the top of her voice which could be heard all over the house.

"I'M NOT BABY! NO BABIES FOR ME!"

"For goodness sake Mother, do be quiet – they'll hear you!" cried Sylvia.

"I'M LEFT, NOT RIGHT! - I'M BACK, NOT FRONT! – IF YOU GO AN' DO THIS BABY SITTIN' THEN I'LL LEAVE THIS JOB!" screamed Mary.

Although she felt blackmailed, for the sake of peace Sylvia said that she wouldn't do it, though for the life of her she couldn't see why her mother was so against it. But how was she going to tell Mrs. Ridgeway's daughter that she could no longer baby sit for her after she had promised that she would? She hated being put in this embarrassing position.

Sylvia did not have to say that she could not do the job. Mrs. Ridgeway's daughter called again at the house the next day and summoned Sylvia to the upstairs sitting room.

"I'm afraid we're going to have to ask your mother to leave Sylvia. She seems to be very disturbed and the whole thing is causing my mother a great deal of distress, and she is too frail to cope with it. Your mother really needs some specialist treatment in my opinion. She should be in a mental home! I'm very sorry my dear, but you'll both have to go by the end of the week".

Sylvia felt very resentful toward her mother for causing havoc in her life once again. Deep down she knew that Mary cared for her a great deal, and wanted her to get on at school. Mary could not be more helpful on her more rational days. It was hard for anyone to comprehend what was going on in Mary's mind which at times was possessed by demons whispering obscenities and warping her perceptions. No one could realise just how frightening and lonely Mary felt. She knew she wasn't right, and she knew that things got out of control, but she did not know how to stop it or even explain it. The demons were whispering that everyone was working against her and that she should fight back!

6. AWAY FROM IT ALL

Back with her grandparents, Sylvia tried to pick up the threads of her original routine. Her grandmother was not too pleased that her own life was once more disrupted, particularly with Mary being so unpredictable. She showed her resentment in the form of lengthy stony silences which often went on for days at a time. One night Sylvia completed a large chunk of homework and failed to take it to school the next day. On returning home that evening, she looked for the work everywhere but could not find it.

"Grandma, I left some work on the sideboard last night. Have you seen it?" she queried.

"I did throw a lot o' papers on t' fire this mornin'. I thought they were rubbish!" answered Lucy.

With a sinking heart, Sylvia realised that her grandmother had burnt her work and she couldn't help feeling that it had been done intentionally. She said nothing. What could she say? With a heavy sigh she sat down to repeat the work, together with the new homework that she had received that day.

The next day at school there was talk of a weekend trip for the Lower Sixth Form, to Staithes on the Yorkshire coast.

"Who would like to go on this trip?" asked the form teacher.

Most of the girls put up their hands, but not Sylvia.

"Sylvia - wouldn't you like to go?" said Miss Burton.

Poor Mary

"Yes I would, very much, but there is no way I could afford it", replied Sylvia.

Later on in the afternoon, Miss Bedford sent for Sylvia to come to her study. Wondering what she might have done wrong, Sylvia nervously knocked on the study door and waited to be summoned in.

"I gather that you would like to go to Staithes with the rest of your form?" said Miss Bedford.

"Well yes, I would like to go, but my mother isn't working now so we can't afford it", said Sylvia.

"We do have school funds for such circumstances Sylvia, and I am prepared to put your name forward to the governors as a worthy cause. You work very hard and I don't think that you should miss out on school trips if we can help it. Just tell your form teacher that you will be going".

Sylvia could not believe her ears. She never dreamed that she would be able to go on the trip if she didn't have any money.

"Oh thank you, thank you!" she cried, and had she dared she would have given her headmistress a great big hug and kiss. Instead she walked sedately from the room and then broke a school rule by running all the way back to her classroom, her heart bursting with joy and eager anticipation. Miss Bedford heard her running but just smiled to herself, glad that she was able to help a girl in difficulty to enjoy school life to the full.

The longed for weekend arrived at last and the Lower Sixth girls took weekend suitcases to school.

They were leaving for Staithes by train on Friday afternoon. The train journey itself was a novelty for Sylvia, and she enjoyed every second of it. She could not believe that she was actually going to spend a whole weekend away from the stresses and strains of her present home life.

"This is the life!" she thought as she chattered gaily with her friends. "I'll travel like this all the time once I'm a teacher".

The party arrived at the little guest house in time for the evening meal which was vastly different from her grandmother's cooking.

On the Saturday morning the girls were going for a long coastal hike. They took with them a sandwich lunch. First they passed through the quaint village of Staithes. There were as yet only a few people about, early morning shoppers talking together, enjoying their weekly break from home chores. Most of them looked comfortably shabby. They were country people who did not feel the need to dress up in their best clothes which were reserved for weddings, christenings and funerals and the like. It did not take long for the girls to find themselves on a path leading towards the cliffs. The early morning rain had left little puddles in the dips along the way. They passed by a small green field that was almost a carpet of primroses. There were cattle grazing in a further field, and they continued to graze, apparently inured to the noise of a group of chattering human beings.

It was necessary to climb an exceedingly steep path in order to reach the cliff top, and the girls' feet were slithering and slipping on the loose stones. Most of the

Poor Mary

girls trod the path boldly and nimbly, like goats, but Sylvia was petrified. When she looked down behind her she went rigid with fear, so her friends gave her a helping hand. Knowing that they would have to return that way, Sylvia spent the rest of the day worrying about how she was going to climb down the cliff.

"Why can't I leap about like the others?" she thought. "They have no fear and seem to have better balance than I do. My legs just don't have any spring in them".

The views of the sea from the cliff top were magnificent. They lingered over their picnic lunch at the top of the cliff and then continued along the cliff path. Eventually it was time to turn back. On their return journey, in spite of her dread of facing the descent of the steep cliff, Sylvia was enthralled by the beauty of the late afternoon. Overhead the larks continued to sing as they had sung all morning, and the girls began to sing too as they felt the freedom of the day. With the help of many willing hands, Sylvia managed to negotiate the steep cliff path, and the little party eventually reached the High Street which was dreaming peacefully in the golden light of the late afternoon.

After the girls had enjoyed a good supper they all went into the large lounge which was lit up by the sunset of that golden day. They played games and entertained each other generally. Rita Green had the most beautiful singing voice and the others asked her to sing for them. She shyly consented to do so and her clear, pure tones rang out as she sang.

'Morning has broken, like the first morning,
Blackbird has spoken like the first bird'.

This was forever after to be a favourite hymn of Sylvia's, and whenever she heard it she was reminded of that magical golden evening. For a while she was able to forget about all the problems at home and just be a carefree teenager.

The next morning, which was Sunday, the girls were allowed to please themselves what they did. A group of them, including Sylvia, went for a local walk. They found themselves in a woodland park. The air was fresh and sweet, and the shady ground was a blue and white carpet of anemones. The dappled sunlight shone through the branches of the trees, lighting up a pretty wooden bridge which spanned a rivulet. The sheer beauty of it all suddenly overwhelmed Sylvia and she could not hold back her tears and began to sob. The other girls attempted to console her, not understanding why she was so upset, nor could she understand herself. All the months of pent up emotion came to a head and she could not contain it. When her tears at last were spent, and she had calmed down, they all returned to the guest house. On the wide stone steps at the front of the house, they arranged themselves in a group for a last photograph together before leaving. It turned out to be a good photograph of the girls who all looked happy and carefree, except one whose eyes betrayed the anguish behind the brave smile put on for the camera!

7. LIGHT AT THE END OF THE TUNNEL

The following September Sylvia returned to school as a member of the Upper Sixth Form. By now she adored the school and every minute spent there was precious to her – particularly as she knew that this would be her final year there. She could hardly bear the thought of leaving the place and did not want to think about it. The school had been her refuge, a place of normality, helping her to keep her head when she could so easily have drowned in the madness which dominated her home.

As Art was one of her Advanced Level subjects, she and other members of the Art Department were asked to design special menu cards for a very important dinner given by the headmistress for the school governors. Sylvia was desperate to please Miss Bedford, so that weekend she put her heart and soul into the designing of her menu card, and spent hours on meticulous ink work followed by careful painting in water colours. When she had at last finished, she left the menu card on the table whilst she went upstairs to fetch a book. Sylvia returned to the room just in time to see her grandmother knock over a cup of tea which ran all over the newly painted menu card. Was it accidental, or a deliberate mean act of destruction? One could never be quite sure, but whatever the reason the menu card was totally ruined and Sylvia wept in despair.

There was nothing else for it but to start all over again, so she wiped her eyes and resolutely settled down to the task which took her well into the next day. This time she put the finished work straight into her school case! She carefully placed it between two hard backed books so that it would not become bent or crumpled. Her efforts were well rewarded when she had the satisfaction of knowing that her menu card had been chosen, along with several others, to grace the dinner table of her headmistress.

The sun was slipping behind a bank of shower filled clouds one Monday morning as Sylvia ran down the road to catch the early morning bus for school. A high wind had sprung up and she had to hold on to her school hat to prevent it from blowing away. As she tussled against the wind, her skirt blew up above her knees. She quickly reached down to secure it at a respectable level but in doing so she dropped her school case which snapped open. Her homework file fell out and landed on its spine, and this caused the clips to spring open. Before she could do a thing about it, the playful wind whipped all the loose leaves from the file and they flew high into the air, some landing on the muddy road to be run over by passing traffic, others being carried by the wind and scattered far and wide over the nearby ploughed field in front of the pit. There was nothing, absolutely nothing that Sylvia could do to retrieve her weeks of work – work which would be needed to revise from for her final exams! She managed to gather up some leaves of paper, but all the notes were destroyed by the wet from the road and they were covered in tyre marks.

Poor Mary

When Sylvia arrived at school, weariness descended upon her and her problems suddenly seemed vast and hopeless. It seemed that things were conspiring against her no matter how hard she tried. The devil certainly seemed to be working faster than the Lord at this point in her life! She dissolved into tears as she told her friends about her ruined notes. She could not stop crying as the first lesson began.

"What is the problem Sylvia?" asked her form teacher.

Trying to control her tears, Sylvia related what had happened to all her notes that morning.

"Well stop crying. It will all be the same a hundred years from now!" said Miss Burton.

"But what about my revision?" Sylvia gulped. "I needed those notes to revise for my exams!"

"We'll all help you", said Rosemary. "If everyone in the class has a little section to copy out it shouldn't take too long to rewrite them".

During the following week the girls were busily writing in the school library whenever they had a spare moment, each one taking a different section of the notes. By the end of the week, Sylvia possessed a complete set of revision notes once more, albeit in a variety of writing styles. This indeed was an act of friendship which gave Sylvia the heart to carry on with her studies against any opposition or set back!

The time came to apply for a place in a teacher training college for the following September. Sylvia was deep in thought about this on her way to school one early October morning. Autumn mists clung round the windows of the houses. Many leaves had fallen from the trees and were drifting about along the pavement. She loved the crunchy, crackling sound they made when trodden on.

"I wonder if I'll get into a training college – and if I do, will I be given a grant towards my expenses?"

She felt so alone suddenly. Most of the girls of her age had two caring parents to love, support and advise them.

"I know Mum wants me to be a teacher, but she hasn't a clue – apart from the fact also that her mind has completely gone! I suppose they'll advise me how to go about things at school".

That day the Upper Sixth Form teachers gave the girls a talk on how to apply for the various training colleges and universities. They were advised to send for a wide range of prospectuses and study them before making their final choices. During the rest of that week, they were discussing their various choices and trying to decide which colleges would suit their individual needs. Sylvia eventually decided that Lincoln Training College was the place for her. One of her friends, Margaret, also favoured this college. Sylvia found this very reassuring and felt not quite so alone. Sylvia wanted to pursue Art and English as her main subjects. She also wished to specialise in the teaching of older children in what were then called Secondary Schools, before the advent of the Comprehensive Schools. Sylvia would dearly have loved to teach in a Grammar School, but one needed to go to university and get a degree in order to do that, and it was a much longer course.

At last the day came when Margaret and Sylvia were invited to Lincoln Training College for interviews. Sylvia wondered how on earth she was going to get there with no transport and no money for a train or bus. Margaret's parents came to the rescue and offered to take her in the car with them. It was so exciting. Sylvia loved every moment of the journey and when they eventually arrived in Lincolnshire with its vast, clean and open fields, it really was a breath of fresh air after the oppressive mining towns with all their grime and pollution. Sylvia thrilled to the sight of the twin towers of Lincoln Cathedral which seemed to grow up out of the ground and rise up to the skies in splendour of carvings, turrets and pinnacles.

Both girls interviewed well and were offered places at the college, subject to their passing their Advanced Level exams this coming summer. Sylvia could hardly believe it. It was like a light at the end of a long dark tunnel! She determined to work even harder on order to make her dream come true. It really was up to her herself now, and she resolved to remain undaunted by any other family opposition, or anything else which tried to obstruct her.

8. SUNDAY DINNER

If Sylvia thought that things were bad on the domestic front she was not mistaken, but they were to get a whole lot worse. Christmas had been and gone and had been fraught with tension, for no one knew how Mary would react to anything that was said or done. Mary's paranoia led her to imagine sinister meanings to everyone's utterances and 'THEY' were always out to get her, steal from her or dirty her things. Consequently she became more aggressive towards everyone except Sylvia who continued to suffer the constant nightly disturbances of her mother's ravings!

It was a Sunday late in January, and a few snow flakes whirled outside in a sharp winter wind. Sylvia had a quick breakfast which consisted of a bowl of cereals and a slice of toast and marmalade. Then she braved the cold wind and went to a Holy Communion Service at St. Mary's Church. It was good to get away from the tensions of the house for an hour. After the service she lingered a while to talk with a few young acquaintances before reluctantly making her way home. It was bitterly cold and although the snow had stopped, the sky now looked loaded with rain. Sylvia quickened her pace as she had no desire to become soaked in the promised rain, and in any case it was far too cold to hang about.

She thankfully reached the warmth of her grandmother's house and realised how hungry she was when she could smell the Sunday roast coming from the oven.

"Is it lamb with mint sauce Grandma?" she asked.

"It is, and there's Yorkshire pudding first", said Lucy.

"Has the Yorkshire pudding got raisins in it?" said Sylvia.

"It 'as. I know that's yer favourite our Sylvia", replied Lucy who was obviously in better temper this day.

"Oh goodie! I can't wait!" exclaimed Sylvia who was partial to Yorkshire pudding with raisins, lashings of gravy and mint sauce.

After the Yorkshire pudding had been eaten, Lucy placed the lamb joint on the table together with dishes of mashed potatoes, cabbage and carrots. There was a steaming hot jug of gravy, and more mint sauce for the lamb. Mary began to chunter about some remark of Lucy's and suddenly a massive row blew up between the two of them. Sylvia could never remember what was actually said because in reality there was no substance to the argument which was based on trivialities and Mary's imaginings. Nevertheless one remark of Mary's caused Lucy to raise her fist to her daughter who was carving the joint of meat at the time. Lucy's aggressive action caused Mary to flinch away from her mother, and in doing so she inadvertently caught Lucy's upraised arm with the carving knife. Lucy's arm was bleeding profusely from the wound made from the blade of the carving knife. There was a sudden silence, and then it seemed that World War Three had broken out in that small sitting room. Arthur was really angry at what had happened to Lucy, and both of them were convinced that Mary had done this thing on purpose, and the three of them were shouting at each other, two accusing and one denying.

Sylvia sat at the table, her head bowed, her eyes closed, and her body rigid with tension. Suddenly something snapped within her and she heard herself screaming at all of them to stop it. Her grandparents stared at her in amazement, and told her to shut up and not to be silly. What happened immediately after that Sylvia did not remember.

The next morning Sylvia said goodbye to her mother, who was now quite calm, and set off for school as usual. She had noticed that her grandmother's arm was heavily bandaged. "I'm sure it wasn't that bad!" she thought. Her mind was not on her school work that day. She felt tired and drained and dreaded returning home that evening. She told no one what had happened over the weekend. It would have seemed a far fetched story to all her school friends whose lives seemed so orderly and carefree.

By the time Sylvia alighted from the bus that evening it was already dark. She walked the rest of the way to her home; her feet were dragging as she was reluctant to face the possibilities of more traumas in the household. "I hope that things have settled down", she thought as she entered the back door. "I've got so much work to do tonight".

The house seemed strangely quiet as she passed through the kitchen. She sensed something was different – something was missing. Arthur was sitting quietly in his favourite chair, his arms folded and his legs stretched out and crossed at the ankles. His face looked drawn and pensive. Lucy was sitting silently on the settee, nursing her bandaged arm.

"Hello!" said Sylvia. "Where's Mum?"

There was a small silence before Lucy spoke. "They've taken 'er away!" she said.

"What do you mean Grandma? Who has taken her away? Where has she gone?"

"They've taken yer mother to a mental hospital", said Lucy.

Sylvia stood stunned and silent. Every vestige of colour had drained from her face. "Where about?" she almost whispered at last.

"Middlewood Hospital in Sheffield", said Lucy. "You'll be able to go an' see 'er at the weekend".

Arthur's blue eyes were full of unshed tears which suddenly spilled out and ran down his wrinkled face. "Our poor Mary!" he groaned, "Our poor Mary!"

Sylvia looked at him silently, and then at Lucy who also had begun to cry. Sylvia herself had lost the power to comfort herself by tears; the ache within her must be kept in bounds. It transpired that Arthur and Lucy had visited Mary's doctor that morning, Lucy brandishing her wounded arm as evidence that Mary had attacked her with a carving knife. That was all that was needed for Mary to be committed to a mental institution. The evidence was there for all to see! Sylvia knew in her heart that this had not really been the case and that her mother had not intentionally wounded Lucy, but she felt powerless to defend her. Besides, something desperately needed to be done for Mary who was certainly chronically mentally ill, so perhaps it was for the best!

9. "YOU PUT ME IN 'ERE SYLVIA".

The next morning Sylvia awoke with a feeling of emptiness and desolation, and she saw the vacant space beside her in the bed, and remembered why. She left the bed to open the curtains and saw a sky that was dark and threatening which only added to her feeling of depression. Downstairs her grandmother remained silent.

"Oh God!" thought Sylvia. "That's all I need this morning!"

Her grandfather was not about, otherwise she would have chattered to him, although he was often reduced to silence when Lucy was in a mood.

Breakfast was eaten in silence and uncertainty. Was her grandmother going to tackle her about leaving school now that her mother was no longer there? How was she going to buy all the normal bits and pieces that a young girl needs? She couldn't ask her grandmother for money, but she thought of the horror of having to wash her hair with household soap instead of the nice shampoo which her mother had normally bought.

"I'll just try to carry on as best as I can", thought Sylvia as she ate her toast and marmalade. "Fortunately I have a bus pass so I don't need money for bus fares to school. My going to college won't cost them anything because I'll get a grant. I've just got to keep going until September, and I must keep working hard for those exams".

After the silent meal was over, Sylvia gathered her school things together and set off for the bus. Her heart felt like a stone within her, and she worried about what

Poor Mary

was happening to her mother and what she must be feeling, shut up in a mental hospital.

She met up with some friends for the walk from the bus station up to the school. They merrily chattered away together as they walked and barely noticed that Sylvia said not a word as she walked beside them, wrapped up in her own thoughts.

"I never thought that one could feel so lonely whilst with one's friends", she mused.

They could not possibly understand her desolation, they who had left their normal home backgrounds that morning, waving their goodbyes to their sane mothers and supportive fathers, and no worries about money. It just wasn't fair! Common sense prevailed and Sylvia told herself that wallowing in self pity wasn't going to get her anywhere!

During the first half of the morning Sylvia sat through her lessons, trying to take in what was being said, and busying herself in writing her notes. The bell rang for morning break.

"You're very quiet this morning Sylvia", said Maureen. "Is there something wrong?"

This remark was all that was needed to tip the scales, and the flood gates opened. Sylvia sobbed inconsolably, and after trying to calm her without success, Maureen went to tell the form teacher that there was a problem. Miss Burton came to investigate and eventually Sylvia managed to gulp out that her mother had been taken to a mental home. After a few sympathetic and reassuring remarks, Miss Burton disappeared for a while, leaving Sylvia sitting alone and still quietly crying. It was not long before she reappeared.

"Would you go along to see the Headmistress? She wants to talk to you Sylvia", said Miss Burton.

Sylvia nodded and went up the stairs to Miss Bedford's first floor study and knocked on the door. The electrical sign outside her door switched from 'ENGAGED' to 'COME IN' so she pushed open the door and nervously entered the room.

"Miss Burton tells me that your mother went into hospital yesterday Sylvia", said Miss Bedford.

"Yes Miss Bedford – a mental hospital – Middlewood Hospital in Sheffield", said Sylvia, now quite calm, her tears having been spent, though her face was all red and blotchy and her eyelids were very swollen.

"How will that affect you Sylvia? I know that you have no father, so how are you going to manage?" asked Miss Bedford.

"I'm living with my grandparents but I don't know what will happen now, I might have to leave school!" Tears once again filled Sylvia's eyes as she thought of this prospect.

"Your grandparents should get some financial help for you whilst your still a student", said Miss Bedford. "It won't be easy for you I know, but we will help you all we can. I can arrange a small grant to fund some of your expenses whilst you are in school, and there would be a small clothing allowance also. You're not going to have to leave the school if I can help it, and once September comes you will receive a reasonable grant towards your college expenses. I will ring up the local authority to arrange for the small grant which I know is available for someone in your position".

Poor Mary

Sylvia murmured an astonished thank you and Miss Bedford gave her a delightful friendly smile and said gently but forcibly, "Now try not to worry, just concentrate on your school work, and we will make sure that you go to college. Off you go to your lessons."

Leaving the study and feeling as though an enormous weight had been lifted from her heart, Sylvia returned to her classroom.

"All I have to do is to work hard", she thought. "If I can qualify as a teacher then I will earn enough money to look after my mother properly – then she'll be better – I'm sure she will!"

The following Saturday arrived and Sylvia was to make her first visit to see her mother at the mental hospital. It seemed that she was to go by herself for no one offered to accompany her. It was a daunting prospect for a seventeen year old girl. A normal hospital she could handle – but a mental hospital!! She found out how to get there and it involved two bus journeys each way. Her grandmother gave her the exact money for the bus fares!

Sylvia had no idea what to expect and she worried all the way during the journey which took a long time. At last she reached the mental hospital, having had a long walk after alighting from the second bus. Crowds of people, obviously all hospital visitors, were making their way towards the grim ugly building which stood at the top of the hill. Sylvia shuddered as she noted the bars at the windows.

"My mother is locked up in there", she thought. Surely this was more like a prison than a hospital. Enormous great doors stood at the entrance to the building and were obviously locked and barred from the inside. A tall clock tower crowned the slate roof and on it was a great clock with Roman numerals and large black hands. It was one minute before two o'clock, and not one second before was any attempt made to open these doors.

The crowd stood patiently waiting. Not many of them were engaging in conversation of any kind, and their faces were gloomy, their feet shuffling uncomfortably. At the stroke of two could be heard the drawing of bolts and the rattling of keys. As the great doors swung back the crowd surged forward, carrying Sylvia along with it. A gaunt, grim faced lady, dressed in a nurse's uniform, went ahead of the crowd, having first pushed the doors closed and relocking them. Again Sylvia shuddered, not relishing the idea of being locked in this prison of a building.

The grim faced nurse led the crowd down miles of corridors and each time they came to another door it had to be unlocked and then relocked behind them. Eventually the crowd was ushered into an enormous hall where rows of chairs were placed round the edges. Sylvia stood a while, uncertain what would happen next. The rest of the people, obviously used to the routine, made a dash to grab a chair each, and to reserve one for the patients they were visiting. Sylvia followed their example and sat down. She looked round at the dismal room, its walls painted a dull brown. There were bars at the large windows and not a picture in sight. A watery

Poor Mary

sunshine flooded through the curtain-less windows and lay in slanting geometric shapes across the floor.

The sound of jangling keys came from behind another door which began to open at the far end of the hall. Several nurses appeared, each wearing an enormous bunch of keys at their waist. Sylvia then froze in horror at the sight which met her eyes. Patients were being herded into the room like animals and Sylvia recoiled from what she saw. There is no doubt that mental illness can drastically change the physical appearance of its victim. Men and women shuffled into the room, their eyes hollow, their cheeks sunken in, and many of them had no teeth. Some of them were muttering to themselves, hardly aware of where they were or who was there. Sylvia of course did not know that they were like this because they were heavily sedated in order to keep them under control.

Suddenly there was a familiar figure shuffling amongst the rest. Surely that could not be her mother, so bowed, her once luxuriant dark hair now grey and unkempt. Why was she wearing that ugly, long brown coat which was certainly not her own? As Mary looked up for a moment, Sylvia noticed that she had two bruised black eyes - eyes which were distant – not registering their surroundings. Her cheeks were sunken and her pale lips had almost disappeared. An icy chill slid down Sylvia's spine. What had they done to her?

"Mother", called Sylvia. "Mother I'm here – it's me!"

There was just the slightest flicker of recognition in Mary's eyes and she followed the sound of her daughter's voice.

"Sit down here Mother. Are you all right?" - a silly question really!

Mary obediently sat down but did not answer the question. For a while mother and daughter sat in silence – one being hardly aware of the other's existence, and the latter at a loss for words in these horrendous circumstances. What Sylvia did not know was that Mary had been subjected to E.C.T. which is electroconvulsive therapy, commonly known as electric shock treatment to the brain. It was an extremely unpleasant experience!

Suddenly Mary spoke. "You put me in 'ere Sylvia!"

Sylvia could not believe what she had just heard. "What do you mean Mother? Of course I didn't!"

"Yer Grandma said yer did. You had me put away, she said!" continued Mary.

"That's a load of nonsense Mother. I went to school last Monday and when I came home you were gone. I knew nothing about it until I came home. Besides I'm too young to be able to do anything like that!"

Mary seemed to accept Sylvia's words as the truth, and relapsed into silence. She had dissolved back into a blank and spinning existence. The hour passed and there was the clanging of a bell to indicate that the visiting hour was over. Sylvia kissed Mary goodbye and having passed through the unlocking and relocking ritual again, she breathed a sigh of relief as she stepped out into the fresh air – and freedom!

10. ONE DAY!

Sylvia tried her best to knuckle down and keep up with her school work, alongside the weekly visits to her mother which took up a great deal of time at the weekends when she would normally have been studying. Each Saturday her grandmother gave her the right amount of money for the bus fares and not a penny more. The promised school grant had not yet arrived so by now she was feeling more than a little deprived of all the small niceties which young girls need. On her way to catch the Sheffield bus an idea struck her.

"I wonder if I can get away with paying half fare on the bus? I'm not very tall and people are always telling me that I look young for my age. If I could, then it would leave me just enough money with which to buy some decent shampoo and soap".

She arrived at the bus stop just in time to catch the Sheffield bus and found herself a seat near the front. As the bus conductor approached her for the fare, Sylvia's heart quailed and she began to sweat with nervousness of what she was about to do. It was not in her nature to be dishonest so she did not make a very good liar.

"Half to Castle Gate, Sheffield!" she muttered, not looking at the conductor as she spoke.

The bus conductor said not a word and produced a bus ticket and some change. Sylvia heaved a sigh of relief as he passed by. She felt really guilty, but after all, she was still at school so it wasn't as though she was earning any money. The change was just enough for her to buy shampoo and soap.

As she grew to know the way through Sheffield, Sylvia began to take an interest in the large departmental stores which she had to pass by on her way to her second bus stop. She would spend ages looking longingly at the lovely coats, hats and dresses which were displayed in the shop windows, and would dream of the day when she would be able to earn enough money to buy what she wanted. Sometimes, if she happened to be a little early for the bus, she would venture into the stores for a closer look at the clothes.

"One day I'll be able to buy a dress like this for Mum", she thought, caressing a pretty cotton dress which was hanging on a rail. "This lovely blue flowery material would just suit her. I wish I could buy it now so that she could wear it instead of those awful clothes they give to her at the hospital. I don't understand why she can't wear her own clothes there. She would be horrified if she realised what she looked like".

Passing by one counter, she noticed some bunches of pretty blue violets which, although artificial, looked very realistic. They were also perfumed with a sweet smelling scent.

"I think I've just enough money to buy a bunch of those for Mum".

Scraping the bottom of her purse, leaving enough money for the rest of her bus fare, she found a sixpence with which to pay for the violets. She couldn't wait to give them to her mother.

By now Sylvia was used to being locked up in that awful place with all its strange inmates, though she never felt comfortable until she was out again. She quickened her pace down the long corridors and seated herself in her usual place in the visitors' room. When the inmates were at last herded through the door, Sylvia tried to close her ears to their strange cries and mutterings, and her eyes to the wild appearance of some of them. Her mother looked pretty wild by now too. The once smoothly dressed raven black hair was now coarse and unkempt. The woman who had once dressed immaculately was now clothed in the shabbiest of garments which were ill fitting and grubby. Sylvia thought of the dress she had longed to buy for her mother, and imagined her wearing it together with smartly dressed hair. As she greeted Mary, who turned her head to look unseeingly at her daughter, Sylvia was appalled at the sight of her. All Mary's teeth had been extracted and her sunken cheeks were covered in bruises.

"Why have they taken all your teeth out Mother, and why is your face all bruised?" asked Sylvia, horror struck!

Sylvia went to a nurse, an over weight abrasive lady, who said that the teeth had been extracted because they were all bad, thus causing ill health, and that the bruises always occurred with the extraction of all the teeth. Going back to her mother, Sylvia placed the violets on her lap. Mary did not look at them; she just stared blankly into space. It seemed to her that she had left the world and had come to a place with devils and monstrous beasts. These beasts she had to fight and they would overpower her, strike her, and throw her into a padded cell where she would scream and shout for hours and beat her fists on the door, but no one would hear, no one would care! When her energies were spent, eventually a beast would come into the cell and stick needles into her, and so she would drift even further away from reality.

Through the hour Sylvia sat by her silent mother who made not the slightest response to her attempts at conversation. The departure bell rang and Sylvia rose to leave. As she said goodbye Mary's fingers stirred on her lap and touched the violets.

"Thank you", - the words were scarcely audible, but at least Sylvia knew that something had reached her mother. The filial bond is not easily broken.

Feeling very depressed, Sylvia made her long journey home, and wondered what mood her grandmother would be in when she finally arrived there. Whilst on the bus she day dreamed the time away by planning all the things she would be able to do if she became a teacher. She dreamed of foreign travel and lying on an exotic beach under a vivid blue sky and a hot, hot sun. She dreamed of climbing mountains and sailing in seas.

"When I'm earning enough money I can help Mother to get better, and I can take her on holidays, and we'll make a nice home of our own together – one day!

11. I'LL TAKE THE POUND!"

The small grant which Sylvia had been expecting had still not arrived, and in the meantime she received a book list and also a list of equipment that she would need at college.

"If that money would only come I could buy some of the essential things on that list", she thought.

One Friday on the way home from school, Sylvia called at the local post office to buy a stamp for the letter which she had written to her old friend in Derbyshire.

"Hello Sylvia! How are you?" asked the post master's wife who was very interested in Sylvia's plans, as she herself had been to the college to which Sylvia hoped to go.

"I'm all right thank you", replied Sylvia.

"How are things at home dear? You seem to be down in the dumps today!"

"Much the same! My Mum doesn't get any better and I think that my grandparents feel that I should be out working instead of being at school", said Sylvia.

"Well you stick at it dear! It will be worth it in the end. You will be able to live your life graciously if you get good qualifications. How are you managing for money at the moment?" said Mrs. Barrat.

"Well it wouldn't be so bad if this grant I've been expecting would come", replied Sylvia. "My headmistress applied for it for me. It's only twenty five pounds, but it hasn't arrived and I need it to buy books and things for college".

Sylvia Hoole

Mr. Barrat, the post master, was serving a customer, but at the same time he was listening in to the conversation between his wife and Sylvia.

"I will ring up the Education Authority for you", he said, and I'll find out what has happened to it".

Mr. Barrat disappeared into his sitting room for a few minutes and he telephoned the Local Education Authority and asked about the promised grant. After a few minutes he put down the phone and returned to the shop.

"Well Sylvia, they say that they have actually sent you the money, several weeks ago, and they are going to look into the matter".

"Thank you for telephoning for me", said Sylvia who felt quite dismayed. "I'll let you know what happens – goodbye!"

Sylvia puzzled over the missing money as she walked the distance home from the post office. Tea was on the table and her grandparents were already seated and tucking in to their meal of cold ham, pickled onions, bread and butter and a pot of tea. There were also some slices of buttered malt loaf to finish the meal.

"You know I was supposed to be getting a small grant from the Education Authority?" Sylvia said as she sat down at the table. "Well I couldn't understand why I haven't received it as it is ages since Miss Bedford told me about it. Anyway, I called at the post office today on my way home from school and Mr. Barrat rang up the Authority about it. They said that they had already sent the money to me, and if it hasn't arrived they are going to look into the matter. I really do need it now because I've got to buy some books and things for college".

Sylvia was so busy babbling on, as well as eating her meal, that she did not notice how quiet her grandmother had become, and even if she had she would have assumed that Grandma was in one of her moods.

The next day, Saturday, Sylvia made her weekly visit to see her mother, and she was pleasantly surprised to find her brighter and more responsive. Also Mary had tidied herself up a little. Perhaps whatever they were doing to Mary at the hospital was working! Because Sylvia had been brought up in the regime which believed that children should be seen and not heard, and because she still felt herself to be not much more than a child, it never entered her head to question anyone as to the treatment which her mother was receiving, and any possible side effects. The sight of her mother without any teeth distressed her very much, and as Mary seemed more aware this week, Sylvia ventured to question her about this.

"Will you be getting some false teeth Mother?"

"I could have some, but I don't want any!" Mary replied.

"But Mother, you look awful without any teeth!" exclaimed Sylvia.

"I don't care", Mary retorted. "I'm not going to have false ones!"

"Well I don't like to see you without them", said Sylvia, "and if you can have false teeth then you should have them – or I don't want to come and see you!"

That seemed to do the trick. Sylvia was learning!

"All right then – I'll have some", said Mary who couldn't bear the thought of her daughter staying away from her.

This was the very first occasion that Sylvia discovered that with her mother it was often better to be cruel in order to be kind if one wished to achieve the best for her. It took her many years to use the technique for the best effect, as it was not in her nature to be unkind. She did not know what had induced her to threaten her mother with no visits.

The following morning being a Sunday, Sylvia went to church, chattered with some of her friends after the service, and then hurried home, looking forward to her Sunday dinner which was her favourite meal of the week.

"Shall I set the table for dinner Grandma?" she said.

"Yes please", said Lucy, "and then go and see yer Granddad in the garden. He wants to talk to ye!"

Feeling very puzzled, Sylvia completed the task of setting the table. She then left the house, walked through the yard to the gate and then crossed the rough lane to her grandfather's allotment garden. She loved it in there, for as well as a good selection of vegetables, Arthur grew rows and rows of beautiful flowers, and as it was now spring time, many of them were in bloom, giving off lovely scents. Sylvia heard the gentle clucking of her granddad's hens and wondered if she might find some eggs, freshly laid in their nests. Arthur was feeding his budgies in the aviary and Sylvia went into him and began to help him, gently talking to the little birds which chattered and chirruped from their perches.

"Grandma said you wanted to talk to me", Sylvia said at last.

"Aye lass! I've got somethin' for ye", and her highly embarrassed granddad took a bunch of paper money from his pocket and handed it to his grand-daughter. Sylvia took it in amazement. There were exactly twenty five pounds – her grant money! She asked no questions and was given no explanations. She was certain that her grandfather would never have stolen her money. He just had to do the dirty work of returning it when her grandmother realised that the Education Authority was going to investigate the missing money. To be in possession of it was good enough for Sylvia, for now she could go ahead and buy the necessary things for college. However, she always puzzled on how her grandmother had managed to cash a cheque which would have been made out to her, and it was a worry that her mail was being intercepted. How many more important letters might her grandmother hide from her?

The pale spring sunshine slanted down through the sky light of the attic where Sylvia was just finishing off some homework. Noisy sparrows were chirruping on the rooftop, performing their ritual dance for the coming of spring. Sylvia closed her books with a sigh of relief and wondered what she should do next. She did not want to go downstairs because her grandmother was in one of her uncommunicative moods and making it clear that her grand-daughter was only there on sufferance. Looking round the attic, which also served as a spare bedroom, having a double bed with a patchwork quilt, a wash stand with a marble top, a couple of chairs and Sylvia's favourite – an old , comfortable rocking chair. She sat down in the latter, rocking to and fro and thinking of her life.

One corner of the attic was used for storage and Sylvia's gaze rested on her mother's trunk which was covered with a rug from India, complete with the picture of a magnificent tiger. The rug had been brought back by her father, Lewis, from his foreign travels when he had been to sea.

"I shall need that trunk when I go to college", thought Sylvia. "I'll see what's inside, if I can open it".

Going over to the corner of the attic, she took off the rug which covered the trunk and was pleased to find that it wasn't locked. Carefully she opened the lid and propped it up with a shoe so that it wouldn't fall on her head. Inside the trunk were some of her mother's few treasures from her youth, jewellery, a beaded evening bag, pretty gloves, and a very pretty frilled handkerchief case in mauve. Attached to the case was a porcelain figure of a naked girl lying on her stomach, resting in the silken frills.

When Sylvia lifted the large tray containing these things from its position, she discovered underneath were all her own childhood books which Mary had bought for her, mainly at Christmas times. Sylvia had always taken great care of her books and they were

Poor Mary

all in perfect condition. She began to browse through some of them, bringing back memories of happier days. There was a large volume of 'Alice in Wonderland' with some magnificent illustrations, and a similarly illustrated volume of 'Stories from the Arabian nights'. She turned the pages of the latter – yes – there he was, Blue Beard, the killer of many wives – the story which really frightened her when she was very small!

"There are pounds worth of books here", she thought as she noted the full sets of all the Enid Blyton series – 'The Castle of Adventure' – 'Five go to Kirren Island' – and many more!

In a box at the far corner of the attic Sylvia espied her old dolls – Baby Pat, Mary, Belinda, the black doll with no name, and Rupert her beloved old teddy. Apart from the teddy, which was well worn, the dolls were in perfect condition for she had never been a destructive child.

Her grandmother suddenly called up the attic stairs, telling her it was time for tea. Thank goodness she seemed a little more amenable today!

"You know Mum's old trunk?" said Sylvia a she began to eat her tea. "Well it would be useful to take to college with me. Is there anywhere else that I could put my old books?"

"What do ye want to keep them for? You're too old for books like that. I think ye should sell 'em an' get some money!"

This had never occurred to Sylvia and she took it as a command rather than a suggestion, and she did find the idea of making some money attractive. She was going to need every penny she could get hold of in order to exist at college!

"Why don't ye take yer books to that second hand stall on the Sheffield market?" said her grandmother. "He's sure to give ye something for 'em!"

The following Saturday, Sylvia found an old suitcase and piled all the books inside it. The case was really heavy when she tried to lift it. Nevertheless, she struggled down to the bus stop with the case, by which time her arms felt as though they were dropping out. When she arrived in Sheffield, she had another long walk with the heavy suitcase until she reached the market. Struggling against the crowds, she eventually found the second hand book stall and set the case down on the ground with a sigh of relief.

"Do you buy second hand books?" she tentatively asked the stallholder, a shabby looking man.

"It depends lass! How many 'ave ye got, and in what condition are they?" said the scruffy individual who owned the stall.

"They're in this case", said Sylvia. "I'll open it and you can have a look".

The man's eyes gleamed when he saw the contents of the case but Sylvia did not notice that. "I'll give you a pound for the lot", he said.

"A pound? But -", protested Sylvia.

"Take it or leave it! That's what I'm offering – a pound!" and the man half turned away as though disinterested.

Sylvia knew that the books were worth far more than that, and it wasn't worth selling them for that small amount. She was too shy to try and get a better price from the man, who was obviously exploiting her, but the thought of lugging the case of books all the way to the hospital and then back across the city, swayed her to accept the man's pittance of an offer, against her better judgment. She just could not carry them any further, even though she knew that the shark of a man was exploiting her youth and inexperience.

"All right!" she agreed in a small voice. "I'll take the pound!"

Walking for the bus to the hospital with her now empty and light suitcase, and a pound in her pocket, Sylvia felt bereft and cheated. Mary did not notice the suitcase, so Sylvia was spared from telling her that she had lost all those lovely books which had cost her mother a great deal of her meagre earnings over the years. It had been a bitter lesson indeed!

12. SAD FAREWELL

Examinations were looming in the not too distant future so when Sylvia was not visiting her mother she generally had her head buried in her books.

"All ye do is read books!" scoffed her grandfather one day.

"I need to keep reading Granddad, if I'm going to pass my exams", replied Sylvia.

Her grandfather snorted and buried his head in his newspaper, whilst Lucy was snoozing on the settee.

Mary was now more stabilized and although Sylvia hated visiting that awful prison like hospital, she could at least now have some conversation with her mother. Sylvia warned Mary that the time would soon come when she would be off to Teacher Training College, and when that happened she would only be able to visit her in the holidays. She promised that she would write to Mary at least once a week.

Mary was now receiving a weekly allowance from her pension. She never spent any of it, as she did not buy sweets, cigarettes, magazines or newspapers from the hospital shop. Consequently she had saved up a considerable amount of cash which she now took from her purse and gave it to her daughter for some pocket money. Sylvia was very grateful, for it meant that she could live like the other girls at school for a while

A trip to Scotland for the Edinburgh Festival was being organized for the Upper Sixth Girls in the summer holidays. The girls were asked to sign up on the school notice board if they wished to go. Sylvia did not put her name down because the cost of the trip was too expensive for her to contemplate. She was a keen member of the school choir and Miss Carter, the music teacher, asked Sylvia if the reason she had not signed up for the trip was because she couldn't afford it. When Sylvia affirmed that this was the case, Miss Carter went to see the headmistress to ask if there were any funds available for this educational trip. The High School certainly looked after its girls who were in financial difficulties, provided that they were deemed worthy of help, and not just time wasters. Sylvia could not believe it when Miss Carter came to the classroom and told her that she would be able to go to the Edinburgh Festival. Her friends were all delighted too, and they were all counting the days to the occasion which would be a wonderful treat once the exams were all finished.

The girls were given their examination time tables, and in between exams they were allowed to stay at home and revise. Sylvia's main subject was Art, which involved four different practical exams and a four hour written paper on Architecture. The latter was a really tough paper on Greek and Roman Architecture, followed by Anglo-Saxon, Norman, Early English and Gothic Architecture. One was expected to provide detailed illustrations with the written work of each of these periods. After completing her practical Art exams and the Architecture paper, the other two subjects, English and Scripture seemed relatively straightforward. At last the examinations were finished. Now all the girls had to do was to sit back and chew their nails with anxiety whilst awaiting the results. Sylvia was dreading the day when she would have to leave the High School forever. The place had been a secure haven for her during the past three turbulent years. She wanted to be able to make the most of, and enjoy her few remaining weeks, but that was not to be.

It was Friday. Mary Bedford stubbed out her cigarette into the ash tray on her desk and then picked up the telephone which was ringing shrilly.

"You need someone now?" she answered the voice on the other end of the line. "Well I should think that would be possible – the girls have all finished their exams now. Leave it with me and I will ring you back later".

After putting down the telephone, she lit up another cigarette and sat for a few minutes in contemplation, the cigarette creating a wreath of smoke across the room. After finishing off the second cigarette, she got up from her desk and went to open her study window. A wash of sunshine flooded down through the big window and the vase of brightly coloured flowers on her desk seemed to ripple in its light. When the air in the room had freshened, Miss Bedford rang down to her secretary and requested that Sylvia Copley should be sent up to her study.

As Sylvia mounted the stairs to the first floor, she felt a little uneasy, wondering if she had done something wrong. Nervously she knocked on the Head's study door and awaited the sign outside to invite her in.

"Hello Sylvia! There's no need to look so anxious, there isn't a problem. I've had a telephone call from the Youth Employment Office in the town. They are looking for a girl to work in the office temporarily, to cover for the holiday period. I thought it might be

Poor Mary

useful for you to be able to earn some money before you go to college. What do you think?"

Sylvia was astonished to think that out of all the girls at the High School who could have done the job Miss Bedford had thought of her.

"When would I have to start?" she asked.

"On Monday", said Miss Bedford, "and I am prepared to release you from school for the rest of the term, and then of course you will be able to continue for the duration of the holidays".

Sylvia's heart sank when she realised that she would have to miss the last few precious weeks of her beloved school, but her face did not betray her inner feelings, and she was extremely grateful for the opportunity to earn some money.

"Thank you very much Miss Bedford. I really do appreciate everything that you have done for me since I have been here. There's just one thing!"

"What is that my dear?" asked Miss Bedford.

"Do you think that I will be able to come into school for the last day of term? I really would like to say goodbye to everyone as we are all going off in different directions".

"I'm quite sure that they won't mind you taking a day off for that occasion, as long as you ask them well in advance", said the Head.

Having received all the details of where the office was, and what time she would be expected to be there on Monday morning, Sylvia bade her headmistress a sad farewell and returned to her classroom. She told her friends that this was to be her last day with them.

"Lucky old you!" Margaret said. "I wish I could go and do some work and earn some money. It'll be better than being in this dump!"

Sylvia made no comment. She was going to miss them all terribly, and more than anyone she was going to miss Mary Bedford who had been a great support for her during her time at the High School.

"I will never forget that wonderful lady", vowed Sylvia as she turned to look back at the High School one last time before leaving for her bus.

13. "IT'S ALL RIGHT LUV!"

The work in the Youth Employment Office was quite interesting and the pay was certainly much better than that from the Post Office. Four pounds a week, instead of nineteen shillings, seemed a fortune for Sylvia, and would enable her to purchase many of the necessary requirements for college, including some much needed underwear and shoes.

In the beginning Sylvia was given filing work to do, and of course the inevitable tea making and subsequent washing up. In time she was allowed to take phone calls and act on them appropriately, and eventually she found herself interviewing young people who had come to the office to seek employment. She had to find out the sort of work that they were prepared to do and then arrange interviews for them at factories, shops, offices and other places of employment. After a few weeks, she was sent out to man remote offices in the surrounding country villages. She found this quite scary and lonely as sometimes she did not see a living soul during the whole day. The only relief from boredom would be an occasional telephone call. She comforted herself with the thought of the pay packet which she would receive at the end of the week.

The longed for week of the visit to the Edinburgh Festival arrived. Fortunately the office manager proved lenient about Sylvia taking the week off work. Excitedly Sylvia met up with her friends and teachers who were going on the trip. Because she had been working for several weeks now, Sylvia had been able to put a little money aside to spend in Edinburgh and she felt very pleased about this.

The party boarded the train which was to take them directly to Edinburgh. The girls were like a gaggle of geese, chattering and laughing, all feeling a great sense of relief that examinations were all over and done with. They could now all relax and enjoy this week.

"It's a shame about Miss Bedford isn't it?" said Liz, one of the girls.

"What about Miss Bedford?" Sylvia queried.

"Oh, don't you know? She's got pneumonia – she's really ill. I'm sure it's all that smoking she does. It can't do her any good anyway, smoking like a chimney!" said Liz.

Sylvia's high spirits suddenly dissipated. Her beloved headmistress was seriously ill. How could she enjoy her holiday now?

The party arrived in Edinburgh during the late afternoon. The sunshine slanted down the stone walls of the ancient buildings, leaving in shadow the deep set timbered doorways. They reached the hostel where they would be staying, and on being allocated their rooms the girls unpacked their bags. Sylvia was sharing a room with Margaret and together they discussed Miss Bedford's illness and hoped that she would soon recover. After putting her own few things neatly in the drawers provided, Sylvia went to the window and sat on the sill, staring out over the sky line of the city in the cool of the evening.

"It's no use moping", she thought. "Miss Bedford wouldn't want me to do that. It would be a waste of all her efforts for me", and with that Sylvia determined

Poor Mary

to enjoy her week to the full, and to drink in all the experiences of the music and drama performances which she would attend that week.

Most of the week was organized by the staff, and the girls were taken to a variety of musical concerts. Midweek they were given a free day in which to do anything they wanted. A group of them, including Sylvia, decided to go and queue for hours in order to see 'Macbeth'. It was a performance never to be forgotten. Another unforgettable experience was to see Dame Margot Fonteyn dance the ballet 'Fire Bird'. Before the end of the week the girls were given time to explore the shops in Edinburgh's Princes Street. Sylvia was fascinated by all the various tartan kilts and materials on display, and by the general flavour of this beautiful city with its granite buildings and imposing castle at its highest point.

The last day of the week dawned and the girls awoke early. There was no sun visible yet, but here and there were hidden gaps in the cloud cover through which streamed golden light. Rain during the night had freshened every square inch of the granite city and as yet there were few people about. The girls came down to eat a hearty breakfast and were chattering excitedly about the prospects of their day. Sylvia ate her breakfast quietly for she was overwhelmed by a deep sadness. This would probably be the last day that she would ever spend with this group of friends. Once this day was over she would feel completely cut off from her refuge, her beloved school, and from Miss Bedford, and from all the friends of whom she had grown so fond. It was the end of another chapter in her life.

Although the weather turned grey and misty they all had a wonderful day. They were taken on a boat trip around the Kyles of Bute, a group of small islands off the coast of Scotland. The beauty and mystery of these islands shrouded in mist took their breath away. It was the end of a perfect week.

Sylvia returned to work at the Youth Employment Office for the rest of the summer vacation. Whenever she could find the time she would go shopping with the money she earned, stocking up with the things she would need for her time at college. Everything she bought was neatly stored in her mother's old trunk which she was going to take to college. The examination results had arrived after her return from Edinburgh and she had passed them all, so there was nothing to prevent her from starting her college course in September.

The Jones' family, who lived next door to her grandparents, was having a hard time. Young Judith, their third child, was in hospital with a T.B. hip, and their father, Eddie, was off work as he was suffering from the lung disease, silicosis, which was caused by the coal dust he had inhaled throughout his years in the pit. Eddie's wife, Helena, was having difficulty in making ends meet, particularly with all the trips to Sheffield in order to visit her hospitalised daughter.

Sylvia spent any spare time that she had with the Jones' girls, keeping them amused by playing games with them in order to keep them from under Helena's feet whilst she tended to her sick husband. She also went with Helena to visit Judith in hospital, and was surprised to see how tanned the little girl's face was. The reason for her tanned face was because the patients' beds were wheeled out through the sliding windows of the ward on to a wide terrace whenever it was warm and sunny. Judith was surprisingly cheerful and glad to see Sylvia who promised to visit her again whenever she could.

One Friday night, Sylvia went to bed early after a somewhat busy day at work. She fell asleep quickly as she was very tired. At least she was getting some decent nights since her mother had gone into hospital. It was about two o'clock in the morning when something caused her to wake. She lay there for a while, wondering what had disturbed her. There was no noise anywhere in the house so her grandparents were obviously in bed and fast asleep. Suddenly she heard a scream in the night, and then a child's cry.

"Oh Daddy, Daddy, Daddy!" and then came the sound of muffled sobs.

Sylvia drifted off to sleep again. In the morning when she awoke, she thought that she must have been dreaming. When she went downstairs for breakfast, her grandparents were already at the table, both of them sitting with sombre looks on their faces.

"Hello", she said. "Is something wrong?"

"Eddie died last night", said Lucy.

"Oh!" gasped Sylvia, going cold all over. "Oh no, I can't believe it!"

She knew that Eddie had been ill, but she had no idea that he had been so ill.

"Then that's what I must have heard last night. I wasn't dreaming after all!"

"What did you hear?" asked her grandmother.

"I heard a child shouting for her daddy and then crying pitifully. Now I come to think it must have been Eileen's voice", said Sylvia.

"It would be", said Lucy. "Eddie knew 'e was going and 'e asked to see his children before 'e died. Eileen, being the eldest, would understand more than t' others. It's a shame about young Judy being in hospital. It would upset Eddie to die without her being there. Just before 'e died 'e made Helena promise that she wouldn't marry again".

Helena, an extremely attractive and wholesome person, kept her promise and never did marry again. She had had a hard life with Eddie who had not been the easiest person to live with. Her four little girls had been born in quick succession and she was quite worn out. The girls had a clean dress on each day so Helena had twenty eight dresses to launder each week, and without the luxury of a washing machine! There was no where clean for the children to play, just the concrete back yard with a large square of hard soil in the middle. By lunch time they were all black bright from grovelling on the dirty ground.

Judith was eventually cured of her T.B. hip. It had been a difficult task for Helena to go to the hospital and tell her sick child that her daddy had died. She had been very surprised at her daughter's reaction.

"Never mind Mum! I'll look after ye when I get better" – and she did.

Poor Mary

Eileen eventually went to college and became a teacher, but her three sisters did not continue with their education. They wanted to be earning as soon as they were old enough.

Bad luck seemed to dog Helena and her family. Her own father became ill enough to go into hospital and Helena took her mother to visit him. As they stepped off the bus, both Helena and her mother were knocked down by a passing lorry. Helena's mother died instantly, and Helena suffered a leg injury which left her permanently lame. The shock of the accident proved too much for her father and he suffered a heart attack and died in hospital!

Sylvia's time at the office was nearly at an end and she now had everything ready for her departure to college. The most difficult thing now was to try and explain to Mary that she would be unable to visit her for a while. Although Mary was fairly responsive she was heavily sedated and it was hard to tell just how much she understood of what was being said.

"Mother", said Sylvia on her last visit before going to college, "Mother – you do realise that I'm going to college in a few days time, and I won't be able to visit you for a while?"

"Yes luv", said Mary dreamily.

"You do understand don't you?" said Sylvia.

"It's all right luv!" replied Mary, still as though in a trance.

Sylvia still wasn't sure if her mother understood what was happening, or even if she would notice if she didn't visit her. To Mary time meant nothing. Half the time she was lost in a dream world and she couldn't differentiate between her dreams and reality.

"I'll write to you every week", promised Sylvia, "and let you know how I am getting on".

"Yes luv. It's all right!" said Mary, and suddenly brightening up she continued, "Don't worry luv. I'll be all right!"

As her daughter disappeared through the door and down the corridor, Mary gazed at the blue sky through the high window of the cheerless room. Her eyes suddenly filled with tears which trickled down her sunken cheeks. She knew that she had lost her little girl!

PART 5

1. TOP FOUR

1992 Her mother had disappeared into the cellar. Sylvia did not exactly see her go but she knew that she was down there. From the top of the steps she peered down into the gloom and then ventured down a few steps. She could still hear her mother moving about in the cellar but, even from her new position, all that she could see was a dark, dark void.

Suddenly there was a strange noise and a scuffle, and then her mother's voice shouting. The shouting changed to a prolonged screaming of sheer terror. Sylvia's blood chilled as she remained rooted to the spot, afraid to go any further. Then there was ominous silence.

Sylvia wanted to rush down the steps and see what had happened to her mother but she was too afraid of what was lurking in the cellar. Whatever it was had silenced her mother in some hideous way and it would do the same to her if she ventured any further. She began to shout for help, for she needed someone to go with her. At the sound of her voice came a movement from the dark shadows below, and then Sylvia could hear herself screaming on and on - - -.

Immediately she was gathered into warm arms and felt the comfort of a warm body pressed close to hers.

"What is the matter darling?" whispered her husband. "What's frightened you?"

"I don't know", mumbled Sylvia sleepily. "I think I had another nightmare". The sweat was pouring from her forehead.

"Well try to go back to sleep. You're all right now. I don't know! You're always having bad dreams and crying out in the night".

As she drifted back into an uneasy sleep, Sylvia puzzled on dreaming about her mother so vividly. After all, it was three years since she had died.

The alarm went off and Sylvia reluctantly roused herself from the deep sleep which had eventually taken over after her troubled night.

"It's my turn to get the tea", she mumbled sleepily, and she groped her way to the bedroom door, tripping over her slippers in the dark. She hated to switch on the bright light first thing in the morning. As she went down the stairs she paused at the tall staircase window on the half landing and peered outside. Autumn had begun its downhill slide into winter and the first of the November frosts had settled on the lawn in front of the house.

Having fed the cats and made the tea, Sylvia took the tray back up to the bedroom and switched on the bedside lamp.

"Here's your tea luv. I don't want to go to that meeting at all this afternoon. I'm just so tired!"

There was a meeting of Independent School Heads in Oxford during the late afternoon, and it would take Sylvia one and a half hours to drive there.

"Never mind!" said Richard. "You'll probably enjoy it once you're there, and the refreshments are usually good!"

Poor Mary

After a busy morning in school, Sylvia went home for an early lunch and then freshened herself for the journey ahead. She set off promptly at two o'clock, allowing herself a little extra time should she become lost in Oxford. It was a pleasant afternoon for the drive. The sun was shining low in the sky and not a shred of cloud desecrated the blue expanse.

"I'm lucky to have a day like this", Sylvia thought, as it had been raining almost daily for weeks, in fact it was one of the wettest autumns on record. Once on the way she began to relax, determined to enjoy the journey and the change from normal school routine. Suddenly there was a sharp bang on the windscreen of the car as a passing lorry hurled up a stone. A small crack appeared at the base of the windscreen.

"Damn!" thought Sylvia. "More expense! The windscreen will have to be replaced now before it shatters. Richard won't be too pleased about that."

The meeting was being held in one of the Oxford colleges and because she managed to follow the directions accurately, and therefore did not lose her way in the complicated traffic system of the city, Sylvia arrived at her destination well before time. As yet there were only a few people there so for once Sylvia had the luxury of a little time to spare and she let her eyes explore her surroundings. The style of the building reminded her vividly of the college where she herself had trained, and her mind conjured up fond memories of her time spent there.

1954 By the time the early morning sun shone through the window, Sylvia was up and dressed ready, her trunk waiting at the front door of her grandmother's house. She looked out of the window and saw the swallows perching on the telephone wires, gathering together to fly away to warmer climes.

"I feel like those swallows today", thought Sylvia, "– impatient to be off to far off lands!"

It was a long time since she had felt so buoyant and light hearted. Her face, usually pensive and anxious, now was bright with merriment at the thought of escaping from this grim and dull place, the home town of her grandparents. She couldn't wait to kick the dust from her heels. She felt like a creature that had been chained up for too long in a cramped space then suddenly let loose in the wild. She was hungry now for new experiences and she felt both nervous and excited. There would be countless new faces, questions, tutors and strange surroundings. Sylvia felt like a long term prisoner who was about to be released.

There was a loud knocking at the front door and her heart beat fast with nervous anticipation.

"I'll go Grandma. It's bound to be Margaret and her parents. They said that they would be here early".

Her friend Margaret's parents were taking them both to college, and as Sylvia opened the front door she was greeted by Margaret's father. He was a cheerful rotund man of middle age, balding and wearing rimless spectacles. He was the manager of a garage and he earned enough to keep his wife and only daughter in a reasonably comfortable manner. At least Margaret had never known what it was like to struggle and she

Poor Mary

was to remain in this blissful state until she eventually married. She married a man very similar to her father and thus her life continued in a cocoon of cosiness but without adventure!

"Hello Sylvia! Are you ready?"

"Yes, I'll just say goodbye to my grandparents", said Sylvia, her face glowing with excitement. She went back into the living room to her grandparents who were finishing off their breakfast. "I'm going now", she said cheerily, and she planted a kiss on each of their cheeks.

"Look after tha sen lass", said Arthur, his voice breaking a little with the lump in his throat. He was going to miss his young grand daughter.

Lucy began to cry, but Sylvia reckoned that her grandmother could turn on crocodile tears whenever she wanted and she was never quite sure how much the old lady really felt beneath her apparent hardness.

"I mustn't keep them waiting any longer", Sylvia said, and she dashed back to the front door. Her trunk was already installed in the enormous boot of the very large car together with Margaret's trunk.

At last they were off, speeding along through the grimy towns and villages of the mining communities which were soon left behind. As they entered Lincolnshire, Sylvia was struck by the pleasantness and cleanliness of the country side. On this September day it was a delight to see the trees flaming out in their autumn glory of rich colour. The car reached the Lincolnshire Wolds and Sylvia gazed at the serene pale gold of the shorn harvest fields, and at the sheep nibbling dry September grass and juicy blackberries dangling in the hedges.

"I can't believe this is actually happening", thought Sylvia. "My life has really begun. It's all too good to be true".

The car sped along the winding country roads until at last they reached the college, entering the grounds by the large iron gates which were flung wide open. They passed a garden crammed with useful herbs, vegetables and sweet smelling shrubs, and the boughs of apple and plum trees were heavy with fruit. Margaret had a room in the main hall of residence but Sylvia's accommodation was in a college hostel a short distance away. Mr. and Mrs. Clark left their daughter to unpack her trunk, telling her that they would be back as soon as they had taken Sylvia to the student's hostel. Sylvia thought wistfully how nice it would be if she had parents there to help her to unpack and settle in, but she soon shrugged off the self pity as the hostel came into view. The hostel was a lovely old detached house set in a large garden. Sylvia gasped at the beauty of the trees in their flaming autumn glory, the deep red maples, golden poplars, rich red oak trees and silvery birches casting a riot of colour.

Hurriedly scrambling out of the car, Sylvia ran up the steps of the front door and tugged on the brass bell pull at the side of the dark oak panelled door. The great door opened and she was confronted by the tallest lady that she had ever seen. The lady's hair was combed back from her face and secured in a roll which encircled her head. Her features were inclined to be masculine and she had a large wart on the side of her chin. Her

Poor Mary

style of dress also favoured the masculine, a drab grey suit with a box pleated skirt and square cut jacket. Her extraordinary large feet sported a pair of heavy, flat walking shoes in dark brown, and on her legs she wore heavy woollen stockings, fawn in colour.

"Gosh! She must be at least six feet tall", thought Sylvia in amazement and feeling somewhat intimidated. "I'm Sylvia Copley", she addressed the formidable looking lady with some degree of nervousness.

"You will be known as Miss Copley from now on", said Miss Bogner, for that was the lady's name. As well as being warden of the hostel she was also a lecturer in Psychology and Education and was a person to be reckoned with.

"You room is on the first floor and it is called Top Four. You will be sharing with three other students".

Having deposited her trunk in the hallway, Margaret's parents said their goodbyes and Sylvia thanked them before they went back to the Main Hall to help their own daughter.

Sylvia walked slowly up the wide polished oak staircase. She noticed with pleasure the beautiful stained glass window on the first half landing. Reaching the top of the stairs she walked along a corridor with a highly polished floor and she noticed a beautifully carved Jacobean coffer standing under the window at the end. Near the window she came to a door on which was a brass plate bearing the name 'TOP FOUR'. Taking hold of the elegant brass knob she turned it and gingerly opened the heavy door. She found herself in an enormous room in which were already three other young ladies all busily unpacking their possessions and placing them neatly in the drawers provided.

There were four beds, one in each corner of the room and, being the last to arrive, Sylvia was left with the bed nearest to the door. By the side of each bed was one chest of drawers, a bureau with shelves for books and a writing top, and a bedside cabinet. A giant wardrobe, which they would have to share, stood centrally along the back wall of the room.

The other young ladies introduced themselves. They were Jane, Kate and Barbara and all of them seemed good natured enough, though Sylvia felt that Barbara, who wore spectacles and who tended to scowl, might be a little bit surly. After some general chit chat about each other, and where they were from, the girls were suddenly startled by a loud knock at the door, and in sailed the tall figure of Miss Bogner.

"Now young ladies, everything in your room must be neat and tidy at all times. Your beds must be made before breakfast and slippers must not be left on the floor but kept in your bedside cupboard. Only breakfast will be taken at the hostel. All other meals will be taken in the main dining room in the college. I shall expect you to be down for breakfast promptly by seven thirty each morning, including weekends. If you go out in the evening then you must be back here not a minute later than ten o'clock. There will be a regular fire drill and if you hear the fire bell in the night you will come down in your dressing gowns and slippers and carry a towel and a torch, then you will line up outside in the garden".

Poor Mary

As suddenly as she had swept into the room then Miss Bogner swept out again without another word.

"So now we know!" said Jane.

"Phew!" said Barbara. "She's a dragon isn't she? I thought we'd left people like that behind at school"

They later discovered that Miss Bogner was generally known as "Bog" by all the students. Although they were careful not to cross her if they could help it, she was often a source of amusement in their conversations as they speculated about her love life, or lack of it. It was said that during one of her psychology lectures she declared, "I have never been kissed and I am proud of it!"

2. A PIECE OF PAPER

The next morning Sylvia woke to light and space and for a moment wondered where she was. The large room was awash with light, a pale rosy white. Outside the window was sunlight on golden apple trees and a glimpse of pale blue sky with fluffy clouds.

"I am really here", Sylvia thought contentedly as she glance round the strange room, observing the still sleeping forms of her room mates.

At seven o'clock came the harsh sound of a bell being rung, obviously the summons to get out of bed. At half past seven there was another signal, this time the mellow sound of a beautiful old gong announcing that it was time for breakfast. In the breakfast room, with its rich dark oak panelled walls, there were two large refectory tables, each having twelve chairs placed around them. The snow white table cloths were set up with breakfast things, toast and marmalade being already on the table. At the head of one of the tables stood an old oak carving chair and this was the permanent seat for Miss Bogner. It was customary that each morning the students would take it in turn to sit next to the lecturer, no doubt in order to learn the art of social intercourse. After they had all tucked in to a hearty breakfast, Miss Bogner announced that all new students must hasten to college and meet in the common room by nine o'clock, when the Principal wished to speak to them and to return their birth certificates which had been sent to the college by the girls prior to them being accepted into that establishment.

Sylvia's heart missed a beat. She had forgotten all about her birth certificate and had never dreamed that it would be handed back to her in public. The birth certificate revealed the fact that her mother had not been married to her father and still bore the name of SYLVIA HOWELL. Only in the margin, in very small writing, was the amendment to say that her name had been changed to COPLEY. In those days there was still a stigma to being illegitimate and it was Sylvia's biggest dread that her friends would find out. She was convinced that they would not want anything to do with her if they knew. Certainly Margaret had no idea of Sylvia's parentage, and as she was something of a prude and inclined to be snobbish, Sylvia had never confided in her on this matter.

"How can I face Margaret when she finds out this morning? The Principal is bound to read out Howell instead of Copley, and then Margaret will want to know why. Then all the other girls will find out and no one will want to know me", and so Sylvia walked up to college with her heart in her mouth. This early autumn day was mild and sunny, and had she not been feeling so worried about that wretched piece of paper, her birth certificate, she would really have enjoyed the walk. The sun shone on the turning leaves and the clear morning sky was bright blue, but for once she did not notice.

All the new students filed into the common room where rows and rows of chairs had been placed in front of a dais. Margaret suddenly emerged from a group of girls with whom she had been chatting.

"Hello Sylvia. Have you settled in all right?" she said.

"Yes thank you. How about you?" Sylvia answered.

"Fine", said Margaret. "I have a really nice room of my own in Main Hall".

"Lucky old you! I share my room with three other girls, but they seem all right and the room is very big so we have plenty of space. The warden is an absolute dragon though. She lectures in Psychology and Education so you'll no doubt come across her", said Sylvia.

The head student came into the common room and mounted the dais. "Can you all sit down and stop talking please. The Principal is on her way and she doesn't want to waste any time", she shouted above the noisy conversations of two hundred female students.

As she finished speaking the Principal of the college entered the room hurriedly. Indeed, wherever the lady went she always appeared to be in a great hurry. Miss Richardson had been the Principal of the college for fifteen years. She was another tall lady, though not quite as tall as Miss Bogner, and she was dressed in a plain brown suit with matching walking shoes. Her features could not be considered to be attractive though there was a kindly look in her eyes. Her hair, steely grey in colour, was drawn tightly from her face and knotted into a bun at the nape of her neck. She talked as quickly as she walked, as though she had not a second to waste. After welcoming them to the college she ran through a list of college procedures and stated what would be expected of the students. She warned that

Poor Mary

although they had all been accepted into the college it did not guarantee their continuance there. It would be necessary to work hard and keep the rules of the college otherwise they may be asked to leave.

"I am now going to give out your birth certificates, so listen carefully for your names", Miss Richardson finally announced.

This was the moment Sylvia had been dreading. She glanced at her friend, Margaret, and felt extremely uncomfortable at the thought of having to explain the other name on her birth certificate. There was no particular order in which the names were being read out, so everyone had to listen very carefully.

"Sylvia -----------". There was a pause as the Principal studied the certificate for a moment. Sylvia went bright red, her heart beating very fast.

"Sylvia Copley", said Miss Richardson.

Sylvia could not believe it! The Principal did not bat an eyelid or make any comment as she handed the certificate to her. Sylvia hastily stuffed the offending piece of paper into her bag and smiled happily at Margaret. She had never felt such a sense of relief and all the tension flowed out of her body. There now would not have to be any embarrassing explanations and her friends would be none the wiser. She could really settle down and enjoy her college days.

3. 'BOG' – AND A RABBIT.

The weeks passed quickly as the days were filled with new experiences and making new friends. Peals of laughter could often be heard coming from Top Four as the girls played pranks on each other. Every Monday evening 'Bog' went out to a meeting in the city. On one such evening the girls in Top Four were all in their dressing gowns, sitting about and discussing the events of the day. They were all studying in different subjects so did not usually see each other until after supper.

"Let's have some fun!" said Barbara. 'Bog' is out at her meeting tonight so let's ring the fire bell and see what happens!"

Barbara and Sylvia crept down the long corridor until they reached the shelf on which rested the fire bell. They giggled together as Barbara picked it up and gave it a long loud ring and then they dashed back up the corridor as all the other students dutifully began to file down the stairs and out into the garden. They were all wearing their dressing gowns and carrying towels over their arms and torches in their hands. They stood on the lawn in the cold night air, shivering as they waited for roll call. The girls in Top Four were splitting their sides with laughter as they watched everyone from their window. Staying in their room was their undoing. They should have gone outside with the rest of the students. It was obvious to Miss Bogner, who after all had not gone to her usual meeting that evening, who the culprits were. The Top Four girls suddenly heard her voice commanding the rest of the students to go back to their rooms.

Poor Mary

"Oh my God!" cried Barbara. "Bog's still here! Now we're in trouble!"

All four girls jumped into their beds and dived under their sheets, pretending to be asleep. Sylvia was stuffing a handkerchief into her mouth in an attempt to suppress her laughter. There was a loud bang at the door and Miss Bogner burst into the room.

"Who in this room rang the fire bell?" she demanded, her voice booming with anger.

There was no reply from any of the girls. Sylvia felt that she would explode with laughter under her sheets and there was no way that she could get a grip on herself to say anything.

"Who in this room rang the fire bell?" repeated Miss Bogner even more angrily.

A small voice sounded from the bed in the far corner. "I did Miss Bogner," said Barbara. "I am sorry!"

"What a despicable thing to do!" raged the lecturer. "Don't you realise that you put people at risk when you do things like that? Come and see me in the morning!"

"Yes Miss Bogner", whispered Barbara.

When the lecturer had slammed out of the room, the four girls emerged from their sheets, shaking with laughter and the tears streaming down their cheeks.

"I'm sorry Barbara", said Sylvia, wiping her eyes. "I should have owned up too but I was just choking with laughter and that would have made Bog even angrier. I'll come with you in the morning and confess".

The next morning the two girls received a stiff admonishment as to the stupidity of their actions and were then sent on their way to their lectures for the day.

Sylvia Hoole

Miss Bogner sighed as she watched them go. It had been necessary for her to assume anger concerning the girls' pranks, but she realised that such behaviour was often an outlet for the built up tensions which students experience from time to time.

About two weeks later Sylvia went back to the hostel after she had finished lectures for the day. There was now a cold bite in the air and the leaves were falling from the trees. She still loved to walk through the crunchy leaves as she had done when a small child. Her cheeks glowed from the nip in the air as she mounted the stairs and hurried along the corridor to Top Four. The three other girls were already in the room, all sitting at their desks and engrossed in their studies. After greeting them, Sylvia began to organize her own desk for the evening's work. Barbara looked up from her own work.

"By the way Sylvia, Bog wants to see you in her study", she said.

"Bog wants to see me?" queried Sylvia. "Why? What have I done now?"

"You didn't pass her the marmalade at breakfast time", said Barbara.

"WHAT! You've got to be joking!" exclaimed Sylvia.

"I'm not", said Barbara in all seriousness.

"But I was sitting at the other end of the table this morning", said Sylvia. "I could not possibly have

Poor Mary

passed her the marmalade unless I had rubber arms which stretched!"

"Well you'd better go ", said Barbara. "I told her that I would tell you as soon as you came in".

With a puzzled expression on her face, Sylvia left the room and made her way to Miss Bogner's study. She knocked tentatively at her door.

"Come in", shouted the lecturer.

Sylvia opened the door and entered the lion's den.

"Yes?" said Miss Bogner.

"You wanted to see me Miss Bogner", stammered Sylvia nervously.

"Did I? What about?" asked the lecturer looking puzzled.

"Er – um – about not passing the marmalade - at breakfast time", Sylvia continued to stammer, now feeling very foolish indeed. It sounded so ridiculous!

"Not – passing – the marmalade – at breakfast time!" repeated Miss Bogner, getting up from her chair. She stood up to her full height and towered over the diminutive figure of the girl standing in front of her. Sylvia squirmed under her gaze and began to fiddle with the brooch she wore at the throat of her blouse. She had a strong desire, born of nervousness, to giggle.

"Now how do you expect me to give you a testimonial if you do not have the good manners to pass the marmalade to me at breakfast time?" continued Miss Bogner.

"I don't know Miss Bogner. I'm very sorry", said Sylvia who could not believe that this conversation was taking place.

Eventually Miss Bogner dismissed her and Sylvia fled from the room, still as puzzled as when she went in. It did not occur to her until some time later that the other girls had set her up and that Miss Bogner had gone along with their joke. Had she been a fly on the wall of Miss Bogner's study then she would have seen that same lady chuckling to herself as she resumed her reading.

Day by day the sun marched in an ever lowering path across the sky, and the nights grew chillier as autumn advanced towards winter.

"I could do with some fresh air", said Barbara. "Anyone coming for a walk?"

The Top Four girls had been engrossed in their work for the past hour on this particular Sunday afternoon.

"What a good idea!" Kate replied. "I'll come with you. Are you coming Sylvia – Jane?"

"I think we all need to get out for a while. It will blow the cobwebs away", said Sylvia.

The four girls wrapped up well against the cold and made their way down the stairs and to the front door. Once outside they decided to explore the countryside as so far they hadn't had any opportunity to do this. They left the main road to venture up a narrow lane which led to a sombre wood. There was the smell of wet leaves from the ditches at each side of the lane, and short gusts of wind sent the still falling leaves spinning in a merry dance.

"What's that over there?" exclaimed Sylvia.

Poor Mary

"Oh – it's a rabbit!" cried Kate.

"Why doesn't it run away?" queried Barbara. "I've never seen one stay so close to people – well only tame ones".

"I think it's sick", said Kate.

The girls cautiously approached the small creature which remained motionless, its breath coming in short gasps. It made no attempt to run away.

"Look, its face is swollen", said Sylvia. "Poor little thing!"

"It's got myxomatosis", said Kate.

"What's that?" asked Barbara who was a city girl and did not know much about country matters, and nor did Sylvia and Jane.

Kate was country born and bred and there was not much that she didn't know about wild life. She explained to the others what it was.

"It's a disease which was introduced into them to keep down the rabbit population. Unfortunately there is now a major epidemic throughout the whole country and the rabbits are dying like flies. It's a very cruel disease and causes much suffering. This rabbit really needs to be put out of its misery otherwise it will suffer a slow and painful death. We will have to kill it".

"WE'LL HAVE TO KILL IT?" exclaimed the other girls all at once. "How could we do it? We just couldn't!" and they continued to protest.

"Look for a big stone", said Kate, and suddenly she came across one at the side of the path.

"What are you going to do?" asked Jane.

"I'm going to hit it on the head with this heavy stone", replied Kate.

"No, you mustn't!" cried Sylvia. "It's too cruel!"

"It's more cruel to let it suffer", said Kate. "I'm being cruel to be kind!" She then began to beat the rabbit on the head with the heavy stone. Sylvia burst into tears and hid her face, not wishing to witness the gory deed. She wondered how anyone could actually bring themselves to take away another creature's life, no matter what the circumstances were. On the grass verge, the small rabbit now lay motionless, and its life ebbed away.

The girls walked back to the hostel in silence.

4. HURT

Sylvia opened the curtains of Top Four bedroom and looked outside at the garden. It was a crisp day and the chestnut leaves flared gold in the early morning sun, and a hint of frost sparkled on leaves already fallen.

"What a beautiful place this is", she thought, "and how lucky I am to be here. I can still hardly believe it". She was now feeling the benefits of some respite from the problems with her mother. She wrote to her regularly each week and Mary wrote back to her with letters full of nonsensical statements, strange poetry and a bit of religious mania thrown in for good measure.

"It's not time to get ready is it?" mumbled Barbara from under her blankets. "Close the curtains, I'm still sleepy".

"I'm afraid it is time", replied Sylvia. "I'm going to be first in the bathroom this morning to make sure that I get some hot water for a change!"

She was now thoroughly into the swing of college life and enjoyed every minute of it. The work presented her with no problems as long as her assignments were handed in on time, and they usually were. Some of the girls left everything until the last minute and then had a mad scramble to get their work in on time.

When Sylvia returned from the bathroom, Jane had just emerged from under her bed clothes and was having a good stretch and a yawn.

"Do you realise that it's half term in a couple of weeks?" she said.

"Thank God!" muttered Barbara still buried deep under her blankets. "I can't wait to go home!"

"Half term!" Sylvia mused. "I never gave it a thought. I suppose I ought to write to Grandma and let her know that I'll be home for that weekend. I'll do that first thing today after my lectures have finished, then I can get the letter in the post".

On the hall table a few days later, Sylvia found an envelope addressed to her in her grandmother's writing and she opened it.

"Dear Sylvie,
I'm writing to tell you that we'll be going out on the weekend of your half term so ye won't be able to come -----------------------"

Sylvia stared at the letter, dumbfounded. Her grandparents never went out for any length of time, except on their annual trip to Blackpool in August. It was just a way of telling her that she would not be welcome in their home. She felt a pain in her heart like a knife twisting, and tears welled up into her eyes. She struggled to fight them back as she went into the breakfast room where she ate her meal in silence. Her grandparents' house was the only place that she could call home, and she was not wanted there.

Her steps lacked their usual lightness and her head was bowed as she made her way up to the college. This morning she did not notice the beauties which autumn offered up to the bright blue sky. She reached the Art Room and prepared her easel and oil paints ready for the morning's work.

"Hi!" said Margaret cheerily as she entered the room.

Poor Mary

"Hello", answered Sylvia despondently.

"Soon be half term", chattered Margaret. "I'm looking forward to it aren't you? Mum says it's all right to give you a lift if you would like that".

At this point Sylvia could no longer contain the floods of tears which she had been trying to stem since before breakfast. Once she had started to cry she could not stop. Her Art tutor, Miss Kelly, came into the room at that moment.

"Come into my room and tell me what is bothering you", she said in a kindly voice. Sylvia, still sobbing, followed her and sat down on the chair offered to her.

"I c can't go home at half term", she cried. "I wrote to my grandma and she d doesn't want me there. My mother's in hospital – and – I don't – know what to do".

During her weeks at college, getting to know a new routine, places and people, Sylvia's anxieties had been alleviated somewhat. Suddenly they all came flooding back, made even worse by the knowledge that she was not welcome in the only place that she could call home. Once again she felt a sense of desolation and loneliness.

"Well you will be able to stay in college so don't worry about that, though you will probably have to move up to the main building for the weekend as the hostel will be closed. There's bound to be someone else around to keep you company", said Miss Kelly.

Once she realised that her accommodation problem was solved Sylvia cheered up and went back to her work. She was fairly resilient and, having got over the initial hurt, she engrossed herself in her work.

Half term weekend came along and the girls packed their weekend cases, chattering happily about being reunited with their families. Sylvia busied herself by packing a weekend bag to take up to the main hall in college. As she left the hostel she saw a row of cars containing the happy smiling faces of mums, dads, brothers or sisters who were all delighted to be seeing a long absent member of their family.

"Oh well! At least I've got somewhere to stay, but I'm going to miss everyone – but it's only for a long weekend and I've plenty to do", Sylvia thought as she made her way up to the college.

She found herself to be limping a little as she walked, and there was pain in her right knee. She did not take too much notice as it had been a regular occurrence since she was eleven. She shrugged it off as growing pains. In the college Sylvia was to share a room with a German au pair girl who was working in the kitchens in order to improve her English. The girl, Helga, had a strong guttural accent. She was tall, heavy of stature, and her hair being cropped short gave her a masculine appearance. However she was amiable enough and Sylvia found it interesting to hear her talk about life in Germany.

On the Saturday afternoon the two girls decided to go to the cinema. The film they were to see was "The Dam Busters" which was the story of the bombing of the dams in the Rurh Valley in Germany. The two girls, one English and one German, sat side by side waiting for the film to begin. Then Helga spoke.

Poor Mary

"My familee – they lived in ze Rurh Valley – and during ze War many of them were drowned when ze dams are bombed by ze English!"

Sylvia was stunned. The film, full of heroism and portraying the ingenuity of the British, gave no hint that many German civilians would lose their lives during this operation, though anyone who really thought about it would realise that this was inevitable. It was an excellent film but Sylvia felt too guilty to enjoy it, and extremely embarrassed in the presence of the German girl whose family had suffered because of the bombing of the dams. It brought home to her the folly of war, that there was good and bad on both sides, and that the reality of war was much more than opposing armies fighting it out on the battle field.

5. KATE

The weeks passed and the trees were finally stripped of all their leaves and the days were shorter and shorter. The bright winter sunlight streaked the pale coloured wall and lit up the mellow wood of the chest of drawers beside Sylvia's bed. She had awoken early and was pondering on the Christmas vacation, and whether or not her grandmother would expect her to go home.

"I'll write to the General Post Office", she thought, "and I will ask if they have any work for me during the holiday period. If they have I can write to Grandma and tell her that I have a job and then she might not mind if I go home for Christmas. Besides, I really must go and see my mother in hospital".

Later that day Sylvia wrote to the General Post Office of the little mining town and several days later she received a letter from the manager confirming that she could have temporary work there. The Post Office employed quite a few students to help out with the Christmas rush. When Lucy received Sylvia's letter to say that she had some work to come to, she wrote back and said that it would be all right for her to come home. It wasn't that Lucy was not fond of her grand daughter underneath that hard exterior which she presented to the world, but she hated having anyone under her feet all day. It was bad enough now that Arthur had retired and she made his life such a misery that he would disappear as often as possible to his garden and his budgerigars.

Now that Mary was reasonably stabilized on her drugs, she was allowed out of hospital for a few days

Poor Mary

this Christmas. The whole family came together as usual for the festivities, and their voices yapped and bayed in a crescendo of family gossip. Apart from her cousin, Ralph, and his wife Doreen, the rest of the family appeared to ignore Sylvia. She had broken the traditional family mould and had ventured into a world beyond their understanding. They did not know how to treat her now and so they remained aloof.

Sylvia was glad to see her mother again, but any hopes of a miraculous recovery were very quickly dashed. She only had to see the glint of malice in her mother's eyes and she knew that trouble was brewing. Before long, Mary was babbling her irritating nonsense, and sometimes cruel words, making everyone feel uneasy and eventually to quarrel amongst themselves. An inward sigh of relief was given by all when Mary had been returned to the hospital.

At the end of the holiday, albeit a working holiday, Sylvia thankfully returned for her second term at college. After two weeks she received a letter from Mary's brother, Ted. This was a most unusual occurrence as he had never written to her ever before. He wrote that he had been to see Mary in the hospital and could not bear to think of his sister locked up in a place like that. Consequently he had taken it upon himself to sign her out of the hospital and had taken her to live with him and his wife, Rose. Sylvia knew instinctively that he had done the wrong thing and that he would live to regret it. Sure enough Mary tormented Ted and Rose to distraction. After eight weeks of misery, Rose put her foot down and said that Mary must leave or she herself would go. Ted, at the end of his tether, took Mary round to Arthur and Lucy with all her bags and baggage. He left her with them, thus shattering their peace once more.

Blissfully unaware of all these problems, Sylvia continued to enjoy the golden moments of her college days. The half term break was approaching once more and she expected that she would have to remain in college as before.

"Why don't you come home with me for half term?" suggested Kate.

"With you?" Are you sure? Won't your mother mind?" said Sylvia.

"Of course she won't. I'll write and tell her", said Kate, and so it was all arranged.

Kate's main subject was English and it was a bone of contention with Sylvia that Kate always said, "I aren't" instead of "I'm not". Kate was a born and bred Lincolnshire country lass but, even so, Sylvia thought that as an English specialist Kate should have known better as she was after all going to be teaching English in schools. Kate's father was dead and she lived with her mother in a small Lincolnshire village. She was a tall girl with rosy cheeks and a fresh complexion, but in no way could she be described as pretty. The way she wore her hair did not do much for her either, for it was cropped exceedingly short in a manly style and emphasized her angular features.

The girls made their journey by train. Earlier it had been snowing and there was still some snow and ice on

Poor Mary

the ground and the sky looked as though it would shed another load of snow any minute. Sure enough, by the time they had completed their journey the snow began again, and continued to drop unceasingly from the sky. Thankfully they arrived at Kate's cottage where they were made welcome by her mother and a nice warm fire, sandwiches, tea and cakes. Kate's mother was totally different from her daughter in appearance, being very short and plump and with insignificant facial features. Her greying hair was permed into that characterless style of crinkly curls so often worn by middle aged women. However she was a very comfortable person who soon made Sylvia feel at ease.

Outside it was still snowing and, when they looked out of the window, the blaze from the lamp light in the lane etched the edges of the whirling snowflakes which were driven sideways by a capricious wind. They turned back to the fire side and chattered together, their talk drifting to matters not personal to themselves. They already knew a little about each other's childhoods and how they had both been deprived of a father because of the War.

The next morning it was still snowing gently, covering the already snow heaped bushes with a new layer of glittering white. By late morning it had stopped and the snow on the ground had softened under the morning sun, only to be stiffened again later to a thin, hard crust.

"Now it's cleared up we'll catch a bus into town and look for the evening dress you want to buy", said Kate's mother.

It did not take long for the bus to reach the square of the little market town and the two girls quickly alighted from it. Kate turned round to offer a steady hand to her mother who was not too sprightly.

"We'll go to the little boutique in the market square", said Kate. "They usually have some nice things in there".

Sylvia was entranced by the display of lovely clothes and experienced feelings of envy as her friend began to try on some of the beautiful dresses. Eventually Kate chose the dress she wanted, a taffeta gown of deep magenta with a tiny waist, a very full skirt and shoulders trimmed with frills. Sylvia longed to possess a dress like that but comforted herself with the thought that she was well on the way to the possibility of earning a decent salary. Then the world would be her oyster!

The trio made their way home and they were glad to be back to the warmth of the cottage. Kate's mother prepared a supper of baked potatoes and beans, followed by tinned peaches and cream.

"I'm going out this evening to the Women's Institute so you girls will have the house to yourselves", said Kate's mother.

After they had washed up the supper dishes and tidied the kitchen, the girls went back into the sitting room.

"Would you like to try on my new dress?" asked Kate.

"Your new dress – really? I'd love to, but it will never fit me I'm sure", cried Sylvia.

Poor Mary

"Try it on and see", continued Kate. "I think it will".

Sylvia changed into the coveted dress and stood in front of the mirror. She couldn't believe the transformation. Although on the long side for her, the dress fitted her body perfectly, showing off her tiny waist and pretty shoulders. She had never felt so glamorous.

"It really suits you", said Kate. "You have such delicate shoulders, not like my broad ones, and you have such milky white skin".

"That's only because they never see the sun", said Sylvia. They would be quite brown if they did".

After pirouetting around the room for a while, Sylvia at last reluctantly took off the beautiful dress and carefully hung it up. She then donned her own mundane skirt, blouse and cardigan, and tidied her hair.

"Come and sit here", said Kate suddenly. "No, not there, here on my knee"

Sylvia thought that her friend was joking and sat down heavily on Kate's knees. Kate threw both her arms around her in order to cuddle her.

"I love you", she whispered into Sylvia's hair.

Sylvia froze. This was no joke and she did not like it. She struggled and broke free from Kate's grasp, her face bright red with embarrassment. She did not know what to say or where to put herself. For her the weekend was completely ruined. She had never heard of lesbianism but she felt instinctively that Kate's behaviour was unnatural, and it certainly offended her. The two girls somehow managed to survive the rest of the weekend together, keeping a polite reserve. Things were never the same again between them. Because she had been rejected by her, Kate felt resentful towards Sylvia, and there were occasions in the future when she incited others to conspire against her.

6. THE SUMMER TERM.

In one of her more lucid moments Mary decided that she ought to be working again.

I want to be helping our Sylvia at college", she said to Lucy. "She needs some new clothes – she's growing up you know!"

"Ye shouldn't be worrying about our Sylvia", remonstrated Lucy. "She's old enough to look after 'erself. She ought to be working now instead o' still being at school!"

Nevertheless, when the better side of Mary came to the fore, all she ever thought about was how she could give her daughter what she needed. Looking through the newspaper advertisements she found several job vacancies, all with living accommodation. On of them was in a children's home on the outskirts of Leeds and this job appealed to her.

Two weeks later Sylvia received a letter from Mary, now in Leeds, and she was overjoyed that her mother was working again.

"Perhaps she really is properly better this time. I do hope so!" said Sylvia to her friend as she put her mother's letter away.

During the Easter holidays Sylvia went to her grandparents who were obviously very relieved to be rid of Mary. Mary had written to tell Sylvia to visit her in Leeds and then they could go shopping in the city for some new clothes. Sylvia was thrilled and she felt very light hearted and excited as she made the bus journey to Leeds. When she eventually found the children's home where her mother now worked, she walked briskly up the long driveway and thought what a pleasant environment it was compared to the mental hospital in which Mary had been an inmate only a few months ago. Mary greeted her daughter affectionately and then showed her the comfortable little bedroom which she had been given. Then she took her to peep at the enormous dining room which still retained the character of the once stately home.

"I have to dust all those chairs. The other youngsters who work here just don't know how to clean! They miss all the rungs and spindles – but I do it properly!" said Mary proudly.

"It's very nice here", commented Sylvia. "It's a beautiful building and such lovely grounds! You should be really happy in a place like this!"

Mary stiffened. "It's all right", she said, then lowering her voice to a whisper – "but they get in ye know!"

"What? Who gets in? What do you mean!" said Sylvia.

"THEY do! THEY come in and muck everything up and dirty my room. The other day they stole my purse!"

Sylvia's spirit suddenly drooped. "Oh dear!" she thought. "She's no different at all. I wonder how long this job will last!"

Mother and daughter took a bus into the centre of Leeds and went into Lewis's, the department store which Mary had often used in her youth when seeking out the latest fashion.

"I'll buy a nice summer dress for you", said Mary. "Maybe two, I've enough money!"

After a session of trying on and deliberating, Sylvia eventually chose a dress of pretty white cotton print bearing a design of small pink roses. Mary pressed her to have another dress so she chose one of a more modern design in shades of green on a white background.

"Look at those little jackets!" exclaimed Mary. "One of those would be useful for you on chilly days. It'd be smarter than a cardigan for you".

Sylvia could not believe her good fortune and she chose a camel coloured jacket which would go with most of her clothes. Mary bought one for herself in her favourite shade of Princess Marina green. The colour still suited her in spite of her greying hair.

"Thanks very much Mother", said Sylvia. "I'm well set up now for the summer term!"

They made their way back to the bus station, each planning to catch a different bus, Mary going back to the children's home and Sylvia back to her grandparents. Before they parted company Sylvia asked her mother if she would be able to visit her at college. She was longing to show off the place to her mother. No other member of the family had visited Sylvia there and she envied the other girls their weekend family visitors.

Mary agreed to visit her at the beginning of the summer term, and this she did. Sylvia met her at the train station in the city centre. She took great pride in showing her mother the lovely old city with its great cathedral which looked as though it were growing out of the ground, its massive towers reaching up to the sky. They climbed together up the very steep hill at the top of which was situated the college.

Sylvia Hoole

"Is your leg hurting Sylvia? Yer limping a bit", commented Mary.

"It always hurts when I walk up this steep hill", said Sylvia. "I don't know why. It must be growing pains or something!"

Once at the top of the hill they wondered down the road to the college. Mary enjoyed looking round and told her daughter that she was proud of her being there. Much to Sylvia's relief, her mother behaved quite normally when she introduced her to some of her friends, and so the day ended without incident. Mary weepily said her goodbyes at the train station and her daughter returned to her studies.

A few weeks later, Sylvia learned from her grandmother that Mary was now living once more with them. She had been given the sack from her work at the children's home due to unreasonable behaviour, causing constant irritation and annoyance to other workers who had threatened to leave their jobs because of this. Sylvia felt very depressed again when she read her grandmother's letter. Was there ever going to be a normal future for her mother? Perhaps when she, Sylvia, was working she would be able to provide a nice home for both of them and then Mary might settle down and behave normally! Perhaps the problem was that Mary did not have anywhere to call her own!

"I'm sure she'll be all right when we get our own home", mused Sylvia as she put her grandmother's letter away. "In the meantime I cannot afford to keep

Poor Mary

getting depressed about things. I must continue to work as hard as I can and pass those exams – then, and only then, can I do something with my life!"

The latter half of the summer term brought three weeks of Teaching Practice for the First Year students. They had completed two weeks before Christmas but that seemed ages ago, and now they were all feeling nervous and on edge. If they did not make the grade this time then it was possible that they would be asked to leave the college.

"What a waste of a year that would be", said Jane as she brushed her short fair hair before going down to breakfast. "Still, we've come this far and, if you remember, a couple of students were asked to leave at the end of the first Teaching Practice, so we can't be too bad – can we?"

"We must make sure that we are really well prepared", said Barbara, cleaning her spectacles. "That's half the battle I think, but it will certainly mean some long hours of work, making all those work cards and writing up our lesson notes in our School Practice files. We'll be burning the candle at both ends, that's for sure!"

Jane, Barbara and Kate had all been placed in local schools in the city, so their day was going to be fairly reasonable as far as travelling was concerned. Sylvia had been placed in a large school which was situated about thirty miles away. This would make a very long day for the students placed there as they were to be taken by coach very early in the morning and brought back each evening, not arriving at college until nearly supper time at six o'clock. These students therefore lost a good two hours of preparation time which had to be made up by working later into the night. This would be far more tiring for them and tempers were to become frayed.

Sylvia had experienced a successful Teaching Practice during the previous October, but nevertheless, like the others she did feel nervous. They all found the journey extremely boring and tiring, particularly at the end of the day. At the beginning of the second week, Sylvia alighted from the coach which had stopped at the hostel for her. She wearily mounted the stairs and made her way to the Top Four bedroom. Her arms were laden with books to be marked and card for making innumerable work cards, and she struggled to open the bedroom door.

She could not believe her eyes when she entered the room. Her bed had been turned upside down and every single book and item from her book case had been tumbled all over it.

"Oh no!" she cried in tired despair. "Who has done this?"

Kate began to titter whilst the other girls pretended not to notice, their heads kept down to their books.

"It's all right for you lot", Sylvia grumbled. "You've all been back a good hour and a half ago and have more time than I have. I can't do with all this!"

Not one of the girls offered to help to restore her possessions to rights and she wearily began to pick them up and put them away. They watched her struggle with the bed as she eventually managed to turn it the right way up. There was a malicious gleam in Kate's eyes which Sylvia did not fail to notice.

The next two nights offered Sylvia the same treatment. How was it that she had engendered such animosity? Could it be her manner towards them, though she had not knowingly offended Jane or Barbara? She came to the conclusion that Kate was behind the irritating prank as she had not ceased to be resentful towards Sylvia since the rejection of her advances on their weekend together.

"The best thing is not to react", stated a fellow student in whom she had confided. "They'll soon get tired of doing it if they don't have the fun of seeing you lose your rag!"

"It's hard not to when you're tired at the end of the day and there's still work to be done – but you are right, I must try to ignore it", said Sylvia.

The next few nights, knowing what to expect, Sylvia took it as a matter of routine to quietly put everything back in its place. She made no fuss nor did she make any comment, thus the prank lost its novelty and was discontinued.

The Teaching Practice was successful and all the students were informed that they had done well enough to return to college for their second year. Sylvia resolved that in her second year she wanted her own bedroom and she asked to be considered for a room in the new modern block within the college grounds. She was delighted to be offered a room opposite her old school friend, Margaret, and looked forward to having a room of her own for the first time in her life.

7. SEASIDE IN WINTER

After a long working summer holiday, Sylvia returned to college for her final year. She was excited to be back and revelled in the luxury of her own room, resolving to keep it neat and tidy at all times, which she did. There was a comfortable modern bed with a spring interior mattress, a built in wardrobe complete with drawers and ample hanging space, a desk and chair, and in the corner of the room was a wash basin. Sylvia was able to keep her trunk in one corner of the room and she covered it with the Indian tiger rug which had once been her mother's. She thought it looked very attractive as well as being a useful place on which to sit.

There was much work to be done and the students would often burn the midnight oil trying to finish essays in time to meet deadlines, or researching in order to begin work on a thesis. Somehow, albeit with many moans and groans, they managed to complete their assignments. Occasionally they would walk into the city in order to do some shopping. At these times Sylvia struggled back up the steep hill from the city, the pain in her right leg now being most severe. It never entered her head to have the problem investigated. She just put up with it, finding it also troublesome in other physical activities such as tennis or netball.

Sylvia did not have much money to spend on shopping expeditions, and could only buy the bare necessities. The cost of her board and lodging and tuition fees were paid for by the Education Authority. On top of that she was granted an annual allowance of £60, therefore she limited herself strictly to spend no more than £1 each week, and if she could help it she wouldn't even spend that amount. By being so frugal she managed to save up a little each term for those few extras, or an occasional visit to the cinema. As she had never been used to having much money at her disposal, she did not find it as hard as some girls to make ends meet.

Final Teaching Practice was looming ahead and due to take place in January for a period of four weeks. Sylvia was placed in a secondary school in the sea side town of Cleethorpes on the east coast, together with three other students. This time the girls were accommodated in a nearby boarding house and so they did not have a long daily journey to their schools. The boarding house was situated on the sea front and Sylvia's room overlooked the sea, or to be more accurate the Estuary of the River Humber. It seemed strange being at the seaside in the middle of winter. Having unpacked her belongings, Sylvia looked out of the window at the view. The light was already fading, dark clouds dropping towards the sea, and rain drifted across the Humber Estuary. The sound of a gong ringing below suggested that a meal must be ready for them.

The dining room and lounge of the little guest house were typical of seaside accommodation. Everywhere one looked could be seen cheap, brash ornaments, some of brass, some of gaudy colours and crude design, and of course the inevitable shells of all shapes and sizes.

"How tasteless!" whispered Dawn, a fellow student.

"Well at least it's cheap and cheerful", replied Sylvia, also in a whisper. "It could be worse! It's clean and warm, and the landlord is quite friendly. Anything is better than a long and drawn out journey everyday anyway!"

The meal which was delivered to them that evening was an example of what they were to experience for the rest of the month, roast meat, three vegetables and lashings of gravy followed by a stodgy pudding with hot custard.

"We're going to put on weight with all this stodgy food", muttered the dark haired Barbara who was a petite girl without a trace of fat.

"Well, we've quite a distance to walk to school each day so we should get rid of some of the calories", said the tall and willowy Dawn.

Staying in the guest house was in itself an exciting experience for Sylvia. She loved the smell of the sea and the freshness of the air – and it was very fresh in January! To be awakened by the cry of the sea gulls gave her a comfortable feeling of security, it somehow felt so homely. The landlord, a short little man of middle age who always wore a white apron, had a great deal to say for himself in his attempt to impress his young female guests. He would fill the girls' ears with gruesome stories of what happened to people if a sea fret, or mist, came down suddenly should they happen to be walking along the sands.

"You start walking in circles", he said, "and you usually end up walkin' towards the sea instead of away from it. Before you know where you are, the water's all around you an' you get drowned!"

Listening to him, the students thought that he was probably highly exaggerating, but in fact what he said

Poor Mary

was true. A tragic incident of this nature took place a short while later. A riding school was nearby and the instructor used to take his group of young riders out along the sands where they had freedom and space to canter with their ponies. One Saturday morning a group of little girls, aged from seven to eight years old, were taken out for a canter along the beach. One little girl who should have been with the group was absent. She had been naughty at home that morning and, as a punishment, she was not allowed to go riding. For her this punishment was a blessing in disguise.

The five other little girls were chattering happily as they trotted their ponies along the sands, following their instructor. They were a good distance away from the promenade as the tide was out, so they could keep well clear of any walkers and their dogs. Without any warning the group of riders found themselves enveloped in a thick sea fret and the visibility was just about non existent.

"Keep close to me", shouted the instructor. "Don't anyone stray away from the group!"

The group of ponies and their riders trotted along the sand in a gingerly manner. The instructor tried to estimate the right direction back to the jetty but, before he knew it, the ponies were floundering in the sea. Naturally thinking that they should turn about, they did so, only to find that they were surrounded by water which was getting deeper by the second. The sea has a habit of creeping up behind and cutting off one's escape, which is precisely what happened on this day. All were trapped, and if their cries for help could have been heard from the shore, no one could possibly have seen where the noise was coming from. Once the tide has fully turned then it quickly flows in deeply, added to which there are very strong and dangerous currents in the Humber Estuary which are capable of sweeping even the best of swimmers out to the North Sea. Sadly all the children, the instructor and all the horses were drowned, and their bodies were eventually washed up on the shore some miles down the coast.

Sylvia had done a great deal of preparation work for her Final Teaching Practice, and she knew exactly what she wanted to do with the class of fourteen year old girls she was to teach. On the third morning she arrived at the school and was told that the class teacher was very ill with pneumonia and would not be back for the rest of the month. Sylvia gulped at the thought of having total responsibility for this Third Year class. Some of its members were taller, and far worldlier than she. They were daughters of local fishermen, dockers and factory workers, and what they did not know about life was not worth knowing!

The month at the school convinced Sylvia that she really did enjoy teaching for she soon acquired the trick of discipline and she taught well. There were incidents, some funny, others not so funny, which stuck in her mind as the lives of these young people, brushed hers. One lunch time she was sitting at the head of the dining table whilst supervising a group of fourteen year old girls.

Poor Mary

"I'm goin' to get 'er after school!" said one of the girls.

"What for?" asked her friend.

"She's not goin' to call my mother a prostitute. I'll get 'er after school!"

Sylvia did not pay too much attention to the conversation, thinking it all bravado. However, at the end of the school day, when most of the pupils had dispersed, there was a great commotion of shouting and screaming going on coming from the pavement outside the school gates. Indeed the young 'lady' who had threatened to 'get 'er after school' had done precisely that! She was sitting astride on top of her victim, who had called her mother a prostitute and had hold of her hair and was banging her head on the pavement. It is a wonder that a murder was not committed, and perhaps would have been but for the intervention of the young needlework teacher, Miss Walker. On hearing the confusion outside, she had quickly weighed up the situation and suddenly appeared with a bucket of ice cold water. This she threw over the fighting girls. The girls picked themselves up, drenched to the skin, gave Miss Walker a mouthful of abuse, and walked off arm in arm!

A few days later, Miss Walker was giving a needlework lesson to some younger children.

"Jean", she called to one of the brighter children in the class. "Please would you go and fetch me the pin tin from the cupboard?"

Jean, a pale dark haired girl with plaited hair, obediently went to the cupboard, rummaged around for a minute and returned empty handed.

"Tint in Miss", said Jean.

"I beg your pardon!" said Miss Walker.

"Pin tin, tint in", said Jean again.

"Oh! You mean that the pin tin isn't in the cupboard. I really do wish that you girls would learn to speak your English language correctly!"

"What Miss?" said Jean.

"Never mind!" Miss Walker sighed.

And so the month of January passed and the Final Teaching Practice was nearly over. On the last day but one Sylvia was sitting in the staff room after lunch, marking some books. The Headmistress entered the room and seeing Sylvia she came and sat beside her.

"Where are you going to apply for a teaching post Miss Copley?" said the Head.

"I don't really know", replied Sylvia. "I hadn't thought that far ahead yet".

"Well you'll soon have to start applying for a teaching post", continued the Head. "There will be a post available here in September, and I would like you to apply for it".

Sylvia felt very flattered that out of the four students placed at the school she was the one to be singled out and asked to go back there and teach. She was very surprised, as the other three girls seemed to be so much more confident than she was. However, she was extremely conscientious and meticulous in all that she did, and it showed in all of her work. Sylvia went back to college and more or less forgot about the Head's invitation, her mind now turning to concentration on the forthcoming Final Examinations.

Poor Mary

One morning at the beginning of her last term at college, a letter arrived for Sylvia. On opening it she discovered that it was from the Head of the school where she had done her final teaching practice. She was asked yet again if she would consider applying for the teaching post at the school for September.

"Well!" thought Sylvia, "I could apply anywhere in the country, but here is a place where someone really wants me. I did like that school, and all the staff, so I might as well apply for the post".

Having applied for the post, Sylvia had to travel to Grimsby by train, and then take a bus to the area on the outskirts of Cleethorpes where the school was situated. She was to be interviewed by the governors of the school, and of course the Headmistress. Sitting in the waiting room was a young lady of similar age to Sylvia. She was also waiting to be interviewed. They chattered to each other nervously as they each awaited their turn.

"I'm Diedre Allen", said the young lady who was very attractive and beautiful dressed. She reminded Sylvia of a piece of Dresden china, so clear and perfect was her skin, and so immaculate her hair with not a curl out of place. She made Sylvia feel quite shabby and mundane.

"I used to go to this school myself as a girl", continued Diedre. "so I've known the Head for a long time".

"I don't stand much chance against that sort of competition", thought Sylvia. "She's bound to get the job!"

As it turned out, both of the girls were offered a post at the school, Diedre for the teaching of Art, and Sylvia for the teaching of General Subjects throughout the school. This suited Sylvia down to the ground as she did not particularly enjoy the teaching of Art although she was good at it herself. All that remained now were the Final Examinations and, eventually having passed those, Sylvia's dreams were realised, her future assured!

PART 6

1. RICHARD

1992 School had been finished since half past three. Sylvia had just seen a pair of over anxious parents and managed to convince them that their son was in fact performing better than they had thought. She accompanied them to the front door, shook hands with them and told them not to worry so much.

"Now they are gone I'll just go and dust those two bookshelves in the computer room. The cleaning lady never seems to think that book shelves need to be dusted. Her eyes don't look any higher than the carpet, I'm sure!"

Taking a duster from the bottom drawer of her desk – she always hid one there otherwise it would disappear – she went into the computer room and began to tidy the offending shelves. On the top shelf were a few personal items, remnants from the days when she and Richard had lived in the flat at the top of the school.

"I really ought to take these things home before they become swallowed up into oblivion!"

She picked up a tiny box of hand painted wood which had once belonged to her great grandmother. She lifted the lid and inside the box was a tiny black cat, the good luck mascot from her own childhood days, and a wedding ring. The wedding ring had belonged to her mother – the ring which Lewis had given to Mary in their pretence of a marriage.

"The black cat didn't bring her much luck", thought Sylvia, "and as for the wedding ring - !" She had a mental image of her mother wrenching off the ring in a frenzy of anger and madness, and remembered how frightened she had felt. The ring had been in that little box for all those years – Mary's last link with Lewis, and a reluctance to sever him completely from her life. Sylvia looked at the rings on her own left hand, an engagement ring, a wedding ring and an eternity ring. She thought how lucky she had been compared to her mother and she began to remember her first meeting with Richard.

1956 Sylvia had completed her very first week of teaching and was on her way back to her digs which she shared with two other young lady teachers. She still had not become used to being referred to as a lady teacher, but it was very satisfying. The digs which she shared with the other teachers, both older than she, were extremely comfortable, and the landlady was a kindly person. They each had their own bedroom and were also provided with a sitting room which was separate from the household.

"Reserved for my lady teachers!" the landlady would say.

She was an excellent cook and Sylvia looked forward to her meals. It was an ideal situation, being well looked after and without the worries of any chores to do. It meant that Sylvia could devote all her spare time making sure that she was well prepared for school.

Poor Mary

"Well, I've survived my first week of teaching", Sylvia thought, "in spite of the problems at the beginning of the week". Her grandmother had been extremely annoyed that Sylvia should even dream of leaving her household – now that she was going to be earning good money!

"All we've done for you, an' now yer leavin' us," she complained. She had had visions of reaping the benefits of Sylvia's good salary!

When Sylvia arrived at the school on her first day, she went to see the Headmistress to ask about her class, and the subjects which she would be teaching.

"But my dear, I sent all those details to you at the end of July together with all the schemes of work. Surely you have come prepared!"

What could Sylvia say? She knew that she had not received these things and could only surmise that her grandmother had once again intercepted her mail and kept it from her – as a ploy to prevent her from leaving. She could hardly say that though – it sounded too far fetched to be believed and it would have seemed like a pathetic excuse for being unprepared. Sylvia felt mortified but could only apologise for being unprepared and mumble that it must have been lost in the post. It had been a struggle for her each evening to do the extra work involved in preparing her schemes, but somehow she had managed to keep her head above water and now she had the weekend to really catch up on herself.

She rose early on Saturday morning as the pale first light framed the window of her bedroom. After breakfast the sun was dazzling, the sky was clear, and she thought that she would go for a walk along the promenade to freshen herself up before settling down to more work. She felt lucky that she had acquired lodgings so near to the sea and determined to take full advantage of it. This autumn day was a day of wind, sending little squalls across the rock pools and spinning the leaves of the promenade trees. The air was chill without being cold and Sylvia walked briskly, occasionally stopping to look out to sea and observe the fishing trawlers, and to gaze at the wheeling gulls as they swooped down hoping for bread. This week she felt as free as they were and revelled in it, but her new found freedom was to be short lived!

"As soon as I can I will bring Mother here", she thought. "She will love it by the sea and it's bound to do her the world of good. It will be a new start for her too and perhaps that is all she needs".

Two young ladies who had been fellow students also lived in this little sea side town. They were Mollie and Angela and, although they had not been particular friends of Sylvia when at college, it was nice to feel that someone she knew lived close by. That morning Sylvia bumped into Mollie as she was making her way home by the main street and the shops.

"Hi Sylvia!" called Mollie from the other side of the road. Coming across to talk to her she asked Sylvia if she had settled down in her digs.

"Everything's fine", said Sylvia. "I've got some good accommodation, really comfortable, and I'm enjoying the work at school".

"Would you like to come with me to a dance tonight?" asked Mollie who was quite an attractive

Poor Mary

dark haired girl, although short and a little on the plump side.

"Oh I don't think so. I need to wash my hair, and I've tons of work to do", replied Sylvia.

"Oh come on, it'll do you good. I won't take no for an answer", insisted Mollie. "I'll call for you at half past seven".

"There's nothing to stop me from enjoying myself a bit now", thought Sylvia as she went on her way. "I've achieved what I set out to do so perhaps I'm entitled to a bit of fun now and again".

Early that evening she washed her hair. Like her mother's, it was naturally wavy and as she wore it quite short it didn't take long to dry. She looked in her wardrobe and took out one of the dresses which her mother had bought for her in Leeds. "I will have to buy myself some warmer clothes when I receive my first pay cheque", she thought. Glancing at herself in the mirror she scowled at her reflection. "Oh well, it will have to do. It will only be a Saturday night hop – nothing special!"

At seven thirty Mollie came to fetch her and together they went up to the local dance hall which was much bigger than Sylvia had envisaged. Angela was also there with a group of friends and Sylvia was drawn into the circle. She felt a little nervous and did not quite know what to do, not being used to this kind of social life. The strains of the music began and couples paired off to dance an old fashioned waltz. As there were a few girls left chattering, Sylvia joined in with them, at the same time watching the dancing with interest.

After several dances, and a lull in the conversation, Sylvia was watching the band when she became aware that a young man was staring at her intently. She had no idea why she smiled at him but she did and, because she did, the young man plucked up the courage to go to her and ask if she would like to dance. They moved into the crowd of dancers, the glitter ball on the ceiling bathing everyone in a blue light.

"I'm Richard", said the young man, and his merry blue eyes twinkled at her as he led her into a modern waltz.

"I'm Sylvia", she introduced herself, "and I'm not very good at dancing. I haven't had much practice!"

Richard was a very good dancer and somehow she managed to follow his lead, albeit with an occasional stumble followed by her apologies. Richard was an intelligent and compassionate young man and from the first moment he pleased her with his meditative blue eyes and lean, sensitive face. She felt comfortable with him and between snatches of conversation they were able to dance in companionable silence. He stayed with her for the rest of the evening and then asked if he could take her home.

"Would you like to go out for a drive tomorrow?" he asked before leaving her at the door of her lodgings, and she gladly assented. Richard was almost at the end of his two years of National Service in the Royal Air Force and this was his weekend leave. He was stationed in Northern Ireland and the following evening he would be travelling back there.

On Sunday afternoon Richard collected Sylvia and took her for a drive into the Lincolnshire countryside.

Poor Mary

Having discovered the previous evening that Sylvia had an interest in Art, he produced an old and battered paint box containing numerous tubes of water colours and a couple of sable hair paint brushes.

"They were mine when I was younger", said Richard. "I would like you to have them".

Sylvia was touched, as the box of paints was obviously one of his childhood treasures and he was giving it to her. She felt the necessity to be absolutely frank with him and told him everything about her background and her mother's mental illness. She wanted him to know everything so that there were no secrets between them. He in turn told her that he was one of three brothers, one of them married and the other engaged to be married. He told her where he lived and that on his next leave, if she still wanted to go out with him, he would take her home to visit his parents. Sadly the afternoon passed all too quickly, and after having afternoon tea in a little restaurant by the by sea, Richard had to take her back to her lodgings and then make haste to catch a train for the first part of his journey back to Northern Ireland. They each promised to write and Sylvia told Richard that she would look forward to his next leave in one month's time. Her heart was singing as she went to bed that night, and she went to sleep dreaming of Richard and their next meeting.

Sure enough, letters were frequently exchanged between them and they each sent the other a photograph. Sylvia kept the one of Richard in her handbag so that she could take it out and look at it whenever she wanted.

2. MARY BY THE SEA

In the meantime Sylvia had to do something about her mother. She had eagerly written to tell her about Richard but Mary had made no comments in her replies to her letters. One Sunday afternoon, Sylvia met up with Angela whose mother ran a small guest house on the sea front. Angela was a jolly girl with flaming red hair and a temper to match. The two girls decided to go for a walk on the sands being as the tide was out.

"By the way Sylvia", said Angela, "you know you wanted some accommodation for your mother?"

"Yes, what about it?" asked Sylvia.

"Well my granddad died a few months ago, and my grandma is very lonely. She hates being alone in the house and she would like someone to share it with her for company".

"That sounds ideal", said Sylvia excitedly.

"Well come and meet my grandma and see the rooms she has to offer, then you can decide", said Angela.

Sylvia went along to meet the elderly lady and everything seemed perfect. She thought it would be an ideal solution for her mother for the time being. She agreed the rent for her mother to pay and then went off eagerly to write to Mary with the good news. Mary was only too glad to be able to join her beloved daughter and so a time was arranged for her journey and Sylvia went to meet her train.

The train steamed into the platform at the station. Sylvia scanned the crowds anxiously for a glimpse of her mother. Suddenly she espied her, clad in her best

Poor Mary

suit and hat and carrying a heavy suitcase. Sylvia ran towards her, kissed her and took the case from her. Mary looked at her daughter through her pale hazel eyes which were mutely accusing.

"You're not my daughter any more!" she said.

"What do you mean Mother?" asked Sylvia, feeling somewhat flattened by her mother's greeting.

"You know what I mean – now you've got a boy friend!"

"Oh dear!" thought Sylvia. "Things aren't going to be easy. She resents the fact that I've got a boy friend, and she's obviously imagining the worst!"

They made their way to Mary's new home in an awkward silence. When they arrived, Sylvia introduced her mother to Mrs. Mason, Angela's grandmother, who showed Mary to her two rooms, one bedroom and a sitting room.

"I hope you like it Mother", said Sylvia.

"It's all right", replied Mary grumpily. "It could be better. It will have to do!"

Sylvia at last had to leave her mother and go back to her own place. Once more she felt as though she bore the whole world on her shoulders, and her old anxieties came to the fore.

The following day, being a Sunday, Sylvia went to collect her mother to take her for a walk along the sea front. Surely when she saw the sea, the gulls, and felt the fresh sea breeze on her face, then Mary would be happy and put the past behind her, and feel that she could make a fresh start in her life. Mary's face was like a thunder cloud as they walked along the promenade. She found fault with everything. She didn't like her room, she said it was dirty, and the old lady was a thief who would steal all her money. Mary's mutterings grew to an angry shouting, and torrents of abuse poured from her lips at the amazed passers by.

"For God's sake shut up Mother!" cried Sylvia who wished that the ground would open and swallow her up. "I'm not going to be seen walking with you if you're going to carry on like this!"

Mary's voice turned to a whine. "I only love you luv. You're all I've got!"

"Well in that case behave yourself or I'll leave you alone", said Sylvia, now beside herself with despair. She had never felt more helpless and she was now worried about the possible reaction of Angela's grandmother if Mary continued in this manner. She took her back to the house, imploring her to behave herself.

"Next weekend Richard will be coming home on leave. I will bring him to see you and then you can judge for yourself what a nice young man he is", said Sylvia before she finally parted from her mother.

When her daughter had gone, Mary went up to her bedroom and locked the door behind her. From all corners of the room, whirling shadows and crouching beasts were coming closed and closer until they fell upon her, and she was swallowed up in blackness.

The troubled elderly lady downstairs heard Mary's rants and ravings, and she was afraid!

3. INTRODUCTIONS

Sylvia could not wait for the following weekend and the prospect of meeting Richard again. Likewise he too was eager for the renewal of their friendship. When he came home he was allowed the use of his father's car so travelling around was no problem. He made a phone call to Sylvia and asked her to be ready on Saturday morning and he would take her into the town to look at the shops, and then they would have lunch together. After window shopping they went into a fish restaurant and had a typical seaside menu of fish, chips, peas, bread and butter and a pot of tea. It was absolutely delicious, for no fish tastes better than that which is fresh from the sea that morning.

"I told my mother that I'd take you to see her this afternoon", said Sylvia nervously.

"Fine", said Richard. "We'll go straight away from here if you want!"

"I must warn you", continued Sylvia, "that my mother can be very strange and she might say some peculiar things".

They arrived at the little terrace house and Sylvia knocked at the front door. It was opened by Angela's grandmother who gave Sylvia a very strange look.

"She's in her sitting room", she said. "You'd better go through".

Sylvia, followed by Richard, went down the dark corridor to Mary's room. Opening the door, they entered the room. Sylvia could not believe what she saw! Her mother, wearing her best clothes and make up for the occasion, was sitting in the corner of the room in an arm chair. On her head she was wearing – a LAMP SHADE – and on her face, an inane grin!

For the second time that week Sylvia wished that the ground would open and swallow her up, she was so embarrassed. The story told years later sounded amusing and made people laugh. At the time for Sylvia it seemed a disaster, having to introduce her very first boy friend to this strange being who happened also to be her mother!

Richard, as said before, was a compassionate person. He went forward with inherent courtesy to greet Mary as though it were quite normal to wear a lamp shade on one's head! If Mary had thought to put him off her daughter her trick did not succeed. He nodded pleasantly and, standing with his back to the fire, he began to chat about the weather.

"Would ye like a cup o' tea luv?" Mary said at length, suddenly defeated by the attitude of this upright young man. He was obviously someone that she was not going to get the better of, and for this she bore him a grudging respect.

"Have plenty o' sugar luv. It gives you energy", said Mary, ladling into his three heaped teaspoonfuls.

"Yuck!" thought Richard as he drank the milky, overly sweet tea politely. "The lamp shade I can tolerate, but this tea is more than disgusting!"

After they had taken their leave of Mary, Sylvia was surprised when Richard asked to see her again the next day. She had convinced herself that he would not want anything more to do with her after meeting her dotty mother.

"I'll take you home to my house tomorrow", he said, "but I warn you, it's not very clean!"

The house was large, detached, and stood well back from the narrow lane and was situated in acres of its own grounds. The building was neglected and shabby in appearance, and so was the garden which was running riot with a mixture of flowers and weeds – although the lawns had been recently cut. Alongside was a big orchard, its trees still bearing many apples waiting to be picked. There were numerous sheds and out houses and at the far end of the garden stood a chicken run where a few hens were scratching at the soil and clucking contentedly. At the rear of the house was a vegetable patch of a good size, and potatoes, runner beans and rows of cabbages were growing there.

Richard opened the front door and they entered a large hallway where what once had been an elegant staircase sweeping up to the first landing. Looking up to the lofty ceilings one could see cobwebs swinging, and dust balls shifting lazily in the draught. Richard's parents were seated in a room which was crowded with furniture from the Victorian era. They were both elderly and were dozing by a fire made from wood collected from their garden.

Mrs. Sanderson was something of a recluse and never left the house except for weddings, christenings, funerals and to vote! She thought that housework was a complete waste of time, and occupied her days by gardening, cooking, looking after the hens, playing the piano for hours on end, or dozing by the fire. She never washed a pot until it was absolutely necessary because there were none left in the cupboard, and then often they would be quickly rinsed under the tap. Mr. Sanderson was a little older than his wife. He had been retired from building since he was forty five, and now he and his wife lived off the rents which their numerous properties produced. He spent a great deal of his time in his workshops where he mended watches and bicycles, and sometimes he made musical instruments.

Mr. and Mrs. Sanderson made Sylvia feel very welcome, though they did not make a big fuss as it was not in their nature to do so. They were not out to impress anyone. One had to take them as they were or not at all! Later Richard apologised for the state of the house.

"Mother never did care for housework", he said, "and now she's getting older even less so. I cut the lawns whenever I can but of course I'm not here most of the time. My National Service finishes at Christmas but I really do want to get away from this place after that".

"Where will you go?" asked Sylvia.

"I don't know – probably to the south of England, near to London, if I can get work down there".

Sylvia's heart sank. Was she going to lose this person so soon? She had already grown attached to him and longed to be with him at all times.

"My brother James and his wife, Liz, live down there", said Richard pointing to the bottom of the garden where a tiny gate led through to an adjoining garden. "We'll go and see them. Come on!"

They walked down to the bottom of the garden, through the tiny gate, and entered a very well cared for estate. They passed some stables on the left and an enormous greenhouse on the right. Then they came to the house of James and Liz. Again it was a very large detached house with well kept lawns and flower gardens, and it was set well back from the main road. On the front lawn was set up a tennis net, and James and Liz were having a game. They stopped playing when they saw Richard and Sylvia, dropping their rackets down on the grass, and came over to greet them.

"I'll make some coffee", said Liz after the introductions. "Come inside and sit down".

All too soon the weekend came to an end and Richard had to go back to Ireland. Sylvia went to the train station with him and he kissed her tenderly before boarding the train, promising to write to her. He hung his head out of the window until she was out of sight. Sylvia's feelings were mixed as she made her way back to her lodgings. She felt elated that Richard seemed to care for her as much as she did for him. She felt desolate now that he had gone, and worried that she might lose him if he went to work in the south of England.

4. LIVING WITH MARY

Having finished school for the day, Sylvia had just arrived at the gate of the house which was her home for the moment. She heard a shout and, looking up, she saw Angela, her bright red hair flying in the wind as she ran along the road towards her.

Hi! Sylvia!" shouted Angela, breathless with running. "I was hoping I'd catch you". She stood panting for a while until she regained her breath. "My mum would like a word with you. Can you come up to my house at about seven o'clock?"

"O.K.!" said Sylvia. "I'll be there as soon as I can. See you later!" Puzzled, she went into the house and straight upstairs to freshen up before supper.

The evening meal was particularly good that night and Sylvia thought how lucky she was to have such comfortable accommodation and such a kind land lady. She really did enjoy living there and, once she had paid her weekly rent, she was fed and watered and kept warm without any worries about having to pay bills. As soon as she was ready after the meal, she put on her coat and set off to Angela's house. The night was cloudless and there was a north wind blowing, and therefore it was cool enough to make her glad that she had also put on a sweater underneath her coat. Arriving at Angela's house she rang the front door bell and soon found herself in front of a blazing fire and a cup of tea in her hand.

"Now Sylvia", began Mrs. Jones. "It's about your mother!"

Poor Mary

Sylvia's heart skipped a beat and she knew instinctively what was coming next.

"She doesn't seem at all well my dear", went on Mrs. Jones, "and really she should be seeing a doctor. In any event, I'm afraid she will have to leave her rooms because she is frightening my mother who is getting very frail now. She can't cope with your mother's strange behaviour. I'm really very sorry my dear, but you do understand don't you?"

"Yes, I'm sorry", replied Sylvia in a small voice. "How long will you give me to find somewhere else for her?"

"Well, at the latest by the end of this month", said Mrs. Jones.

"That gives me just three weeks", thought Sylvia despondently.

The following weekend Richard wangled an extra leave so that he could see Sylvia. She told him of the further problems with her mother.

"The best thing for you to do", he said, "is to look for a flat for both of you, then she won't be affecting anyone else".

"I never thought of that", replied Sylvia. "I didn't feel ready to take on anything like that just yet, but I suppose you're right, it would solve the problem".

The following week Sylvia scanned the newspapers each evening for furnished flats to let. At last she saw one advertised and it was not too far away from school, so she went to have a look at it. It was a very small flat, if indeed it could be called a flat. It was situated on the first floor of an old terrace house and afforded one bed sitting room, one small kitchen and a W.C. – that was all! The rent was just about all that she could afford at the moment. Had she not been in such a hurry, and had she had more experience and maturity, she would have turned it down and looked for something better. But there it was – she took it for better or worse!

Mary was overjoyed at the prospect of being able to live with her daughter again, and in their very own flat. Sylvia felt depressed at having to leave the comfort of her lodgings where she had her own bedroom. Now, not only would she be sharing a room, but the same bed settee with her mother! No doubt she was going to be kept awake every night again by her mother talking to herself all night long.

"It's a pity there is no bathroom", sighed Sylvia.

"Never mind!" said Mary. "You 'ave to wash as far as possible one way and as far as possible the other!"

Having spent all her life in other people's homes, Sylvia had never been allowed to have any pets. Now that she and Mary had their own place, such as it was, when Sylvia saw an advertisement saying 'Puppies for Sale', without any real thought she rushed to buy one! It was a sweet little dog, black with a bushy, pale brown curly tail. Its mother was a Pomeranian bitch who had escaped one day. Her puppies resembled her with their long silky fur, pointed muzzles and pricked ears.

Poor Mary

"She will be company for you Mother, when I am at work", said Sylvia. "You will be able to take her for walks and that will give you some fresh air and exercise. It will do you good to get out more".

"What shall we call her?" said Mary.

"Well, she's small and has very pointed ears. Let's call her Pixie", suggested Sylvia.

Mary doted on the little dog and was paranoid about its safety, quite convinced that 'They' would hurt Pixie if she wasn't watched every second. A few weeks later a kitten was added to the family, a pretty tabby which they named Whiskers. The two animals got on well together, and they gave Mary something to think about other than herself. Also she did take the dog out regularly each day and this was good for her too. When Richard came home for his next leave he was not at all enthusiastic about the animals. It was not that he did not like them, for he had been brought up with animals all his life.

"This flat is just not suitable for animals Sylvia", he said firmly. "It's not fair to them. They need space and a garden!"

Sylvia looked so crestfallen that he melted towards her.

"Well never mind, you've got them now, and you're right in that they will occupy your mother which is no bad thing. But don't say I didn't warn you. Animals can be very destructive, and it's not your furniture remember!"

Sylvia Hoole

The weeks passed and Sylvia attempted to draw Mary out of herself and to encourage her to become interested in other people and events, but it was a useless exercise! Mary refused to be interested and would not make friends with anyone.

"I only love you luv!" she continued to proclaim. "I don't want anyone else, they're all dirty!"

Of course, as might have been expected, Mary bitterly resented Richard and made it quite clear that she did not like him. He took all of this in his stride and remained always courteous and helpful towards her. He was a very caring person. He even suggested that they took Mary out for a day but of course she made the day an absolute misery for them, deliberately embarrassing them in the restaurant and other public places by drawing attention to herself in some inane way.

On one occasion, Sylvia took her mother to an evening concert to listen to a famous pianist playing classical music. The hall was full of 'important' people. The ladies were dressed in furs and fancy hats, the gentlemen in evening attire. They were the sort of people who prided themselves on being 'cultured and intellectual'. The hubbub of chatter died down as the pianist entered the stage and took his bow.

"He looks just like your father!" exclaimed Mary in a loud voice. "Sh!" whispered Sylvia, squirming with embarrassment. "He's going to begin".

The pianist began to play and one could have heard a pin drop amongst the audience. Mary suddenly began to snigger. Sylvia glared at her but said nothing. Then Mary began muttering to herself and then laughing

Poor Mary

loudly and heads were turned to see what was going on. Not wishing to cause a scene, Sylvia just nudged her mother and gesticulated to her to be quiet. It was all to no avail! It seemed that Mary's soul intention was to draw attention to her self in any way that she could. In despair Sylvia said in between piano pieces, "Come on, we're leaving!" and she took her mother's arm and ushered her out of the concert hall as quickly as she could. She felt so angry and ashamed that she couldn't say anything for the rest of the evening. Mary continued to talk and laugh to herself, and there was no way that Sylvia could escape from it. She had to lay awake for most of the night, listening to her mother beside her going on and on and on and on - !"

After several disturbed nights in this manner, Sylvia was at the end of her tether. She was feeling tired at school and she was suffering from a habitual slight headache. She had been to see a doctor about her mother. In fact she had taken her mother along with her on the second occasion. Mary was crafty enough to assume an air of meekness in front of him, so what ever Sylvia said to him in private sounded highly exaggerated.

"Your mother is not doing anyone any harm", said the doctor, "and unless she is willing to be admitted to a psychiatric hospital voluntarily, then there is nothing to be done".

There was no way that Mary could be persuaded to go into hospital voluntarily.

"I'm not hospital!" she shouted. "No hospital for me! I'm Felixstowe! All I want is a little cottage in the country!"

Sylvia Hoole

Sylvia climbed into bed one Wednesday night, longing for a good night's sleep. Mary undressed for bed and then began with her incessant muttering and grumbling. Her mother's carping voice set Sylvia's teeth on edge.

"Oh for goodness sake Mother, get into bed, shut up, and go to sleep like any normal person!" Sylvia cried.

Two angry spots of colour burned Mary's cheeks. "You're tired of me - your own mother - after all I've done for you! You know you're all I've got. I only love you, but since you got mixed up with that Richard ye don't care about me. You're nothing but a little trollop now!"

That was enough for Sylvia. She threw back the bed clothes, dressed herself hastily, and fled down the stairs and out into the night. She did not want to go back to that flat and wished that she had somewhere else to go. Looking at her watch she saw that it was one o'clock in the morning. She could hardly disturb anyone at this hour anyway.

"I can't keep wandering round all night. I'll never be fit for school tomorrow. It's really cold now! It looks as though I shall have to eat humble pie and go back to the flat", she thought.

Wearily making her way back, she pushed open the gate of the small back yard and went to the flat door to open it. It was locked! Her own key was in her handbag which was in the bed sitting room, but even had she had the key it would have been no use as Mary had locked the door and left her key in the lock.

Poor Mary

"Damn!" thought Sylvia. "Damn, damn, damn! So much for all your love Mother!"

Eventually Mary came down and opened the door for her daughter, her face full of glee and malice. "That'll teach you to cheek yer own mother!" she said.

The next incident which Sylvia recalled vividly happened a short time later. Sylvia was scheduled to go on a school trip to Switzerland with a group of fourteen year old girls, two other teachers and the Headmistress. The trip was to take place in May and the Headmistress advised Sylvia to get her passport organised in good time. Sylvia obtained the necessary form from the post office and filled it in. As she was still only twenty years old, and parental consent had to be obtained until a person was twenty one in those days, the form required her mother's signature.

"Can you sign this passport form for me please?" asked Sylvia.

"No I won't", said Mary.

"What do you mean, you won't?" said Sylvia in surprise.

"I don't want to sign it, and I'm not going to. I'm not Switzerland. I'm Felixstowe!"

What an ironical situation! Here was a young professional lady in charge of senior school girls. She earned a good salary, paid rent for the flat, paid heating and lighting bills, and generally looked after her dotty mother whom the law said was responsible for her twenty year old daughter!

"Look Mother, are you going to sign this or not?" said Sylvia angrily. "You surely realise that this trip to Switzerland is part of my job?"

"Going on holiday an' leaving me isn't a job", grumbled Mary.

"Well in that case", said Sylvia, "I'm leaving this flat straight away, and I won't be coming back! You can jolly well look after yourself!"

"I'll sign it", said Mary.

"Thank you - Mother!" said Sylvia.

5. TWENTY FIRST BIRTHDAY

That Christmas Richard was finished with his National Service and came home to his parents for a while. He kept extremely busy by helping his father with the property maintenance and was also looking for work. He was still adamant that he wanted to work in the south of England. Before his National Service he had been training to be an accountant, but now he was unsettled and wanted pastures new. In the meantime he saw Sylvia regularly, and she found it a great comfort knowing that he was close by. Often when they were together she found herself dissolving into tears for no apparent reason. Probably the realisation that there was no hope for her mother's sanity being restored was taking its toll. Richard found it difficult to handle these emotions so he often became quite cross, telling her to pull herself together. Because he had no sisters, and because his mother and aunt never displayed any emotions, it made it hard for him to understand the average female mind.

What Sylvia had been dreading at last became a reality.

"I have a job", said Richard shortly after Christmas, "and I start work at the end of January".

"Oh! What is the job, and where?" asked Sylvia, dreading to hear the answer to the latter part of her question.

"I'm going to work in a Building Society office in Newbury", said Richard. "The salary is low to begin with, but the prospects are good and there is the possibility of promotion in the near future".

Knowing that he did not like to see her cry, Sylvia restrained the tears which welled up in her eyes and tried to be excited for him. She loved him and longed to be with him at all times, and now he was going. He felt the same about her, but he was ambitious to make something of his life, and have some degree of security to offer before he settled down.

"I'll write to you whenever I can", he said, "and I'll come home once a month, so we can look forward to that. I do love you!"

"I love you too", said Sylvia, "but I do wish that you didn't have to go so far away".

Richard left at the end of January and Sylvia felt wretched without him. They wrote lengthy letters to each other, both expressing their desire to be together permanently one day. March came and with it Sylvia's twenty first birthday. She had been to a round of twenty first birthday parties lately, as all her friends were coming of age.

"What can I do for my twenty first birthday?" she asked her mother. "Would you mind if I had some friends here for a little celebration?"

For once Mary was agreeable and even said that she would have a special birthday cake made at the local bakers. Sylvia invited Angela and Mollie and the two young teachers with whom she had shared her lodgings, and also Diedre from school. The flat was just not big enough for anymore people. Salmon sandwiches, birthday cake and a cup of tea for all provided a simple

Poor Mary

but enjoyable tea for all and, much to Sylvia's relief, her mother behaved reasonably well.

Richard had a present for her but he wrote to say that it was too big to post. As it happened, Sylvia was taking a group of girls to Wembley the following Friday, to watch an England versus Ireland hockey match. She wrote to Richard and suggested that he might meet her there in the car park and he agreed and said he would bring her present with him. He also said that if it were possible he would like to travel back on the coach with the school party and then they could have the weekend together.

The coach party of chattering, giggling school girls, and their two teachers, duly arrived at Wembley Stadium. As they stepped down from the coach, Sylvia's heart sank. The car park was vast and contained hundreds of coaches, and there were thousands of people milling around everywhere.

"Never in a thousand years will Richard find us in these crowds", she thought dejectedly. "The car park goes on for miles and miles. I had no idea it would be so huge".

The two teachers shepherded their charges into their allocated places and settled them into their seats.

"Do you mind if I go and look to see if there is any sign of Richard?" Sylvia asked her colleague.

"You'll be lucky in that crowd, but off you go. I'll keep an eye on the girls", said Miss Leake, the games teacher.

Sylvia had an idea. She knew that Richard would come out to Wembley by tube train from London, so she asked an official from which direction anyone would approach from the Wembley tube station. That would eliminate three possible directions. The man casually waved his hand in one direction and Sylvia began to walk that way. She did not dare venture too far in case she became lost. She kept her eyes skinned on the hordes of people pouring from that direction.

"There isn't a hope of finding him", she muttered. "It's like looking for a needle in a hay stack in these crowds."

As she said these words, she suddenly saw a familiar figure in a familiar trench coat, dejectedly walking her way, and carrying a most cumbersome parcel. It really was Richard! She waved frantically and called his name, and his face lit up when he saw her.

"A fine place you choose to meet me! Wembley car park indeed!" he scolded. "I've had an awful time carrying this thing around in all these crowds, and I was just about to give up and go back to Newbury!"

"Well never mind, you're here now and it's wonderful!" exclaimed Sylvia. "Come with me - I'd better get back to the others".

After the match, Richard journeyed back to Lincolnshire on the coach with the school party so that he could be with Sylvia for the weekend. He gave her his present which was a beautiful standard lamp of dark oak with a pretty shade. No wonder it was awkward to carry!

6. LIFE WITH AUNT EMILY

The months passed and in August Sylvia and Richard became engaged to be married. Although Mary showed no enthusiasm for this forthcoming event, she did not quibble too much about it at this stage. Richard had been saving up to buy the best ring that he could, and as he placed it on Sylvia's finger she declared that it was the most beautiful ring in the world. The couple did not intend to marry immediately as they hoped to save up for a while so that they could buy a house and furniture.

Aunt Emily, who was the sister of Richard's mother, had bought for herself a large house across the road from the family home. It was much too big for one person and lent itself to being split down the middle into two self contained units. One weekend Sylvia was visiting her future mother-in-law and they sat drinking tea together in the garden.

"Aunt Emily is looking for a tenant for the other half of her house Sylvia", said Mrs. Sanderson. "Why don't you and your mother rent it from her and get out of that poky little flat you're in? It would do your mother good to live in the country and to be able to sit outside in a garden. Also, when you get married she will be able to stay there and Aunt Emily will keep an eye on her".

This seemed to be a splendid idea and it would certainly solve the problem of what would happen to Mary after Sylvia and Richard were married. Sylvia knew that Richard was not keen to have her to live with them, and obviously his mother and Aunt Emily recognised that it would not be a good thing either!

When Richard next came home for a weekend, he borrowed a van and helped Sylvia and Mary to move into their new home. Sylvia was thrilled. She would have her own bedroom again, as well as the use of a pretty garden. She was over the moon! The prettiest room, which she would really have liked for herself, was at the back of the house and overlooked the beautiful garden with all its trees. She thought it would be better for her mother to have this sunny bedroom as it would be quieter being at the back of the house. Sylvia therefore took the front bedroom which was very large but much darker as it was north facing. Never mind, she had her own bedroom and a bed to herself again. It would be absolute bliss! Last but not least, they had their own bathroom!

Downstairs they had their own very large sitting room which was pleasantly decorated and comfortably furnished. There were two enormous bay windows which let in maximum sunshine. Richard had bought Sylvia a sewing machine and this was set up in the corner of the room where a good light streamed through a smaller window. Across the hallway led to a pleasant kitchen where they were also able to take their meals. The animals had a field day, being able to run freely out into the garden. It was much healthier for them. Aunt Emily was a great lover of animals, and the cat and the dog would be spending a great deal of time at her feet in her own sitting room.

Poor Mary

"Surely this will work", thought Sylvia. "Mother has now got what she said she always wanted - a place in the country!"

Sadly it was not to be, and at last Sylvia had to realise that her mother was never going to be any different. If you gave her Buckingham Palace, then she would want Windsor Castle. If you gave her a saucepan, then it should have been a frying pan! Nothing was going to please her, but that Sylvia could have coped with, for many people become cantankerous as they grow older. The thing that got everybody down was Mary's irrational behaviour, the shouting in the night, and the accusations that everyone was persecuting her when in fact they were all bending over backwards to please her. Aunt Emily herself was a somewhat eccentric lady, and therefore tolerated Mary's strangeness far more than the average person. She was able to accept her as she was, and if things became too bad, then she would lock herself in her own room, sometimes with the animals, and get on with her sewing. It did not seem to worry her unduly for which Sylvia was truly grateful.

Sometimes when Richard came home for the weekend he liked to meet up with his old friends and they would all go out together. One Saturday, Richard and Sylvia and their friends, Don and Cathy, returned from an outing and decided to have a cup of tea at Aunt Emily's place. As Sylvia was making the tea, Cathy asked if she could use the W.C.

"Yes certainly", replied Sylvia, "but it's an outside toilet and the light switch is on the outside of the door".

Cathy went outside, switched on the light, and then locked herself in the W.C. After a few minutes there was a sudden shriek from Cathy who had been plunged into total darkness! Mary had crept up to the door of the W.C. and wickedly switched off the light, knowing full well that Cathy was in there. Don and Cathy laughed about the incident afterwards, but Sylvia was embarrassed at her mother's treatment of Richard's friends, and felt it to be yet another malicious trick on her mother's part!

One Thursday evening, Richard telephoned to say that he had bought a car and would be travelling home in it the following weekend. Sylvia was excited at the prospect of a weekend of jaunts in their own car. Late on Friday evening Richard arrived and laughingly showed the car to her. It was a very old Austin Seven, and it had cost him twenty pounds!

"It's not much of a car", he laughed, "but it goes well. It got me here didn't it? The journey is two hundred miles you know!"

"I think it's sweet", said Sylvia, "and if it gets us around that's all that matters!"

The next morning the sky was azure with fleets of fair weather clouds sailing from the estuary.

"What a wonderful day for a drive in our little car", thought Sylvia as she waited for Richard to come across from his own home after breakfast. It was a late autumn morning, crisp and sunny, as they set off on their first jaunt into the Lincolnshire Wolds. They turned a corner

Poor Mary

and there, spread beneath the autumn sunshine, was a pretty little village nestling into woodland.

"Shall we go for a walk in these woods?" said Sylvia who was still delighted in walking through crunchy leaves, and picking up horse chestnuts and beech nuts. She remembered how, as a small child, she used to enjoy threading the latter and making necklaces from them. It was a wonderful day and the youngsters were so happy to be strolling hand in hand through the woods. After a good walk they decided it was time to make tracks for home. As they journeyed along the narrow, twisting country lanes, Sylvia broke the silence.

"Richard"

"Mm!" he replied, his mind intent on the road ahead.

"Every time this car goes round a bend, should the hooter go off on its own like it does?"

"Not really", said Richard, and laughed.

That evening they decided to go to Cleethorpes in the little car. It was now dark and the car was bobbling along the road, following the path of the tram lines on the sea front road. A tram was following slowly behind them. There was a sudden bang and the car sat on its nose in the middle of the tram lines. The king pin had sheared clean in half and both the front wheels were resting at a crazy angle on the road.

"Oh dear!" exclaimed Richard.

The tram behind them halted in its tracks and the irate driver alighted from it.

"Ye'll 'ave to move that!" he shouted.

"We can't", said Richard. "The wheels have fallen off!"

Richard, the tram driver and the bus conductor, lifted the old car from its front end and wheeled it like a barrow into a large garden which belonged to the Youth Hostel Association. The tram was then able to continue on its journey. Richard ran up the steps of the large building which was the hostel and rang the door bell. A funny little man, who was the warden of the place, opened the door.

"Please may we leave our car in this garden, just for tonight? The wheels have fallen off", said Richard.

The little man shuffled down the steps and stood looking at the car and scratching his head.

"Mm, they'ave, 'aven't they? It's all right, ye can leave it there. Don't ye think that ye should put a stone behind the back wheels so that it won't run away?"

"I hardly think that it will do that", said Richard, trying to keep a straight face, but he put one there just to keep the man happy. Richard loved tinkering with cars and he quickly managed to get hold of some spare parts and eventually had the car on the road again. He then sold it for fifty pounds so making a good profit. With the money he bought for himself a motor bike to use for his journey from Newbury as this was a much cheaper way of travelling than by train.

Sometimes Richard took Sylvia back to Newbury on the back of his motor bike – if she should be on holiday from school! She was rather frightened but

Poor Mary

found it an exciting way to travel, though she hated it when they were overtaken by massive lorries and she thought how awful it would be to fall under those big wheels. After four hours of constant riding on the pillion of the bike, Sylvia found great difficulty in getting off the machine. Her hips had seized up completely and she could barely walk.

"I'm just very stiff", she would say. "I'll be all right when I've thawed out. It's so very cold riding on a motor bike".

On one of these visits to Newbury they came across a three wheeler Bond Mini car for sale at twenty pounds,

"Just look at that!" exclaimed Richard. "I'd really love that!"

"Can we afford it?" asked Sylvia. "Remember we are trying to save up for a deposit on a house!"

"Well I can do it up and then sell it for a profit, and in the meantime we can have some fun in it", said Richard.

So the car was bought and Richard said he would take Sylvia back home in it.

They set off in the open top car on their two hundred mile journey. Sylvia was wearing a warm suit and a scarf round her head to keep her ears warm. Placed on the front seat between the two of them was a shoe box. Inside the shoe box was a tortoise which Richard had bought for Sylvia that weekend. She had called it Timmy and she would occasionally take a peep inside the box to make sure that her pet was all right. The ride was much more comfortable than on the motor bike, and of course a great deal warmer. They stopped in a small village near Oxford for a coffee, and then they wandered down the main street looking at the antique shops as they went. When they were ready to leave, they went back to the car and climbed in. Richard pulled the starting handle but nothing happened. He pulled again and, with a sudden TWANG, the starting cable snapped!

"We'll have to push start it now", said Richard. "It's not very heavy so you push whilst I steer".

"Not so easy in a tight skirt and high heeled shoes!" shouted Sylvia, but eventually the engine fired and they were once more on their way. Every time they stopped the car for any reason, this performance had to be repeated in order to start the car again.

Half way on their journey they came to a place called Six Hills where the six hills converged together at a massive roundabout at the bottom of the valley. They had to negotiate an extremely steep hill down to the roundabout, and then carry straight on. The car was gathering speed - more than it should!

"The brakes have gone!" yelled Richard, slamming the car into its lowest gear in an attempt to slow it down. The car ran down the hill at great speed and, unable to stop at the roundabout, Richard steered to the left and they zoomed round the corner as though on a railway track. Fortunately for them the roundabout was clear of traffic at that moment, otherwise there would have been a nasty accident. They both gave a sigh of relief as the car came to a stand still as the road began to incline upwards.

Poor Mary

"Phew!" exclaimed Richard. "That was a near thing. Fortunately there are no other hills as steep as that one".

Once more on the right road, being extremely careful now that they knew that the brakes weren't functioning properly, they at last reached the Lincolnshire Wolds. Coming to a manned level crossing, they managed to stop the car before it ploughed into the gates which were closed. The man in charge of the gates came out of his hut in order to open them.

"Ye'll have to reverse before I can open the gates!" he exclaimed.

"We can't", said Richard. "There's no reverse gear on this car".

The man pushed the car backwards until there was room enough to clear the gates before he opened them.

"Right! Off you go!" he shouted.

"We can't", said Richard again. "The starting cable has snapped. You'll have to push!"

"What is this?" asked the man. "Is it a bubble car?"

"No," said Richard as they set off once more. "It's a bloody car!"

By now it was getting dark and the moon had risen. They reached a very steep hill in the Wolds and the little car refused to climb it and came to a sudden stop. By the light of the moon, Sylvia struggled in her high heels and tight skirt to push the car as Richard steered, but the hill was too steep and she couldn't manage it. Together the two of them pushed the car all the way to the top of the hill and then, quickly jumping back in, they were able to free wheel down the other side, coming to rest on the outskirts of a small village. It was now midnight.

"We're not too far away from home now", said Richard. "There's a phone box on the corner. I'll ring my brother and he'll come and get us".

Richard's brother, James, eventually arrived. He was still wearing his pyjamas underneath the trousers he had quickly thrown on. The tired youngsters were eventually delivered to their respective homes and were thankful to arrive in one piece. The next morning the little car was retrieved. It started immediately without any problems - which is the way with cars sometimes! After a great deal of tinkering, the car was thoroughly overhauled and painted bright red which made it look very sporty. It was sold for a handsome profit!

7. A MARCH WEDDING

The months went by and before they knew it two years had passed. The summer prior to their intended wedding was exceedingly hot and dry. Sylvia did not go out socially very much when Richard was away. They had a good time together once a month when he was at home and she was quite contented with that. Many of the summer evenings and weekends were spent playing tennis with her future brother and sister-in-law. She found this very enjoyable except that after all the running about during the tennis games caused her to experience a great deal of pain in both her knees. Many were the evenings when she would limp home, declaring that the game had stiffened her joints!

One day she was walking down the corridor at school when an older member of staff commented that Sylvia was limping, and also drew attention to the fact that her right foot turned inwards as she walked.

"You ought to see a doctor young lady. By the way you are walking now you'll be in a wheel chair when you are older!"

Sylvia laughed, but said that she would go to a doctor, for she was concerned about the persistent pains in her legs. She never found it easy to explain illnesses or discomforts to a doctor and usually made light of them, not wishing to be a nuisance. The doctor listened to what she had to say but did not examine her.

"You are a young girl! There's nothing wrong with you. You've probably just strained the muscles with unaccustomed exercise!"

Sylvia was only too ready to believe this simple explanation and continued to put up with her discomforts.

Autumn approached and Richard announced that they should set the date for the wedding before April, and so it was arranged that their wedding day would be on the first day of the following March. During the long dark nights of that winter, Sylvia's sewing machine could be heard whirring away as she busily made garments for her trousseau. She made pretty night gowns, a negligee and a fully tiered underskirt to go beneath her wedding dress, and many more bits and pieces.

There was no way that Mary was going to be able to contribute to her daughter's wedding, so it was decided that it should be a small occasion, everything limited to a strict minimum, the customary family, witnesses, and only a few close friends. Sylvia sent an invitation to her grandparents but they declined it and said that they would not be able to come.

"I have no one to give me away Richard", said Sylvia one evening when they were discussing the arrangements.

"Well I'm quite sure that my Uncle Henry will be delighted to do that", said Richard. "He'll make a good job of it too. He likes to do everything correctly; he's not a bit like my mother and Aunt Emily. Everything has to be 'just so'!"

Uncle Henry was flattered to be asked to perform the task of giving away the bride at his nephew's wedding. He was a widower and had no children of his

Poor Mary

own, so he took a great deal of interest in the sons of his sister.

As the wedding was going to be in term time, and on a week day, Sylvia had to apply to the local Education Authority for a week's leave of absence from school. Much to her amazement, not only was she granted a week's leave of absence, but also with full pay! After all this had been officially confirmed the couple felt that they could send out the wedding invitations.

"We'll have to invite certain members of the staff from my school", said Sylvia. "Naturally we'll invite the Headmistress and the Deputy Head. Mrs. Jackson is kindly making our wedding cake so she'll have to come. Miss Miller, the needlework teacher, is making my dress so she must have an invitation. Diedre of course is my one and only bridesmaid so she'll be there anyway". Diedre, in spite of her immaculate and attractive appearance, was destined to be always the bridesmaid, never the blushing bride!

"How will the school manage without all those staff members?" queried Richard.

"Oh they'll manage somehow, one always does. It is only for half a day anyway!" replied Sylvia.

Sylvia spent much of her spare time looking at catalogues and at dress patterns and materials for her wedding dress. Eventually she selected a pattern and the material and took them along to her colleague, Miss Miller, who was going to make it up for her. The next thing to buy was the head dress and veil and Sylvia chose a simple circlet of white rose buds attached to a veil of fine tulle. On returning home from her shopping expedition, the headdress and veil were carefully placed, still in their bag, on top of the dressing table in Sylvia's bedroom. The next day, when she returned home from school, she noticed that the bag on the dressing table looked different and was curiously flat! She hastily opened the bag. The headdress was still in there but it had been squashed as flat as a pancake. All the delicate white rose buds were crushed and misshapen. Sylvia burst into tears. Mary hotly denied having anything to do with it and blamed Aunt Emily's cat.

"But I shut my bedroom door!" cried Sylvia, "and it was still shut this evening when I returned home from school".

She never did find out how the headdress had come to be crushed or whether or not the cat had somehow managed to get into her room, or whether it had been deliberately let into her room, or whether her mother had flattened it in a fit of anger over the wedding! Anyway, Aunt Emily saved the day. When she was younger she had once worked in a milliner's shop and knew a few tricks of that trade. She carefully steamed the silk roses, gently coaxing them back into shape with the end of a spoon. When she had finished the headdress looked as good as new, and no one would have known that it had been so ill treated.

The month prior to the wedding, Sylvia and Richard went through all the arrangements to make sure that all was in order. The month sped by and before they knew it there was only one day left.

Poor Mary

"I won't see you again now until we are in church tomorrow", said Richard as her kissed her goodnight.

"I'm going to have an early night", said Sylvia. "I must have my beauty sleep for tomorrow. I can't believe that our day has arrived at last".

After a long, hot bath, Sylvia climbed into bed and began to dream about her wedding the next day. Mary had gone to bed early that night too. Suddenly Sylvia was aware of some disturbance and was immediately wide awake. It was her mother! She was talking to herself in her bedroom and before long her voice became louder and louder until she was almost shriekiug. She seemed determined to wake up the whole neighbourhood!

"I'm not wedding!" she cried, and she came out of her bedroom and paced up and down on the landing outside Sylvia's door.

"I'm not wedding! No wedding for me! It's dirty! When the vicar asks if any one knows of any just impediment, I'm going to stand up and say 'YES'. I'm going to say "His nose is too long!"

All night long this went on, and Sylvia cringed beneath her bed covers and tried to block up her ears. She was now terrified that her mother was going to deliberately ruin her wedding day. She did not go to sleep until the early hours when her mother eventually settled down.

On the morning of the wedding Sylvia awoke to find the sun streaming into the bedroom through the gap in the curtains. She looked at the alarm clock. It was seven o'clock. Jumping out of bed she opened wide the curtains and looked out of the window. The sky was cloudless and the sun brilliant, though a playful March wind shook the yellow headed daffodils which blazed in the garden like an army of soldiers. When Sylvia went down to breakfast Mary was already in the kitchen making a cup of tea. Much to her relief, her mother seemed fairly rational this morning.

"Perhaps she got it all out of her system last night", Sylvia thought. "I do hope so!"

Diedre arrived early to help Sylvia to dress. She had made her own bridesmaid dress of deep blue velvet in a simple style with a neat waist and a very full skirt. Its only adornment was a blue velvet bow secured from the waist at the back of the skirt.

"She looks like a Dresden china shepherdess", thought Sylvia. "She is so dainty and her skin so clear".

Peeping out of the window she was just in time to see Richard setting off with the best man in the wedding car to the village church. She herself was almost ready.

"Are you wearing all that you should?" asked Diedre. "Something old?"

"Yes", replied Sylvia. "These pearls were given to me years ago by my grandfather".

"Well your dress is new, so what about something borrowed?" continued Diedre.

"Oh no! I haven't got that. It's good to tell that you are an experienced bridesmaid".

"Then I will lend you my spare handkerchief. I brought it just in case! Now what about something blue?"

"I put little blue bows on the petticoat that I made for under the dress, so that is covered!" replied Sylvia.

By now Mary had departed to the church together with Aunt Emily who would no doubt try to keep her under control. Sylvia's heart was fearful nevertheless, lest her mother should cause an unpleasant scene in the church. At last her car arrived and Uncle Henry was there to open the door for her. She carefully climbed in, arranging her dress so that it would not be trodden on.

When they arrived at the church, Uncle Henry gave her his arm as they walked up the long drive to the church porch. The sky was still a clear morning blue, with a few harmless clouds drifting light as thistledown. The little March wind took hold of Sylvia's veil and the skirt of her dress, and playfully teased them until they billowed out. As she neared the church, outwardly Sylvia appeared the traditional bride, young, composed and ethereal but beneath her skirts her legs were trembling so much that she thought they would not bear her weight during the long walk up the aisle.

As the Bridal March began there was a stir of movement among those present. Richard turned and saw his bride, shrouded in white and with pearls shining like drops of new milk round her neck.

"Pearls are for tears!" whispered one of the older guests. "She ought not to be wearing those on her wedding day!" Strangely, these words proved to be right. She still had the pearls years later but there had been many tears shed since she had worn them on her wedding day.

Sylvia's dark eyes lifted and fleetingly swept over the small congregation, and then down the aisle to where Richard was nervously waiting. His fair hair was shining in the sun's rays which poured through the stained glass windows. She advanced step by gliding step towards him, her gown whispering about her. After the ceremony the newly weds were ushered into the vestry to sign the register. Husband and wife then left the church to the sound of wedding bells. At the door of the church Richard bent his head to kiss his bride's lips with reassurance and promise.

After the small wedding reception, Diedre helped Sylvia to change out of her bridal attire into a suit of powder blue. The newly married couple were then rushed to the train station and showered in confetti as they boarded a train bound for London. The honeymoon was a surprise destination for Sylvia, and she was astonished to find herself boarding a plane which was to take them to Jersey. Richard was an extraordinary considerate and attentive companion, always seeking to please his wife, and was to remain so during the rest of their life together.

Mary went back to the house with Aunt Emily and each went to their own quarters, Emily to snooze and Mary to brood. She went into her daughter's bedroom and wept now that she had lost her. In the night her own bedroom was full of shadows waiting to pounce and she was possessed by a vast sense of emptiness and the ache of loneliness.

PART 7

1. A WITCH'S CAULDRON

1993 It was Monday evening, approaching ten o'clock. Richard was out at a meeting and Sylvia was enjoying a good television program. When the program had ended, Sylvia switched off the television set and walked into the kitchen. "I'll make myself a cup of herbal tea", she thought, filling the kettle and switching it on. She heard the sound of the front door so prepared another mug with coffee for Richard.

"Cheese and biscuits with your coffee?" she shouted so that he could hear.

"Yes please darling - then I'm going straight to bed. I'm just so tired".

"Me too!" said Sylvia.

After finishing her drink, Sylvia was just about to go upstairs when the phone rang. The time was a quarter to eleven!

"Hello Mum. I think I've started!" It was Anna, her daughter.

"What do you want me to do?" asked Sylvia.

"I don't know", said Anna tearfully. "Oh! - It hurts so much!"

"I'll come and spend the night with you", said Sylvia. "Then I can stay with Ruth when you have to go into hospital and you won't have to worry about her".

"That's a good idea", said Anna.

"I'll be with you as soon as I can – but I shall have to get a few things together, and the journey takes me about three quarters of an hour in the car".

Sylvia replaced the receiver and called upstairs to Richard.

"You'll gather that Anna's baby is on the way. I'll go and spend the night with her in case she has to go into hospital before morning, then Ruth will be cared for.

"Is there petrol in your car?" asked Richard.

"Oh no, damn! I forgot to fill it up and it's almost empty. I'll never make twenty two miles!" exclaimed Sylvia.

"There's an over night garage if you go the long way round to the motor way. Now do be careful. Drive slowly – it's a wild night outside", warned Richard.

Sylvia, now fully awake, put her over night bag in the car and started up the engine. She switched up the heating because the night was so cold. The roads were deserted at that time of night and this would enable her to travel more quickly. After filling up with petrol she headed for the motor way and Bristol. Even above the sound of the engine she could hear the howl of the wind, and there was a pelting of sleet against the windscreen. Instinct told her to keep her speed down as the roads were treacherous with ice.

On the motor way the wind was worse, buffeting the car and gusts blew the rain into huge sheets so that she could barely see through the windscreen. On reaching her daughter's house, she parked the car on the street and battled her way through the wind and the rain to the door. After having a couple of false alarms it was now obvious that this time Anna was definitely

Poor Mary

in labour. During the early hours of the morning Anna went into hospital whilst Sylvia stayed to look after her first born grandchild. Ruth. At seven thirty that morning Maria was born.

The coming of the day turned the eastern sky to a musky ruby and then to a pale lemon. By the time that Sylvia and Ruth had breakfasted the sky was relatively clear.

"When can we go and see my baby sister Grandma?" The five year old Ruth queried.

"I think this evening, if we are allowed, because Mummy needs to rest today as she has been awake all night. It is hard work having a baby!" said Sylvia.

That evening Sylvia took Ruth to the hospital to see her mummy and new baby sister, Maria. Anna looked very tired and tearful but was relieved that her child was now born. Sylvia picked up her new granddaughter from the crib and gazed at her. New babies have the most beautiful aroma, the scent of pure freshness. There is no other fragrance like it. And such sweet innocence! "Welcome to the family Maria", Sylvia said, "and may you have a happy upbringing!"

Sylvia thought of her own upbringing – how she had lived in fear and dread of her mother's mood changes, and how a spot of dirt on her dress earned her a good whipping. A few drops of fruit juice on her dress had been enough to unleash Mary's fury. Her own children had experienced nothing like that and had been encouraged to make something of their lives. Sylvia's thoughts drifted back to the birth of Anna, her first born.

1960 After their wedding Richard was transferred to an office in Halifax and that was where he and Sylvia bought their first house. Sylvia fully intended to work for at least a couple of years before starting a family, so that they could collect a few things together and be more established. The town of Halifax is situated in a bowl which resembles a witch's cauldron with its black stone factories and mills from which smoke belched and drifted upwards. As the couple sat in their car at the top of the hill, and looked down on the town for the first time, Richard shuddered.

"Oh it's awful! I don't think I'm going to stand living in a place like this. It's so dirty and smoky, it can't be healthy. Just look at that – row upon row of grimy back to back terrace houses, and all their smoking chimneys!"

"We'll manage!" said Sylvia. "As long as we're together, that's all that matters".

"I still won't like it any better", said Richard. "I hate it!"

They were searching for a house to buy and it seemed that there weren't any nice ones on the market. Richard was used to having plenty of space and didn't want to be hemmed into a place where there wasn't enough room to swing a cat round – as the saying goes! Their luck changed however, and they found something which pleased him. It was a very old house dating back to the fifteenth century. It had once been a beautiful manor house surrounded by fields, and Oliver Cromwell was reputed to have signed a treaty within its walls. Now it stood, like a jewel, amidst the rows of back to back terraced houses and factory buildings. The ancient stone work was blackened by years of smoke from the factory chimneys and coal fires of the houses. Although the garden was now small, it was pretty and enclosed by high walls and bordering trees, thus affording some privacy. A short flight of steps led from the front lawn to an attractive terrace in front of French windows. Once one was actually inside the garden, the ugliness of the rest of the street could not be seen.

There were five bedrooms, four of them situated across the front of the house and having been constructed on what had once been a minstrel's gallery. Down stairs were an enormous sitting room and a large dining room with a great chimney between the two. There was an open, dark coloured oak staircase leading from the sitting room to the first floor. The sitting room itself was richly panelled in dark oak. A long narrow kitchen ran alongside the dining room, and a door underneath the staircase led to another extremely large kitchen at the back of the house. The latter had an enormous stone fireplace through which one could see daylight when standing inside the chimney place and looking up. From this kitchen another staircase led to the fifth bedroom which had retained its old oak beams in the ceiling, as had the kitchen.

"There's not too much room outside", said Richard, "but there's plenty of space inside the house. What do you think?"

"I like it", replied Sylvia. "It's certainly the most attractive house that we have seen in this area so we'd better snap it up before someone else does!"

Everything was set in motion for the purchase of the house. In the meantime Richard found them some accommodation in a small guest house until the completion of the contract. Sylvia had acquired a temporary teaching post in a nearby school.

Mr. and Mrs. Phillips ran the little guest house and they were kindly people. Mrs. Phillips was a big woman, Yorkshire born and bred and with a heart of gold. Her husband was a Londoner and he equalled his wife in size, but he was a very quiet person and always did his wife's bidding! Each morning they prepared an enormous breakfast for their guests and a good meal in the evening. Richard and Sylvia expected to be living there for about two and a half months, as the completion date for the purchase of their house was in July. It was now the beginning of April. Sylvia's favourite breakfast was bacon and eggs and she always looked forward to it. She came down to the breakfast table one morning and sat down in her usual place. A few minutes later Mrs. Phillips sailed into the room, bearing the plates containing their hot breakfast and set them down on the table in front of her guests. Sylvia looked at her plate and suddenly her stomach revolted.

"I can't it eat", she whispered to Richard. "I suddenly feel really sick!"

"Just try", said Richard. "We don't want to offend our landlady".

"No, I really can't – honestly! I'll throw up if I try!"

Ten minutes later found Richard apologizing to Mrs. Phillips for his wife's untouched meal.

"Ee lass!" she cried in a loud voice for all to hear, "If ye're pregnant suck 'spanish'. That'll help wi' the sickness!"

The 'spanish' to which the lady referred was a stick of hard black liquorice.

Sylvia turned bright red. "I can't be", she whispered to Richard. "I haven't even missed a period!"

Poor Mary

But the next period did not arrive and each morning Sylvia felt even more nauseous. At last she visited a doctor who confirmed that indeed she was pregnant. She no longer ate the delicious cooked breakfast which she had enjoyed in the past. Instead she had strange fancies for beetroot or banana sandwiches for breakfast.

"Beetroot or banana this morning?" Mr. Phillips would shout up the stairs.

Sylvia was working in a small junior school in Halifax. She often felt tired and irritable, but she was determined to carry on with her teaching until the end of the summer term as they needed all the money they could earn. At last the term ended, and with the summer holidays came the completion of the contract and so they were able to move into their new home. There was a great deal of decorating to be done and they wanted to do as much as possible before the arrival of their baby. They decided to tackle the bedrooms first. In one of the bedrooms was a strange and unpleasant smell.

"It smells like urine", said Richard. "Perhaps an old person who was incontinent had this room at some time. I think we'll start work on this room first".

The next day Sylvia awoke to a summer sky in which luminous masses of pearly clouds seemed to be themselves a source of light.

"I'll start work on that bedroom today and strip off the old wallpaper", she said in the middle of a yawn and a stretch as she got out of bed.

"Just be careful you don't reach up too high", said Richard. "It is supposed to be bad for you when you're pregnant, so I've heard my mother say!"

Sylvia Hoole

"I'll be careful", replied Sylvia. "I'll leave the high bits for you. I don't really want to be climbing ladders anyway".

Once Richard had left for work and she had tidied up the breakfast things, Sylvia tied up her hair in a headscarf and, taking a bucket of water, a sponge and scraper, she began to strip off the old wallpaper as far as she could comfortably reach. She felt happy as she beavered away and was singing to herself. Suddenly she stopped what she was doing and listened. Yes, there it was again! She could hear a pitter-pattering noise somewhere above the ceiling in the false roof, just like tiny feet scrambling about. This noise continued intermittently during the course of the morning. At twelve thirty Richard came home for his lunch.

"I think there must be birds in the roof", Sylvia said as they were eating their lunch. "All the time I was working in the bedroom I could hear this pitter-pattering noise. It was very disconcerting!"

Richard went up to the bedroom but now all was quiet. "Perhaps it was a bird up there", he said. "These old houses lend themselves to birds getting inside the roof easily. It must have found its way out again".

After a good week of hard work, the bedroom was finally finished, looking pretty and smelling fresh and clean. They had chosen pale pink flowery wallpaper, and had painted the woodwork white.

"It will be an ideal guest room", said Sylvia, looking round with pride. "I do hope that someone will come and stay with us soon. Perhaps we should ask your brother and his wife!"

2. ANNA

The baby was due to be born at the beginning of January so Sylvia and Richard were intent on doing as much decorating as they could before this event. In September, Sylvia took another temporary teaching post in a different school and intended to work until the November half term holiday. By now she was feeling cumbersome and found the long walk to and from the school very heavy going. She had not yet learned to drive a car so she had to walk or take a bus whenever she went anywhere on her own. After finishing school one day, she set off to walk the distance home. She walked about half a mile when she suddenly experienced the most intense sharp pain in her right hip. It was so agonizing that she had to lean on the nearest garden wall, and was struggling to hold back her tears. She felt that she could not go a step further.

"The baby must be resting on a nerve or something", she thought as she gritted her teeth to try and overcome the pain. Somehow or other she managed to get herself home, but her face was ashen by the time she lowered herself into the nearest chair. She was still sitting in the chair when Richard came home from work.

"I'm very sorry but I haven't prepared a meal yet. I had these awful pains in my hip and could hardly walk home from school. I thought I'd better stay off my feet until it settles down", said Sylvia who was still very tearful.

"Never mind!" said Richard. "You rest whilst I rustle up something simple. I think I'll cook a – mm – a salad!"

By now they had decorated all the bedrooms and had decided to leave the rest of the house for the time being. Richard went upstairs to shut all the bedroom windows before the dampness of the autumn evening crept in. When he came downstairs he looked puzzled.

"I've just been into the pink bedroom and that awful smell is back", he said.

"You're joking!" said Sylvia. "You must be imagining it!"

But sure enough, the unpleasant smell, from whatever the cause, had seeped back into the room.

"Whatever can it be?" said Sylvia when she went to investigate for herself. "I wonder if there is a dead bird up in the false roof."

"I'll go up there at the weekend", said Richard, "and have a good look around".

He finished work at mid-day on Saturday so after lunch he mounted a pair of steps and raised the hatch of the false roof. He shone a torch around but could not see anything in the immediate vicinity, and he did not fancy clambering around up there in case the timbers were rotten.

"I really can't think what it can be", he said. "It certainly smells pretty foul up there but I can't see any bodies!"

The week of Christmas came and Mrs. Phillips, their previous landlady, invited Sylvia and Richard to have Christmas dinner with them.

"It'll save you from 'avin to cook ", she said, "and after dinner ye can put yer feet up an' watch t' telly in t' kitchen".

Sylvia felt extremely uncomfortable after eating the massive Christmas dinner. She felt restless and could not make herself at ease no matter which way she sat in the chair. As the evening wore on she grew increasingly agitated and at last whispered to Richard that she would like to go home. When they felt that there was an opportune moment to make their excuses without appearing ungrateful, they did so, and Richard ushered Sylvia out of the house to the car.

"Thank goodness for that" sighed Sylvia wearily as she sank into bed at last, "though I don't think that I'm going to have a very comfortable night!"

Something awakened Sylvia very early on the following Boxing Day morning. She looked at her watch which said six o'clock. There it was again – a sudden sharp pain in the small of her back. She groaned and tried to turn over. "I must have eaten too much Christmas pudding", she thought. Ten minutes later she felt another stab of pain in her back, causing her to gasp.

"What's the matter?" mumbled Richard, still half asleep.

"I keep getting these really sharp pains in my back", replied Sylvia. "I think I ate too much Christmas pudding last evening. Perhaps I'm constipated!"

"Are you sure that the baby hasn't started to come?" queried Richard, now fully awake.

"I don't know. I've no idea what to expect really", said Sylvia, wincing as she experienced yet another severe pain.

Richard began to time the pains. "They're coming every ten minutes exactly", he said. "I think we'd better ring the hospital!"

"But the baby's not due for another two weeks", she protested," and first babies are usually late – or so they say!"

Undeterred, Richard telephoned the hospital and was told to take his wife in at once. Sylvia was examined and there was no doubt that the baby was on the way. Hours of suffering went by and at last relief came, and with thin infantile wailing a baby girl was born. Sylvia noticed that it was exactly twenty past six on Boxing Day evening before she sank into slumber.

The next morning Sylvia looked in wonder at the marvel that was her child. Every mother thinks hers is the most beautiful, and when looking upon the baby for the first time, they see a miracle. As Sylvia gazed in awe at her child, she was consumed by a new emotion, a mother's pure and unquestioning love.

"What are we going to call her?" asked Richard as he looked down proudly upon his new daughter later that evening.

"We'll call her Anna – after your grandmother – and Mary after my mother. That way both families are represented so no one can grumble. Anna Mary Sanderson – that sounds nice don't you think?"

3. RATS

December was ushered out in a swirl of dazzling snow. The sun peered occasionally through watery clouds and, although it was not freezing, the weather was extremely cold. During the first few weeks of Anna's life, Sylvia was confined to the house. The child had weighed a small five and a half pounds at birth, and it was necessary to keep her in an even temperature for the first few weeks. These weeks passed and at last came the daffodils, heralding the spring and milder weather. Sylvia took great delight in walking out in the fresh air with her baby in the pram.

"I don't call this fresh air", grumbled Richard one day. "It's solid pollution! Just look at those factory chimneys belching out their smoke, let alone the rows and rows of houses with their smoking chimneys. You never see a truly blue sky here – there's always a haze of pollution!"

"You're quite right", said Sylvia. "Every time I leave Anna out on the patio she is covered with flecks of soot when I bring her in, and so are the white nappies when they've been hanging on the washing line. It's also very noticeable how quickly the house gets dirty. No matter how many times I dust, a few minutes later it's as bad as ever!"

Richard was growing more and more disgruntled with his life in Halifax. He hated having to live there. "I don't want my child to grow up in this environment!" he exclaimed one day. "I want her to have the freedom of space and the clean air which I enjoyed as a boy".

The climax of his despair came when they discovered that the noises and the smell in the guest room were caused by rats in the roof. Everyone has a pet hate and rats were Richard's. He could not even bear to look at a picture of one, let alone confront a live one! The thought of them was intolerable to him. They never actually saw the rats, but every night the creatures could be heard scampering around in the false roof and behind the skirting boards. Things came to a head when they heard a terrible gnawing sound above the ceiling of Anna's bedroom. Sylvia was terrified lest the creatures should gnaw their way through the ceiling and perhaps attack her tiny baby daughter in her cot.

"That's it!" cried Richard. "I've had enough of this house, and this town. I'd rather be a car park attendant in Lincoln than stay here any longer. I'm going to give in my notice at the office tomorrow!"

Sylvia did not object to her husband's decision, rash though it may have been. She would prefer to live away from this dismal place and often longed for the freshness of the little Lincolnshire village where Richard had been brought up. She herself had been teaching games in a senior school in Halifax for one afternoon a week, having hired a baby sitter for Anna. She had started off the year playing at netball herself with the girls in her class, but as the weeks went by she had suffered increasingly more pain in her hips and knees. Eventually she had to give up playing the game herself, and could only supervise the game from the side of the court.

"I'm sure that you will find work in Lincolnshire", she said, "and your mother might look after Anna if I can get some teaching work. That would be better than having a child minder. Also it would be better for my mother if we were nearby".

"We'll be able to live with my parents until we sort out another house", said Richard. "Don't worry about the state of their house. I'll make it nice for you and Anna, and if I do some decorating and repair work on the house it will be beneficial for my parents too. Just think how lovely it will be for Anna to play in that large garden when she's old enough!"

"Just think how lovely it will be for me not to have to contend with all this coal dust and soot. Mm! I can't wait!" said Sylvia.

4. "I'VE GOT THE UNKNOWN ONE!"

Having sold their Halifax home at a good profit, Richard and Sylvia and baby Anna moved to the family home in Lincolnshire. The house was large enough for them to have their own separate accommodation and Richard spent time in painting, decorating and generally modernizing the old house. He replaced the electrical wiring and put in new power points. He decorated a large sitting room, a kitchen and two bedrooms and, by the time he had finished, at least part of the house was spick and span.

Sylvia awoke one morning to the early summer sunshine pouring through the bedroom window. She felt decidedly unwell and, as it tuned out, she was once again pregnant. The doctor's practice was nearby and Sylvia had become friendly with Dr. Clare Henderson who looked after her very well if she ever needed medical attention. Clare Henderson was tall and slim and she had mid brown hair and grey eyes which took on the colour of what she was wearing. When she wore blue they seemed blue, but she seldom wore that colour. Mostly she was clad in grey or buff coloured suits of good material which she felt was in keeping with her profession. Her face was rather thin and she had a neat straight nose and arched eyebrows some shades deeper than her hair. Clare was a very private person, presenting to the world a calm and efficient manner, but underneath this veneer she was a very caring person. Clare was particularly attentive towards Sylvia during this second pregnancy, making sure that her patient and friend was kept fit and well.

Poor Mary

"I really do not want our new baby to be born into this house", said Sylvia to Richard. "Your mother is bound to interfere. She never agrees with the way in which we bring up Anna and it will be much worse with a new baby. Also I can't bear the thought of a baby crawling on your mother's dirty floors. You know she never washes them and I can hardly keep the child away!"

Richard could not disagree with his wife's opinion with regard to his mother's lack of hygiene, and promised that they would look for a house of their own as soon as he found work.

In the meantime, Aunt Emily had decided to sell her house. Secretly she had had more than enough of coping with the craziness of Mary and selling her house was a good enough excuse to ask Mary to leave without hurting Sylvia's feelings. As soon as Sylvia knew that the house was to be sold then she began to look for some new accommodation for her mother. At last, after many days of telephone calls, bus journeys and inspections, Sylvia found a small self contained flat which she knew Mary would be able to afford. It was not much of a place but the rent was reasonable, it provided Mary with everything that she needed, and it had the advantage of being situated in a nearby village and so would not be difficult to visit.

In her usual form, Mary was not going to give anyone the satisfaction of knowing that she was settled. She did every conceivable thing to annoy the other occupants of the large tenanted house, and to upset the landlady. A few week's later Sylvia received the now familiar, "Will you come and see me?" summons from her mother's landlady. She did not need to be told how the conversation would go! This time however, it turned out rather better than expected. After the usual complaints about the irrational behaviour of Mary towards her fellow tenants, the landlady made a suggestion.

"I have a very old terrace house on one of the back streets of the town", she said. "Actually it is due for demolition but it is still habitable. If your mother rented this house from me, then the local council would automatically re house her when they started work on demolishing that block of houses. Once she gets a council house then she will be secure as far as housing is concerned, and that might help her a lot!"

This seemed a good solution to Mary's problem and Sylvia was extremely grateful to the lady for giving her mother this chance. On the day of Mary's move to her new home, the sun was shining and the clouds in rapid retreat, blown away by a sharp wind that came from the east. Mary had only personal things to gather together so it did not take too long. The little terrace house, such as it was, had adequate furniture, albeit shabby, and in some cases quite ramshackle. Near the ill fitting door the damp seeped up and on the walls the wallpaper was damp and peeling. A naked light bulb hung from the ceiling in the sitting room.

"I don't think much to this", grumbled Mary.

"I know it's not very good", said Sylvia, but it's only a very temporary arrangement. You will be re housed by the Council soon, and then you'll have a nice new place from which no one can remove you provided that you keep paying your rent.

Poor Mary

Afterwards Sylvia expressed her concern to Richard about the dilapidated house.

"Well love, you've done your best. Your mother won't behave herself anywhere and people just won't put up with it, and why should they? The trouble is that she doesn't learn. She had a lovely home with Aunt Emily and she didn't appreciate it. As I've said before, if you give your mother Buckingham Palace then she will want Windsor Castle",

---

When her daughter had left, Mary organised her few things and made herself a cup of tea. After sitting in the shabby old armchair for a while, she suddenly jumped up and began pacing the room with unsteady steps, gesticulating, pulling her dishevelled hair and uttering strange sounds. She knew that 'they' would come through the electrical power points. She was unable to hear, unable to feel. Her mind had become a terrifying void and fear gripped her. She struggled to return to normality but was only drawn back down deeper. A few hours later she awoke to find herself still sitting in the armchair. She was too afraid to go to bed.

When Sylvia visited her mother the next day, Mary locked the door behind her. All the electric power points had been stuffed with rags and the walls in the sitting room were running with water.

"However did these walls become so wet?" asked Sylvia. They were not like this yesterday".

"I threw a bucket of water with some Domestos in it. Domestos kills all known germs ye know! The trouble is – I've got the unknown one!"

Sighing, Sylvia glanced at the table on which had been placed a carving knife. She felt uneasy knowing that she was locked in with her mother. She didn't really think that her mother would hurt her, but nevertheless she breathed a sigh of relief when Mary unlocked the front door and she could escape, back to normality.

5. A COUNTRY COTTAGE

As the early days of June simmered and baked, Richard and Sylvia were house hunting. Richard now had a temporary job as a visiting officer for the Social services – until he decided what he really wanted to do with his life. Sylvia remembered clearly a hot afternoon when she, Richard and Anna who was now a toddler and talking, made their way up a long lane leading to a pretty little house which they had come to view.

"That's my house and I'm going to live in it!" young Anna suddenly exclaimed, pointing to the house.

These words were so unexpected from so young a child, and perhaps this is why they decided to buy the house.

The sun was indulgently warm where it spattered through the branches of the trees in the orchard, speckling the ground with light. In the orchard the trees had crowded about an old and disused hen house.

"That would make a lovely playroom for Anna if we cleaned it up", said Sylvia. "This is a wonderful garden for children to play in and so far away from the main road and traffic – and just look at those beautiful red roses on the driveway!"

The house itself was quite small, having only two bedrooms, bathroom, sitting room and tiny kitchen.

"It's big enough for us at the moment", said Sylvia", "and much easier for me to handle than that great barn of a house in Halifax, lovely though it was!"

"Yes", said Richard, "and we won't need a big mortgage this time, having made a good profit on that house".

So it was decided. The couple went ahead to buy the house and were eventually able to move in during August, giving Sylvia plenty of time to prepare for the arrival of her second baby. In the meantime, Richard had decided that he would like to become a teacher himself and had successfully applied for entry into training college.

In September Richard began his training college course whilst Sylvia literally enjoyed the fruits of her own garden. She was kept very busy making fruit pies, preserving black currants, gooseberries and blackberries, and of course making endless jars of jam. During this period she also had a course of driving lessons and when she was eight months pregnant she took her driving test. To her great surprise and delight she passed the test, this giving her life a new dimension.

"I'm sure the examiner only passed me out of sympathy", she said to Richard. "I'm so big with this baby that I could barely fit behind the steering wheel!"

"Well, you passed", said Richard," and that will be an asset to you for the rest of your life – particularly as we live so far out in the country".

Typical of Richard's thoughtfulness, and although he was not at all fond of Mary, he bought her a bicycle so that she could easily visit her daughter whenever she wished. One day each week Mary rode out to the little village and stayed with Sylvia for the whole day.

Poor Mary

Someone had been stupid enough to give to Mary a mongrel dog. Aunt Emily had kept Pixie and Whiskers the cat when Mary had moved into the flat where pets were not allowed. The dog seemed a good idea at the time and Mary doted on the creature, but it was a great nuisance being totally untrained and therefore wild and noisy. However Lassie as the dog was called, went everywhere with Mary. It was a comical sight to see Mary riding on her bicycle, the dog perched in a basket which was strapped to the front handlebars.

6. SUGAR COATED PILLS

Summer was ending and the long and dismal winter threatened. In November another daughter was born to Sylvia and Richard. They named her Rebecca after Richard's paternal grandmother. She was a much easier baby than Anna had been, sleeping contentedly in her pram in between feeds. Perhaps it was because Sylvia was more relaxed with her second child, now being a more experienced mother! Sylvia was now feeling the benefit of having passed her driving test, for it enabled her to visit her mother, Richard's parents and her friends without the hassle of struggling with a baby and a small child on public transport.

The advent of Rebecca affected Anna adversely. One always imagines that a second child would be company for the first one but this is not always the case. Anna should have been an only child. She resented Rebecca from the minute she set eyes on her, and there seemed to be enmity between the two of them which lasted well into their teenage years.

Richard arrived home late from college one summer evening, and as he drove his motor bike up the long drive to the house his heart sank as he observed the usual mess of toys strewn all over the garden. His mouth compressed into a line of irritability as he strode into the back door of the house.

"Why do you always leave the garden for me to clear up?" he commented impatiently. "You've nothing else to do all day, except look after the house and the kids!"

"I'm sorry!" said Sylvia. "I will go and clear up, but bending and stooping really hurts my hips and knees, so I keep putting it off".

Sylvia was now feeling the pain in her legs an intolerable imposition. Her sleep was broken night after night, and she would wake to discomfort every morning. It made her bad tempered and irritable and she would often snap at the children unnecessarily.

"I think that you should see a doctor", said Richard.

"Well I did just before we were married", said Sylvia, "but he just dismissed it as nothing to worry about – just muscular pains!"

"You should have mentioned it to Clare Henderson whilst we were still living at my mother's", said Richard. "Anyway, we have a different doctor now in this village. Perhaps this one might investigate further".

Sylvia made an appointment to see the village doctor and in the first instance she was fobbed off with sugar coated pills which had no effect whatsoever. Eventually, after many visits and Sylvia's insistence that she had a problem, the doctor arranged for her to have her knees x-rayed at the local hospital. The results were negative! Several more months of sugar coated pills went by before Sylvia determined to insist upon further investigations. Reluctantly the doctor arranged for her to have another hospital appointment, this time for x-rays of her hips. After the appointment she was sent home to await the results of the x-rays. Almost by return of post she received a letter from the hospital, urging her to return for further x-rays.

"I've had a letter from the hospital this morning", she said to Richard when he came home from college that evening. "They want me to go back for further x-rays tomorrow, so perhaps the first lot did not take properly".

The next morning dawned with the carefree persistent singing of a meadow lark in the neighbouring field. When Sylvia opened the bedroom window she could smell the sweetness of the fresh raindrops which sparkled in the hedgerows like a thousand diamonds. She sighed contentedly, glad that she lived out in the country where her children could play in safety, glad that they had made their decision to leave the grim industrial town of Halifax.

"I'll take the children to your mother's whilst I go to the hospital", she said to Richard at breakfast time. "I don't suppose that I shall be too long. Thank goodness I can drive the car now otherwise it would be such a hassle!"

When she eventually arrived at the hospital, Sylvia was ushered to a cubicle and asked to remove all her clothes and put on the long white gown which was handed to her. She was puzzled. This had not happened last time. When she had stripped off her clothes and put on the gown, she sat down on the bench in the cubicle and awaited further instructions. After a few minutes the curtain was drawn back swiftly and a white coated doctor stood in front of her.

"Mrs. Sanderson?" he asked.

"Yes", replied Sylvia, now even more puzzled.

"I am Dr. Askew", he said. "Tell me about these pains that you are having. Has your mother ever had any problems with her hips?"

"No, I don't think so", answered Sylvia.

"What about your grandmother?" Dr. Askew continued.

"Well, I know that she had arthritis very badly", said Sylvia.

"Have you any brothers and sisters?"

"No", replied Sylvia.

Dr. Askew paused for a moment before he continued.

"Well I'm very sorry to tell you my dear, but you have osteoarthritis in both your hips. They are already in the state of a seventy year old person with chronic osteoarthritis. By the time that you are fifty you'll be in a wheel chair!"

At that moment in time Sylvia was twenty eight years old!

"We are now going to take x-rays of the rest of your bones to see if they are also affected!" said Dr. Askew.

After the second lot of x-rays had been examined it was clear that the arthritis was confined to Sylvia's hips and the base of her spine.

Sylvia drove home in a state of shock. She told Richard who was equally shocked and very worried. Every six months she had to visit the consultant at the hospital, and every time he examined her he would say exactly the same thing, "Poor lass! Poor lass! There's nothing to be done for you at the moment. Come back in six months time".

There was of course hip replacement surgery, but that was still in its infancy and could easily go wrong. Also Sylvia was considered too young for such drastic surgery for in those days the risk of failure was high and she could have ended up in a wheel chair for the rest of her life. As she had two young children to look after it was not considered right for her to take such a risk.

One day she was asked to go to a medical conference of surgeons in Sheffield, and to be subjected to their examinations in the interest of medical science. She went along willingly in the hope that one of these eminent persons might come up with some remedy for her condition. The group of consultants concluded that her arthritic condition was the result of a bilateral Perthes' disease in early childhood. Perthes' disease is a malformation of the bones during the process of ossification. In other words, when the bones were still gristle during babyhood they had malformed as they hardened. Instead of the hip bones being smooth and rounded, they had lumps and nodules on them. The arthritis had attacked the already diseased bones when Sylvia was about eleven years old. It was suggested that the reason for the original problem could have been malnutrition as a baby. Knowing the stories of her infancy, when her mother was unable to feed her, and could find no milk to suit her so that she drastically lost weight, Sylvia could well see that malnutrition at that crucial stage of development was the answer. She was not to have any more children because her hips were not strong enough for the weight bearing involved. Everything now fell into place in Sylvia's mind – the painful walking from an early age, the limping, never being able to run fast and always being last in races. She had never been able to climb a rope or jump over the gym box in gymnastics, like her friends. Then there was all the pain she had experienced during her two pregnancies.

Now that she knew there was a genuine reason for all her pain and discomfort it helped her to come to terms with it. Sylvia had a resilient nature and after the initial shock, with Richard's help she set about arranging her life differently. Anna was now big enough to help more, and it was going to be necessary to insist that both the children should gather up and put away their own toys at the end of the day. Richard made a weekly visit to the super market and stocked up the larder for the whole week, and he also helped with any heavy household chores whenever he could. Thus the family adapted to the situation to keep the household running as smoothly as possible.

7. RAT POISON

Richard was half way through his last year at teacher training college. He had been thinking a great deal about his wife's disability and how it might affect all their futures, particularly if she did become wheelchair bound.

"I think we need a bungalow Mother", he said one day when visiting his parents. "Then there won't be any stairs for Sylvia to climb and it will be easier for her to manage. There are some days when she can hardly walk, especially in the damp cold weather."

"Why don't you build one here?" said Richard's father. "I'll let you have a piece of land in this garden. We don't need it all now that we are getting older".

Richard thought that seemed a splendid idea and it would kill two birds with one stone. Not only would he be able to provide a suitable home for his wife, but he would also be on hand to help his aging parents without actually living with them. Also it would cut down travelling time to and from school should he acquire a teaching post in the town.

During the summer months he designed the bungalow himself and had the plans drawn up by an architect. The design was for ease of maintenance, with extra wide corridors and doors in case his wife ever came to needing a wheelchair. The bungalow would be 'H' shaped with a central kitchen and main hall, the bedrooms and bathroom to the left, and a large sitting room and dining room to the right. He had thought of the position of the sun during each part of the day and placed the windows to gain maximum benefit.

That August they sold their little house in the country and moved back to live with Richard's parents until the bungalow was finished. Richard was going to be involved in a great deal of the work himself, subcontracting tradesmen to do the skilled jobs which he could not do. He did much of the labouring, the plumbing of the central heating system, and all the electrical wiring. Once the craftsman had completed his work on the roof then Richard completed the roof by laying the tiles.

Sylvia acquired a teaching post in a nearby private school where she was able to take Anna. Rebecca went with her in the mornings and was installed in the nursery there. At lunch time each day Aunt Emily went down to the school to collect Rebecca and to take her home for her afternoon nap. Rebecca loved her Great Aunt Emily very much. She loved to hear the stories about the 'olden days' when Aunt Emily was young. Sometimes they would go on a long walk together or, should it be raining, they would stay indoors and Aunt Emily would play games with her. Richard had objected to Sylvia going back to work, particularly to a full time job.

"Look!" said Sylvia, "You know I love teaching and it's a job I can do which doesn't hurt my hips. The money will help with the cost of the bungalow and eventually, when we move in, I can afford to pay someone to do the housework which I hate doing anyway".

Richard saw the sense of this and they could certainly do with the money.

Sylvia did not relish living with her in- laws again but she knew it was only a temporary arrangement. It was not that she was not fond of them, but there were occasional clashes as her way of thinking was so different from theirs. Richard did his best to smooth the way, understanding his wife's point of view as well as his parents, so things did not work out too badly.

Sylvia was thoroughly enjoying her work at school. She had been trained to teach much older children but found the younger children much easier to handle as well as being very keen to learn.

"You can actually go into a classroom and begin to teach straight away!" she exclaimed. "At secondary school age half the children don't want to be in school at all and one spends half one's time battling with discipline. They're just not interested in learning!"

It wasn't that Sylvia was ineffectual in this area. She knew the trick of discipline and generally had her classes under control. Her amazement was that the toughness she had acquired from teaching older and disinterested children was not required with the children now in her care. She could really enjoy pure teaching and with good results, so she felt it to be much more rewarding.

One November day, damp with mist and fog, she came home from school with a raging sore throat.

"I'll just have to go to bed Richard. Can you see to the tea for you and the children please?" asked Sylvia.

Poor Mary

"Will beans on toast be all right, or toast on beans?" said Richard grinning. "Then perhaps my mother will see the children to bed as I want to work on the bungalow again the evening".

Sylvia made herself a drink of hot milk with treacle and a tot of whisky, and took a cold cure powder. She went up stairs and collapsed into bed, her hips throbbing with pain and burning with inflammation. Any infection she picked up seemed to seek out her damaged bones very quickly. Richard came to bed much later having spent his evening doing some more plumbing work in the new bungalow.

The house was quiet as everyone slept. Only Sylvia tossed and turned as the fever manifested itself in hot sweats. Suddenly she heard a noise and she sat up in bed, causing her head to throb even more painfully. There it was again – someone knocking at the door! It couldn't be – not at three o'clock in the morning! She staggered out of bed and peered through a chink in the curtains. Outside, the dark street was still damp from the November rain which had fallen earlier. There was definitely someone knocking at the front door. She could hear the shuffling of feet in the porch way. It couldn't be a burglar – he wouldn't knock! Besides it was hardly the sort of house to be burgled, being shabby and tatty in appearance. With that in mind Sylvia made her way down the dark staircase to the front door. She observed the shape of a person through the frosted glass of the door.

"Who is it?" she whispered loudly.

"It's your mother!" was the reply.

"Oh God! What now?" thought Sylvia as she unlocked and opened the door.

Mary thrust a tin of something into Sylvia's hand.

" 'Ere! I've brought this to finish you all off with. I've taken mine!" said Mary, and then quickly disappeared on her bicycle into the night.

Sylvia stood on the doorstep, shivering and sweating, and looking in amazement at the tin in her hand. It was labelled 'Warfarin'!

"Oh God!" she thought again, and hurried up the stairs to the bedroom to Richard who was now fully awake.

"What the hell is going on?" he whispered loudly as his wife came into the room and sat down shakily on the bed.

"It was my mother", whispered Sylvia. "Can you believe it? She shoved this tin into my hand and said that we should finish ourselves off with it. It is rat poison I think!"

Richard took the tin from Sylvia and removed the lid to reveal the powder within. He moistened his finger and dipped it into the powder which immediately turned blue on contact with the moisture.

"It's definitely rat poison", he said.

"She says she's taken some. Do you think she would?" said Sylvia anxiously.

"I don't know. Anything could happen with your mother!"

"It's no good", said Sylvia. "I feel really awful but I shall have to go down and see her".

Wearily she struggled into her clothes, the sweat pouring down her face with the effort. She went out into the cold night air and climbed into her car and set off. It was now about four o'clock in the morning. As she reached her mother's home, her head was pounding and she shivered violently as she knocked at the door. She heard the sound of a key being turned in the lock and the door slowly opened to reveal Mary standing there, an inane grin on her face. Then she retreated down the dark corridor to the back of the house without saying a word, allowing Sylvia to follow her.

Sylvia switched on the electric light as she entered the shabby room which smelled of dampness and mould.

"Have you taken any of that powder?" demanded Sylvia in a croaky voice as her head was now thick with cold.

Mary responded by sticking out her tongue which was bright blue, exactly the same colour as Richard's finger when he had tested the powder.

"You stupid woman!" Sylvia shouted hoarsely. "I'll have to telephone the hospital now and you'll have to go in. Why ever did you do that?"

Dashing out of the house, she rushed to the nearest telephone box and rang for an ambulance, telling the operator that her mother had taken rat poison. Within a short time an ambulance came and whisked Mary off to the local hospital where she had her stomach pumped. No trace of the poison could be found in her stomach, only on her tongue. It had all been a ploy to attract attention to her self and to cause maximum distress to others. She had certainly achieved her goal.

8. THE LITTLE BOAT

Sylvia's full time work was certainly boosting the finances. Richard was now also teaching so with two good salaries coming in they were able to afford luxuries which otherwise would have been impossible. They bought a small motor boat which they often used on the nearby river.

"There's a sailing course in the docks during the next few weeks", said Richard. "I think we should go on it, and then we will be better equipped to take our boat out on the sea".

During the next few weeks the couple went regularly on the sailing course which taught them a great deal. The problems for Sylvia arose because she lacked agility and she was not sure footed. Climbing down the iron ladder down the steep wall of the dock, and clambering into a rocky boat in the choppy water, she found terrifying. It was also difficult for her to avoid being struck by the swinging boom. It was however valuable experience in handling any boat on choppy waters.

It was seven o'clock on a spring evening in April. Richard suggested that they should take the little boat to the slip way at Cleethorpes and then motor down to the docks and back. Leaving Anna and Rebecca asleep in their beds and in the care of Grandma, they set off, towing their boat behind their car. On reaching Cleethorpes they struggled to launch their boat from the slip way and at last found themselves chugging along and hugging the coast as they made their way to the docks. It was a beautiful evening and they were

Poor Mary

finding it exhilarating as they made their way down the estuary of the River Humber. They bobbed along the crest of the waves and listened to the cries of the gulls which swooped down towards them, hoping for a morsel of food. Sylvia turned her face up to the bright windy sky and sighed with contentment.

"This is the life", she thought, "We should do this more often".

"I don't think we should go any further. We'll turn round and go back now", said Richard. "We shouldn't really take this small boat into the dock". He steered the little boat around and they began to make their return journey.

"I'm really enjoying this", cried Sylvia above the noise of the engine and the wind. "It gives you a great sense of freedom doesn't it?"

At that moment the engine spluttered and then there was silence!

"Oh dear!" exclaimed Richard. "I think we've run out of petrol. Never mind, we have a gallon tin of petrol with us. What a good thing I brought that!"

Clouds scudded across the sky, driven by brisk winds. The sea had suddenly become choppy and trying to fill up the petrol tank whilst the boat was bobbing up and down was no easy task, but at last it was done. Richard then picked up the starting cable to restart the engine, but just as he did so an extra large wave caused him to totter and, in trying to regain his balance, he managed to drop the starting cable over the side of the boat into the murky water. Within seconds it had been swept out of reach and the tide had turned and an off shore wind had sprung up. They were heading at an alarming rate towards the open sea and by now the coast was already too far away for anyone to heed their cries for help.

"We're nearly in the deep sea fishing lane", said Richard who was now desperately trying to row the boat with the one oar they always carried with them. For every stroke he made forward the little boat was thrust five paces back by the powerful pull of the tide. It was impossible to make any headway.

With her heart in her mouth Sylvia had never felt so petrified in the whole of her life. She couldn't swim a stroke and Richard was not a strong enough swimmer to swim against the nasty dangerous currents of the Humber Estuary. Sylvia thought of the regular newspaper stories of swimmers and boats being carried out to the North Sea, and bodies being recovered from miles down the coast. She was convinced that this was about to be their fate. She thought of her two little girls lying asleep in their beds, and she imagined them waking up the following morning to the news that they had lost their mummy and daddy. Whatever would become of them, for Richard's parents were too old to have full time care of two young children!

"This is it!" she thought. "We're really going to die. No one knows that we're out here so no one will look for us until it's too late". She wondered what it would be like to drown and she began to cry with fear.

Richard was a practical chap who always functioned best when all the chips were down. He quickly realised that rowing was a waste of time and energy and that no one was going to see that the boat was in trouble. If he didn't do something quickly then they were in danger

Poor Mary

of being run down by a passing trawler or engulfed by the much larger waves which they would shortly encounter. His eyes scanned the bottom of the boat and, tucked underneath one of the seats, he espied an old piece of rope. He quickly made a grab at it.

"I'll try and splice this rope", he said, "and with any luck I should be able to restart the engine with it!"

Several more precious minutes went by whilst Richard struggled to splice the rope so that he could have a thin enough piece to fix round the starter motor. Having made sure that the spliced rope had a firm grip, Richard gave the loose end a sharp pull and miraculously the small engine spluttered back to life. Quickly grabbing the tiller, he steered the boat towards the shore but it was no easy task. They were fighting the outgoing tide and the off shore wind, but very gradually the tiny craft gained ground until at last they were in striking distance of the shore. It was not until they were in shallow waters that Sylvia felt herself begin to relax and give way to relief. For her the sea had lost its charm and was forever to be feared.

At last and thankfully they were on dry land, heaving the boat up the slip way to its trailer. They were both very quiet as they drove home, each thinking what a lucky escape they had had, and never to underestimate the power of the sea. When they reached the house, Sylvia went straight upstairs to look at her sleeping children who lay there in their beds, peacefully oblivious of how near they had been to losing their parents.

9. NEW LIFE

Birds filled the early morning air with twittering, chirpings and raucous calls. A world of green, still wet from the rain, glittered in the morning sun. The blue sky and sunshine were welcome after the rain of the day before. Sylvia rose from her bed and went down stairs to make breakfast for her husband and two small daughters. As she busied herself in the kitchen she was suddenly overcome by a wave of nausea. Trying to shake it off, she continued with her tasks and then went back upstairs to make sure that the children were awake and getting ready for school. Anna could manage to dress herself, but Rebecca still needed a little help. Having made sure that the children were ready, she went into the bedroom to Richard.

"I think I'm pregnant!" she announced.

"You can't be!" exclaimed Richard. "We've taken every precaution. Have you missed a period?"

"Not yet", answered Sylvia, "but I feel terribly sick this morning, exactly like in my other pregnancies. I just know that I am!"

Sylvia's period did not arrive and so she paid a visit to her doctor.

"Yes, you're definitely pregnant Sylvia", confirmed Clare Henderson. "You must not go through with this – not with the condition of your hips! You'll have to have an abortion. I'll make an appointment for you to see a consultant".

Later that day Richard and Sylvia were worriedly discussing this new dilemma.

Poor Mary

"I don't think that I can go through with an abortion", said Sylvia. "I don't agree with them. I just can't make that decision".

The firm grip of Richard's hand, resting on hers, was as always strong, vigorous and comforting.

"Don't try to make a decision until you've seen the consultant", he said, "and then follow his advice".

A few days later found Sylvia sitting in a consulting room facing Mr. Dunkerly, the consultant who had just given her a thorough examination. If she had expected a decision to be made for her then she was to be disappointed.

"It's entirely up to you whether or not you go ahead with this pregnancy", he said. "Your hip condition, bad as it may be, is not a life threatening situation, so you must decide".

Sylvia knew that another pregnancy would be difficult for her, causing more discomfort to her damaged hip bones as her weight increased. It would also mean that she would have to give up her well paid teaching post, just as they were beginning to feel the benefit of two steady incomes. Her salary was going a long way towards the cost of their new bungalow, and they also had plans for nice new furniture. She also knew that she could not deliberately destroy the new life growing within her.

"I'll get through this somehow", she said later to Richard, "and it's only for nine months!"

"You'll just have to rest more", said Richard, "and you know I'll do anything to make life easier for you. Don't worry about the money. We'll manage on my salary I'm sure!"

"We'll just have to go without the new furniture that we'd planned to buy", said Sylvia. "Anyway, what's the point of having posh furniture for three young children to jump on?"

Sylvia had stayed behind at school in order to finish marking her pupils' books. The door of the classroom opened and in walked the Principal of the school. She was an elderly, white haired lady who had been a handsome woman in her time. Sylvia rose to her feet as Miss Macdonald approached her desk.

"Hello Sylvia", said Miss Macdonald. "I just wanted a word with you. Do sit down again". She drew up a chair and sat down herself. "I'll come straight to the point", she continued. "As you aware, I'm not getting any younger and I need to think about the continuity of the school when I retire. I'm looking for a partner to run the school with me for a while and who will be able to take it over completely when I eventually go. Are you interested?"

Sylvia was flabbergasted and then, as the realisation of what was being offered to her sunk in she felt thrilled. This would be a dream come true, a share in the running of a school which would one day be hers. Then she suddenly remembered and flushed bright red!

"Oh dear!" she said. "I would absolutely love the opportunity – it's what I've always wanted – but – I must tell you now that I'm pregnant. I was going to tell you soon anyway – except that the doctor thought that I should have an abortion, but I've realised that I couldn't go through with it. It's all been very unsettling!"

"I see", said Miss Macdonald in a voice full of disappointment and dashed hopes. "So you'll be leaving us then? When do you think that you will finish here?"

"I hope to be able to stay on until Christmas. The baby is due in February. I would like to come back to work here though – once the child is old enough to be left with someone else – just part time of course – so that I can earn the money for the school fees for Anna and Rebecca – if it would be possible!"

Miss Macdonald went away feeling very disappointed. She really thought that she had found the right person to help her run the school, and who was capable of taking over after she had retired. "Never mind!" she thought, not being a person who was daunted for long. "I'll wait a little longer until someone else comes along".

10. JAYNE

The weeks passed and the summer holidays arrived. For some time, Sylvia had been threatened with the miscarriage of her baby and was advised to rest more. With two young children to care for this was easier said than done, so she carried on normally and thinking that if she did miscarry then it was nature's way of protection and that it would probably be for the best.

Richard had bought a cheap caravan which he towed to the Lincolnshire coast and placed it on a camp site there.

"I would like you and the children to stay in the caravan during the holidays", he said, "whilst I get on with the building of the bungalow".

"It sounds a lovely idea to me", said Sylvia. "There won't be any household chores to do, and the girls will love being by the seaside for a good long stretch. It will be good for them to be out in the fresh air all day".

"I'll come down each weekend", said Richard, "so that will give me a break as well as making sure that you are all right".

Although she often had a nagging back ache and a persistent loss of blood, Sylvia continued to carry on doing normal things with Anna and Rebecca. They went walking by the sea, played games in the sand, and even had rides at the nearby funfair. If it had been intended that Sylvia should miscarry then it certainly would have happened, but the baby hung on tenaciously.

"What is to be will be!" thought Sylvia, and so she passed through the first months of her pregnancy and eventually things settled down.

The summer passed and once more the leaves on the trees turned golden as Sylvia returned to teaching for one last term before her baby was due to be born. As her weight increased with the pregnancy, she found life increasingly difficult with the pain from her arthritic hips. There were many days when she felt that she would never get up from the place where she was sitting, nor did she often want to do so. Being of resolute spirit, she gritted her teeth with grim determination to work until the end of the term.

In the meantime Richard worked every moment of his spare time on the bungalow. He knew that Sylvia wanted to be settled in there well before the baby was born. Also he knew that she did not find it easy living in his parent's house, particularly with the two girls. His mother had different standards of discipline, and cleanliness, the latter leaving a great deal to be desired. Sylvia did not want her new baby to begin life anywhere less than wholesome.

Somehow she managed to stagger through the term but Richard gave a sigh of relief when she arrived home, puffing and panting at the end of her last day at school.

"I want you to have a good rest this Christmas", he said. "Then I hope that we will be able to move into the bungalow early in January, even though it might not be quite finished it will be habitable. That will give us five or six weeks to get organized before the baby arrives".

At last the great day came when the little family could move into their home. They couldn't afford to buy any new furniture as they had originally planned, but that didn't matter. The bungalow was double glazed and had central heating, so it was always going to be warm and snug and with plenty of hot water. A second hand automatic washing machine was bought to take the chore out of the washing. What more could they want?

"This is such an easy house to clean", thought Sylvia as she vacuumed the carpets one day in mid February. It was freezing cold outside but the bungalow was snug and warm, and Sylvia was actually perspiring heavily as she dragged the vacuum cleaner along the carpet. Suddenly she felt a sharp pain in the small of her back!

"Ouch!" she exclaimed, straightening up quickly. She glanced at the clock on the book case in the sitting room. It was exactly four o'clock in the afternoon. "I'll hurry up and finish this room before I make the evening meal. Ouch! There it is again!" It suddenly dawned on her that this could be the onset of labour. "I'd better phone Clare", she thought.

Ten minutes later it was confirmed that Sylvia was in labour. By now Richard had arrived home from school and helped his wife to prepare her bag for the Maternity Home.

"Peter is on duty tonight", said Clare, "so he will probably deliver your baby".

Poor Mary

"Well tell your husband that I will see him at four o'clock in the morning", said Sylvia. "Both my other pregnancies were exactly twelve hours from start to finish and I had my first pain at four o'clock this afternoon".

"That doesn't mean that it will be the same this time", laughed Clare.

Peter Henderson arrived at the Maternity Home to deliver Sylvia's baby. At exactly four o'clock in the morning Sylvia gave birth to her third daughter!

Richard took Anna and Rebecca to see their mother and new baby sister as soon as it was convenient later on in the day.

"What are we going to call her Mummy?" queried Anna as she gazed in wonderment at the perfect tiny baby resting in her crib by her mother's bed.

"Do you like the name Jayne?" asked Sylvia.

Everyone agreed that the name suited the baby so Jayne she was called. Sylvia looked at her two elder daughters, Anna with her blue eyes, blonde hair and peaches and cream complexion, and Rebecca with her dark brown eyes so much like her own, the darker straighter hair and golden tanned skin. Then she looked at baby Jayne.

"I think that Jayne resembles Rebecca", said Sylvia. "You are more like your Daddy Anna, and Rebecca and Jayne look more like me. You all have a strong family look though – you can tell that you are all sisters".

Several nights later, Sylvia fell into a deep sleep and she began to dream. She dreamed that she had lost her baby. She was searching for her but she was no where to be found. In desperation she ran across the garden until she came to Clare's house and hammered on the door.

"I've lost my baby", she wept as Clare opened the door. Clare slammed the door shut in her face and Sylvia crumbled to her knees, sobbing.

Sylvia gave a loud cry of anguish, and woke up in her bed, sweating with fear. "My baby!" she thought, and then she gave a sigh of relief. Jayne was there in the crib beside her bed. It had just been a bad dream!

The next morning Sylvia awoke feeling very uneasy, and then she remembered her dream. She leaned over to look at the sleeping infant. The child was perfect in every way, but still Sylvia worried. She remembered some anti-inflammatory drugs that she had been prescribed for her painful arthritic hips. She was supposed to take them everyday, whether she had pain or not. In the early stages of her pregnancy Clare had given her a sample pack of these tablets. In the pack was a leaflet about the drugs. The small print clearly stated that there was no proof that this drug did not harm the unborn foetus. Sylvia had recoiled in horror, being three months pregnant, and threw the tablets away immediately, vowing never to take them again. She has worried during her pregnancy that her unborn child might have been harmed in some way. Seeing her baby lying there, so perfect, dispelled her fears somewhat. Then another thought came into her mind.

Poor Mary

"You look perfect on the outside, but what if you have been damaged inside your little body!"

As the day wore on and visitors came to admire her baby, exclaiming how beautiful she was, Sylvia told herself that she was worrying unnecessarily over a silly dream. "I probably only dreamed it because of my worry over the tablets", she told herself.

11. A CHRISTENING

Sylvia was proud of her three daughters. Anna was now seven and favoured her father in appearance with her blue eyes and fair hair. Rebecca had the same warm brown eyes and darker skin of her mother. She tanned easily and without burning, whereas Anna had to be careful not to burn in the sun. Rebecca's hair was not as dark as Sylvia's but it had the same natural wave and thickness. Baby Jayne was almost a replica of Rebecca, except that her eyes were a darker shade of brown. She was an extremely good baby who never cried without good reason. In fact Clare said that Jayne was too good to be true.

"This baby is unnatural", said Clare whose own children had all been troublesome babies. "You can set the clock by her waking up for her feeds - eight, twelve, four and eight o'clock, on the dot each time!"

Sylvia thought that it was perhaps that she had been lucky in being able to establish a good routine from the start with Jayne who seemed naturally a good natured baby.

As May departed and June arrived, Sylvia awoke one morning to a bright sunlit day, warm with the fullness of summer. The trees were leafed out but still a shade lighter than they would be later.

"It's a lovely day to put Jayne out in the garden in her pram", she thought as she looked up at small puffs of cloud drifting lazily on a light wind.

Poor Mary

At lunch time she discovered that Jayne had diarrhea in her nappy and during the course of the rest of the day it was necessary to change her nappy at frequent intervals.

"I'd better let Clare see Jayne", said Sylvia to Richard when he came home from school. "She's had diarrhea all day and it doesn't seem to be clearing up".

Clare gave the usual medical advice for a baby with diarrhea, and prescribed some anti-biotic medicine. Jayne's condition did not improve and the medicine was changed.

"I can't understand why she doesn't respond to the treatment", puzzled Clare.

Jayne's condition lasted for three weeks before eventually clearing up and naturally she had lost weight. It was a relief to all when the child began to feed normally again and to regain some of her weight. After that episode Jayne began to thrive again, but Sylvia still had a niggling worry.

"I'm probably being really stupid, but I still wonder if those tablets I took during her pregnancy did some harm to her somehow. Perhaps they damaged the lining of her stomach and that is why she did not respond to treatment quickly. I don't suppose we'll ever know and I suppose any doctor would think I am being a paranoid mother!"

As the months passed and Jayne blossomed into a bonny, bouncing child, full of smiles and laughter, Sylvia forgot about her worries.

In November Rebecca had her fifth birthday followed by Anna's eighth birthday in December. The two little girls were eagerly looking forward to Jayne's first birthday in February. They wanted to have a party, complete with a birthday cake and one candle. When Jayne's first birthday dawned on a bright February morning, Anna and Rebecca were up very early to greet their baby sister with their gifts for her. Anna gave her a miniature rubber doll, just big enough for a tiny hand to hold – and a little mouth to chew! Rebecca gave her a rag book with pictures of baby animals. Sylvia and Richard's present to their daughter was a teddy bear which, when wound up by a key in its back, played the tune of 'Three Blind Mice'. Anna helped to decorate the birthday cake and they all enjoyed the birthday tea along with a few friends.

"Jayne is now one year old", said Sylvia, "and she hasn't been christened yet. I'd better go along and see the vicar and arrange for him to christen her".

Because the area in which they lived had grown rapidly and several new housing estates were shooting up all over the place, it was now thought large enough to have its own church, other than the old church which served the original village. A vicar had been appointed but, as the church was not yet built, the services were held each Sunday in the local school hall. There was however a new vicarage and the new priest already lived there with his wife and family. Sylvia went along to the vicarage and soon found herself sitting in the vicar's study. The Reverend John Wentworth was a tall well built man with a jovial countenance and a keen sense of humour. His wife, Francis, was tall, slim and

Poor Mary

very pretty. John and Francis had one baby daughter who was a few months older than Jayne. She was sitting outside the vicarage in her pram and talking to the trees when Sylvia had walked down the garden to the front door.

"When would you like your baby to be christened?" asked the Reverend Wentworth. "I can do it next Sunday if you wish!"

"That would be perfect", replied Sylvia.

"Being as we have no church building yet", continued Reverend Wentworth, "I can christen the child in the school where we have our services, or alternatively I can hold the christening in your own home"

The latter seemed an unusual idea to Sylvia and it appealed to her, and so it was agreed that the christening service should take place at home.

"If you like I can also bless your new house at the same time", suggested the Reverend.

"Thank you", said Sylvia, "I would like that. Also if your wife would care to come along to the christening and bring your baby, I would like that too".

During the following week, Sylvia busied herself sending out invitations to relatives and close friends, and arranging who should be godparents to her daughter. She then had to organize refreshments for the christening party afterwards.

On the morning of the christening, raindrops glistened in the shafts of sunlight which splashed along the garden. However, as the day wore on, the February sun dried up the paths and the afternoon proved to be sunny and crisp. Whilst Sylvia prepared for their guests, Anna and Rebecca amused baby Jayne whilst Richard took the car to go and collect his mother-in-law, Mary. He dreaded the thought of the embarrassment she might bring to his family, but for once she came along meekly and in one of her rare reasonably rational moods, and looking suitably dressed for the occasion.

At last the time was near and friends and relatives began to arrive and chat together in the sitting room. Anna and Rebecca were clothed in their prettiest dresses, and Jayne wore a simple white dress trimmed with a single pink bow at the collar. She bounced up and down in her baby walker, enjoying all the extra attention from her aunts, uncles and cousins.

"Oh look!" cried the five year old Rebecca, jumping up and down with excitement. "Here comes the vicar with his mummy!"

Sylvia looked up to see the Reverend Wentworth, and his wife who was pushing her baby's pram, walking down the driveway. "I don't think that Mrs. Wentworth would be very flattered if she heard that Rebecca. The lady is not his mummy, she is his wife, and the baby is their little girl".

"Oh!" said Rebecca, pressing her nose to the hall window as she watched the vicar and his family approach the house.

The christening service and the following party were enjoyed by all, including the Reverend and his wife.

"Do come round to see me for a chat and a coffee whenever you want", said Francis to Sylvia as they were leaving the house.

"Thank you, I would love to", said Sylvia as she bade them goodbye. Thus a friendship began which was to last for the rest of their lives.

12. PAULA

Her three daughters were all tucked up in their beds and fast asleep. Sylvia did her nightly check, pausing at each little bed to gaze at the face of each sleeping child. She stood looking down at Jayne who was sleeping contentedly in her cot. Suddenly a cold shadow seemed to pass through the room and Sylvia shivered. A terrifying thought came into her mind, a flash of premonition swept over her, a sense of tragedy so strong that she felt faint.

"What if one of them had to die", she thought. "Which one would I have to lose? How could one make a choice like that if put to the test?" She then shook herself, telling herself not to be so morbid and to cast away such unbearable thoughts.

About a week later Richard came home from school, had his evening meal, and sat down to rest for a while before going outside in the garden to do some work.

"Something really strange happened to me in the staff room after lunch", he said.

"Oh!" said Sylvia. "What was it?"

"Well I know this may sound silly. I was sitting in a chair, marking some books, when my eyes felt really tired. I closed them for a moment and suddenly saw three figures all dressed in white".

"That is strange," said Sylvia. "Perhaps it was because you're over tired."

"Perhaps", said Richard, "but the funny thing was, I opened my eyes and rubbed them, and when

I closed them again the three white clad figures were still there".

A sense of unease came over Sylvia .This was not like Richard at all. He had a scientific mind and was not given to fanciful imaginings, nor did he believe in the supernatural, but obviously he was disturbed and troubled by the incident. She remembered her own experience of a sense of foreboding a few nights ago and she shivered.

A few days later, Richard stood looking out of the window and watching the March wind play havoc with the garden.

"Sylvia!" he suddenly cried out. "You need a friend!"

Sylvia looked up, startled at this sudden outburst from her husband.

"What do you mean, I need a friend?" she asked. "I've got Clare and she doesn't live far away".

"No, she'll let you down", said Richard. "You must have a friend who will be reliable!"

Sylvia recognized that this was no casual observation but a cry from the heart. She remembered her dream in the maternity home when she had lost her baby and Clare had closed the door on her. She quickly went to check on Jayne in her pram. The child was sleeping contentedly, a rosy bloom of health on her cheeks.

Sylvia had not seen her cousin Ralph and his family for about eighteen months when they had all come across from Yorkshire for the day. Ralph's daughter, Paula now sixteen, was an extremely pretty girl on the verge of blossoming into womanhood. Sylvia had marvelled at how grown up she was, remembering the days when she used to push Paula out in her pram when she herself was only sixteen. Paula had always had a special place in Sylvia's heart. The family had left them with promises on both sides to meet up with each other again soon.

One evening Sylvia went across to talk with Richard's mother for a few minutes. The old lady liked to hear about the events at school, and how the girls were getting on there. Sylvia was now teaching for a couple of afternoons each week and by doing so she managed to pay the school fees and also pay for someone to do her cleaning. It was easier for her to teach than to do housework, the latter being a painful experience for her arthritic hips. A neighbour who loved babies was delighted to look after Jayne for the two afternoons. By the time Sylvia had paid all of these expenses there was no money left for her self but she preferred these arrangements. Apart from saving her temper by not having to painfully struggle with household chores, it also gave her something else to talk about.

The telephone rang shrilly in her mother-in-law's hall and Aunt Emily, who was also talking to her sister, went to answer it.

"It's for you Sylvia", called Aunt Emily.

"For me? Why should anyone telephone me here?" said Sylvia. She was puzzled as she went to the phone and picked up the receiver.

"Hello! Is that Sylvia?" said a female voice with a strong Yorkshire accent.

"Yes it is", replied Sylvia.

"It's Maureen here".

Who?" Sylvia asked.

"Maureen, your Ronald's wife".

"Oh I'm sorry. I didn't recognise your voice and couldn't think who it could be. How are you?"

"I'm afraid I've got some bad news for you Sylvia".

The smile faded from Sylvia's face as Maureen continued with news of a most distressing nature.

"It's Paula. She got pneumonia – and she died!"

Sylvia cried out, left the phone dangling, and ran sobbing out of the house to her own bungalow. She did not stop to ask why, or how, she was so totally devastated.

"Richard! Richard!" she cried. The girls, Anna and Rebecca, looked up in amazement as their distraught mother stumbled through the door.

"Whatever is the matter?" said Richard.

"It's Paula – she's dead!"

"You must have got it wrong. She's only sixteen. It must be your grandmother who has died. You've misheard", said Richard.

"No, no I haven't. It was Maureen on the phone", said Sylvia in between sobs, - and she said – that - Paula had caught pneumonia - and that – she died!"

Poor Mary

It happened that Paula had been having uneasy dreams and, although she was now sixteen, she had asked her mother to stay with her during the night.

"I don't know why Mum, but I'm frightened", she had said. Her mother had stayed with her, trying to reassure her that everything was all right.

A few weeks later Paula caught a very nasty cold which turned out to be a bad dose of influenza. She had a really high temperature and a terrific headache, but she was supposed to be going out with her boy friend to a dance.

"You can't go out tonight", said her mother. "You've got 'flu – do have some sense!"

"Oh stop fussing Mum. I'll be all right. I'll probably feel better for going out".

As she disappeared up the garden path in her new high heeled shoes, her head throbbed with pain and sweat trickled down her back, in spite of the cold night air of early March. Two hours later her boy friend brought her home. She could barely stand up and her clothes were drenched with sweat as she shivered on the doorstep.

"I told ye not to go out", scolded her mother. "Go straight up to bed and I'll bring you a hot drink and a couple of aspirins."

During the night Paula was thrashing about in her bed and she was delirious. Her mother rushed into the bedroom on hearing her daughter's cries. Suddenly Paula sat up, holding her chest.

"I can't breathe Mum", she gasped, "and my chest is so painful".

"Ralph! Ralph! Go and telephone for the doctor – quickly!" shouted Doreen.

Paula's condition grew worse by the minute whilst her parents anxiously awaited the doctor's arrival. As soon as he saw the girl he wasted no time in sending for an ambulance.

The hospital staff did everything they could to make her comfortable and to stabilize her. Ralph and Doreen kept vigil by her bedside for the whole night. In the early hours of the morning as the first light broke, Paula seemed strangely quiet, but she was breathing gently. Suddenly she sat up in bed and removed her ear rings from her pierced ears and gave them to her mother.

"I won't need these any more Mum", she whispered.

Doreen's heart tightened as she looked at her daughter's ashen face, beads of perspiration on her forehead. Paula took the watch from her wrist and handed that also to her mother.

"I won't need any more time!" she whispered.

Then she lay back exhausted on her pillows, and her life ebbed from her fragile body.

13. DOCTORS DON'T ALWAYS KNOW BEST!

During the next few weeks Sylvia felt a great heavy sorrow pressing down upon her. Her sense of loss was painful as she grieved for her favourite niece.

"If I feel like this, whatever must Ralph and Doreen be feeling?" she sad to Richard. "It must be unbearable for them".

For a variety of reasons they had not been able to make the long journey to go to Paula's funeral. They therefore planned to visit Sylvia's bereaved cousins and Paula's grave on the Tuesday of Easter week which fell on the second week in April. On Easter Monday Sylvia prepared for their journey of the following day whilst Jayne bounced up and down in her baby walker, gurgling happily and trying to stick everything she laid hold of into her mouth. As Sylvia passed through the sitting room she lingered a while to play with her baby, marvelling at the beauty of the child who laughed at her with merry brown eyes so like her own. Aunt Emily had taken Anna and Rebecca to the seaside for the day and they came home at teatime full of the excitement of their day. At the funfair Rebecca had won a little bracelet which she proudly showed to her mother.

"Look what I won Mummy", cried Rebecca, flourishing the bracelet in front of Sylvia.

"Oh, how lovely! Let me have a look. Oh, it's a snake bracelet – and look, the snake has its tail in its mouth. That is a symbol of Eternity", explained Sylvia.

"What does that mean Mummy? What's ternity?"

"Eternity means for ever and ever", said Sylvia, "Now come along and eat your tea".

After tea the two little girls were told to get ready for bed so that they could have an early night, ready for their early start of their journey the following day. Rebecca left her snake bracelet on the kitchen table and then scampered off to her bedroom.

It was still dark when they got up on the day of their departure, and the multi hued leaves were just starting to show their true spring colours as the sky lightened. Ragged tatters of clouds streamed far to the south. Anna and Rebecca were both dressed and having their breakfast in the dining room. Sylvia glanced at the kitchen clock and thought that she had better see if Jayne were awake.

As she entered the bedroom a sickly smell invaded her nostrils. Jayne had been sick in her cot. Sylvia was alarmed when she saw her little daughter lying in a pool of vomit but Jayne grinned happily up at her.

"Oh dear Jayne! We'll have to put you in the bath now", said Sylvia as she stripped off the infant's soiled night dress. "Anna, will you come and watch Jayne in the bath for a minute. She's been sick and I need to change the sheets in her cot".

"Is she all right Mummy?" asked Anna as she gently splashed her baby sister with warm water.

"Well I hope so! She seems happy enough now and I think that she would be grizzling if she didn't feel

Poor Mary

well. Perhaps she's just got rid of something which disagreed with her".

At last the family was seated in their car and their journey began. Jayne was strapped into her baby chair on the back seat and was constantly kept amused by her two sisters. They had completed about half of their journey when Anna shouted.

"Mummy! Jayne must have dirtied her nappy and it really smells horrible!"

Richard stopped the car so that Sylvia could change Jayne's nappy. They glanced at each other, concern in their eyes, as they saw the contents of the nappy.

"She's not well", said Richard. "We'd better get on with the journey, and we'd better not stay too long with your cousins".

At last they reached Ralph's house and Sylvia wept as she embraced her bereaved cousins. They visited Paula's grave and Sylvia looked at the hard, cold black of the headstone which bore her niece's name.

"How can this be?" she thought. "It's just not fair! She had a whole life ahead of her, and now there's nothing but this cold stillness".

During the course of the day Jayne produced several more obnoxious nappies and had become quiet and pale.

"I really think that we should get home as quickly we can", said Richard. He felt very uneasy as he sped the car along the roads as fast as he dare. They eventually arrived home safely and the older children were put straight to bed. Jayne soiled her nappies frequently throughout the night, and the following Wednesday morning she looked flushed and was very hot. Sylvia wrote a note to Clare telling her of Jayne's condition and asked if she would come and see her as soon as possible. She then asked Anna to take the note to Clare. Ten minutes later Anna came back.

"Did you give the note to Clare?" asked Sylvia.

"Not exactly! Her cleaning lady said that she had gone shopping and wouldn't be back for a while. I left the note with her and she said that she would give it to Clare as soon as she got back", replied Anna.

Lunch time came, and lunch time passed and still Clare had not visited her little patient, who now lay listless and unsmiling in her pram, her cheeks burning with fever. Richard was outside mixing concrete so that he could complete the driveway to their house. At three o'clock Sylvia went out to him.

"When do you think Clare will come, Richard? I don't like to pester her but I really am worried now. It would be all the same if she were dying wouldn't it?"

As she said these words her stomach churned and tightened into a knot as fear brushed the edge of her mind. An hour later Clare could be seen as she walked from the inter-joining gate at the bottom of the garden. She apologised for not coming sooner but had only just received Sylvia's note.

"I had a few other things to do as well as my shopping and I only arrived back home ten minutes ago. I came as soon as I saw the note".

Clare examined the very quiet child as Sylvia explained how Jayne had been since the previous day. She looked up to be met by Sylvia's troubled eyes.

"There's nothing to worry about. I've seen babies like this hundreds of times and they always bounce

Poor Mary

back. Give her plenty of boiled water and glucose and cut out all milk for the time being".

"She's not taking food anyway", said Sylvia. "She can't keep anything down!"

During the night Sylvia kept Jayne in bed with her so that she could tend to her needs and constant nappy changing. The infant's eyes were rolling about and she needed to be close to her mother. Sylvia felt that her baby needed more medical attention, yet she was governed by Clare's words that there was nothing to worry about, and after all, Clare was the doctor, she should know best! If only Sylvia had listened to her own instincts as a mother! Doctors do not always know best!

As the new day dawned Jayne's breathing was shallow, dark circles rimmed her eyes, and her skin was warm, dry and pale. Sylvia fed her with glucose and water from her bottle, but even that she could not keep down. During the course of the morning, as she lay in her pram, her little hands continually plucked at the sheet which covered her. Not wishing to make a fuss, Sylvia did not know what to do.

"Surely Clare will come across and see Jayne this morning", said Sylvia on the verge of tears. I don't like to pester her again but she does know that she is poorly!"

"I'm going across to see Clare", said Richard resolutely. "That child needs urgent attention now!" It was totally out of character for him to be pushy but he was now very alarmed about his baby daughter. He returned a few minutes later.

"Did you see Clare?" asked Sylvia.

"Yes", replied Richard.

"What did she say?" queried Sylvia.

"She said that there is no cause for alarm and that babies are often like this", said Richard, his mouth drawn in a tight line.

"I'm sure they're not as bad as this", cried Sylvia. Her breath caught in her throat as the ice claw of fear once again gripped her heart.

A few minutes later Clare appeared at their door and she had brought an anti biotic prescription for Jayne. Inwardly she was disturbed by the drastic change in the child's appearance but her manner portrayed none of this to the parents.

"You must keep giving her the water together with the medicine", said Clare.

"But she can't even keep water down", cried Sylvia who was now very distressed.

"Keep persevering", said Clare as she left by the back door." I'll come back later!"

Sylvia cradled the listless child in her arms and rocked her gently. She stayed seated at the kitchen table so that she could continue trying to feed her the water from her bottle, but there was no strength in the baby to even suck now.

On the red kitchen table Sylvia noticed the little snake bracelet which Rebecca had won on Monday at the fair. Suddenly an amazing thing happened. The thirteen month old child, who appeared to have lost all her strength, reared herself up to a sitting position,

Poor Mary

reached out her little hand and picked up the bracelet. Instead of putting it in her mouth as she normally would have done, she slipped the bracelet on to her small wrist and then lay back in her mother's arms, her eyes closed as she laboured with her breathing. Sylvia gazed at the snake bracelet – the symbol of Eternity – on her child's wrist – and she shivered.

She carried her baby into the sitting room and sat down on a more comfortable chair. Richard, who had been outside and working on his driveway, came in through the front door.

"How is she?" he enquired anxiously.

"I don't really know", replied Sylvia. "She appears to be resting at the moment. Perhaps she's a little better – she actually sat up and grabbed Rebecca's bracelet from the kitchen table. It was quite amazing the way she put it on her wrist – in such an adult way – not like a baby! It made me feel quite funny!"

Suddenly the child on her lap stiffened and went rigid, her head thrown back and her eyes rolling up to the top of her head.

"Quick! Quick! Go and get Clare - quickly!" shouted Sylvia.

Richard flew down the garden like the wind and a few minutes later he came back with Clare. Clare took one look at Jayne and her face paled.

"I'll go and get Peter. He'll take her to the hospital. She's had a convulsion!" she said quietly.

As they waited anxiously for Clare's husband, Peter, Sylvia and Richard stared in fear and dread at the unseeing eyes of their infant daughter. They were both now aware and frightened that even if she should survive she might only live in a compromised fashion. A convulsion of this magnitude could only have caused massive brain damage.

After only a few minutes which seemed like hours the doctor, who had delivered Jayne just over a year ago, came into the house. His face looked grim as he saw the child. Sylvia let Richard take Jayne from her arms. She did not move from the chair, nor did he ask her to go with him. In his clothes made dirty from the concreting work he had been doing, he carried his baby to Peter's car. All the way to the hospital the child was in difficulty and as Peter steered his car with one hand, he was resuscitating her with the other. They arrived at the hospital within five minutes and oxygen tent had already been set up. Richard gently lowered his tiny daughter down into the crib, and as he did so he felt her writhe for a moment, and then he felt her stop moving!

Sylvia did not know why she did not go with Richard. She should not have let him go through this experience on his own, but she sat there as though mesmerized. Clare came and took her back to her house and the two women sat in silence in the kitchen – waiting!

Sylvia knew before Richard came back what the outcome would be, and yet when he at last entered the kitchen, shaking his head in silence, she still fought against it.

"No- no- NO- NO!" she screamed louder and louder. Her mind refused to acknowledge that her child was dead. She clung to Richard and the tears streamed down her face and mingled with his own as they wept together for their daughter.

14. ALL THINGS BRIGHT AND BEAUTIFUL

On Friday morning Sylvia woke early to bright sunshine and the peaceful sound of a wood pigeon cooing from a tree in the garden. Then the agony of the loss of Jayne passed across her heart and left a long stinging scratch. Her sprit took a downward plunge as though a black wall of water closed over her head and she felt that she might drown in her grief. The realisation of the finality of death is an awesome thing, when one knows that there is nothing at all that can be done to change it. Maybe in an earlier time, when couples had many children and infant death was common, perhaps women coped with it, but it is doubtful. The death of one's child tears out one's heart. "If only we had done this – if only we had done that – if only – if only!" So the tortured mind forever seeks an escape from the finality. One does not get over the death of a child. One only learns to live with it!

"Richard!" cried Sylvia, and she turned towards him in their bed. He could find no ways of comfort and he held her as she began to weep for their child. She wept silently, clinging to him, sobs shaking her. He let her expand her grief, and slowly the sobs abated.

Anna and Rebecca could be heard talking together in hushed voices. Sylvia got up from her bed and went to them, drawing them close to her and kissing the tops of their heads. How does one explain the death of a sister to two little girls? Then she went into the room where Jayne's cot stood silent and empty. Going up to it she gazed down at the vacant place where her baby should have been. The pillow still bore the indentation of the child's head from when she had last rested there. At the foot of the cot sat Jayne's teddy bear. Sylvia picked it up and turned the tiny key in its back and listened to the tune it played. The tune of 'Three Blind Mice' came from the musical teddy in sweet soft tones. She had never thought it possible to experience such physical pain in her heart. Reaching down into the cot she picked up the tiny rubber doll - Jayne's birthday present from Anna – just big enough for tiny fingers to hold. The head of the doll bore the imprint of two small teeth marks.

"It's best if we clear all her things as soon as possible", said Richard's voice behind her. "It will only hurt more if we delay!"

Sylvia nodded and they went into the kitchen for breakfast. Later on that morning the Reverend Wentworth came to see them to offer as much comfort to the family as he could. As they sat talking together, a great banging and clattering could be heard coming from the kitchen. Going to investigate, Sylvia found Anna on her hands and knees madly scrubbing the kitchen floor. The eight year old girl had never done anything like that before. As they had a cleaning lady there was no need.

"It's her way of coping", thought Sylvia. "She's trying to help us and it's the only way she can". She smiled at Anna. "Thank you very much Anna, that's very helpful, and the floor will look lovely when you've finished it".

Inwardly she wondered how Anna's little heart was coping with the pain and grief. Rebecca was playing her usual games and appeared to be acting quite normally. At her tender age she did not really understand what was going on. She only knew that Jayne was not in the house anymore!

That afternoon Sylvia and Richard were going to the Chapel of Rest to see their baby.

"I want to go too Mummy!" Anna cried.

"I'd rather you didn't", said Sylvia. "It's better for you to remember her when she was well and happy".

Anna didn't argue, but Sylvia never knew if she had done the right thing or not. One never does know until it is too late!

The little chapel was dimly lit and icy cold as Richard and Sylvia approached the white coffin which looked so tiny and lonely in this empty room. Sylvia gasped as she beheld her child, for her eyes had not been closed. Two beautiful orbs of soft brown pools stared unseeing at Sylvia who felt as though she were looking into her own soul. At that moment a little of the mother died with the child. Such a beautiful infant she had been! Distraught, Sylvia looked down upon the perfect waxen creature lying motionless in the white coffin. She gently touched the child's cheek and felt the coldness, like marble, and then she brushed a kiss on the icy forehead. The anguish of that moment and the intolerable frustration were unbearable.

The day of Jayne's funeral brought together the same group of people who had gathered at the house only six weeks before to witness her christening. The vicar who had christened the child six weeks ago was now going to bury her. As the relations arrived they met together in the sitting room and talked amongst each other with occasional lapses into hushed sepulchral tones.

The moment Sylvia had dreaded finally arrived. The hearse drew up outside the house together with the funeral cars. Before Richard could stop her, she dashed out of the house, running up the driveway and to the hearse which contained the tiny coffin lying on a bed of flowers. She touched the glass of the window, longing to take her child from this cold bed to the warmth of the house where she belonged. Her head was bowed for a few moments and she struggled to recover her composure before going back to her guests.

When the funeral party arrived at the old church where Richard and Sylvia had been married, Richard assisted his wife to the front pew. Once everyone was seated, the choir lifted their voices in the hymn;

> 'All things bright and beautiful,
> All creatures great and small,
> All things wise and wonderful,
> The Lord God made them all'.

Richard took Sylvia's hand and linked his fingers with hers as they turned together towards the tiny white coffin and followed it to the graveyard. As the Reverend Wentworth performed the last rites he too openly wept for the little one whom he had welcomed into the Church such a short time ago.

15. PICKING UP THE THREADS

The emptiness after Jayne's death was indescribable. Sylvia cried in bed, she cried in the kitchen, she cried in the car. She visited the tiny grave and she cried there too. One has to let out the tears and go through with those bone shakings of grief – and one has to be alone. Eventually one has to accept the enormous void and get on with living one's life.

It was perhaps as well that, due to illness, a member of staff was absent for the following summer term and Sylvia was asked to cover this full time work. Iron self control achieved through years of practice enabled her to carry out the school routine. Nevertheless, as she stood in front of her pupils at the small private school, her heart was like a cold stone as she taught them their lessons. There was emptiness within her that nothing could fill. At least her mind was occupied, there is no other way in a class room, and her sanity was preserved.

As Richard had strangely prophesied when he said that she needed a friend and just as she had dreamed at Jayne's birth, Clare let Sylvia down when she most needed her. Clare stopped coming to see her socially and made excuses to prevent Sylvia from visiting her. This was doubly hurtful to Sylvia at this moment of her life, and it was fortunate that she was able to go to school each day and therefore was not left alone to grieve in the house for long periods. Thinking of Clare's attitude later, Sylvia came to the conclusion that Clare was not able to handle the situation and was also grieving in her own way. Months later, when wounds were healing a little, their friendship was resumed.

Every night Sylvia dreamed about Jayne, or if not Jayne there would be other babies in her dreams. Perhaps these dreams could be interpreted as a yearning to put back the clock and start again. This time she would not make any mistakes! Every morning she woke up crying for her baby.

After several months of these dreams, Sylvia went to bed one night and as usual began to dream, but this time it was different. Sylvia found herself being taken by an unseen presence to a place not unlike the cloisters of a cathedral. She stood in the shadows of the cloisters and looked on to the sun lit lawn in the centre. There, sitting with her back towards her, was Jayne. Her fair hair curled into the nape of her neck and she was wearing her little yellow dressing gown. The infant was intent on picking the daisies from the lawn and plucking the petals from them, as babies will. Sylvia stretched out her hand towards the archway of the cloister and wanted to go through to her baby, but she was prevented from doing so by an invisible barrier. All she could do was to look. A voice came from the presence beside her.

"Look! She's all right isn't she?"

"Yes", said Sylvia. "She's all right!"

At that moment Sylvia awoke from the dream and experienced a strange feeling of peace and calm. She never dreamed again about babies. Working through grief is a long slow process and it can sometimes take years. Her grief had passed its lowest ebb and now she had the strength to pick up the threads of her life and look to the future.

"I really would like another baby Richard", she said one morning at breakfast.

"There is a lot to consider darling – the state of your hips for instance!" replied her husband.

"Well I've managed to struggle through three pregnancies. I'm sure I could get through one more. I know it won't be easy, but I'm desperate for another baby. I know Jayne can never be replaced, but a new baby in the house would be good for all of us, particularly the girls. It would make us all look forward again!"

"Well let's be careful!" said the ever cautious Richard. "Wait for a year and then you will know whether you really do want another child".

This seemed a fair compromise and so it was agreed. Sylvia now had a full time permanent post in her school where she had now been teaching for a few years. Once more she was approached by the Principal who asked her again if she would like to go into partnership with her.

"I must be honest with you", replied Sylvia, "but I really would like to have another baby, and it wouldn't be fair to accept your offer, feeling the way I do!"

16. THE FIRST GREAT GRANDCHILD OF QUEEN VICTORIA

Jayne's death preyed on Mary's mind and she had no resources to cope with it. For all her strange ways and irrational behaviour, she loved her grandchildren. Her mind was convinced that the Devil had been at work, taking this baby grandchild from her, and the Devil was everywhere and in everybody.

A few weeks later, Sylvia made one of her regular visits to her mother and found her to be quite deranged. Mary's immediate neighbour came out to greet Sylvia as she stepped out of her car. They complained that Mary was threatening them and banging on their door at all hours of the day and the night. Mary was sitting in her dingy darkened room when Sylvia entered the house. The carving knife was, as usual, placed on the table in front of her.

"The neighbours have been complaining about you Mother. They say that you are keeping them awake every night, and threatening them. If you are not careful you'll find yourself back in hospital and then you won't get your nice new flat".

"It's THEM!" muttered Mary. "THEY did it!"

"Did what?" asked Sylvia.

"They killed our Jayne. Then they ate her. Her bones are buried in their garden".

Sylvia went cold. These words were too awful to comprehend and she had to remember that they were a product of a deranged mind. However, feeling so raw her self, it was hard to shrug them off. When she arrived back home she telephoned Mary's doctor to

Poor Mary

ask if he would pay her a visit. He was actually on holiday so Mary was visited by another doctor within the practice. He declared that he'd never seen anyone as bad as Mary outside a mental hospital but there was nothing he could do as he wasn't her doctor. When Mary's own doctor returned from holiday, he was of the opinion that Mary should stay where she was as she hadn't actually harmed anyone! He was not concerned with the nuisance value for the people who had to tolerate her!

A few weeks later, Sylvia received a telephone call from Mary's doctor. This time he was of the opinion that Mary should be committed to a mental hospital. One night, in desperation, Mary's neighbours had called the police as she continued to batter their door and shout obscenities through the letter box. When a policeman had arrived, Mary threw a milk bottle at him. The milk bottle was full of water! This was the reason for the doctor's change of heart!

"Well that's the limit!" exploded Richard in disgust. Anything can be done to the neighbours and to other people and nothing is done about it – but because it's a policeman it's a different story. There's no justice!" In Richard's opinion the doctor should have hospitalised Mary years ago.

The problem was now going to be getting Mary out of the house because she certainly wouldn't come willingly. Her doors were locked up like Fort Knox at all times, and the carving knife was always ready, a constant threat! Mary was due to be 'captured' on the following Monday morning.

"I don't really want to be there", said Sylvia, "– otherwise she'll think that I'm the one who is sending her to hospital".

"We'll take the car and sit and watch from a distance", said Richard. "That way she won't see you but you'll be on hand in case you are needed".

The dreaded Monday morning arrived and very early Richard, having had to take time out of school for the occasion, drove Sylvia into the town where her mother lived. When they turned the corner into the street where her house was situated, they saw a group of people clustered round her front door, an ambulance parked in front of her window. There were two people from the Social Services, a couple of policemen, and Mary's doctor who also happened to be a Justice of the Peace. Apparently it was required by law for a J.P. to be present when a person was forcibly committed to a mental hospital. They were all talking together and discussing how they were going to get into the house, as both doors were locked and bolted. Mary was screaming at them from behind the door and telling them that she had a carving knife and she would use it if anyone came near her. She was frightened out of her wits. Who wouldn't be with that threatening crowd outside one's door, and an ambulance which was going to cart you off from your home!

Richard could not bear to see the ineffectual way they were dealing with the situation and got out of the car in exasperation. He strode across the road towards them.

"Oh God!" thought Sylvia, "Now she'll say it is Richard who is putting her away. That's all I need!"

Poor Mary

"You'll have to force the door", said Richard to the two policemen. "The back door is very weak and should be easy enough to manage".

The company of people filed like sheep to the back of the house. The two policemen each tried to force the back door open by using their shoulders, but without success.

"That's not the way to do it", muttered Richard. Whether he liked it or not he was going to be involved and Mary was going to blame him for putting her away. Still it couldn't be helped, she needed treatment. He made his way down the garden path.

"Let me have a go", he said.

The little group opened up to let him through. Richard took a run up to the back door and gave it an almighty kick which, not only sent the door crashing down into the house, but also the whole of the door frame. As the captors swarmed into the back of the house, Mary ran out of the front door, brandishing the carving knife! No one had thought to leave someone on guard for that eventuality! However, as she could no longer get back into the house to lock herself in again, it wasn't a difficult job to catch and restrain her, and to remove the knife from her possession. Like a frightened animal she was then bundled into the ambulance with a nurse and two social workers.

"I'd better go with her Richard", said Sylvia, and she ran towards the ambulance and climbed into the back, sitting opposite her mother. The mental hospital was forty miles away on the far side of Lincoln.

"We've just got to call in at the General Hospital in the town before we go to Lincoln", said the ambulance driver.

It took only a few minutes to arrive there, and would you believe it – everyone except Mary and Sylvia – got out, leaving the back door of the ambulance wide open!

"We're just going to have a cup of tea", said the nurse. "We won't be long".

Sylvia could not believe that after all the trouble they'd had to 'capture' Mary, they had all disappeared, leaving her virtually unattended, and with an open door!

All this time, Mary had not said a word but was sitting and looking accusingly at her daughter. Then she spoke!

"I think I'll just get out and go for a walk".

"No, no, you mustn't", cried Sylvia frantically. "Stay sitting down where you are".

"I want to go home!" said Mary.

"Well you can't just yet", said Sylvia. "After a little stay in the hospital you'll feel much better. Then you'll be able to go home"

"There's nothing wrong with me!" shouted Mary. "It's THEM!"

At last the ambulance was on its way on its forty minute journey to the mental hospital near Lincoln. Sylvia shuddered as it entered the grounds and she saw the barred windows of the hospital building. They brought back unpleasant memories of the time that Mary had spent in the mental hospital in Sheffield years ago. The usual red tape of admittance had to be

Poor Mary

gone through and then a defiant Mary was ushered into a room where two white coated doctors were waiting for her.

"Now my dear!" said the elder of the two men. "What is your name?"

Mary stood up proudly, her head held high. "I am Mary Alice, the first grandchild of Queen Victoria. This is my daughter, the Princess Sylvia of Wales".

"I see", murmured the doctor, and began asking more questions, making copious notes as he did so.

During her time in hospital, the house in which Mary had lived was demolished. When at last the doctors thought her stable enough to leave the hospital, the local council was informed and she was allocated a first floor council flat. Richard and Sylvia took possession of it on her behalf and so were able to redecorate it for her. They gathered together some second hand furniture, including a bed, and so Mary had a comfortable little flat to which she would come home.

"This must be the first real home of her own that she's ever had", said Sylvia. "Perhaps she'll settle down now, if she feels more secure".

"Hmm!" said Richard. "I very much doubt that!"

17. THE PROFESSOR

Four years after the birth of Jayne, Sylvia bore yet another daughter. Due to constant threats of miscarriage, the pregnancy was tense. At any moment Sylvia had expected the worst, and each week passed safely was another milestone. Because the baby was lying in a breech position it had to be induced prematurely. After the birth, which was the most difficult Sylvia had experienced, the baby was handed briefly to her, and then placed in a ward for premature babies where she was tube fed. The baby was there for a whole month during which time Sylvia could only look at her through the glass window of the ward.

When Sylvia was released from the maternity home, nearly a week after she had been admitted, it was hard to walk out of the hospital empty handed. Going home without a baby was agony for her. When she entered her home and saw all the baby things laid out in readiness, and no baby, it brought back vivid memories of Jayne's death, and she knelt down and wept.

Everyday she could not get to the maternity home quickly enough to see her baby daughter. She needed to be with her, even if it just meant standing and looking through the glass screen at the child in the incubator. At last the baby was deemed strong enough to be taken home and once there she thrived into a beautiful fair haired child, not at all like Jayne in appearance. She was christened Kathryn.

Poor Mary

By the time she was two years old, Kathryn had bright golden hair that ran riot over her pert little head in shining curls. Her blue eyes were fringed by long dark lashes and her winning smile could melt the hardest of hearts. She was bright like quicksilver and both Anna and Rebecca adored her. The coming of Kathryn restored the spirits of all the family, though none of them would ever forget Jayne.

Sylvia's hip condition was becoming worse. There were times when she sat down that she would gladly have remained in the chair permanently, so great was the pain.

"I think that you should see a consultant privately", said Clare one day after seeing Sylvia limp painfully down her garden path. "Can you afford to do that?"

"I'll have a word with Richard", replied Sylvia. "I'm sure he'll agree. We've both reached the stage when we'll try anything. It's such a worry for him and I feel such a burden".

Richard was only too pleased to pay for a private consultation for his wife. He worried himself sick over her, knowing how much pain she was in and watching her increasing difficulty in walking. He did his best to help her in every way he could, but he was powerless to prevent her pain. An appointment was made to see an orthopaedic consultant the following week. Having examined the x-rays of the damaged hips, watching Sylvia walk, and realizing how limited her movement was, he had no hesitation in referring her for consultation at the Wrightington Hospital, the National Hip Centre. Hip replacement surgery had been pioneered at this hospital. People came from all over the country to have their surgery done there as it had the reputation of being the finest centre in the country. Sylvia was very lucky to have been referred there.

A clear autumn sky showed just a touch of cumulus clouds as Richard and Sylvia set off on their journey to the other side of the country to Wrightington Hospital. The damp chill of morning hung in the air and Sylvia shivered, part with cold and part with apprehension. She rubbed her arms as she waited for the car to heat up. She felt more and more nervous as they drew nearer to the hospital. On the one hand she was desperate for something to be done, but on the other hand she was terrified at the prospect of surgery.

The first noticeable difference about Wrightington Hospital, compared to the average hospital was the speed and efficiency with which patients were dealt. No one was left waiting about for hours, and indeed if a patient let it be known that they had travelled a great distance, then they were dealt with even more quickly so that they could begin their return journey as soon as possible. Richard parked the car in the hospital car park and he and Sylvia walked to the reception area. Her teeth chattering with nervousness, Sylvia presented herself at the desk and, before she knew what was happening, she found herself in a cubicle stripping down to the minimum of clothing in readiness for the x-ray unit. After being x-rayed, these were handed to her and she took them to the waiting area for seeing the consultant.

Poor Mary

Professor Charnley was a short, bespectacled and balding man, the sort of person who would pass without notice in a crowd. Beneath that insignificant exterior was a brilliant brain. It was told to Sylvia that this great man had begun his career as an engineer, but when his mother became crippled with arthritic hips, he decided to train as a surgeon. Having done this, he used his engineering knowledge and skills to design artificial hip joints and the tools with which to perform the hip replacement operation. When Sylvia entered his room he looked at her with kind twinkling eyes and then spoke crisply.

"Do you use a stick?"

"I use a long umbrella when the pain is really bad", replied Sylvia.

"Do you take pain killers?"

"Only if I'm really desperate", said Sylvia, remembering the drugs she had taken when she was pregnant with Jayne. "I don't like taking drugs on a regular basis if I can help it".

"Let me see you walk across the room" said the Professor.

Sylvia did as he asked, then she had to clamber up on to the surgery couch where the professor tested the span of her movement and flexibility of her hips. After a few more short questions he told her to get up from the couch.

"You don't take pain killers, you don't use a stick regularly and you are too young to have the operation! I don't care how much pain you have – if the operation went wrong – which it could – you'll be on crutches for the rest of your life, and you still have very young children to consider. Make an appointment to come back in three years' time. Goodbye!

The interview had lasted for all of five minutes and Sylvia left the hospital with her hopes dashed and a sense of anti climax!

PART 8

1. CAR TROUBLE

1993 It had rained for days, then had come the muggy period with a hazy sun followed by damp cold nights. That particular Saturday morning in February it was cold. As Sylvia drove along the M4 motorway she congratulated herself for having made such an early start. She might even be in Dover for the eleven o'clock boat instead of the mid-day boat which she had booked. Richard had travelled to their French apartment by train some days ago and Sylvia was going to join him now that it was half term. She was driving his Volvo diesel estate car which was much cheaper on the fuel than her own car.

As she neared London the car's engine suddenly missed a beat, and so did Sylvia's heart! She knew instinctively that there was a problem and she tensed up as the car began to lose power. Before she knew it the car had slowed down to twenty miles an hour on full throttle.

"Damn!" thought Sylvia. "Damn – damn- damn!"

At the next junction she pulled off the motorway and trickled down the nearest road. The car stopped completely in the middle of the next cross roads. After a few minutes she managed to restart it and slowly drove along the road until she came to a garage. Explaining what had happened to the mechanic, she was dismayed when he said that he knew nothing about diesel engines but after a casual look he declared that he could not see anything wrong with the car, and of course it started immediately and with full power!

"I'll push on and try to reach Dover", she thought. "I have time to spare and I might find a Volvo garage there".

The M25 motorway was as usual horrendous with four fast moving lanes of traffic with no let up! Suddenly the car lurched, the engine spluttered, and within seconds it had slowed down to twenty miles an hour again – a very dangerous situation on any busy motorway, let alone the M25. Road works were ahead and the traffic was diverted into a single lane for a couple of miles. The car came to a sudden stop and Sylvia cursed again as the traffic piled up behind her, several drivers beeping their car horns impatiently.

"I've just got to get this car back home somehow", she thought. There's no way I dare risk taking it across the Channel now, even if I did get as far as Dover!"

At the next junction she left the M25 and then re-entered it on the opposite side and headed for home. It took her three hours before she finally drove into her own driveway, and she felt absolutely shattered. The cats were glad to see her back so soon anyway! They were banned from the main house and lived in the hallway whilst she was away. Sylvia's neighbour would feed them in there and then they could get out from a cat door in the wall of the integral garage.

Sylvia transferred all her bags and baggage from Richard's car to her own, thankful that it had an exceptionally large boot. She then made several phone calls, one to Richard to let him know that she would not be arriving until much later, one to the ferry company to see if she could catch an evening boat, and one to her daughter, Anna, to let her know what had happened. After fixing herself some lunch, Sylvia set off once more for Dover. By now the fog had lifted and it proved to be quite a pleasant drive, although she was now already feeling very tired. She reached Dover at half past four in the afternoon and felt very light hearted when she realised that she would be able to get on the five o'clock ferry instead of the half past six boat which she had booked.

"Good!" she thought. "That gives me an extra one and a half hours of travelling time before I need to find a hotel for the night".

She flourished her ticket through the half open window and the attendant waved her on to board the ferry. Just as her car went over the ramp there was a loud bang and the electric window on the driver's side disappeared down into the door of the car! When the car had been parked on the boat, Sylvia sat and fiddled with the knob which controlled the electric window, but there was no response! Two members of the ship's crew examined the window but both of them thought that nothing could be done by anyone other than a garage mechanic.

"There is an A.A. base on the Calais terminal. I'm sure someone will be able to help you", she was assured.

By now feeling very uptight, Sylvia went to find something to eat but did not enjoy her meal of fried cod, peas and chips. It was so tasteless and almost cold. Also she was worrying herself sick about the permanently open window of the car. Unless she could get it fixed there was no security in the car and she had a long way to go.

The boat docked in Calais and began to unload. The darkness had fallen as the cars rolled off the ferry, and it was very cold indeed. Sylvia gulped down the clear sea air through her open window. It was a welcome relief after the stale fug of the boat and the masses of people who had been crowded on to it. Slowly the line of cars inched towards the customs shed and, having passed through, Sylvia parked the car and went to look for the A.A. office. She found it quickly, but it was in darkness and locked up for the night. Dismay entered her heart.

"What on earth shall I do?" she thought. "I can't possibly stay in a hotel in Calais because it won't be safe to park the car on the street. I think I must drive out of Calais and find a country hotel which has a garage."

She had given up the idea of driving on for an hour or so as she was now quite exhausted. Starting up the engine, Sylvia headed for the auto route out of Calais. By now a damp fog had descended, swirling round the car and entering it through the open window. Her hands were frozen, in spite of her gloves, and she began to have earache from the cold gale which blew through the car as she sped along. There was a road sign ahead but she had taken a wrong turning before she realised, not being able to see properly in the fog.

Oh shit!" she cried in despair. "Where the hell am I now?"

The fog was now so dense that she could barely discern the road ahead.

Poor Mary

"I'll just keep driving steadily. There's bound to be a hotel eventually", she thought.

Spying lights and signs of life ahead, she at last pulled up and parked at the edge of the road by a wayside bar. Wearily she climbed out of the car and picked her across the uneven path to the door of the bar. Nervously she entered to be met by several pairs of eyes immediately weighing her up. The local middle aged men were having their nightly chat and drink and were gathered together at the bar counter.

"Est ce que un hotel par ici?" she asked the barman nervously, as her French was never very good.

"Deuz kilometers Madame, tout droit".

"Merci beaucoup", Sylvia said and made a hasty retreat from those staring eyes.

Sure enough, after a short drive she came across a very pretty little hotel situated in the square of the village. She parked the car in the square and entered the hotel, again somewhat nervously.

"Avez vous une chambre pour une personne s'il vous plait?"

"Oui Madame".

"Avez vous une garage aussie?" asked Sylvia, and her spirits lifted when she was told there was.

"Thank goodness! At least I can sleep tonight without worrying about the security of the car", she thought. After the stresses of the day she felt extremely tired so she went straight to bed, having ordered breakfast to be brought to her room at seven thirty the next morning.

Feeling refreshed the next day Sylvia paid her bill and went to the hotel garage. She was pleasantly surprised to find that someone had been kind enough to cover the gaping window with a large piece of card, so the car was not too damp inside.

"I must get some petrol as soon as possible", she thought. Travelling towards the auto route at eighty miles an hour, Sylvia realised that it was going to be unbearably cold and she had eleven hours of travelling in front of her. As it was now Sunday, there would be no garages open for repair work so she had no alternative but to carry on with her journey with the broken window. She pulled in at the first filling station and filled up the car with petrol. Having done that she opened up the boot and fished about in her travel bag for some warm clothing which she then took into the ladies' toilet area. Fortunately she had a pair of ski trousers with her and she put these on over her track suit. Then she put on an extra sweater over her tracksuit top, followed by a polar fleece jacket, a padded waistcoat with a hood, and lastly a cagoule. She then pulled the hood over her head and bound a warm scarf round it to keep it secure and to protect her ears. Catching a glimpse of herself in the mirror of the ladies' room she laughed.

"I look like the Michelin Man", she thought. In spite of all these clothes, her body and legs were only just warm, and her hands were freezing cold as she drove along at speed. Her eyes and lips soon became sore with the wind whistling passed them for the length of her six hundred mile journey. Somehow she endured the long and lonely journey, deep in thought as she sped along. She thought of the events which had led her and Richard to buy their own school and eventually their properties abroad.

2. A SCHOOL OF OUR OWN

1976 Kathryn eventually joined her sister, Rebecca, at the private school where Sylvia taught, whilst Anna went to the local grammar school at the age of eleven. Now that all three girls were at school Sylvia was teaching full time again. Richard let her have the car for her journey to school whilst he went to work on his bicycle. He did not want her to be standing around in all weathers waiting for buses, nor having to walk too far. He did not really want her to go to work at all, but he realised that it was more fulfilling for her to be doing the job for which she had been trained, and certainly the money she earned made life easier for them all.

In spite of her increasing difficulties and severe pain, Sylvia never took time off school because of her arthritic condition. She enjoyed teaching enormously and it enabled her to pay for a cleaning lady to do the heavy household chores which for Sylvia would have been a very painful task. Richard was becoming more and more disillusioned with his teaching career and longed to be his own master. Consequently, in due course, an idea grew in Sylvia's mind.

"Why don't we both finish with our present jobs and buy our own school?" she said to Richard one day.

"What do you mean?" he said, staring at her in surprise.

"Well Miss Macdonald has offered me a partnership with her on more than one occasion. It's a pity that I wasn't ready at the time, and now someone else has taken up her offer I'll never get another chance in that school. Besides, I could do with a change, and I know that you are fed up with your school and would like to run your own business. You are trained to teach and also you had some training in accountancy – so together we ought to be able to make a go of it. What do you think?"

"Mm! It will take o lot of thinking about", mused Richard. "It means we would have to sell this house and move from the area, and if we did I would prefer to be in the south of England".

"Well let's start looking then", said Sylvia excitedly. "We don't have to commit ourselves just yet and it costs nothing to look around".

The next day, full of enthusiasm, Sylvia called in at the local newsagent on the way home from school, and bought a copy of the Times Educational Supplement. When she arrived home she skipped through all the columns which advertised teaching posts until she came to the section titled 'Businesses for Sale'. There she found the name of an agent who specialized in the buying and selling of independent schools. Without wasting a minute, she sat down and wrote to the agent and asked him to send her details of any independent schools which were for sale in the south of England.

The light morning frosts of autumn brought a nip to the air and the leaves outside the bedroom window were scarlet on this late October day. Richard heard the click of the letter box and jumped out of bed to fetch

Poor Mary

the post. He took the mail into Sylvia and then went to put the kettle on for their early morning cup of tea.

"Perhaps there's a letter from the school agent", he shouted from the kitchen.

"It doesn't look like it", called Sylvia as she examined all the post marks before opening the letters. "There is one from Wrightington Hospital though. I wonder what that is about!"

Opening the envelope, Sylvia read the letter as Richard came in to the bedroom with the tea tray.

"Well, what is it then?" he asked.

"They've sent me an appointment date to see me next week. I can't believe that three years have passed so quickly. I suppose I'd better go but I know they'll only say what has been said before – I'm too young for hip replacement surgery!"

The following week saw Sylvia and Richard on their second cross country journey to Wrightington Hospital. It had been raining heavily when they set off, but by mid morning the rain eased to a dreary drizzle, and by the afternoon it had stopped altogether. By the time Sylvia was sitting in the hospital waiting room, after having had her hips x-rayed, shafts of sunlight streamed through the windows, creating dappled patterns of light on the pale green carpet. After a short while Sylvia found herself ushered into a small consulting room. Behind his desk was sitting a tall lean man with a weather beaten face and dark grizzled hair. This was Mr. Monroe, the consultant who was now in charge of the team at Wrightington. It seemed that Professor Charnley was now out of the country, demonstrating his knowledge and skills abroad.

Mr. Monroe wasted no time beating about the bush but came straight to the point.

"Well the ball is now in your court Mrs. Sanderson", he said to Sylvia, and leaned back in his swivel chair, his chin resting on his hands.

"What do you mean?" asked Sylvia nervously.

"We are now in a position to be able to operate on you. A new and longer lasting material has been discovered and artificial hip joints should now have an approximate 'life' of nineteen years. Even then it is not the material which will wear out but rather that the joints have worked loose. Of course there is always the risk of the artificial joints being rejected by the body, and an infection could set in and smoulder there for ages before being discovered. This could make it necessary to remove the joints completely and you would be in a wheel chair for the rest of your life. It would take five years before we could give you the all clear on that. Now that you know all the risks do you still want to go ahead with the operation?"

"Yes", said Sylvia weakly.

"Good, then we will send for you when we have a bed. It may be in six months time or longer. We will operate on your right hip first, as that is in the worst condition. Then, if you have not lost too much blood, we will continue straight away with the left hip".

Sylvia met up with Richard a few minutes later, a stunned look on her face. After years of people exclaiming and 'tut-tutting' over her, with no prospects of any release from her painful condition, like a bolt from the blue, everything was suddenly happening – and she was afraid!

"Well, what do we do now about our search for a school?" queried Richard.

"I've been thinking about that", answered Sylvia. The operations won't take place for at least six months so we have time enough to sort that out. If we do have our own school by then, and the operations did go wrong – thinking of the worst scenario – then at least I could do some work from a wheel chair. I could tutor individual children or do secretarial work, there's bound to be something I could do! If we stay where we are and the operations went wrong, then I would lose my job completely. If everything goes well, then it would be a brand new start for the whole family!"

3. THE SEARCH

Details of several schools for sale were sent by the agent, and Richard and Sylvia studied them carefully.

"I think we must be very careful in our choice", said Richard. "The place that we buy should at the least be as pleasant to live in as this house, and preferably better. Also the income we derive from the business should be at least what our joint income is now, otherwise it would not be worth our while to uproot from here".

"I agree with that", said Sylvia, "and there also needs to be the opportunity for expansion, so the building and site are important. The problem with my present school is that there is absolutely no room for expansion and it does not allow for any flexibility".

With these criteria in mind the couple made arrangements to visit a number of schools in the south of England, and they managed to see three schools before Christmas. One of them was far too small and did not provide enough income or work for them both. The second school was highly profitable but was situated in the centre of a rather unpleasant city. The accommodation there was crude to say the least. The third school was very pleasing and situated in a pretty market town. They would have been happy to settle for that one but it was far too expensive and their bank manager said that it was not a viable proposition as far as they were concerned.

They had three more schools on their list, but it was now the week before Christmas. Anna was scheduled to spend Christmas in France with a family they knew very well – having done several holiday exchanges with them. Also François and Anne-Marie Pascale had both visited the Sanderson family in England in order to perfect their English, so Anna was already very friendly with the youngsters. However, by the time that Anna was due to be taken to Southampton for her boat to Le Havre, she was protesting that she did not want to go.

"You've left it a bit late now Anna", remonstrated Richard. "Your ticket is paid for and François will be waiting at Le Havre to meet you. Also Mme. Pascale is bound to have prepared a special French Christmas for your benefit, and they would all be terribly disappointed if you didn't turn up. You can't let people down like that!"

The Pascale family in Rouen was an interesting group of people. During the War, Andre and Cecile were engaged to be married. Cecile said to her betrothed that should he be captured by the Germans and work for them, then she would never speak to him again. On the other hand if he managed to avoid working for them, then she would call all their children Marie! Andre was captured by the Germans but he managed to escape and by doing so did not have to work for them. When he and Cecile were eventually married all their seven children were called Marie! They were Marie-Claude, Dominique-Marie, Bernard-Marie, Jeanne-Marie, Pierre-Marie, François-Marie and the youngest was Anne-Marie. The boys of the family did not take too kindly to being named Marie and they were often teased at school.

Their second child, Dominique-Marie, was a remarkable person. At two years old she had contracted polio. Consequently both her legs were underdeveloped and had not grown in proportion to the rest of her body, and she had to wear callipers and walk with crutches. However, she was a very determined lady and learned to drive a specially adapted car which she drove all over Europe. Also she had won a Gold Medal for swimming in the Olympics for paraplegics. Eventually she married another disabled person who was an equally determined young man. With ease he could beat any person at table tennis whilst resting on one crutch and batting with his free hand. Daily he drove the two hour journey to Paris where he worked as an accountant. The brave couple did all their own decorating, shopping and gardening, often putting the average couple to shame.

Against her doctor's advice, Dominique was determined to have a child. At last a perfectly normal little boy was born to her. As he grew into a toddler, seeing both his parents walking with sticks or crutches, he thought that was the way to walk! They gave him two little sticks so that he could be like Mama and Papa, but the child soon realised that he did not need them and threw them away. Later a delightful baby girl was born. The perfect little girl modelled herself on her brother who was of course walking normally by this time, so she never used sticks. The courage and determination of this little family were a shining example to us lesser mortals who constantly grumble and grouse our way through this life.

Poor Mary

The journey to Southampton was long and dreary and was not made easier by Anna's sulking and teenage awkwardness. However she began to cheer up and show some excitement as they approached the port.

"I know exactly what François will say when he meets me", said Anna.

"What will that be then?" asked Richard, pleased that his daughter was showing some enthusiasm at last.

" 'ello, 'ow are you? Did you 'ave a good journee?" said Anna. She was trying to imitate a French person who has difficulty in aspirating the letter 'h'.

As it happened that is exactly what François did say when he met Anna. At the port they met another family with a teenage daughter named Avril who was also travelling alone on the ferry. Anna and Avril decided to accompany each other on the boat so both sets of anxious parents felt much happier that their daughters were not entirely alone on their journey. Sylvia waved her daughter a tearful farewell before she and Richard went to find the car.

They had three more schools to look at on their list, and it had seemed sensible to combine this with their journey to Southampton. The first school on the list was not too far away from Southampton. They found it a rather drab establishment and there was no parking facility outside the school. They also discovered that the school was not very profitable.

"It's no good", said Richard afterwards, "there must be adequate parking outside a school, not only for teachers and parents but also for delivery vans and such like. It would be bad enough for us with our own car let alone anyone else who came to the school. There is no room for expansion at all either. I wonder how the school keeps open in this day and age!"

They looked at the remaining schools on their list. One was a small school near Newquay, the other a larger school on the edge of the Mendips. They looked at the wintry sky which was grey with the promise of snow, and then they looked at the map.

"What shall we do?" asked Richard.

"Well", said Sylvia, pondering over the map. "The weather doesn't look too good. I think we are in for some snow. It as far from here to go to Newquay as it is to go back to Lincolnshire. I think that we should scrap Newquay, in view of the weather, and visit the bigger school in the Mendips which is virtually in the right direction for home.

As they started up their car, rain mixed with snow began to fall against the windscreen and they were glad of a good heating system. After a couple of hours they reached the little town where the school was located. They stopped the car outside the school gates and peered through them.

"This is it!" cried Richard excitedly. "That is the place for me. That is where I would like to be!"

The Abbey School, situated on the site of an ancient abbey, was a large eighteenth century house of stone, and set within spacious gardens of about three acres in all.

"It's beautiful!" exclaimed Richard. "I could really do something with this place. Look at all that space! There would be no parking problems here, and plenty of room for expansion. It has enormous potential!"

Poor Mary

They walked up the gravel drive and rang the brass door bell of the great white front door. At last the ring of the door bell was heard, but not by anyone who could help them. Only workmen were in the building, the owners being away for the Christmas break, and they would not be back until just before the new term began. Before the door was closed, they caught a glimpse of a beautiful wide staircase with a large Georgian window letting in the light on the first half landing.

"We'll go home now before the roads become snowed up", said Richard. "Then we will write to the owners of the school and make a proper appointment for a visit. I must say that it is the sort of building that I've always wanted".

An appointment was made to visit the Abbey School during the half term holiday of February so that it would not interfere with the school routine of all concerned. This time the door was opened by a tall, gaunt and bearded man who was wearing Wellington boots, a tatty woollen jumper and an old, shabby rimmed hat. His blue eyes twinkled merrily as he welcomed them and asked them to come in.

Richard and Sylvia were both well experienced teachers who knew what to look for as they were shown round the classrooms of the school. The living accommodation was on the top floor of the building. It was primitive by modern standards, but very spacious. There were no carpets on the rough wooden floors, no electrical power points, and no bath room or W.C. on that floor.

"Don't worry about it!" whispered Richard. "I can fix all these problems – as long as there is plenty of space, that's all that matters. When I've finished with it we will have a very desirable living accommodation!"

Outside, the vast gardens were full of daffodils, snowdrops and aconites. A gravelled path led to another walled garden, the walls of the building were smothered in jasmine and honeysuckle, both about to burst into bloom the minute the sun gave out its spring warmth. After the couple had been shown round every nook and cranny, both inside and out, it was time to discuss business.

"My wife actually runs the school", said Mr. Fletcher, "but she has been seriously ill. I've been trying to keep the place ticking over but I'm not a teacher. We are both getting on in years and need to retire so that Mrs. Fletcher can regain her health".

It turned out that the Fletcher's did not actually own the buildings, only the school business. This of course was reflected in the asking price and it would make it possible for the Sandersons to purchase the business after selling their own home without having to borrow money from the bank. There was also the possibility that they would be able to buy the buildings at a later date. It would all be an enormous gamble of course, because if the school did not work well for them they would lose everything. The discussions with the Fletchers went well and Richard and Sylvia decided to risk all and buy the school business.

"There is just one thing though", said Mrs. Fletcher. "As you know, this property is leased and before the lease can be transferred to another tenant it would have to be agreed by the landlord. I'm quite sure that there will not be a problem, but the landlord would want to meet with you, and approve of you, before the lease changes hands. I would suggest that you gather some references to show him".

The Fletchers offered Sylvia and Richard a bed for the night which they gladly accepted. As Sylvia peered out of the dormer window of the second floor bedroom, a wraith like moon, brightening as dusk deepened, lit up in dark relief the abbey buildings. The stillness and silence of the gardens were absolute.

Two weeks later, armed with their bank and character references, Richard and Sylvia returned to the Abbey School. They had an appointment to meet the owner of the school property. He was a big landowner by the name of Major Smythe-Patterson, a hunting, shooting and fishing man with a reputation of being somewhat eccentric. His wife had died early on in his marriage and since then he had devoted his life to his animals on his vast estate, declaring that they were far more trustworthy and loyal than people. Although he preferred to live alone in his mansion house, he did a great deal of good for the local community. Sadly this was not always recognised or appreciated by the locals who tended to run him down at any opportunity. After all, he was not 'one of them'!

Richard and Sylvia drove up the long drive of the ancient mansion house with its vast parklands surrounding it. They parked the car and approached the grand stone flight of steps which led to the massive oak door of the house. They felt nervous as Richard pulled the old brass bell. A serving woman opened the door and led them down a long wide passage, panelled in dark oak, until they reached the sitting room of her employer.

The room was absolutely enormous, and lined with books from wall to wall. By one of the tall windows was standing a beautiful grand piano. An enormous old settee rested in front of an impressive stone fireplace where a log fire crackled merrily. Over the mantel piece was an oil painting of a very beautiful woman who was wearing an evening gown of deep blue, matching the amazing blue of her eyes. A honey coloured gun dog was sprawled by the side of the settee, and Major Smythe-Patterson stood with his back to the fire, his hands clasped behind him.

"Come in, come in. Sit down, sit down", his voice boomed, echoing through the lofty ceiling. He remained standing whilst Richard and Sylvia sank down, down and down into the softness of the settee. The Major appeared to tower over them and they felt very small and intimidated. With some difficulty, Richard fumbled about in his pockets and eventually managed to extract a bundle of papers. He handed the references to the Major who scanned them through very quickly.

"Yes, yes, yes!" he blustered. "These all seem to be in order. Just want to make sure you were not 'reds under the bed'! You know what I mean? I think that

Poor Mary

will be all. I'd offer you a sherry – trouble is – I haven't got any! Perhaps we could go to the Gun Club and have one there!"

"Thank you very much", said Richard, "but if all is in order then we would really like to make our way back to Lincolnshire – if you don't mind!"

"Certainly, certainly! Goodbye then! We'll meet again no doubt!" and Major Smythe –Patterson ushered them out of the room, calling for his serving lady to see them out of the house.

"Phew!" said Sylvia. "He puts you in your place doesn't he?"

After further discussions with the Fletchers about the drawing up of a contract of sale, the Sandersons agreed to return at the beginning of April when the contract could be signed by both parties.

"We'd better put our house on the market straight away", said Richard as they were driving home.

"I shall be sad to sell it", said Sylvia, "but I think it will be good for all of us to have a complete change. After all, if we don't do it now we never will!"

4. DILEMMA

The beginning of April saw the signing of the contract for the purchase of the school. This time Anna, Rebecca and Kathryn went with their parents so that they could see what was shortly going to be their new home. Rebecca was very excited and looking forward to the move. Kathryn, at only five years old, remained indifferent, not really understanding what was going on. Anna, now sixteen, was definitely surly about the whole idea. She did not want to uproot and leave all her friends and made no bones about letting everyone know how disgruntled she was!

"You'll make some new friends my dear", said her mother, "and your old friends will be able to come and visit you whenever they want, and I'm quite sure you will be able to visit them".

"I don't want new friends, I want my old friends. You're ruining my life!" cried Anna.

"Oh dear!" said Sylvia impatiently. "I do wish you wouldn't be like this. I had to move schools at your age, and I didn't carry on like you are doing, nor did I have any choice in the matter".

"Well I'm not you", muttered Anna angrily, "and I don't want to leave my friends!"

The gardens of the Abbey School were at their best. The flowering trees were exploding into bloom and clouds of white blossom scented the air. In the large walled garden the bluebells looked like blue lace under the old apple trees, and a cuckoo could be heard calling from some distant tree. Even the grumpy Anna had to acknowledge the beauty of the place. Rebecca was enchanted and young Kathryn danced with excitement to see a group of ducks swimming with their ducklings on the large pond within the walled garden.

In the evening when the sun had sunk below the horizon, the last dim after glow outlined the leafy silhouettes of dark foliage rustling in the gentle breeze. The trees, almost in full leaf, were outlined against the sky in rounded shapes of velvet darkness. It was warm and mild and soon the deep dark sky was full of stars. From their bed, Sylvia and Richard gazed through the un-curtained window at this beautiful night sky.

"I'm sure we've made the right decision", whispered Sylvia before going to sleep. "Anna will be all right eventually, when she gets used to it".

"She'll have to be", mumbled Richard. "It's too late to turn back now!"

At the beginning of the summer term, Sylvia and Richard gave in their notices at their respective schools. It was a very damp start to the term, with blustering east winds which stirred up the pains in Sylvia's bones.

"Well, it's the last day of the week", she thought as she began to ascend the rather splendid wooden staircase of the school where she worked. Suddenly, both of her hips buckled under her weight and, had it not been for the fact that another teacher steadied her from behind, she would most certainly have fallen backwards down the stairs.

"Gosh! That was a near thing", said Sylvia, badly shaken. "If you hadn't been behind me Elaine, I'd be lying in a heap at the bottom of the stairs by now! My hips have never let me down as badly as that before. They really must be crumbling away!"

That weekend she rested, as far as one can rest with three children to look after, and hoped to be better for work on Monday morning. Monday morning arrived and the postman pushed a letter through their letter box. Richard picked it up, saw that it was for Sylvia, and put it on the tea tray which he took to the bedroom.

"It's from Wrightington Hospital!" exclaimed Sylvia. "Oh! I don't believe this! They want me to go there in two weeks time for my hip operations. Now what are we going to do? We've just signed that contract and are now committed to going to the Abbey School for September. I really did not expect this to happen so quickly. It's no where near six months since I was there!"

"Perhaps it's for the best", said Richard. "The worst will be over for you by September, and it will all be behind you".

"But how do I know how I'm going to be? I don't want the parents to see me disabled and on crutches. That wouldn't give them much confidence would it?"

"You can't afford to put it off. Look what happened to you at school last Friday. Your hip condition is getting much worse so go and get it over with and the sooner the better!"

Poor Mary

"But I'm really scared now it's come to it. What if it all goes wrong?" said Sylvia.

"That's a risk you'll have to take", replied Richard. "The way things are going at the moment you are going to be in a wheel chair anyway, just as you were told, and sooner than you thought. I can't see that you have anything to lose, but everything to gain – hopefully!"

5. 'NIL BY MOUTH'

Only a few distant clouds marred the clarity of the early morning sun as once again Richard and Sylvia sped along the road towards Wrightington Hospital. It was a journey of about a hundred miles.

"I'm really scared Richard", said Sylvia as they drew nearer to the hospital.

"You'll be all right", said Richard soothingly.

"Yes, but what if it goes horribly wrong?" continued Sylvia.

"I'm sure it won't. Wrightington has an excellent reputation for this kind of surgery. People from all over the country go there. You're in the very best hands – really you are!" said Richard.

"It's going to be painful!" muttered Sylvia.

"Yes, it probably will be, and I'm sorry", said Richard. "If I could have the operations for you I would. Try not to worry darling, and remember what my father always used to say –'One day follows another – and everything passes'. That is inevitable so keep thinking positively!"

A short while later, having deposited Sylvia's small travel bag in the hospital ward and helped her to put her things away in the locker, Richard said that he really should set off on his return journey.

"I must get back to the girls as soon as possible", he said. "I don't like leaving Anna in charge for too long – she and Rebecca quarrel too much – besides which she has a lot of revision to do for her forthcoming examinations. You know what she is like – any excuse not to settle down to her school work".

Poor Mary

"Poor Anna!" said Sylvia. "It's hard for her to have her mother in hospital at the most crucial time in her school life. Make sure that she has adequate revision time and that she gets to bed reasonably early".

The couple hugged each other in an emotional farewell, then Richard disappeared through the door and Sylvia was left standing forlornly in the hospital corridor. The worst thing was going to be lack of visitors during her time in hospital. Nobody could be expected to travel over a hundred miles for a hospital visit, and in any case Richard would have his hands full looking after the girls. He had promised to bring the girls to see her the following weekend.

"It's strange to think that the next time I see him I will have had the operation", mused Sylvia as she made her way back to the ward.

Half an hour later she was undressed, in her night gown and sitting in the chair beside her bed.

"Would you get into bed", a nurse said. "The doctor will be round in a minute to ask you some questions and give you some tests". The doctor gave Sylvia a thorough examination to make sure that she was fit for major surgery. Blood samples were taken, and skin tests for allergies were given.

"By tomorrow we shall have all the test results and, if all is well, we will operate on Thursday. As you have probably been told, your right hip will be done first. If you haven't lost too much blood then we will continue to operate on your left hip. I think you should know that you are one of the first persons to have both hips operated on at the same occasion. Normally we operate on one hip and then wait for six months before doing the other. You are an experiment!" said the doctor laughingly.

"Isn't it all a bit drastic?" said Sylvia.

"Well yes, I suppose it is, but you are young and strong, and if you can tolerate the two operations together then your recovery period will be considerably shortened".

Sylvia was on tenterhooks the next day as she waited for all the different test results. By the end of the afternoon everything was complete, and she was told that the operations would take place on the following day – Thursday 26th of May.

"No supper for you tonight!" said the nurse, putting a 'NIL BY MOUTH' notice at the head of Sylvia's bed, "– and no breakfast in the morning – not even a cup of tea!"

"How will I survive?" laughed Sylvia, trying to assume an air of cheerfulness.

That evening, unable to settle down to reading her book because she was so apprehensive, Sylvia chattered to the other patients. They were all laughing and joking in an effort to mask their fears, in fact some were almost hysterical. When supper time came, Sylvia absented herself from the ward. She felt very hungry and the smell of the cooked meal was too tantalizing. She wondered down the ward and found a door leading into the Day Room. Here she sat, looking out on to the beautiful gardens of the hospital. The evening was bright and sunny and she could see a small lake nearby where ducks and ducklings swam contentedly. Soft soothing music was being played through a loud speaker. It was Albinoni's 'Adagio for Organ and Strings' and it was

Poor Mary

so beautiful that Sylvia wanted to cry. Moving into the next room, which was a toilet area, she was surprised to see a small saw on a shelf. It was a gruesome reminder of what would actually be happening to her on the following day, though she could hardly believe that this particular saw was actually used in operations! Thinking about it again, they would have to use a saw, for how else would they cut off the head of the femur! Shuddering, she put these thoughts out of her mind and returned to the peace of Albinoni.

The next morning when she opened her eyes, fear and dread took possession of her. "This is the day!" she thought. "There's no turning back now", and she tried not to think too much about the details of the operation. "I'm not going to be hung, or drawn", her thoughts continued," but I am going to be quartered – just about!"

One hour later a nurse, carrying a tray, came to Sylvia's bed. "I've just come to prepare you for the operation", she said. "Then I'll give you your pre med. and you'll soon be nice and drowsy. Sylvia's legs were shaved and covered with iodine so that she was thoroughly disinfected! They had been checked for any sore spots which may be there.

"Gosh! You are careful", said Sylvia.

"That's right", said the nurse. "If Mr. Monroe saw that your legs had one spot with a scab he would immediately cancel the operation, and all the operating theatre would be disinfected before it was used again. What a waste of time that would be for everybody!"

"It's comforting to know that they are so careful", said Sylvia.

"Well", said the nurse, "the most likely cause of failure in this operation is infection setting in – that is why they have to be so fastidious".

After the nurse had completed painting Sylvia's legs with iodine, both legs were wrapped up in a white sterilized material rather like muslin. Sylvia was by now already wearing her theatre gown and cap. "I feel like an Egyptian mummy!" she said.

When all was finished, the nurse injected Sylvia's arm. "There now, you'll soon feel nice and drowsy. You'll be taken down to theatre in about one hour".

Sylvia felt her body and mind being taken over by the drug and let herself go with the flow. She was now too drowsy to be afraid and did not care what happened to her. An hour later, two white coated men came into the ward wheeling a trolley which they stopped alongside Sylvia's bed. She was aware of strong arms lifting her from the bed to the trolley then suddenly she was being wheeled down endless corridors until at last they reached the operating theatre. The trolley was thrust through stainless steel doors and, from her prostrate position, Sylvia was aware of bright lights, masked faces peering down at her, and a conglomeration of machinery, instruments and other equipment. A masked face peered down into her eyes.

"Just one little injection into your hand, and then I want you to count to ten", said a kindly voice from behind the mask.

"1,2,3, - 4 --- 5 -------------", then Sylvia was totally submerged into unconsciousness and knew nothing of what was happening to her during the next few hours. Both operations completed, she was about to be carefully lifted from the operating table back to the trolley. Pain killer drugs had not yet been administered. For a fleeting moment Sylvia drifted back to consciousness and felt her self to be momentarily suspended in mid air as she was transferred to the trolley. The most agonizing pains seared across her hips. She screamed out loud and then sank back into merciful, dark unconsciousness.

6. FRED

She awoke to bright white light and two white robed people, both wearing masks, were bending over her, intently busy working on her operation wounds. She now felt no pain, only a curious numbness in the lower part of her body. Sylvia was in the recovery room where she remained for a few hours before being taken back to the general ward. Both her hips had undergone surgery and by the time the second one was finished she had lost a lot of blood and was to feel weak for some time.

When she was fully awake Sylvia took a peep under the bed clothes. She saw that her legs were set apart and her ankles secured by white tape to a triangular cushion placed between them. Her thighs were covered in complicated dressings, several white fluffy balls attached to each wound, and each wound was about twenty centimeters long.

"Why is that triangular cushion there?" she asked the nurse who came to take her temperature and check her pulse.

"Oh! That's Fred!" said the nurse. He makes sure that your legs stay in that position for a few days, until things have settled down – otherwise you might dislocate your hips. The muscles round your hips have to re-establish themselves you see!"

"Does that mean that I have to stay in this position?" asked Sylvia.

"I'm afraid so", answered the nurse. You must sleep on your back for the next eight weeks. Even if

Poor Mary

you wanted to move you wouldn't be able to turn over just yet. That will take time".

A few minutes later another nurse came to Sylvia's bed, carrying a bed pan.

"Let me put this underneath you luv. Put your weight on your good leg and pull yourself up with your arms using this pulley".

The pulley was fixed to the wall behind the bed.

"I haven't got a good leg", said Sylvia.

The nurse flung back the bed covers. "Oh my God!" she exclaimed. They've operated on both legs at once. I've never seen that before!"

"What shall I do?" asked Sylvia.

"You'll have to try and take all your weight with your arms", said the nurse as she handed Sylvia the handle of the pulley. "It's going to be painful but it can't be helped".

The movement involved in this little exercise sent agonies of searing pain through the lower half of Sylvia's body. Now that the numbness was wearing off she was aware of just how much pain she was going to have to bear. Her face was pale and beads of sweat stood on her brow. She gritted her teeth, trying not to cry out as she tried to take all her body weight on her arms.

"I'll bring some pain killers for you", said the nurse, seeing her distress.

Sylvia's heels became unbearably sore with lying on her back continuously. In the dark hours of the seemingly endless night, the tears flowed freely from her eyes and she tried to stifle her sobs. The night duty nurse passed by and heard the muffled sniffles coming from under Sylvia's sheets. "Are you all right?" she whispered.

"It's my heels", answered Sylvia. "I can't bear the pain from them. It's worse than the pain from my hips".

The nurse disappeared for a moment and then came back with some ointment which she gently applied to Sylvia's heels. Then she produced some special socks with little pads which fitted snugly under the heels, thereby taking off some of the pressure.

"These will ease the weight and take off the pressure", she said. "Now would you like a nice cup of tea?"

"Thank you so much", said Sylvia. "Yes please, I would love a cup of tea – if it's not too much trouble"

The tea was soothing, and with her heels now more comfortable Sylvia managed to settle down to sleep. In her mind, and perhaps unreasonably, she was blaming her mother for all her present agonies, and fell asleep cursing her.

After three days Fred, the triangular cushion, was removed, though Sylvia's legs remained locked in the same position. Very gradually during the next couple of days her legs began to resume a more natural position.

"You must keep exercising your feet. Rotate your ankles and keep wriggling your toes", said the physiotherapist who came to exercise her legs daily.

On the fifth day a different physiotherapist came trotting down the ward towards Sylvia's bed. "You're going to get out of bed and stand up today", she said. "Come along now –operation leg first!"

Poor Mary

"Which one?" Sylvia said. "They've both been operated on!"

"Oh dear! That's most unusual. I haven't come across that before. Well then, always use your right leg first", and the young lady helped Sylvia out of bed. As she stood up for the first time Sylvia felt faint and her forehead and hands were clammy with perspiration. "Take your time, there's no need to hurry", continued the physiotherapist. "Today you only need to take one or two steps". Then she showed Sylvia how to use the crutches which she had brought for her.

Learning to walk again was a slow and painful process, but it wasn't long before Sylvia's grit began to surface and her fierce determination was to carry her through those first few gruelling weeks. We are all far more capable than we imagine. A strong mind can control the body and if you make up your mind that you are doing well, then you eventually will.

Although Richard could not come to see Sylvia until the weekend, she was able to telephone him each evening. After she had walked for the first time, she excitedly told him over the telephone. "The trouble is though", she said, "I now walk like a penguin!"

"Never mind", said Richard, "you walked like a duck before!" –a remark which was typical of his sense of humour and Sylvia did not take it seriously.

Gradually Sylvia improved and was able to get around quite swiftly on her crutches. The nurses had told her that the more she practised walking, the quicker her recovery would be, so everyday she could be seen determinedly walking on her crutches up and down the ward and a little way outside in the garden.

7. DETERMINATION

At last it was time to go home and Sylvia waited excitedly for Richard to bring her outdoor clothes. When she was dressed she was taken by wheel chair to the waiting car, and then came the difficult task of getting her legs in the car without bending the hips too much. Keeping her legs as straight as possible, she had to carefully lower herself down into the front seat which had been pushed back as far as possible. Then the nurse took hold of both of her ankles and carefully swung both legs round into the car.

Anna, Rebecca and Kathryn were all waiting anxiously for their mother's homecoming. They had cleaned and tidied the house and all the washing and ironing were up to date. Anna had prepared an evening meal and set up the table in the dining room. Richard thought that Sylvia should go straight to bed after her long car journey.

"I will go for an hour", said Sylvia, "but I would like to get up and eat at the table when we are ready".

The front doorstep was the most difficult thing to negotiate. It was extremely painful to lift either leg up and to bear the weight necessary for stair climbing. "Thank goodness we have a bungalow", she said. "At least I don't have to struggle with a whole staircase".

"Well the house was designed with all your problems in mind", said Richard, " – and shortly we're going to leave it for a big, rambling old house with thirty nine steps up to the living accommodation on the top floor. We must be mad!"

Poor Mary

Three days later, two teaching colleagues of Sylvia came to visit her. One of them gave her a bag of toffees. "Here you are", she said. "These will keep you quiet and stop your nagging at Richard from your chair!"

"Thank you very much", laughed Sylvia, handing them round.

Later that evening, Sylvia was chewing one of the toffees when suddenly there was a horrible crunching sound from within her mouth. One of her back teeth had snapped off at the base, leaving nothing but a jagged edge. "Oh no!" she exclaimed, extracting both the toffee and the tooth from her mouth.

"What is the matter?" asked Richard anxiously.

"I was chewing a toffee and it has caused one of my back teeth to snap off", she replied. "Whatever can I do? I'm in no condition to sit in a dentist's chair".

Clare came to see Sylvia later that evening, which was a Saturday.

"I can arrange for you to go into the local hospital and have private treatment tomorrow, although it's Sunday", she said. "It's going to be the only way to deal with it quickly. You're going to need an anaesthetic for that job as the remaining tooth needs digging out!"

The next morning, Sylvia was once again transported to hospital. She was given a general anaesthetic for the removal of the tooth. When it was extracted her blood, which was extremely thin due to blood loss during her recent operations, shot straight up to the ceiling like a fountain, and the hospital dentist had great difficulty in stemming it. As Sylvia came round from the anaesthetic her body began to shake uncontrollably, and her teeth were chattering together in her mouth. It was a most unpleasant experience. When she arrived home later that day, Clare took a blood test and it was discovered that Sylvia's blood count was exceedingly low.

"I am very surprised that you were not given a blood transfusion after your operations", she said as she wrote out a prescription for a course of iron tablets.

After that little set back, Sylvia worked determinedly to strengthen her legs. Each day she set herself a goal which was always a little further than the day before. Her aim was to be able to walk unaided before September when they would be taking over the Abbey School. "I don't want the parents to think that I'm a cripple", she said. "I've got to be walking properly before the September term begins".

In the meantime they had found a buyer for the bungalow and they had to pack up all their belongings, ready for their move. It was no easy task to operate this exercise from crutches, so Sylvia had to direct her daughters and her cleaning lady to do the packing up of all their possessions.

After six weeks, Sylvia went back to Wrightington Hospital for a check up and her crutches were replaced by two sticks. It seemed like starting the process of learning to walk all over again, as the sticks were not as supportive as the crutches, nor could she rest on them. However she had exercised well and her muscles had strengthened, so she soon acquired the technique of walking with sticks.

Poor Mary

At the end of July, sad farewells were said to family and friends before Richard, Sylvia and the girls departed for their new home in the south of England. Clare was upset by Sylvia's departure and felt bereft of her friend. Partings are usually harder for the ones left behind than those who are sustained by the excitement of a new venture!

Mary was in a state of melancholy about Sylvia's going, as was to be expected. She relied greatly upon her daughter's regular visits, and no one else could replace her, for she would not allow any one else into her life. "I only love you luv!" she said. "I don't want anyone else".

"Never mind Mother", said Sylvia. "I shall visit you whenever I can, though not as often as it is too far. Once we have sorted things out we might be able to find a little place for you near to us. You'll just have to be patient for a short while".

8. "THERE'S NOTHING WRONG WITH ME!"

Throughout the month of August, the roses in the Abbey School bloomed riotously, salmon and white, blush pink and scarlet, wine and crimson. There was a drone of bees in the air, and birdsong from the tall trees. The beech trees were now in full leaf overhead and the light summer wind rustled through them plaintively. Sylvia and Richard spent much of their time in the garden, being able to work outside at the garden table. There was a great deal of work to be done before the school reopened in September, and the more they did now, the more they realised what a marathon task lay ahead of them.

"Never mind", said Richard, "at least we are our own bosses now, and we couldn't be working in a lovelier setting. This garden is delightful".

"Yes", replied Sylvia. "Thank goodness we were able to complete the sale of our bungalow in time for the completion of this contract. I must say, I was very sad to leave our bungalow – we'll never get another one as nice at a price we can afford – particularly in this part of the country. The property prices here seem so much higher than in Lincolnshire. One seems to pay twice the price for half the value! Do you think that the girls will settle? It was a big thing to uproot them from all their friends".

"It's hard to say", replied Richard. "I think that Kathryn will be all right as she is young enough not to worry about anything, except perhaps which kind of sweeties she should buy with next week's pocket money. Rebecca will probably adjust fairly quickly, but I do so worry about Anna. She's so moody and secretive these days".

"I think most teenagers go through that", said Sylvia. "She'll grow out of it – I hope – particularly when she begins to make new friends. I suppose she's feeling nervous and insecure!"

Before the term began, Sylvia had to go back to Wrightington for another check up. By this time she had managed to abandon both of her walking sticks, unless she was going walking for a long distance. She felt very pleased with her progress, especially when she noted that some people who had only one hip replaced were still using their sticks. The consultant was satisfied that everything was as it should be and said that there was no need to go back for another year, unless of course there were any problems.

The school opened with a flurry of anxious parents, all eager to meet the new Heads, and the chatter of excited children who were eager to be back at school with their friends after the long summer holiday. Kathryn was of course to be educated at the Abbey School until she was eleven. She soon settled down and made new friends. Anna and Rebecca went to an independent day school for senior girls in the nearby city. Rebecca took to it like a duck takes to water, but Anna was resentful and was to cause her parents a great deal of anxiety by her constant rebellion and flaunting of authority. All that would be another story!

After the term had settled down to a reasonable pace, Sylvia thought that she would pay a visit to her mother. Mary had been devastated by her daughter's move to a place far away, although Sylvia had promised to visit her whenever she could. The journey was two hundred miles each way, so it was not possible to go more frequently than once a month. Each time Sylvia went, she found her mother in a worse state than the time before. She just was not looking after herself, nor was she taking her all important medication.

"I don't know what we can do", said Sylvia to Richard, after returning from one of her visits. "We are so busy with the school I can't possibly visit her any more than I do!"

"Well if she gets really bad", said Richard, "we'll just have to look for a cheap property in this area and move her here".

Richard went with Sylvia on her next visit to Mary. They found her, and the house, in a very bad state. She had returned to her old tricks of stuffing rags round all the electrical sockets, and she would not eat or drink as she was convinced that all the food and water had been poisoned. She had therefore lost a great deal of weight.

"You must get back on those tablets Mother", remonstrated Sylvia.

"I don't need any tablets", said Mary, "There's nothing wrong with me. I'm left luv, not right! It's all in the shape!"

"Oh God!" thought Sylvia. "Now listen carefully Mother. If you go and see your doctor and go back on your tablets, then Richard and I will look for a little

Poor Mary

house for you, near to where we live. If you don't go back on those tablets then I'll never come to see you again!"

"All right!" said Mary. "I'll go back on them", and she did. In the meantime Richard and Sylvia began their hunt for somewhere for Mary to live. They had now sufficient income with which to buy her a small place, so long as it wasn't too expensive.

9. INCIDENTS

The Abbey School being situated in a small country town which was surrounded by pretty villages one would imagine life to be all peace and tranquility, but that was not always so. It was a dusky evening and a chill wind moaned across the street, carrying a scurry of leaves with it. Richard and Sylvia were going out for a drink together with a member of staff and her husband. Richard was driving and they went to a delightful country pub in the prettiest of villages. They left the pub about ten o'clock and drove down the dark country lane which led out of the village.

It all happened so quickly! One knew it was going to happen a few seconds before it did, but there was nothing to be done to prevent it. As they were driving, Sylvia, who was sitting in the back seat of the car with Mrs. Taylor, glanced up to see a group of youths illuminated by the head lights of the car. They were all armed with rocks and were poised ready to attack. One second later the front windscreen was shattered and the occupants of the car were showered with fragments of broken glass. It was in their hair, in their shoes, and even down their necks. With presence of mind Richard did not stop the car as other rocks hurtled towards them and smashed against the sides. He accelerated quickly in order to drive away from the trouble, and did not stop until they were within the safety of the town. It was no pleasant ride with a howling gale blowing through the smashed windscreen.

As soon as they reached the Taylor's house they phoned the police. Richard's hand was badly gashed from the rock, which measured thirty centimeters in diameter, falling through the glass and trapping his hand on the steering wheel. Had it not been a laminated windscreen which delayed the impact of the rock, then he would probably have been killed, for the rock would have struck his head! There were seven other direct hits, including a smashed headlamp and a badly dented car bonnet. Two policemen spent ages interrogating the victims with the usual questions, "Where have you been and why? - How old are you? - Where do you work?" etc. In the meantime the gang of thugs got clean away and they were never caught!

It transpired that earlier in the evening, the same gang had gone on the rampage in the little village, causing a great deal of damage to one of the pubs and the next door hairdressing salon. They had smashed windows, mirrors, glasses and anything else they could. They had then crossed the road and entered another pub and were intent on a similar destructive course of action. There they met their match as a local rugby team of young men of great strength and fitness happened to be drinking at the bar. The young ruffians were forcibly evicted from the pub by the members of the rugby team, and they went running off down the dark lane and disappeared into the night. There, in the shadows of the overhanging trees, the gang planned revenge on the young men who had ousted them. They collected together as many rocks as they could, mainly from a dry stone wall, and lay in wait. They saw the headlights of an approaching car and assumed that the occupants would be members of the offending rugby team. When the car was in striking distance the hooligans hurled their rocks towards it, intending to cause maximum damage and hurt.

After that incident, the Sandersons and the Taylors did not sleep for nights, reliving the horror of that moment of attack, when at least one of them could have been killed. Richard was so unnerved by the incident that for many months after he drove with the sun visor down, as he felt it offered him some sort of protection in the unlikely event of a similar attack.

That first winter brought with it icy winds and darker days and finally the snow. The boys of the school were not able to have football lessons until the snow had cleared towards the end of February. The football pitch was very muddy, having been water logged by melting snow.

"I'll take the boys out for football today", said Richard. "They have been cooped up long enough this winter and they need some exercise, and so do I!"

As they had not been able to play for a few weeks, Richard began the lesson with some preliminary coaching. Some of the boys were quite young and did not have any idea how to kick a ball effectively.

"Watch me carefully!" shouted Richard, and he sped towards the football, but as he lifted his right foot to kick it, his left foot slipped on the mud. He fell backwards and felt a searing pain across his right shoulder. When he picked himself up, he realised that his right shoulder level had dropped dramatically and he was in great pain. Gritting his teeth, he stuck his

Poor Mary

right hand into his track suit pocket, thus giving some support to his injured shoulder, and carried on with the football lesson.

An hour later, ashen faced, he staggered up the stairs and into Sylvia's study. "I think I've broken my collar bone", he said, and stood there, his right hand still in his pocket.

"Stop acting the fool!" exclaimed Sylvia, convinced that he was only joking.

Richard removed his hand from his pocket and immediately his shoulder level dropped about four inches, causing him to cry out with pain.

After x-rays at the hospital, Richard was tightly strapped up in a figure of eight bandage and was instructed to go back to the hospital the following morning for the bandage to be tightened.

"If you can take me early in the car, then I will take a taxi back. That way we won't both be off the premises for too long", said Richard, "I just don't know how long I might be kept waiting at the hospital".

Sylvia delivered her husband to the hospital and then hastened back to school so that she would be in time for the morning assembly. Driving the car through the school gates, and up to the steps of the front door, she hurriedly jumped out and was just in time to follow the last class of children making their way into the hall for morning prayers. Richard later came back in a taxi, arriving back at school in time for lunch. When school had finished for the day, and everyone had gone home, daylight had disappeared and it was very dark outside.

"I'd better go and lock up all the out buildings and put the car away for you", said Sylvia, taking the large bunch of keys from the drawer of the cupboard in the entrance hall. She opened the front door. "Oh! It's gone!" she exclaimed.

"What's gone?" asked Richard.

"The car – it's gone! I parked it at the front door this morning and now it's not there!"

"I don't believe you", said Richard. "You must have parked it on the street".

"I never park it on the street. There's no need to park it on the street. I parked it really close to the front steps. I remember distinctly because I was only just in time for assembly".

The police were informed and the next day a parent confirmed that the car had been parked by the steps of the front door. "I know it was there about five o'clock last evening", he said, "because it was so close to the steps that it caused me to trip up on them – in my haste!"

About three days later the car was found in the car park of the local swimming pool. It was unharmed and nothing was stolen from it, except that all the petrol from the tank had been used up.

"It must have been joy riders", said the policeman who came to tell them where to find it.

"Well at least we've got it back", said Richard, "but we'll have to remember to keep it locked at all times from now on!"

It was a day of full sunshine in April. The apple blossom cast drifts of white petals which carpeted the grass like lace. The sun sent shimmers of light through the lime trees, the lilac which scented the air hung in heavy mauve masses, and the laburnum tree dripped yellow clusters. Under the beech trees in the walled garden, the ground was carpeted with bluebells, and the buds on the pussy willows had burst out of their silvery fur into fluffy yellow catkins.

The Easter holiday was almost ended and Sylvia was busy sewing, making summer school dresses for Kathryn. Within the school buildings it was chilly as the main heating had been switched off for the holidays. Sylvia had set up her sewing machine in the front classroom where there was plenty of space to spread out her materials. She would do the machine sewing in the classroom, and then go into the library room opposite to do the hand sewing. It was much warmer in the library with a gas fire switched full on.

"Rebecca!" shouted Sylvia. "Can you come here a minute please?"

Rebecca raced down the hallway to answer her mother's call. "What do you want me for?" she asked.

"Would you mind going up the High Street to buy some more sewing thread for me? I've nearly run out and I really would like to finish this dress today".

"All right Mum. I like shopping in the High Street", answered Rebecca.

Sylvia took her wallet from her handbag which was on the floor of the library. "Here is money for the thread, and you may buy your self some chocolate, or whatever you want, with the change".

"Oh goodie! Thanks Mummy!" and Rebecca shot off from the house, through the great wrought iron gates, and up the High Street. She soon came back with the thread, her cheeks bulging with the chocolate which she had bought from the sweet shop on the way back.

At one o'clock, the whole family was eating lunch in the enormous kitchen which was situated at the back of the building. The school cook, Mrs. Hawkins, was busying herself cleaning the kitchen equipment in readiness for the start of the new term. At two o'clock the telephone rang and Richard answered it. It was a call from Barclay's Bank in the High Street.

"Has Mrs. Sanderson lost her Barclay Card?" asked a female voice on the other end of the line.

"Have you lost your Barclay Card Sylvia?" asked Richard.

"No of course I haven't", replied Sylvia. "It's in my wallet in my handbag which is in the library. I'll just go and get it if you don't believe me!"

Sylvia's bag was sitting on the floor in the centre of the room, exactly where she had left it, and it was open. That did not surprise her because she had used it that morning to get money for Rebecca to buy the thread. She rummaged round the bag for her wallet. "That's funny, it doesn't seem to be here", she thought, tipping the contents of the bag on to the floor. There was no wallet!

"Richard!" she cried. "My wallet – it's gone from my handbag!"

"Well you must have dropped it on the road", said Richard, "and someone has picked it up and tried to use your Barclay Card at the bank this lunch time. Fortunately the man was too stupid to realise that the

Poor Mary

card is in a woman's name, and that is why he was spotted so quickly. Apparently he fled from the bank and they now have your card in their possession".

"But I haven't been out of the building with my bag", remonstrated Sylvia. "I only had my wallet – in this room – shortly before lunch time. I gave Rebecca some money to buy thread and then returned it to my handbag".

"Well however it went there are other problems", said Richard.

"There certainly are", continued Sylvia. "All my other credit cards are in the wallet, together with my driving licence and a considerable amount of cash. We'll have to put a stop on all the cards – and phone the police!"

A short while later two policemen came to the school and interviewed everyone on the premises. One of them noted the unlocked front door.

"If the door was unlocked", he said, "then anyone could have walked in during lunch time whilst you were all at the back of the building having your lunch!"

Having made all the necessary phone calls to the various credit card companies, Richard went upstairs to his top floor office in order to do some work. Sylvia, feeling very disturbed, continued with her sewing. She sat in front of the warm fire whilst she completed some hand sewing, and she was thinking what an inconvenience the whole thing was – apart from the horrible thought that someone had actually come into their home to steal – and in broad daylight! Suddenly there was a ring at the door bell and she dropped her sewing and went to answer it. When she opened the door she instantly froze! Standing in front of her were two dirty, unshaven youths with tattoos on their arms and several ear rings in each of their ears.

"We wanna speak to Mrs. Sanderson – outside – on 'er own", one of them growled menacingly, and in his hand he was holding the rest of her credit cards.

At that moment Richard, having heard the door bell ring, came dashing downstairs, much to Sylvia's relief. Astutely he assessed the situation correctly, whipped out a five pound note from his wallet and flourished it in front of the noses of the two youths. One of them thrust the cards into Richard's outstretched hand and grabbed the money being offered.

"Someone gave them to us", he muttered, "but they weren't any good – being in a woman's name", and both the youths made a hasty retreat through the school gates.

"Why ever did you do that?" said Sylvia in astonishment.

"It was the cheapest way of getting the cards back into our possession", said Richard. "Just imagine how much they might have been able to buy at our expense, before the credit card companies put their stop on them. There is no limit with American Express – they could have had a whale of a time this afternoon! I'll now telephone the police and the credit card companies again to let them know what's happened!"

Apparently a well known petty thief of the area had entered the school through the front door. Seeing Sylvia's bag through the open door of the library, he had slipped in and stolen her wallet.

"What would you have said if you had been apprehended on the school premises?" a policeman had asked him later at the station.

"I'd 'ave said that I wanted my daughter to come to this school", he answered.

After stealing the wallet he had gone to Barclay's Bank where he had tried to draw money on the credit card. The assistant immediately realised that the card could not belong to him and the scoundrel had fled from the bank as she raised the alarm. Along the High Street he had encountered two other ruffians and had tried to sell them the rest of the credit cards and Sylvia's driving licence. They, however, realised that the cards would not be much good to them, being in a woman's name, but they craftily thought they might be able to make some money by returning them to the rightful owner. They managed to snatch the cards from the original thief, but not the driving licence.

In the meantime, whilst the two criminals now holding the cards were visiting the Abbey School, the original thief stole their battered old car. Eventually they all ended up having a good old 'punch up' at the police station whilst the two policemen on duty looked on with some amusement before locking up all three miscreants. The wallet was eventually recovered, minus the driving licence and the cash, but having been stuffed down a drain it was completely ruined.

"At least we've got all the credit cards back", said Richard, "but so much for this sleepy little town. We never had cause for any dealings with the police in our Lincolnshire home, but since we came to the south of England we've had nothing but trouble – and we haven't been here a year yet!"

10. MOVING MARY

Their first year of running the Abbey School proved to be a very successful one. It was extremely hard work but also very rewarding. As Sylvia had promised, they had been looking for a small place which they could afford to buy for Mary, and at last they had found one. It was situated in a little market town about sixteen miles away from the Abbey School.

"It's not too far to visit your mother regularly", said Richard, "but it's far away enough to keep her from under our feet. The last thing we want is your mother to be coming here and making trouble, it would be very bad for business!"

The place which they bought for Mary was newly built and therefore would not require too much maintenance. It was a two bed roomed maisonette with kitchen, bathroom and living room, and it had its own tiny garden and garage.

"It's perfect!" exclaimed Sylvia. "I'm sure she'll love it. What more could she want? I wouldn't mind if I had to end my days in a place like this".

"You know your mother", retorted Richard. "Nothing ever suits her and she won't get on with anybody – so don't expect too much!"

They were to take possession of the property a few days before Christmas.

"That will be nice for her to be in her own proper house for Christmas" said Sylvia.

"Yes, but just think of the horrifics of my having to go and fetch her, and clear all the stuff out of her present flat", said Richard. "It's not going to be a pleasant task for me!"

Mary was aroused in the early hours with the sound of rain lashing against the windows. A wild wind was blowing the rain in slanting lines on this dark December morning. Then she remembered that this was the day that her son-in-law was coming to fetch her and take her to live near her beloved daughter. She got out of bed and went to the bathroom. Filling the basin, she splashed icy cold water over her face. She had packed up her few clothes and wrapped up her ornaments in newspapers and put them in cardboard boxes. She made herself a breakfast of bread, butter and jam, and a pot of tea. After that she sat down in her old armchair to wait for HIM!

Richard was dreading the removal, and even more he dreaded the two hundred mile long journey back, with Mary muttering and grumbling to herself continuously by his side. He had taken the seats out from the school mini bus, leaving plenty of space at the back for Mary's few bits of furniture. He knew that her flat would be in a dreadful state and that he would have to clean it up before taking the keys back to the council.

At last the distasteful job had been accomplished and with a sigh of relief Richard bundled Mary into the front passenger seat of the mini bus.

"How am I going to stand two hundred miles of this?" he thought as Mary began her irritating nonsense talk almost immediately.

"I'm A.B.C. luv. Don't think you can get round me – I only love our Sylvia!" she growled.

"Yes, all right!" said Richard. "Now we've got a long way to go. Have you made yourself comfortable and fastened your seat belt?"

"You can't fasten me luv! Nobody can fasten me. I'm not seat!" ranted Mary.

Richard sighed as he started up the engine. It was not good weather for travelling, with the rain lashing the windscreen which continually misted up. They had travelled about six miles and were passing through the small village near to Richard's old home.

"Are we nearly there?" asked Mary.

"What?" spluttered Richard.

"Are we nearly there? I want to get out. I don't like it in this bus", moaned Mary.

"We've only done six miles. We've another one hundred and ninety four miles to go. You'll just have to be patient", said Richard, trying not to snap.

"I want to go to the toilet", said Mary.

"Well you can't just yet because there aren't any. You'll have to wait until we get to a service station", snapped Richard, his patience now stretched to the utmost.

"I'm not in service!" said Mary. "No service for me! I hope I don't wet myself!" she continued wickedly, enjoying winding Richard up!

"And it's only the beginning of the journey", muttered Richard under his breath. "What have I done to deserve this?"

Half an hour later, Richard drew up the mini bus on to the forecourt of a service station. He helped Mary down and pointed her in the direction of the toilets and then went to lock the mini bus.

Poor Mary

"I might as well use the toilet too", he thought. "A wise man goes when he can!"

As he approached the toilet area he heard a commotion coming from the men's side of the block. "Oh no!" he thought. "She can't have!"

But Mary had gone into the men's toilets and she was most indignant to find two men in there, relieving themselves, and in no uncertain terms she was shouting how disgusting they were. Full of embarrassment, Richard took hold of her and managed to steer her towards the ladies' block.

"There – that's where you should be", he said, pointing to the sign. "Now please hurry up. We've have a long way to go and we've wasted enough time".

Sylvia was at Mary's new home, making sure that her mother would have everything she needed. They had bought her an electric cooker and a bed complete with a duvet, pillows and pretty covers. Sylvia had fixed curtains at the windows and was filled with pride as she looked round at the sparkling new home for her mother.

"She's bound to be pleased with all of this", she thought. "The neighbours seem very nice people, and it's a lovely walk to the shop round the corner. The gardens will be really pretty in spring time, they are all so well cared for. Perhaps she will even make some friends here". Another little voice inside Sylvia's head said, "Chance would be a fine thing – she'll never alter – she's been like it too long!"

The kettle was on and a good meal ready by the time a weary Richard and his disagreeable companion arrived. Sylvia hugged them both and then led her mother round the little house, showing her each room.

"There, isn't it lovely? Do you like it? On a clear day you can see the Mendip Hills from this sitting room window", she said excitedly.

"It's all right", said Mary in a half hearted manner.

Sylvia's spirits plummeted in the old familiar way, but she refused to be put down.

"Come and sit down and have a nice cup of tea", she said, "then when you've both had something to eat, we'll get the rest of your things upstairs. You'll feel better when you've had a meal and a drink – you'll see!"

11. "WATER'S COMING THRU' ELECTRICS!"

The following week Sylvia took her mother to the Medical Centre in the town so that she could register with a local doctor. Mary was most reluctant to go.

"I don't need a doctor! There's nothing wrong with me!" she exclaimed.

"Everyone has to have a doctor whether there is anything wrong with them or not", said Sylvia. "Besides, you couldn't get your tablets without a doctor's prescription, and you must never be without those!"

Remembering Sylvia's threat to leave her completely if she failed to take her tablets, Mary put on her outdoor clothing and went out to the car with her daughter. For once she did not cause any disturbance whilst they were sitting in the waiting room and remained quietly in her seat. Sylvia was relieved, knowing how her mother loved to aggravate people and liked nothing better than to disconcert others around her.

At last it was their turn to go onto the doctor's surgery. Mary sat down demurely, giving the impression of being a meek little old lady who wouldn't say 'boo to a goose! It made it very difficult for Sylvia to say anything about her mother's mental condition, and she wished that she had made a prior visit to see the doctor on her own. She would just have to rely on her mother's medical records – when they were eventually sent by Mary's previous doctor. She did however tell the doctor that her mother has spent periods of time in mental homes, and she gave him the names of the two drugs normally prescribed to Mary.

"Do you know what dosage she is on?" asked the bespectacled doctor looking keenly at Mary, trying to weigh her up.

"Three hundred milligrams a day", replied Sylvia.

"That's a very high dosage", remarked the doctor, looking even more intently at the meek little figure of the woman sitting in front of him.

"Well I wouldn't know about that", said Sylvia, "but I do know that without the tablets – things get – very difficult!"

"Well then Mrs. Copley", continued the doctor, "we'll have to get you into some social life now that you have come to live here. We can't have you being lonely".

"My daughter will look after me", said Mary primly.

"Yes, I'm sure she will, but I suppose that she has her own young family, and a job to do, so she can't be with you all of the time. What about joining the Derby and Joan Club where you can meet people of your own age?"

"No thank you!" said Mary curtly.

"Well then, what about the Church?" said the doctor, "You're bound to make some friends if you go there. The local Church has a lot of activities for Senior Citizens".

"I used to go to Church but I don't anymore. I've nothing to do with Church", said Mary, a deep frown now on her forehead. She felt that she was being pressurized and she didn't like it.

Poor Mary

"I see", said the doctor. "Then perhaps you'll make friends with your new neighbours. I'm sure they will be very glad to meet you".

"I don't want neighbours! No neighbours for me!" replied Mary, her voice becoming really taut now, and the demure façade beginning to crack badly. "I only want my daughter. I only love our Sylvia!"

The doctor sighed, giving Sylvia a sympathetic glance as he handed her the prescription for Mary's tablets.

Sylvia and Richard did their best for Mary in her new home, but it was a thankless task. They had central heating installed because she kept meddling with the gas fire and breaking it, and then complaining that she was cold. They bought her a television set which she would never switch on because it was 'dirty'! They put in a telephone so that she could contact them if she had any problems, but she only used it to be a nuisance. The phone rang whilst Sylvia was working at school one day and it was Mary. Sylvia could not make out what her mother was saying and kept asking her to speak slowly and clearly. Suddenly there was complete silence at the other end of the phone, but obviously the receiver had not been put down.

"Oh dear!" said Sylvia to Richard. "I don't know what's happened but I'll just have to leave my work and go out to see her".

When she arrived at Mary's house she let herself in and went up the stairs, dreading what she might find up there. The phone in the hallway had been left swinging loose on its cord. Sylvia went into the sitting room and there was Mary, resting in her easy chair, a smug grin on her face. Sylvia was so cross that she had lost an afternoon's work for no good reason, particularly when it was obvious that her mother had been deliberately winding her up!

Sylvia went regularly each Friday afternoon to visit her mother, and she tried to keep the place clean for her.

"I won't be able to come next Friday as Richard and I are going away for the weekend. We will bring your Birthday present this coming Sunday and next week I'll come on Thursday instead of Friday", said Sylvia who always told her mother exact arrangements so that she would not be worried.

On Sunday, as promised, Richard and Sylvia delivered Mary's Birthday present together with some flowers. Mary never failed to appreciate flowers, no matter how ungrateful she might be about her present. The next few days Richard spent in doing some practical work in the school – as it was a school holiday and there were no children on the premises. When Thursday came he was very involved in what he was doing and did not want to leave the work unfinished.

"I would like to come with you when you visit your mother today, then I can call at the builders' merchants on the way", he said, "but I would like to finish this job first".

Poor Mary

"All right", said Sylvia. "I'll ring up my mother and tell her that we are going to be late", and she picked up the phone and dialed the number. "Hello Mother! I will be coming today but I'm going to be a bit late so don't worry"

"Water's coming thru' electrics", said Mary.

"What do you mean?" asked Sylvia irritably.

"Water's coming thru' electrics", repeated Mary, "but I've put a bucket under it so it won't go on the carpet".

"We'll be there as soon as we can", said Sylvia wearily, sighing as she put down the phone. "I don't know if it's just my mother's usual nonsense or whether it's true", she said to Richard after repeating her mother's words.

"We'll find out soon enough", said Richard.

Sure enough, when they arrived at Mary's house, water was actually dripping through the ceiling via the electric light cable in the centre of the room where Mary had indeed placed a bucket. A watery stain discoloured the majority of the living room ceiling.

"How long has this been going on Mother?" Sylvia asked her mother.

"It started just after you left last Sunday", said Mary enjoying the attention.

"WHAT? But it's now Thursday – why ever didn't you telephone and let us know?" remonstrated Sylvia.

"Don't like phones!" said Mary.

"Well you could have asked the neighbour to telephone for you!"

"I'm not neighbours! THEM at number 21, they're all dirty! THEY get in and dirty my house!" Mary snorted.

"Well this is an awful lot of damage", said Sylvia. "I suppose you would have just sat there and let yourself be burned to death if it had caused a fire – which it easily could have done!"

Mary had been fiddling with the controls of the central heating boiler and by doing so she had turned up the temperature on the thermostat. The water in the tank in the false roof had reached boiling point and was continuously bubbling and spilling out through the ceiling, its main exit through the cable hole of the central light fitting.

"You know", said Richard as they drove home," your mother really ought to be in a home. She's not fit to be on her own, but if she ever came to live with us I would walk out. I just couldn't stand it!"

"I think I would join you 'cause I couldn't stand it either!" said Sylvia. "We'll just have to persevere and see what happens. We can't do any more for her than we are doing".

Sylvia was very disappointed that her mother did not make the most of her lovely new environment. Mary could have had a very full life if she had made friends with her neighbours, gone for walks in the nearby park, or joined a social club for the elderly. Instead she just sat there all day and everyday. She did not read, sew, knit or watch television. She just sat brooding and vegetating, then feeling very sorry for herself because she hadn't seen anyone since her daughter's last visit.

Poor Mary

Another problem which Sylvia found horrific was the state of the lavatory in the bathroom. There was excrement everywhere, on the toilet seat, on the flush box, and even down the wall at the side if the lavatory. Every week it was a major and revolting task for Sylvia to clean it up, and it made her feel sick. She often felt like just leaving it for Mary to wallow in, but she knew that she had to keep on top of the situation for the sake of the property.

"However do you get the lavatory in this dirty state every week?" she said to her mother.

"It's not me. It's THEM from number 21. THEY get into the house and dirty it. THEY pinch my purse as well!" said Mary.

"Don't you sit down properly on the lavatory?" said Sylvia, ignoring her mother's nonsense talk.

"I never sit down on a lavatory", said Mary. "It's too dirty. You don't know who has been on it!"

Mary's not sitting down on the lavatory was obviously part of the problem. It also turned out, as Sylvia discovered later, that she was consuming two large tins of Epsom salts each week, and so she had permanent diarrhea! She was obsessed with her bowel functions and inner cleanliness, according to a psychiatrist who later studied her behaviour.

12. CRACKED CEMENT

Due to their hard work the school continued to flourish and remain profitable. Sylvia and Richard were soon able to pay off the loan on the maisonette which they had bought for Mary.

"Well at least she's secure in a home of her own", said Sylvia. "No one can be telling her that she has to move out anymore, and when eventually something happens to her we will still have a house to sell or let".

"Your Mother will never die", said Richard. "She'll outlive both of us and she'll torment us to the end of our days, and if she does die she will continue to haunt us!"

"I must say, I dread the prospect of her becoming physically ill or infirm, and all that would be involved. It's bad enough now", sighed Sylvia.

"Never mind, you can only do your best", said Richard.

It was necessary to pay visits to other schools in the area from time to time. Part of their job involved advising parents on suitable schools for their children after they had outgrown the Abbey School. One morning Richard shuffled through the pile of letters and circulars which had dropped through the letter box that morning.

"Mm!" he murmured as he read one of the letters. "We've been invited to have lunch and to look round

Poor Mary

St. Edmund's School in Castleton next week. It would be good to look round there to see if it would be suitable for any of our boys".

"All schools are suitable for some children", said Sylvia. "We just need to know if it is high powered academic or whether it accepts children of average and below ability, or children with learning difficulties. These schools vary so much. I know that Mrs. Thompson is looking for a suitable school for her son who is not too bright!"

The following morning they set off on their ten mile journey to Castleton. The long bleak winter had given way to a blustery spring and it was good to see the hedgerows and trees beginning to green up. At last they turned their car into an enormous gateway at the end of a long and winding drive up to St. Edmund's School for boys. The building was very impressive with its towers of grey stone and mullioned windows. Richard rang the brass door bell of the great, studded oak door which was opened almost immediately by a slender woman with a warm smile on her face.

"I'm Mrs. Dyas", she said, holding out her hand. "I am the Head's secretary. If you come this way, Mr. Bamford is waiting for you in his study to have a sherry before lunch".

A wide stone staircase swung in a gracious curve up to the first floor on which Mr. Bamford's study was situated. After an exceedingly pleasant lunch Sylvia and Hugh were invited to look round the rest of the school and to see the pupils at work. The Head Boy was to be their guide. They all began to descend the stone staircase leading down to the main entrance hall, as all the classrooms were situated on the ground floor of the building. The steps were shiny and slippery from years of wear and, as they neared the bottom, Sylvia's foot slipped from under her and she fell down the remaining stairs. Every bone in her body was jarred by the fall.

"Gosh! Are you all right?" asked the Head Boy in a fluster, thinking that perhaps he had been going too fast for her.

"Yes, I'm fine thank you", said Sylvia as Richard helped her up, a look of concern in his blue eyes. She bit her lips to hold back the tears and struggled to keep her composure.

"That was a nasty fall", said Richard when they were at last driving home.

"It certainly didn't do me any good!" said Sylvia. "I feel bruised all over".

A few months later Sylvia went up to Wrightington Hospital for a routine check up. The x-rays revealed that the cement which secured the shaft inserted into her thigh bone was now slightly cracked.

"You'll have to watch that!" said the consultant, looking closely at the x-rays. "Have you fallen down at all?"

"As a matter of fact I have", said Sylvia. "I fell down some stairs a few months ago".

Falling down is bad for the replacement hip joints", said the consultant. "It can loosen the wiring and the joints, and in this case the cement has been cracked. Let us know immediately if you have any bother!"

After a period of time, Sylvia was troubled by her right hip. She often had referred pain in her right knee and was inclined to limp again. Some days it was worse than others, and certainly damp weather conditions seemed to affect it.

"I can't understand how it is that damp weather can affect an artificial hip joint, but it does", said Sylvia to her husband.

"Perhaps you are going rusty!" said Richard in jest.

Sylvia did not bother the hospital at that time. Firstly she felt that she was far too busy for yet another long trek up to the north of England, and secondly she did not want to have further surgery if she could possibly manage without. She did however visit her local doctor, Dr. Davies, and he declared that the pains she was experiencing were probably muscular pains and there was nothing to worry about.

After a few spells when her right hip ceased up and she couldn't walk at all for a few days, Sylvia made another visit to Dr. Davies and requested a private consultation with a specialist at a nearby clinic. Here x-rays were taken and once again she was assured that there was nothing to worry about. Even the fact that the cement was cracked appeared to go unnoticed.

"I'm sure this right hip is now loose", said Sylvia as she was getting into bed one night. "It feels different and it doesn't always take my weight comfortably. It's the same old story – no one ever believes me!"

One morning, out of the blue a letter arrived from Wrightington Hospital asking her to go for a check up.

"Oh dear!" said Sylvia. "I thought they wouldn't send for me again just yet. I can't see the point of going all that way when I've recently had x-rays locally. I'll go all that way and they'll only tell me that there is nothing seriously wrong. It's such a long journey from here and it will serve no purpose".

"You must go!" insisted Richard. "They know what they are looking for, having done the operations in the first place".

Sylvia made the long journey to the hospital alone and she wore her track suit for comfort and convenience. The usual speed and efficiency saw her through the x-ray department and waiting her turn to see the consultant. Professor Charnley was now dead, sadly, but his trained team of experts carried on his good work. At last it was Sylvia's turn and she knocked nervously at the door of the consulting room.

"Good afternoon Mrs. Sanderson – how are you?" asked Mr. Knowles who was quite new to the Wrightington team.

"Fine thank you", replied Sylvia, thinking that there was no point in saying anything else.

"No you are not!" said Mr. Knowles. "You are in pain, you are limping and your right hip is coming loose!"

Poor Mary

Sylvia was stunned. Mr. Knowles had put in a nutshell what she had been experiencing for the last two or three years.

"Oh!" she gasped. "What will that mean? How long ------?"

"I don't know the answer to that", replied Mr. Knowles shrugging his shoulders, "but you must be very careful indeed. Come and look at the x-rays and I will explain to you what is happening".

On his screen were two x-rays. One of them was the original taken immediately after the operation, the other one had bee taken that day. There was clearly a difference in the position of the stem of the right hip.

"Let us know immediately if it becomes worse", Mr. Knowles advised. "You'll certainly know about it when it happens!"

13. MOUNTAIN RETREAT

Time passed by and the school remained successful. Many scholarships were won by its pupils, and Richard and Sylvia were generally regarded as a dedicated couple who would make every effort for the children in their care. The Sanderson's own children were a source of worry from time to time. Both Anna and Kathryn showed a wayward streak in their characters. Their father seemed to fill them with violent and conflicting emotions. He dominated their lives and they hated and loved him for it! In their teenage years they both tried to reject every value of his, including their education which they terminated abruptly. Kathryn would promise the sun, moon and stars, but then she would do exactly as she pleased. She was going her own way and no one was going to stop her.

In between the two rebels, Rebecca tried hard to please her parents, and took it upon herself to compensate for the disappointment caused by her two sisters. She worked hard and set herself a goal, and did not deviate from the path until she had successfully gained an honours degree. No one could have worked harder, and no one deserved to be more successful than Rebecca.

Richard loved France, and he always declared that his one regret was that he was born on the wrong side of the Channel. Most years he took his family to France for their summer holidays. When the children had left home he and Sylvia continued to explore the many parts of France.

"I really would like a property in France", said Richard.

Whenever they went to France they would investigate property prices and sometimes go to view the properties. After visiting many areas of France they came to the conclusion that a mountain property would be the best buy because it was attractive all the year round. A seaside resort was limited to three months of summer. The mountains were beautiful in the summer without being too hot, and in winter they were amazing! Richard had learned to ski and it was his favourite sport. Because of the problem with her artificial hip joints, Sylvia did not attempt to ski for fear of falling and loosening them further. However, she enjoyed the wonderful winter sunshine, brilliant blue skies and fresh air of the Alps. So, they eventually bought an apartment in a ski-ing village in the High Alps near to the French Italian border.

Sylvia would never forget the magic of their first Christmas there. Outside the windows of the apartment the snow was dazzling, glinting with a million specks of light. It was a shining wonderland of icicles, drifts of snow and an indigo sky. The first snows came early here and winter could be from October until the beginning of May. Even by the end of April the snow was deep where winter still clung tenaciously to northern exposures.

May was the wettest month and it could rain for days on end, the snow line retreating with the rain. Suddenly cascades of white flowers would break into blossom. Mountain goats nursed their kids, and the shrill cry of marmots could be heard as they emerged from hibernation. The air is so special in the mountains, like wine, and there is nothing better than to breathe it in, whilst feeling the warmth of the sun and smelling the scent of fresh budding trees and flowers.

After their first Christmas, Sylvia and Richard could not wait to get back to their idyllic retreat for the Easter holiday. When they returned, typical for April, was a mixture of snow storms one day and brilliant hot sun and blue skies the next. Spring had come with boisterous tumult and colour.

"Let us walk over into Italy today", said Sylvia. I'll make a picnic and we can eat it high up on the mountain".

"Are you sure that you're up to it?" said Richard. "It will be very heavy going. I don't fancy having to carry you back down the mountain."

"I'll be all right if we take it steadily. I'll wear my tough walking boots, and the exercise will do me good – and you!"

It was a hot day and the snow of the previous day had disappeared on the lower slopes. They only needed to wear light cotton tops with their trousers, but they did carry a warm jumper in case the weather changed suddenly. On the hottest day it can be really cold high up on the mountain if the sun disappears behind a cloud for a few minutes. As they climbed the path they had to pick their way across icy patches of snow. It was an exhilarating walk, and hard work, and they were glad to stop for a rest and their picnic before taking the descending path on the Italian side of the mountain.

Poor Mary

"Are you sure that you shouldn't go back the French way?" said Richard. "I don't want you to overdo it!"

"I'm fine", said Sylvia. "These walking boots are marvellous. They really do support my ankles and prevent me from slipping on loose stones, and they're wonderfully comfortable".

"I'm still not happy about you walking much further", said Richard. "We've an awful long way to go back if we take the Italian path".

"I need to achieve things now in case there comes a time when I can no longer do them", said Sylvia. "Once I've done it I will be satisfied, even if I never do it again!"

Richard understood her point and so they carried on.

That evening they were having a French family for supper so, as soon as they arrived back, they busied themselves in the kitchen to prepare. A pleasant evening was had by them all. Their friends did not stay too late as they did not want to be driving down the mountain which would later be icy. After clearing away the supper things Sylvia and Richard went to bed. They both fell asleep straight away after an exhausting day. During the night Sylvia turned over in her sleep and was awakened by the most agonizing, searing pain which caused her to cry out. Her cry did not wake Richard who was dead to the world in his deep sleep. She tried to move her right leg and again the awful pain seared through her. The source of the pain seemed to be where the metal stem was inserted into her thigh bone. She lay there not daring to move again, hoping that the pain would go away. The rest of the night she spent on her back and was unable to sleep. When the first light of day dawned from behind the mountain she thought that she would get up and make a cup of tea. Lifting the upper part of her body from the bed using her arms, she managed to drag herself into a sitting position without actually moving her right leg too much. She tried to move her legs carefully from the bed so that she was sitting on the edge of the bed. The sweat glistened on her forehead as she attempted to stand. As she did so, she experienced the most agonizing pains of her life, far worse than any arthritic pain had ever been. She managed to stand up but her back was twisted and she found that she could not put one foot in front of the other to walk.

"Richard", she said quietly. "Richard – my hip – I think the joint has broken. I can't walk!"

Richard jumped up immediately and saw his wife in a stooping position, her face now ashen with pain.

"You get back into bed. I'll go and make a cup of tea. Perhaps it will ease off if you rest it. You did too much walking yesterday you know – I did tell you!"

They were travelling home to England that day. Richard made Sylvia stay in bed as long as possible whilst he loaded up the car. When it was nearly time to go Sylvia managed to dress herself, albeit with the greatest of difficulty.

"I don't know how I'm going to get down to the car", she said miserably.

"We'll take your walking stick with you and that will help a little. What a good thing that you brought it!"

Poor Mary

Very slowly and painfully, Sylvia made her way down to the car. She felt like the little mermaid from Hans Anderson's fairy tale, every step was like a thousand daggers piercing her body. When at last she reached the car, she carefully lowered herself into the front seat and then Richard took hold of both of her ankles and gently swung them round to the front. The first two hours of the journey were spent getting out of the mountains so there were many hairpin bends to negotiate. The slightest bend in the road caused agonies of pain and Sylvia held on to the grab handle above the door to try and keep her body steady.

Over two painful hours passed before they reached the motorway which proved to be a little more comfortable for Sylvia as her body was not thrown about so much. It was soon time to stop for their picnic lunch and petrol, so Richard drew into a service station. He filled the car with petrol and then re-parked.

"I've parked as near as I can to the toilet area so that you don't have to walk too far", he said.

With the greatest difficulty Sylvia heaved herself out of the car and Richard handed her the walking stick. A piercing cold wind was holding off the threatening rain as Sylvia began the short distance to the toilet area. It was a slow and agonizing process and she bit her lip to prevent herself from crying. There was a long queue of women and children at the entrance to the toilets. Sylvia leaned against the wall as she waited, and tried to keep back the tears which threatened to spill out. When her turn came at last, and she was behind a locked door, she could no longer prevent the tears from falling as she battled with rearranging her clothes. People stared at the woman who was obviously in great pain and could barely walk, as she made her way back to the car. Richard was dismayed and extremely worried when his wife began to sob uncontrollably once she was seated in the car. In the past Sylvia had been irritable and bad tempered with pain, but he had never seen her react like this before.

"I know it's hard love", he said, "but we've got to get home as quickly as possible – it's the only way. It will only prolong the situation if we hang about!"

14. "I WILL NOT GO!"

They arrived back in England to a cold, grey drizzle, whipped into their faces by a blustery wind. After the brilliant skies of the Alps, England had never seemed more dismal or less inviting. By the time they had driven from Dover it was late in the evening by the time they arrived home. The following day was Sunday. Richard went downstairs to make breakfast and took it back upstairs on a tray so that Sylvia could have hers in bed. After breakfast he telephoned the emergency doctor who came along about half an hour later to see her. After he examined her he realised that there was a serious problem with her hip.

"I will write to Wrightington Hospital and tell them", he said. "What is the name of the consultant you normally see?"

"Mr. Monroe usually, though I have seen others from time to time" replied Sylvia. "Mr. Monroe is the one who operated on my hips though, twelve years ago".

An appointment was made for her to see Mr. Monroe for the following week. Richard drove Sylvia to the hospital and after they arrived it was not too long before she found herself in Mr. Monroe's consulting room, nervously awaiting his opinion.

"Now you are in serious trouble", he said. "The stem is now completely loose and is moving around all the time. That is why you are experiencing so much pain in your thigh. We will have to operate as soon as possible and, of course, you must realise that the revue operation will be as complicated as the original one, and will carry al the same risks. You will be in here for about ten days and on crutches for six weeks, just as before".

"When do you think you will be able to do it?" asked Sylvia. She had mixed feelings, fear and dread of another operation, but relief that something was going to be done to put her out of her misery.

"We will have a bed vacant in two weeks time", said Mr. Monroe. "Please make arrangements with my secretary before you go and then she will send you details of the exact time, and what you will need to bring with you".

Richard was relieved that something was going to be done so quickly. As they were driving home, they mulled over the various problems that would arise from Sylvia's lengthy absence from the school.

"I think we will advertise for a teacher to do your classroom work for the whole of the summer term", said Richard. "Then you'll have until September to recover, which will be almost six months".

"That's a good idea", agreed Sylvia, "but we've also got the problem of my mother. I won't be able to drive my car for at least eight weeks or so, and you certainly won't have the time to be going out there every week to muck her out and do her shopping!"

"Perhaps we should try to find a nursing home for her. She really does need looking after now", said Richard.

A few days later they paid a visit to Mary's doctor. They explained what the situation was and asked him about the possibility of a nursing home for her, even if

Poor Mary

it should only be a temporary measure until Sylvia had recovered from the operation.

"Well, if you want my opinion", said the doctor", the best thing that could happen to your mother is that she falls down the stairs and breaks her neck!"

Sylvia and Richard were shocked at his words!

"Well. I know I've often thought that myself", said Richard to Sylvia later on, "but you don't expect a doctor to say anything like that. It's hardly professional! He obviously knows what she is like though"

An arrangement was made by Mary's doctor for a consultant in geriatrics to visit her in order to assess her needs. Sylvia and Richard obviously had to be at the meeting. The difficulty was going to be in persuading Mary to go into a nursing home voluntarily.

"Look Mother, I'm going into hospital myself next week and I won't be able to drive my car for at least two months. I just cannot look after you for a while. Once I'm back to normal then you can come back here again". Sylvia tried to reason with Mary.

Mary was not going to be persuaded no matter what was said. Two days later Sylvia and Richard met up with Mr.Rathbone, the consultant, at Mary's house. Sylvia was sitting down and her sticks, which she now had to use, were resting against the table when he at last arrived.

"Are these your sticks?" Mr. Rathbone asked Mary.

"They're mine!" said Sylvia. "I assume that my mother's doctor has explained to you what is happening!"

Mr. Rathbone did not answer but turned his attention to Mary. She had discarded her frail little old lady act and deliberately gave the impression of being a strong, fit person.

"I don't believe this", thought Sylvia as she watched her mother's show of strength when Mr. Rathbone asked her to grip his hand – which she did with a grip of iron!

"Well done!" he said. "There doesn't seem to be much wrong with you. Why do you want to go into a nursing home?"

"I don't want to go into a home" said Mary tearfully. "They only want to put me away so they can go on holiday!"

"I'm going into hospital Mr. Rathbone", said Sylvia quickly. "I won't be able to do anything for her for a couple of months or more!"

"Well – I don't think there's any need for your mother to leave here", said Mr. Rathbone. "The Social Services will visit her frequently and make sure that she is all right".

"But she won't let them into the house!" said Sylvia.

"Oh I'm sure she will", said Mr. Rathbone patronizingly, "–won't you my dear!"

When Mr. Rathbone had left the house, Mary stood up to her full height, albeit only five feet and two inches, and shouted defiantly at the top of her voice which rose to a crescendo.

"Mr. Rathbone says I needn't go into a home – and I WILL NOT GO!"

"All right Mother! Have it your own way. I have to go into hospital next week – and there's nothing else I can do for you. Be it upon your own head!"

15. WRIGHTINGTON REVISITED

When Sylvia awoke, the sun was streaming through the bedroom window. It looked like a perfect spring day in this month of May. Then her stomach knotted with a feeling of fear and dread. This was the day she was going to Wrightington for her operation.

"At least it's a good day for travelling", said Richard as he sipped his early morning tea.

"I'm scared though!" said Sylvia.

"Well you've got to go through with it", said Richard. "Just concentrate on getting yourself right, forget about everything else. People, including your mother, will have to manage without you for once".

"What if it goes wrong this time?" continued Sylvia. "I might not be so lucky this time. I can't bear the thought of not being able to walk in those beautiful mountains again".

"Don't worry, you'll be all right", said her husband. "Let walking in the mountains be a goal to aim for!"

After their four hour journey they at last reached the hospital car park. As they turned through the big gateway Sylvia gave an involuntary shudder and was subjected to a strong sense of foreboding, a premonition of disaster passing through her mind. She tried to shake it off but she was trembling when she reached the door of the hospital ward. After Richard had helped her to sort out her bag, and she had put her things away in the locker, he picked up her empty travel bag.

"I'd better be getting back now", he said. "It's a long drive home and there will be a lot to do when I get back to school".

Bearing her weight on her walking sticks, Sylvia limped to the main door with him, her teeth still chattering with fear.

"You'll get through it", said Richard, taking her into his arms. "You did it before and you'll do it again. One day follows another and the time will pass."

"I wish that you were not so far away", Sylvia said tearfully. "It was bad enough last time, but now you're twice as far away".

"Never mind, you're in the best place for the operation", said Richard. "You'll be able to telephone me everyday, and I'll be here again at the weekend. I'll stay at the little hotel down the road from here so that I can visit you on Saturday and Sunday!"

"That will be nice", said Sylvia, trying to put on a brave face.

When Richard had gone she limped back to the hospital ward. A television in the corner churned out canned laughter, and was watched by indifferent faces – faces that would turn hopefully when someone came into the room. They were hoping for visitors who seldom came because of the distances involved in travelling. Most of the patients on the ward were from different parts of the country – too far away for regular visiting.

As on her first occasion twelve years before, Sylvia was subjected to further x-rays, blood tests and endless questions. Now that the inevitable was near, Sylvia wanted to get it over with as quickly as possible. She was doomed to disappointment. For one reason or another, her operation was cancelled on two occasions.

Poor Mary

The nurse, a plump and cheerful soul, came bustling into the ward to do her duties.

"It's because they're short staffed in the theatre", she announced. "There's been a flu epidemic amongst the staff and that's put all the operations behind".

It was suggested that the waiting patients could go home and wait until they were sent for again.

"No thank you", said Sylvia when she was asked. "It is much too far and would eat up too much of my husband's time. If it is all right then I would prefer to stay here".

At long last Sylvia was told that her operation would take place on the following day. The usual preparations took place and the 'Nil by Mouth' notice was stuck above her bed.

"I'm pleased that I had a good dinner", thought Sylvia. "I'll be starving by the morning".

The operation went through successfully and she awoke to find herself back on the ward.

"At least it's only one hip this time", she thought as she struggled with bed pans during the first three days of being confined to bed. "I don't know how I managed last time with two gammy legs. It's amazing how one forgets how painful it is".

Sylvia did not feel at all well. After the initial three days in bed the physiotherapist came along to help her out of bed and to have a trial walk on the newly done hip joint. A few days later she was told that she could get up whenever she wanted, and it was advisable to walk about as much as possible.

"I don't know what's the matter with me", thought Sylvia. "I don't seem to have a scrap of energy and only feel like lying in bed and sleeping. I'm sure I didn't feel like this last time!"

Nevertheless, she forced herself to get out of bed regularly and walk up and down the ward, sometimes venturing out into the sunshine of the garden.

"You don't look very well at all Sylvia", commented Mollie, a patient with whom Sylvia had become very friendly. "Your face looks really pale and drawn".

That night Sylvia struggled to make her self comfortable for sleeping. But it wasn't easy. Sometimes cramp seized her tired back, knotting and twisting her body until she gasped with pain. Then she experienced a different kind of pain in the middle of her back, near the lower part of her lungs. It was a sharp pain which took her breath away.

"I must have pulled a muscle or something when heaving myself around on those crutches", she muttered to herself. "I'll get out of bed and have a walk round and perhaps the pain will go away".

In the darkness of the ward, Sylvia padded around on her crutches, seeking some relief from the intense pain which was now making her cough. As she passed the nursing station, the night sister looked up from the notes which she was writing.

"Are you all right?" she asked.

"I think I've pulled a muscle in my back", replied Sylvia, coughing again. "I thought some exercise might relieve the pain".

Poor Mary

"Show me where the pain is", said the sister.

A few minutes later Sylvia was back in bed, propped up with pillows, and with strict instructions not to get out again and to keep as still as possible.

"Keep the buzzer in bed with you, near your hand, and don't hesitate to press it if you feel any worse", she said.

Sylvia at last fell into the dark drugged sleep of exhaustion. When she awoke the next morning, the pain in her back was much sharper and she could hardly breathe. A hospital doctor visited her before breakfast and listened with his stethoscope to what was going on in her lungs.

"I think you have a pulmonary embolism", he said, putting the stethoscope back into the large pocket of his white coat.

"What's that?" queried Sylvia.

"It's a clot of blood caused by the operation, and at the moment it appears to be lodging in your lungs. In the meantime I'm going to give you an injection of heparin which will help to thin out the blood. It's very important that you keep as still as possible for the moment so that the clot doesn't move. We don't want it travelling to your heart.

Sylvia felt very frightened, poorly and tearful. After breakfast a wheel chair was brought for her and she was quickly transported to the x-ray unit. An x-ray did reveal a blood clot in her right lung.

"I'm afraid this means that you won't be going home for a while", said the doctor later that day.

"But I was supposed to be going home in two days time", said Sylvia miserably.

"That is out of the question now", said the doctor. "We are prescribing Warfarin for you. This is a drug which thins the blood and helps to prevent clotting, but until we can establish the correct dosage for you, then you'll have to stay here".

"How long will I have to take it?" asked Sylvia.

"It could be weeks, months or even years", said the doctor, "but once the correct dosage is established then you can go home and continue the treatment there. It will mean regular blood tests in order to adjust the dosage from time to time".

When the doctor had gone, Sylvia stared miserably at the ceiling. She felt so alone, and so far from Richard and her family. She began to cry softly, not only with disappointment but because she felt so unwell.

"Don't worry!" called out Mollie from her bed across the ward. "I told you that you didn't look well – but at least you're getting the right treatment. That's one thing about this hospital, nothing is left to chance!"

"Yes", called out another patient, "In any other hospital ye could 'ave died! Did ye know that Warfarin is what they give to rats? It's rat poison!"

"Thanks!" muttered Sylvia under her breath. "That's all I need to know!" She had not associated the little coloured tablets she was being given with rat poison, but now she thought about it then it made sense. Warfarin thinned the rats' blood until they died! That is why so much care was being taken to give the correct dosage! Too much could be dangerous!

Richard was very worried when Sylvia telephoned him that evening to say what had happened, and that

Poor Mary

she would not be able to come home. He was even more worried and shocked the following weekend when he saw her drawn pinched face, though he tried not to show it. He comforted her as best he could, but when he left her his heart was troubled.

After two weeks the hospital doctor decided that Sylvia could go home and continue with her treatment there. As the day of her release from the hospital was to be a Monday, it was not possible for Richard to collect her because he was teaching in school. So that she did not have to wait until the following weekend, Mavis, a friend of Sylvia, said that she would motor up to the hospital and bring her home. Sylvia waited all day in eager anticipation for Mavis to appear. Although her blood count was reasonably stable with the treatment, she still felt quite ghastly. Several times during that day she had diarrhoea, and experienced a dull fairly low down ache on the left side of her abdomen.

"No wonder I've got diarrhoea, having to take rat poison" she thought as she struggled on her crutches to the toilets for the umpteenth time that day.

Mavis arrived shortly after lunch, but it was not possible to leave the hospital before she was given the final 'all clear' from the duty doctor of that day.

"It is very important indeed for you to have another blood test tomorrow!" said the doctor. "I will telephone your own doctor and ask him to visit you, and he should test your blood every other day. I cannot stress how important this is!"

Sylvia had not mentioned the diarrhoea problem to anyone except Mavis.

"They'll probably keep you in longer if you say anything", said Mavis. "Best to keep it quiet and I'm sure you'll feel better when you get home. You've probably got an upset stomach through being on edge about getting out of here!"

"Either that or the rat poison – warfarin stuff – is upsetting my gut!" said Sylvia.

It was a difficult journey home, and it took a good four hours. The motorway was packed with traffic, particularly in the Birmingham area. Also Sylvia needed to stop several times because of her gut problem, and it wasn't easy to get her in and out of the car with her crutches, and having to prevent her new hip joint from bending at the wrong angle. The last thing Mavis wanted was a dislocated hip joint on her hands, and having to take Sylvia back to the hospital. However, the journey ended at last and Richard was waiting to greet them, having prepared an evening meal for them all.

"Oh it's so lovely to be back", sighed Sylvia as she sank back into her favourite chair which had been raised by wooden blocks to ensure that she sat at the correct angle. A chair too low could cause a newly done hip to dislocate in these first few weeks.

"I've been in hospital for over a month – can you believe it? Thank you for travelling all the way to Wrightington and back Mavis. It really is very good of you and I do appreciate it."

After they had all eaten, Mavis declined the offer of money for petrol she had used and said her goodbyes.

"I'll come and see how you are in a few days time", she said. "I hope your stomach settles down. Take care now!"

16. THE CONCERT

It seemed a long and drawn out night to Sylvia as she tried to make herself comfortable with pillows under her knees to take the strain off her back.

"Another six weeks of misery!" she thought.

Every time she thought that she had made herself comfortable she needed to go to the bathroom again, and had to struggle to find her crutches in the dark. She did not want to wake Richard if she could help it, but more often than not she would knock over her crutch as she felt for them in the dark. Morning came at last and Richard said he would make breakfast and bring it up to her.

"I don't think that I can eat too much", Sylvia said. "My stomach feels really grotty and I still have diarrhoea. I'm sure it's that wretched rat poison which is upsetting me".

"I must say I don't like you being on the stuff", commented Richard who was averse to taking drugs of any kind, even aspirin.

After he had finished his breakfast, Richard went to school leaving Sylvia established in her adapted chair, a telephone to hand, and also the remote control for the television. Rebecca was at home for the time being, having taken a few days off work to help out at home. Sylvia thought that she'd better check with the surgery that a doctor was coming to take a blood test, having been told at the hospital how crucial this was. Rebecca busied herself around the house and prepared lunch for them both. Just before lunch time the front door bell rang and Rebecca went to answer it. Dr. Davies was a man approaching retirement age who had become very cynical during these latter years of his medical career. He was white haired, bespectacled and of a gaunt appearance and he did not endear himself to his patients! He had a very impatient manner. He breezed into the sitting room, rudely pushing passed Rebecca and ostentatiously looking at his watch.

"Really Mrs. Sanderson, I don't have the time to be coming here and taking blood tests. You'll have to get into the surgery!"

Sylvia was aghast at his brusqueness and Rebecca stood there open mouthed in disbelief.

"But my mother can't walk that far, or drive her car. She's just had a hip operation followed by the complication of a blood clot and she's feeling really poorly!"

"Then she'll just have to get someone to bring her into the surgery", said Dr. Davies curtly.

"There isn't anyone available", said Sylvia. "My husband is at work, my daughter doesn't drive, and all my neighbours are working. Also I am really feeling very unwell and would not want to attempt to leave the house just yet"

She could not believe his nonchalant attitude. In the past she had always thought him to have a careless and dismissive manner whenever she had the cause to visit the surgery, but she had thought that he would be a little more sympathetic towards a patient who had just had major surgery followed by a pulmonary embolism.

"I really am feeling very unwell", continued Sylvia as Dr. Davies tried to find a suitable vein in her arm from which to take the blood. "I have a really upset stomach and frequent diarrhea".

"That will be because of the antibiotics", he blustered. "Stop taking them and drink plenty of water".

"I should complain about him", said Rebecca angrily when Dr. Davies had left. "I know a lot of people who have had similar treatment from him, and sometimes with serious consequences. My friend Jane's father died because Dr. Davies did not take him seriously until it was too late!"

"Well, your father said that it was a good thing that the embolism happened at Wrightington, for had it happened here Dr. Davies would just have told me to take some cough mixture! Clare Henderson would have been far more careful. If you remember, she came to visit me within the hour of my getting home from Wrightington last time, and I didn't even have to ask her!"

"I don't remember that", said Rebecca. "I was only a little girl at the time. I was probably out in the garden playing with my dollies!"

The next morning Sylvia felt so ill that she stayed in bed. She was now vomiting as well as having diarrhea, and it was most distressing having to cope with these problems whilst using the crutches and trying to remember not to bend her hip too much.

"You must phone the doctor", said Richard. "You look really ill now!"

"I will when the surgery opens, but I don't expect to get much joy out of Dr. Davies", said Sylvia wearily.

As soon as she could Sylvia telephoned the surgery and asked to speak to Dr. Davies. She immediately sensed his impatience in his manner when he eventually spoke to her.

"Mrs. Sanderson", he said curtly, "you've just got gastro enteritis and my magic presence is not going to make any difference. Just keep drinking plenty of water and I'll leave a prescription for Dioralyte for someone to pick up from the surgery".

Rebecca was furious at her mother's treatment. "How does he know what's wrong with you when he hasn't even examined you. It's not as though you are well anyway! That man is no good. You should change your doctor!"

Sylvia still felt ghastly a few days later, and the dull ache in her lower abdomen continued to disquiet her, though the diarrhoea had settled for a while, probably due to the medicine.

"I really must force myself to do some walking to exercise this hip Rebecca, but I don't seem to have the energy".

Nevertheless, she forced herself to take short walks up and down the street, but she felt bowed low with the discomfort in her abdomen. She was also very worried about the lack of blood tests given to her by Dr. Davies. The hospital had stressed how important it was to have them every other day during this early stage, but there seemed to be no regular testing and when Sylvia queried this she was told it wasn't too important. Sylvia had more faith in the hospital doctors and worried because their instructions were not been carried out.

Poor Mary

One Friday evening, Richard came home from school feeling very angry. Before going into hospital, Sylvia had been producing a musical play in readiness for the summer concert which was due to take place the following week. The bulk of the work had been done before her departure, the children knowing their parts very well, and Sylvia had instructed the pianist who worked with her to keep them well practiced whilst she was away. Of course she had not envisaged that things could go so wrong, and had thought that she would be back in action, at least for the concert evenings.

"Mr. Butler has flatly refused to do the concert on his own", said Richard. "He says he will walk out if there is no one to help him next week, and as he's a part time self employed music teacher there is nothing I can do about it"

"Whatever is the problem?" asked Sylvia. "I know that the children know their stuff. All he has to do is to play the piano and they will do the rest. They are very versatile and good at improvising if things go wrong. Most of those children are really intelligent and would carry it off on their own, but they do of course need a pianist."

"Well, were it not for the children", said Richard, "I'd tell Mr. Butler to go and not come back, but the concert is arranged for next week, and they and their parents would all be very disappointed if I had to cancel it".

"That would be a great pity", said Sylvia. "They have all worked so hard and I know that the parents have made the children's costumes. We can't let it all go to waste. I suppose Mr. Butler feels he cannot be responsible for the whole thing. He is an excellent pianist but not experienced in handling and directing large numbers of children. I suppose I might feel the same in his shoes. I'll just have to try to get into school and direct the children from a chair and my crutches – if you could take me down!"

The following Monday was the first dress rehearsal. Richard was reluctant but Sylvia was insistent, so he took her down to school for the rehearsal. Her face was ashen as she struggled up the staircase, with her crutches, to the concert hall which they had rented for the occasion. The children were excited and pleased to see their Headmistress, and she managed to muster a smile for them.

"Are you sure that you should be here?" said one of her teachers. "You don't look at all well!"

"I'll be all right", said Sylvia. "It would be an enormous help if you could move the children around as I direct you. I'm hardly going to be darting around myself at the moment!"

After the rehearsal, Richard took Sylvia home and she went straight to bed, sleeping for the rest of the afternoon. She hardly ate any of the evening meal which Rebecca had cooked for them.

"I'm sorry Rebecca", she said. "It's not your food – it's just me – I feel sick when I try to eat".

The following morning there was another rehearsal and, in spite of all her difficulties, Sylvia managed to lift the concert out of its doldrums, and inspire some enthusiasm and sparkle back into the children. When the chips were down, Sylvia had the ability to work through pain and discomfort, only collapsing when

Poor Mary

the job was completed. The first performance was due to take place on Wednesday evening, followed by a Thursday evening performance.

"I really do need to have my hair done before the concert", said Sylvia. "It looks such a mess and dull and lifeless".

"I'll take you to the hairdressers near to your mother's on Wednesday afternoon", volunteered Richard. "Then you can make a quick visit to see her when you've had your hair done".

Never had Sylvia felt as ill as she did that afternoon in the hairdressers! Her face was drawn and pale and the dull ache in her lower abdomen gave her no respite.

"Do you want to do some shopping before we visit your mother?" asked Richard when he collected her from the hairdressers.

"No!" I just want to go straight home now and go to bed. Perhaps If I get some sleep I'll feel better for the concert this evening. We can visit my mother when the concerts are over, at the weekend".

All Sylvia wanted to do was to curl up on the bed, but of course she was restricted to lying on her back which did nothing to ease the nagging ache within her. She worked out at what time she would need to take her pain killing tablets in order to see her through the concert performance that evening. She couldn't afford to take too many, too early otherwise she wouldn't have her wits about her for the concert. After managing a short nap she struggled out of bed and went to the shower room. She could not negotiate the bath yet, so she was thankful to be able to take a shower, though she had to be careful not to slip. By the time she was showered and dressed it was six thirty.

"If I take the tablets now", she thought, "they will have started to take effect by seven o'clock and with any luck should see me through the two hours of concert time. After that it does not matter, for I can go home and collapse into bed".

She began to apply a little eye make up and lip stick.

"God, I do look dreadful!" she exclaimed, looking at her own pinched and drawn features in the mirror. "My cheeks look really sunken in. I suppose it's because I've hardly eaten anything since I came out of hospital. Oh well, I'm always wanting to lose weight, but I must say this is a bit drastic!"

Somehow or other she managed to get through the evening. The children, uplifted by her presence, rose to the occasion and did a splendid performance. Years of practice enabled Sylvia to present a smiling face to the audience, and not until the last person had departed did she let it slip.

"Get me home quickly Richard, before I pass out!" she said urgently. "I now have the most awful pain in my right side".

By the time they arrived home Sylvia was doubled up with pain.

"I'm going to ring the doctor", said Richard.

"But it is ten o'clock!" said Sylvia. "He won't want to come out at this time. You know what he's like – he can barely be bothered to make a normal day visit!"

Sylvia went to bed but Richard did telephone the doctor. Half an hour later Dr. Lane, another doctor of

Poor Mary

the practice, was ringing their front door bell. They were both relieved that it was not Dr. Davies. Dr. Lane examined Sylvia's tummy, pressing gently but firmly on the right side where she described the severe pain to be.

"It's possible that your appendix might be the problem", he said. "Don't hesitate to let me know if it gets any worse. In the mean time take your painkillers and rest in bed and things may settle down."

"Well at least he takes some notice", said Richard after Dr. Lane had gone. "It does give one a bit more confidence!"

When she woke up after a restless night Sylvia was no better, but neither was she any worse.

"If I stay in bed all day, I might just manage to make the concert this evening", she said. "If I can survive those two hours then I'll be satisfied. I really do want to see this thing through, and after that it doesn't matter".

Reluctantly Richard once more took his wife to the concert hall that evening. He knew it was no use to argue with her once she had made up her mind. He had to admire her determination but he was exceedingly worried about her. He was working behind the scenes during the concert, operating the lighting and the sound effects. From time to time he would peep out from behind the curtain to observe Sylvia, her face taut as she conducted the singing whilst trying to rest on her crutches, but she kept on until the concert was ended.

It was a hot and sultry night and Sylvia was restless throughout the dark hours. Had she been mobile she would have been tossing and turning. As it was she had to put up with lying flat on her back when all she longed to do was to curl up in the foetal position to relieve the now increasing pains in her abdomen. She slept fitfully and when she did she found herself being sucked into a long dark tunnel with no light at the end of it. Throughout the night she was plucking at the bed covers with restless fingers.

At six in the morning she opened her eyes and knew that she was in serious trouble. She pressed her hand to her mouth so that she would not cry out with the pain which enveloped her. She lay there for a few moments, her eyes closed, the dark tunnel still waiting to engulf her.

"Richard!" she said, her voice now urgent. "Richard, get the doctor NOW!"

Although he had been fast asleep, Richard responded immediately to the urgency of Sylvia's plea. He'd never heard her sound like that before and he knew she was in trouble. He jumped out of bed, ran downstairs to the phone and telephoned the doctor. Dr. Davies was on duty – unfortunately – but having been alerted by Dr. Lane that his patient might have an appendicitis brewing, for once he did not argue but went straight to his car.

Sylvia was desperate to ease the pain in her abdomen. She heaved herself out of the bed in order to manoeuvre herself to the foot of the bed. Then she slowly lowered herself face down on to the bed and lay there, inert, with little thought as to how she was going to get up again. She was still in that position when Dr. Davies came into the bedroom ten minutes later.

Poor Mary

"Let's have you on the bed on your back", he said curtly.

Sylvia somehow dragged herself upright and then got back into bed, lying down on her back so that Dr. Davies could examine her. After poking and prodding and questioning, he stuck a thermometer into her mouth. Her temperature was 104 degrees.

"Roll over on to your side", demanded Dr. Davies.

"She mustn't!" cried Richard in horror. "She's just had her hip joint re done – it will dislocate!" He thought to himself, "Surely the man knows that!"

"She'll have to go into hospital", muttered Dr. Davies. "I'll ring for an ambulance"

After a few minutes he reappeared in the bedroom. "The ambulance is on its way. It will be here in about fifteen minutes. Goodbye"

Rebecca began to make up a bag for her mother to take to the hospital. She was furious with Dr. Davies for being so casual with his patient and also very, very frightened for her mother. She had never seen anyone look as ill as her mother did at that moment in time. The ambulance arrived and was soon speeding on its way to the city hospital, its siren wailing all the way. Richard and Rebecca felt desolate and helpless as they watched it disappear from their sight.

"I'll go into school and make sure that everything there is all right, and then I'll go to the hospital", said Richard.

"I'll come with you Dad", said Rebecca tearfully.

17. DEATH'S DOOR

The ambulance man helped Sylvia into a wheel chair and then rushed with her to the Acute Assessment Ward of the General Hospital. A young female house doctor came to examine her and take blood tests, and then she administered Pethidine, a powerful soluble pain killing drug. Sylvia could feel the immediate effects, a soothing flow through her abdomen and lulling her into a relaxed state. The pretty young doctor then went in search of a consultant. She did not want to make a wrong diagnosis and Sylvia's condition puzzled her. The notes sent in by Dr. Davies suggested that Sylvia might have appendicitis but she was not too sure, Certainly there was extreme tenderness in the appendix area, but equally so the lower left side if the abdomen gave her cause for concern, and she did not feel experienced enough to give an accurate diagnosis.

The consultant bent over the patient who had recently been admitted with suspected appendicitis. Her stomach was extremely swollen and distended and he did not like the look of her at all. His face looked grim and intense as he gave her a thorough examination.

"Will you please breathe up my nose Mrs. Sanderson?" he asked.

"What an odd request!" thought Sylvia dreamily as she exhaled close to the nose of the consultant. She did not know that some medical conditions can be diagnosed by the smell of the patient's breath.

"We are going to have to operate on you Mrs. Sanderson or you will die. First we will look at your appendix, but I'm going to have to explore further

Poor Mary

than that. I must tell you that you are in a very serious condition. You need to be operated on immediately, but I can't do that because you would bleed to death. Your blood is much too thin because of the warfarin you are taking, and we will try and thicken it up before we can operate. We don't have too much time because whatever is causing your problem is obviously now in your blood stream and you have peritonitis. Will you please sign this form to give permission to do an exploratory operation and to act according to our findings?"

In a dreamlike state, Sylvia signed the consent form. She had understood what the consultant had said, and vaguely realised that she was in a dangerous situation, but somehow none of this information applied to her. She floated off into a merciful darkness.

Each of her three daughters had rung up the hospital to ask about their mother. Each one was told that they should come to the hospital immediately as there was a strong possibility that their mother would not survive the operation. By coincidence they all arrived at the hospital at the same time, and together they went to the Acute Assessment Ward. Sylvia opened her eyes to the vision of her three daughters standing in an awkward silence at the foot of her bed.

"What are you all doing here?" she murmured, and sank back into her drugged state, thinking how odd it was that all three of her daughters should be there together. She was aware of hushed conversation, and then someone taking her hand. It was Richard, his face taut with anxiety.

Anna and Kathryn eventually had to leave, but Rebecca stayed with her father at the side of her mother's bed. The young lady doctor had set up a drip for the purpose of administering plasma into Sylvia's blood, in order to thicken it. It took half an hour for the plasma to be absorbed into the blood stream before the blood could be tested. After three precious hours and several bags of plasma, Sylvia's blood was still too thin for a safe operation. In the meantime violent bouts of sickness brought her out of her lethargic state, and then more Pethidine would be given.

She had been brought into the hospital at eight o'clock that morning. It was seven o'clock in the evening, and still her blood was too thin! Her condition was worsening by the hour.

"Why don't you go home and get some sleep Dad?" said Rebecca. "I'll stay with Mum until they can operate, and then I'll take a taxi home".

Richard acquiesced, for he knew that he was exhausted, and it was necessary for him to keep the school running properly in spite of their personal problems. He did not want to add to their troubles by things going wrong at school because he had failed to do something important. He kissed his drowsing wife on the forehead, and with a heavy heart he made his way down the corridors of the hospital, and out into the car park. Rebecca sat in a chair by the bedside and her heart quailed when she observed her mother's sunken eyes and cheeks. From time to time she held a bowl for her during the bouts of sickness, her lips

Poor Mary

mouthing comforting words of reassurance she far from felt herself. It was now ten o'clock in the evening and still the blood was too thin. Another bag of plasma was hastily set up by the young doctor whose own face now looked tired and drawn. She had been on her feet since seven that morning, now already fifteen hours!

At one thirty the following morning another blood test was taken.

"We're almost there Mrs. Sanderson", said the tired doctor as cheerfully as she could. "One more bag should do it". Even then she thought that it would be touch and go for her very sick patient, but they couldn't leave the operation any longer or she would die anyway!

Rebecca was dozing fitfully in the chair beside the bed when the last empty bag of plasma was removed. There was another half hour to wait until a blood test was completed.

"That's it!" the young doctor cried at last. "She's ready! Get her down to the theatre as quickly as possible. There isn't a moment to waste. Everyone and everything is ready and waiting for her!"

Sylvia became aware of a great rush and flurry of people, and then she was being whisked down the long corridors on a trolley as the porters, nurses and doctor ran with it to the operating theatre. She remembered seeing a large clock above her head and the time said two thirty, but she did not know whether it was morning or afternoon. It had taken seventeen hours to de warfarinise her, no one wasted a second of time. The young lady doctor bent over her and peered into her eyes, then the anaesthetist applied a needle to the back of her hand, and he too bent over her.

"Look into my eyes and count up to ten", he said.

As Sylvia began counting, her last memory was of a pair of large, red, framed spectacles, behind which were intense and concerned eyes.

The surgeon applied his scalpel to the appendix area of his patient. He delicately probed until he found the appendix.

"Well, it's very inflamed, but that is not the source of the problem", he said shaking his head. "I'll take it out anyway because it's obviously going to cause trouble. Then we will have to carefully explore the rest of the abdomen, but we have no time to waste!"

As he began to probe about he gave an exclamation when he discovered numerous tiny pouches along the intestines.

"This patient has diverticular disease of the colon", he said to the junior doctor who was helping him with the operation. "Look at these little pouches in the mucous lining of the large gut wall. Faeces will gather in them and as they have no muscle of their own, they cannot empty by normal muscular contraction. The contents sometimes harden, blocking the mouth of the pouch which becomes infected, causing diverticulosis. This is why she had the aching pains in the left side of the abdomen. Now we know what we are looking for!"

When the surgeon eventually found the source of the infection he was horrified. An inflamed pouch had burst through the gut wall forming an abscess which in turn had burst, thus causing peritonitis.

"What a mess!" he exclaimed. "If we could have known about this days ago the patient could have been properly prepared for this operation, and antibiotics would have reduced the infection. The bowels need emptying and flushing out and there is no time. I'm afraid we're in for a very dirty operation which could also infect the patient – and we do not have time on our side!"

"We're losing her!" cried the anaesthetist. "Both her lungs have collapsed!"

The team worked furiously to keep the patient breathing, and managed to get the lungs working again.

Sylvia was looking at an all blue sea, white buildings and golden sunlight, a city sky line floating on the bay shrouded in mist, and tall masts of sailing ships. Then she saw a sunrise, clear and beautiful. Great wings of glowing cloud stained the sky with crimson veils across the dawn sky. Then she saw a sea which was calm and blue as gentians, and the sky had become clear and windswept. She saw Richard swimming alone, drifting in the swell and surrendering to its limitless power. Then she heard a murmur of voices and she opened her eyes. The pretty young doctor was bending over her and taking her pulse.

"Are you still here?" murmured Sylvia.

"I'm always here!" she answered.

"She must be - - very - - - tired", thought Sylvia as she drifted back into unconsciousness.

Rising to semi wakefulness once more, again Sylvia heard the murmur of voices. She heard her name mentioned as the night nurses discussed with the day nurses the details of her operation before the change over. She heard words which she did not understand, before drifting off again into sleep. The next time she opened her eyes she was more fully awake and she gradually became aware of her own condition. She was wearing an oxygen mask and there was a tube going up her nose and into her throat. Other tubes were attached to other parts of her body, and a blood transfusion drip was attached to her right hand. An intravenous drip feed administered a salt and sugar solution via a tube going into her left hand. She suddenly realised that she was very, very thirsty. Then she began to remember the previous day – or was it the day before – she didn't know! She did remember about her appendix though, and took a peep under the bed clothes. Her stomach was covered by a large dressing, but on the left hand side emerged a sort of plastic bag which appeared to be attached to the side of her stomach. She also saw that she had been fitted with a catheter, a tube inserted into her bladder for the removal of urine.

Poor Mary

I must have got cancer!" she thought. "I've heard of people having to wear bags when they've had part of their bowel removed because of cancer"

She felt surprisingly calm about it, probably due to the fact that she was heavily sedated, though she did spend the rest of the day trying to come to terms with that possibility. All of the nurses were rushed off their fee and could not answer her questions.

"The doctor will tell you later", seemed to be the stock answer.

Later on that day the surgeon who had operated on her came to visit Sylvia. He assured her that she did not have cancer, but a diverticular diseased colon which had had a 'blow out'.

"I'm sorry that we have had to give you a colostomy", he said, with reference to her plastic bag, "but it was the optimum. We had to cut out a large piece of your colon and now it needs time to heal and recover from the heavy infection it has suffered. However, the colostomy is a temporary measure and in about five months time, if all goes well, we will be able to reverse it and then you will be back to normal.

A short time later the anaesthetist came to Sylvia's bedside. He wanted to check her breathing after the collapse of her lungs during the operation. She was actually coughing a great deal which was extremely painful to her stomach wounds.

"Can you tell me Mrs. Sanderson, what is the last thing you remember before your operation?" he asked.

"Yes", answered Sylvia. "The last thing I remember was seeing your large, red spectacles. They seemed so much bigger than they really are!"

The anaesthetist then checked her lungs, her throat, mouth and eyes but he did not say anything. Sylvia ventured a question which had been troubling her for some hours as she lay there in bed.

"Do you think that I was over dosed with warfarin when I came into hospital?"

"Yes, you most certainly were!" he answered, and then continued on his rounds.

Sylvia drifted off once more into a drugged sleep. If she had been her normal self she would have been horrified at what had happened to her. As it was she was so heavily sedated that most things drifted over her, and though she understood all the implications she just accepted them – for the moment!

So began a long, slow and painful recovery process. She had a dreadful cough as a result of the lungs having collapsed, and this in turn caused agonies of pain to the enormous wound which was like a big grinning mouth in her stomach. Above that, a hole had been cut into the wall of the stomach for the attachment of the colostomy bag. On top of all this, she had the added complication of her very recent hip operation, and the encumbrance of her crutches. She was in a sorry state!

18. ROAD TO RECOVERY

On more than one occasion Sylvia thought that she was going to die and it took enormous willpower to keep going when it would have been so much easier just to slip away. However, Nature's healing process had begun and day by day she gained a little more strength, and each day brought release from one or more of her trappings. First the tube was taken from her nose, and then the blood transfusion equipment was removed. At long last the catheter was removed from her bladder. She still needed an oxygen mask from time to time, and she was still being fed intravenously in order to give the colon time to heal. The colostomy of course was going to be with her for several months to come.

When she was out of intensive care, Richard had her moved to a private clinic where she had the peace and quiet of a private room. It was absolute bliss after experiencing the noise and bustle of a hospital ward for the past two months. Richard was able to visit her each evening and eat supper with her, and she had the very best of nursing care. After her initial fear, Sylvia eventually mastered the technique of changing the colostomy bags, though she found the whole procedure extremely distasteful.

Once she began to feel stronger, she realised that her newly operated hip was sadly lacking in exercise and it felt very weak and needed strengthening. She forced herself to walk on her crutches up and down the corridors of the clinic several times each day. Each time she had completed a circuit she would return to her room on the point of collapse, sweat dripping from her face. At the end of July she was allowed to go home, but she was far from strong. Kathryn, her youngest daughter, came home for a while and took it upon herself to clean the house, do all the washing and ironing, and to prepare all the meals each day. Every evening Richard and Sylvia were able to enjoy an excellent three course supper which their daughter had prepared with care.

Richard began to worry about their property in France.

"I really think that I should go out and check it over", he said.

"I wish I could go too", sighed Sylvia. "I'm longing to see those beautiful mountains again".

Sylvia had changed her doctor, having completely lost faith in Dr. Davies. She now saw Dr. Lane and she asked him what he thought about the possibility of going to France.

"I think that it would do you the world of good providing that you are sensible. Your blood count is now stable enough to last for two weeks without testing, so you could go for about ten days. You must wear surgical stockings for travelling though. They will help the circulation. Also you must stop and get out of the car and walk around for a while every two hours. You need to keep the circulation moving so try not to fall asleep in the car. Don't forget to take with you the special card which states that you are taking warfarin. It's important for people to know that should you have an accident!"

"Heaven forbid!" exclaimed Sylvia," I think I've had enough problems to last me a life time!"

Poor Mary

Richard booked the ferry crossing and Sylvia was overjoyed. The very thought of going to France again lifted her spirits. Richard drove her to see her mother for a brief visit before they left.

"This time we really are going on holiday, but just for ten days", said Sylvia to her mother. "I'm sorry I haven't seen you for such a long time, but I've been very ill indeed. It's going to be some time before I can drive my car again, so I won't be able to see you regularly for a while".

Mary made no comment and seemed unusually quiet and withdrawn.

They took their time on their long journey to the French Alps, and it passed uneventfully. They eventually arrived and Sylvia was glad to at last be free of the confines of the car, and the first thing that she did was to open the curtains of the apartment. The views from their window were breath taking, and Sylvia felt immediately uplifted and strengthened, spiritually as well as physically. She managed to walk to the village on her crutches, and each day she became a little stronger. The air was like wine, and so relaxing, and though the sun was hot and the sky a brilliant blue, the heat was tempered by the cool mountain breezes. During one night there was a spectacular storm and the day that broke the next morning was the purest pastel blue with air that was like something for drinking. That day Richard made up a picnic and they went in the car to the beautiful valley below. They came to a clearing that opened into the river, a mile upstream from a little village. It was a spot of rare beauty, a grassy porch shaded by sparkling trees. Here they settled themselves down to have their picnic lunch. All this was exactly the tonic they both needed after the gruelling time they had both experienced during the past months.

"Surely this is the most beautiful place on earth", said Sylvia. "I'm so pleased that I managed to get here. You know – when I was in hospital I thought that I'd never see these mountains again, and I felt really cheated. By next year, I'm going to make sure that I can walk unaided to the top of that mountain!"

"Let's have you walking properly on the flat ground first!" said Richard, laughing.

"I'm so sad to be leaving", said Sylvia, "but at least I know that we will be coming back!"

19. POOR MARY

They arrived back early on Friday evening on August 18th, and after unloading the car, Richard went to fetch a 'Chinese Take Away' for their supper. They went to bed quite early, being tired after their long journey. Richard rose early the next morning and found Kathryn already in the kitchen making breakfast. Sylvia came downstairs slowly on her crutches after Kathryn had shouted that breakfast was ready.

"I really miss those mountains", said Richard as he munched his toast and marmalade, "but at least it's a nice day here for a change. For once the sky is blue, and it's going to be quite warm I think".

They were all having coffee at the breakfast table when the telephone rang. Kathryn went to answer it.

"It's for you Mum!" she shouted from the sitting room.

"Who is it?" asked Sylvia as she slowly hobbled from the kitchen.

"Don't know!" said Kathryn, going up stairs to put on a noisy pop record in her bedroom.

"Hello!" said Sylvia as she put the phone to her ear.

"This is the matron of the Victoria Hospital", said the voice on the other end of the phone. "I'm afraid we've got your mother here in the hospital".

"My mother? Why? What's happened?" cried Sylvia.

"Apparently her neighbour noticed that your mother had not taken her milk into the house this morning. She managed to find some help to get into the house and they found your mother collapsed on the floor".

"Oh dear!" said Sylvia. "I'll be there as soon as I can", and she put the phone down. "It's my mother", she said in answer to Richard's questioning look. "She's in the Victoria Hospital. The neighbours found her collapsed on the floor this morning. Is it possible for you to drive me there?"

In three quarters of an hour, Richard was driving the car through the gates of the hospital car park.

"I'll wait here in the car", he said. "I don't want to go in there. You know I hate hospitals and I've seen enough of them lately!"

"Well I've certainly had more than my share of them recently", said Sylvia tartly. However, she understood how he felt, and certainly her mother was not his favourite person.

When she entered the ward she found Mary sitting in a chair by her bed. She looked distressed and exhausted, and beads of sweat stood on her brow. Her eyes were closed and for one fleeting moment she looked as Sylvia remembered her years ago when she, Sylvia, had been a child.

"Mother!" she said quietly.

Mary opened her eyes and her face lit up when she saw her daughter. She opened her mouth to speak but her words were incoherent and Sylvia couldn't make out anything that she was saying.

"What's wrong with her?" Sylvia asked a nurse.

"She's got pneumonia love. I think she may have had a little stroke as well. By the way, she has no clothes except for those which she is wearing. Do you

Poor Mary

think that you could go and get some for her?" said the nurse.

"Yes certainly", replied Sylvia. Then she told her mother that she was going to fetch some clothes for her and that she wouldn't be long. Hobbling back as quickly as she could to the car, she asked Richard to drive her to Mary's house. There was no problem in gaining entry as Sylvia always carried her own key to the property. Once in the bedroom, Sylvia found a suitcase containing two new night gowns, a dressing gown, and a new black pleated skirt with some bright blouses and cardigans. Sylvia had bought all of these things before she herself went into hospital, thinking that her mother would be going into a nursing home for a while.

"Well I must say that this is all very handy", said Sylvia to Richard as they inspected the contents of the suitcase. "It's all complete, even to the toilet bag, new flannels, toothbrush etc. What a good thing we had it all ready!"

They returned to the hospital and Sylvia opened the case for her mother to see inside. For a moment, the old stubborn look passed across Mary's face, but then she sank back in her chair with exhaustion.

"Well I'll give these to the nurse", said Sylvia. "You'll probably feel like changing your clothes later".

Mary did not reply, and just leaned back in her chair, her eyes closed and a puckered frown on her forehead.

"I'll have to go now Mother. Richard is waiting for me outside. I'll come again first thing tomorrow morning".

Again Mary mumbled something. She was desperately trying to convey her thoughts to her daughter, but Sylvia could not make any sense of her mother's jumbled word.

That evening there was another phone call from the hospital.

"Your mother is in a critical condition at the moment", said the matron. "However, there is nothing that you can do and she may pass through it. I will let you know immediately if I feel that you should come – so be ready just in case!"

Both Sylvia and Richard kept a track suit by their bed that night, in case they had to get up hastily and make a journey to the hospital. The morning of August 20th arrived, and being a Sunday all was still and quiet. They had heard nothing from the hospital so, at eight o'clock, Sylvia telephoned to see how her mother was.

"Oh she's much better this morning", said the nurse on duty. "She had a very bad night, but now she's sitting on her chair by her bed and she seems quite cheerful. By the way, would you please bring her a pair of slippers? There were none in the suitcase".

"That's just typical of my mother", said Sylvia to Richard. "She frightens everybody to death and

Poor Mary

when she's got everyone scurrying round after her she bounces back as fit as a fiddle".

"She's an attention seeker!" proclaimed Richard as he finished his morning coffee.

In her own poor condition, Sylvia found it impossible to rush about, so knowing that her mother was getting better, she didn't even try.

"I think that we'll go straight to my mother's house for her slippers. I can't think why we failed to see them yesterday. Also we'd better change her bed covers. They're bound to want her out of hospital as soon as possible. We might even have to take her home today!"

It was nearly mid-day by the time that they reached Mary's house. Sylvia hunted round for the slippers and found them under the bed.

"Would you mind helping me to change the bed now please?" asked Sylvia. "Oh my God! Just look at this bedding! It can't have been changed since I did it before I went into hospital last May, and now it's August!"

The bottom sheet, pillow cases were saturated with grease. Mary's latest foible was to lather herself in night cream before going to bed, not just her face but her whole body. The bedding was dripping with oily cream. On the dressing table stood six jars of Nivea cream!

"The Social Services were supposed to come in and change her bed regularly", said Sylvia. "They promised faithfully!"

"Well perhaps she wouldn't let them in", said Richard. "You know what she is like!"

Sylvia Hoole

"In my opinion", continued Sylvia, "the Social Services should have someone experienced enough to deal with these sort of problems. They just give up too easily! I don't think that this grease will ever come out of this duvet cover, even in a hot wash. I might have to throw the bedding away. I'll see what happens in my washing machine first though!"

As soon as clean linen was on the bed, the couple set off to the hospital, making sure that they did not forget the slippers. Sylvia suddenly felt very tired and a little faint. She was in no condition to cope with these further problems and all the running about involved.

"I'll wait outside again – if you don't mind" said Richard.

Sylvia hobbled wearily through the main door and down the hospital corridor. She peered through the ward door but could not see her mother anywhere. A nursing sister glanced up from her work and saw Sylvia standing and leaning on her crutches in the doorway.

"Have you moved my mother?" Sylvia asked the sister.

"Come into the office with me Mrs. Sanderson", said the sister, leading the way. When they were in the office she turned to Sylvia. "Your mother died at quarter to one my dear. We tried to ring you but there was no reply".

Sylvia gasped. "But she can't have! They said she was better this morning! I've just been to get her slippers and change her bed!"

She began to shake all over and felt that she might faint. Then she burst into tears.

"Sit down my dear. I'll go and get you a cup of tea", said the sister.

As Sylvia sipped her tea the tears continued to stream down her cheeks. "If only I'd got here sooner! If only I had known! It's difficult for me to rush you see – I'm recovering from two major operations – but I would have tried to get here sooner had I known. My husband and I have just been to her house to get her slippers. We changed her bed because we thought she might be coming out. They said she was much better this morning! How did it happen?"

"She died suddenly, but very peacefully, as she was sitting in her chair", said the sister.

"If only I'd been here sooner! If only I'd come here first!" wept Sylvia.

Her weeping paused for a moment and, finishing her tea, she stared miserably out of the window, though she did not notice the blue sky, or the trees rustling in the breeze.

"Can I see her?" she said suddenly. "I want to see her".

The sister led Sylvia down a dark corridor and into a dismal room which served as a temporary mortuary for the hospital. Mary was lying on a bed as though she were asleep, but so still, so very still. Sylvia approached the bed fearfully and looked down at her mother who looked at peace, possibly for the first time in many, many years. Sylvia bent down to kiss her forehead – it was still warm, and damp with sweat.

"If only I'd known that you were so ill", she thought. "I'm so used to your pretending".

She took one last look and for a fleeting moment she remembered Mary again in her younger days, with her white skin, her flawless complexion, raven black hair, and the proud tilt of her head. Then the vision faded and all that was left was a frail, white haired old lady who had drawn her last breath.

"Good bye Mother", she whispered, and then she turned and left the room.

Richard was as shocked as Sylvia when she came back to the car and told him. They had both expected a long, drawn out and messy ending to Mary's life. Neither of them could believe that she had gown without a murmur and without a fuss.

On Monday morning Sylvia had to go into the surgery for yet another blood test. She'd had so many blood tests that the nurse was having difficulty in finding a vein in her arms willing to relinquish some blood. Sylvia had always been very stoical and put up with all these discomforts but this morning it was all too much. As the nurse repeatedly and unsuccessfully jabbed her arm with the needle, she broke down and wept.

Later that day, arrangements were made for Mary's funeral which was to take place the following Thursday. The day before the funeral Sylvia asked Richard if he would take her to the Chapel of Rest so that she could see her mother for one last time, and to make sure that everything was as Mary would have liked it to be. She entered the chapel and approached the coffin diffidently. Mary was laid out in cream satin and looked very, very small, but Sylvia's heart skipped a beat when she saw the expression on her mother's face. Gone was the tranquil appearance. Mary's face had become twisted with bitterness and cynicism – the look of which Sylvia had been so afraid when she was a child, and a cold bleakness filled her heart

----

The day of the funeral dawned, warm and sunny, and Mary was laid to rest. Now she was beyond fear, beyond despair, and no longer heard the screaming of devils. Her daughter was at last free from the shadow of her mentally ill mother.

Six months later, now without crutches but never as strong in health again, Sylvia stepped back to get a better view of the newly erected headstone of white marble, adorned with the carving of a single rose. The inscription on the stone read quite simply;

MARY ALICE COPLEY

1907 – 1989

REST IN PEACE

"I have done all that I can now for you Mother", she whispered as she walked away.

THE END

About the Author

Sylvia Hoole was born in Yorkshire. Her father was killed in the Second World war and she was brought up solely by her schizophrenic mother, hence her interest in schizophrenia.

She trained to be a teacher and eventually became the headmistress of a preparatory school in the south of England.

She married and had four daughters. A great deal of her time is spent in the French Alps where she and her husband bought a house.

At the age of twenty six, her youngest daughter was murdered by a schizophrenic man.

Printed in the United States
109303LV00001B/4-9/P